The Fringe Dwellers
Nene Gare

Text Publishing Melbourne Australia

textclassics.com.au
textpublishing.com.au

The Text Publishing Company
Swann House
22 William Street
Melbourne Victoria 3000
Australia

First published by Heinemann, London 1961
This edition published by The Text Publishing Company 2012

Cover design by WH Chong
Page design by Text
Typeset by Midland Typesetters

Printed in Australia by Griffin Press, an Accredited ISO AS/NZS 14001:2004
Environmental Management System printer

Primary print ISBN: 9781922079541
Ebook ISBN: 9781921961823
Author: Gare, Nene, 1919–1994
Title: The fringe dwellers / by Nene Gare ;
introduction by Melissa Lucashenko.
Series: Text classics
Subjects: Aboriginal Australians—Fiction. Sisters—Fiction.
Dewey Number: A823.3

CONTENTS

Fighting in the Margins
by Melissa Lucashenko

'THEY look like people, that's the trouble,' wrote Judith Wright, referring to the salesmen who arrive at your front door, masquerading as human beings. Wright's phrase often does good service for Aboriginal people too, faced with the endless task of telling allies from enemies.

This was my dilemma as I came cautiously to *The Fringe Dwellers*. Research soon revealed, though, that in the 1950s Nene Gare had welcomed Aboriginal women into her home in Geraldton as friends, rather than as servants (an unthinkable act to many white West Australians of the time—probably still unthinkable to many white Australians today). Of poor and marginalised origins herself, Gare witnessed the vicious racism that scarred Aboriginal lives, and she wrote perceptively about what she saw.

But, I also learned, she was married to Frank Gare, who in 1962 was reluctantly appointed the Commissioner for Native Welfare—and the words 'Welfare' and 'Protector' sit bitterly in Aboriginal mouths even now. Go to any Aboriginal community in Australia and you will soon find the victims, the stolen generations, and also the unacknowledged children and grandchildren, of many so-called Protectors. The Gares, by all accounts, were of a different stamp: people who genuinely tried to force legislative and political change, and who were active in resisting the mores of the time that said that Aboriginal children were 'better off' being raised by strangers in white institutions.

The Fringe Dwellers was Nene Gare's response to the commonplace West Australian racism that kept Aborigines segregated from white society. It was an attempt to speak out about the injustices she was confronted with on her doorstep, living as she did a stone's throw from a fringe camp on the aptly named Mount Misery.

When I opened the novel, a sentence on the first page leapt out: 'Trilby was classified as a half-caste.' These days we avoid the term, for its imprecision as well as its offensiveness. But Gare doesn't write that Trilby *was* a half-caste, but rather that she was *classified* as one. The phrase underlines a hard, ongoing fact of Aboriginal life: as a black girl Trilby was one thing, but white Australia insisted on seeing her as another, and as a mere category at that. This was encouraging; I read on.

In *The Fringe Dwellers* the teenage Comeaway sisters, Trilby and Noonah, reluctantly leave their younger brother and sister behind on the mission, and return to their parents' ramshackle existence on the fringes of a country town. Here, a few hours north of Perth, is the freedom that Trilby has longed for: a chance to escape the stifling oppression of mission life, and, she hopes, the trap of her Aboriginality. Pragmatic Noonah begins training as a nurse, bringing in money to the near-destitute family. Trilby dreams of working in a shop—of anything except 'kids or cleaning'.

It soon becomes evident that her dreams are one thing, and life in an unwelcoming West Australian country town is quite another. Grey-eyed Trilby meets a scattering of unambitious relatives and comes to know her extended family for the first time. Seduced by a young Aboriginal lad, Phyllix, she regrets the indiscretion, and quickly rejects him. Trilby determines to go back to school for a year so that she can get a 'good job in an office, something like that'. Overt racism dogs the girls wherever they go, from sneers in the town milk bar to stares on the train. When Trilby punches a racist white student in the face the principal calls her in, but she is not expelled, nor is her dream of escape extinguished.

Life in the fringe camp is simple but sociable: 'Ten

yards to the liveness and laughter of other people.' There is never much food, as the feckless Mr Comeaway is more inclined to yarn his days away with his brother Charlie than to make the journey down to the wharf for paid work. But, through a combination of gambling skill, child endowment, calling in of favours and communal obligation, Mrs Comeaway scratches together enough tucker to go around.

All is well enough until Noonah persuades her parents to attempt the move to the Wild-Oat Patch— a new housing development in town, designed to assimilate the 'coloured' population. Here there will be respectability, and the chance for young Bartie and Stella to come back to the family. And so the slide to isolation and 'civilisation' ('Only Noonah worried about things like rent') begins. The inevitable horde of Comeaway rellies soon arrives to stay. Trilby, despairing of life in a house designed for four and accommodating closer to twenty-four, discovers that she is pregnant. Jail, madness—'It's not really my baby'—and worse soon follow. The move towards white society has, it turns out, been a move towards annihilation.

What are we to make of this story, first published in 1961, from the vantage point of the early twenty-first century? Nene Gare was a writer far ahead of her time, and her sympathies are unmistakable. Trilby and Mrs Comeaway are heroes, with a supporting cast of Aboriginal characters who are mostly rounded and nearly all likeable. Gare had a good grasp of many of the ways white civilisation, or white racism (the two are sometimes indistinguishable for Aboriginal people, something she also understood), affected black Australians. And she doesn't fall into the trap, common to outsiders who decide to depict Aboriginal life, of thinking that she is the only white person ever to sympathise. There are plenty of racist whites in *The Fringe Dwellers*, but there is a variety of others too: a man in a milk bar who interrupts the intolerable rudeness of the other patrons; the insufferable but well-meaning neighbour at the Wild-Oat Patch; the school principal who gives Trilby the benefit of the doubt.

There are anomalies. For this Aboriginal reader, it seems unlikely that two prodigal daughters arriving in their parents' home after a long train ride from the mission would not be offered food and drink, when both are available. Other than the term 'monarch' for police, no Aboriginal language is spoken until well into the final third of the book, and then sparingly. And only old Skippy the 'full-blood' has a country— the Kimberley, to which he longs to return. The other fringe dwellers have been forced away from their tribal life to a degree that is almost unrecognisable today, a forcing-away described by May, a camp dweller, in the final chapter: '"An now they wants to push us further back." The black eyes sparkled. "Jack says we moved all we gonna move. We stay put now. They can all just damn well move themselves…"'

May has guts and grit in spades, for like all Nene Gare's Aboriginal characters she is a real person, with the strengths and weaknesses of all humanity. And Gare saw, too, the inherent cruelty of the system Aborigines were subject to. Not long after arriving home from the mission, Noonah argues that Bartie is desperately unhappy there, and needs to come back home. Their mother resists the idea.

> Mrs Comeaway's lower lip was pendulous, her smooth brow puckered…'It's like this here,' she said at last. 'You kids don't understand proper…Up there, theys all the same, nothing to choose between em. Nobody don't call em names just because they coloured. An even if they don't like it for a little while…'
> 'I hated it,' Trilby burst forth. 'All the time I was there I hated it.'

Three chapters later Noonah is forced to explain to her mother what incarceration on the mission felt like:

> 'happiness isn't just food and a bed and clothes. Not for children…they feed you and teach you to brush your teeth and they give you a bed in a proper room, but they could never teach us to stop wanting our mothers and fathers and our own homes…It's like being sick all the time. Not in your stomach, but up

here.' She put a thin hand against her heart. 'The little kids pretend Mrs Gordon is their mother. Whenever she walks round they crowd up against her and hold onto her hands or her frock...I know they're pretending she's their mother, because I used to pretend myself.'

Gare saw what it was for the children to live torn away from a mother's love. And she recognises Aboriginal pain for what it is: simple human pain. But Mrs Comeaway has surrendered her children voluntarily, afraid of the racism they will be exposed to in the outside world. While he has his concerns, Mr Comeaway too has come to terms with his children being raised hundreds of kilometres away in a white institution. And pregnant Trilby rejects her unborn baby, planning to send it off to the authorities. I found this parental acquiescence an odd contrast with, say, the heroic stance of the Aboriginal father in Archie Roach's 1990 anthem 'Took the Children Away': 'Dad shaped up and stood his ground / He said, "You touch my kids and you fight me."'

Nene Gare knew a lot of Aboriginal people well, and wrote Aboriginal lives that ring true on the page. But the idea of Aborigines resisting missionisation and organising their own affairs, rather than being the happy subjects of the 'partment' man beloved of old Skippy, isn't raised in this novel. Mum Comeaway is wise in a sloppy, take-life-as-it-comes kind of way, and Trilby is both ambitious and angst-ridden about the number she has been dealt in Australia's racism lottery. But neither they, nor Mrs Green who lives on the hill, nor the hard-bitten Rene Riley who has known and rejected white city life, are shown to have the capacity to run their lives independently, to exercise real social or political power. But then, perhaps it is too much to ask a white writer at the start of the 1960s to have envisioned self-determination for black Australians.

What Nene Gare did do so successfully, in the most popular of her books, was to speak out in the face of a white Western Australia that held Aboriginality in withering paternalistic contempt. She had the imagination and the life experience to portray for a white audience—and maybe for the first time—a world in which Aboriginal men and women are both decent and normal, despite their being treated as far less than that. Perhaps this, as much as anything, was the reason that Judith Wright's old friend Oodgeroo Noonuccal agreed to play a role in Bruce Beresford's 1986 film of the novel. I think she very probably recognised herself in its pages.

And it is the reason why Gare's story deserves to be read today. Her protagonist may feel forever trapped in the margins, but she is determined to keep fighting for the rights that she knows she deserves. Critically, like her mother, her sisters and her brother, young Trilby Comeaway is still alive at the end of *The Fringe Dwellers*, fiercely alive.

The Fringe Dwellers

To my friends, with love

ONE

Trilby paused to look back at the mission. The box-like buildings straggling either side of the wide roadway were ugly, utilitarian, and the only graceful note was lent by the tall wide-reaching gums which shaded them. At this distance the children's voices sounded like the carolling of birds, echoing and re-echoing as they laughed and called to each other.

Trilby stuck a long leg over the boundary fence, lifting her skirt high above the line of barbed wire at the top. Safely over, she bent her head against the wind and continued her walk. Outside the fence the slender-leaved wattles spread circular skirts to break the force of the southerly. In this dry red land of North-Western Australia the southerly blew all summer long, strong and straight. It blew Trilby's hair back from her face and down her faded cotton skirt between her legs. It inclined her figure at an angle and only her down-bent gaze shielded her eyes from the flying red dust.

Soon the mission was just a block of indistinct outlines, and the bell-like voices were truly those of the birds. A line of river-gums appeared and as they grew more distinct Trilby speeded her steps. Under the trees was the river-bed, dry and sandy now, but still cool beneath the low trailing branches of the ghost gums. Trilby stopped to look wistfully at a mud-bottomed hollow that sometimes, when there had been good rains farther north, held water all through the long dry summer; but the rains had been sparse this year and the pool was dry. She stooped to brush a scurrying line of big black ants from a sandy spot beneath one of the trees, then she settled herself down, her back against its trunk. Here, where the force of the wind was broken, there were small bush flies by the hundred. They settled on the girl's face and arms and legs and lost themselves in her hair. She leaned over to pick a frond of leaves to use as a fly-switch.

Trilby was classified as a half-caste. For years now she had lived at the mission. There were four of the Comeaways there—Trilby's older sister Noonah, and the young ones, ten-year-old Bartie and the baby Stella, who was six. Trilby had always hated the life, though the active rebellion of her first year or so had dwindled to a dreary acceptance, lighted only by wild plans for the life she would lead when she was free. She dreamed of excitement and gaiety and laughter and joyous adventure, but these things did not belong to mission life, and until now there had always been the cold awakening to this fact. Not today, though. Today she could dream as much as she liked. Only one more night at the mission for herself and Noonah. One more night between herself and the wonder of pleasing herself what she did. Her mouth curled upward in ecstasy.

With her face turned to the clear strong light, it seemed that most of the dark blood in this girl had drained into hands and feet, leaving the skin of her face a glowing amber, highlighted with gold. There were stripes of gold in her hair too, over dark honey. But her eyes were her most outstanding feature. Between curving black lashes they glinted like silver.

Trilby's grandfathers, both of them, had been white. The cold arrogance of one had been centred in the narrow grey eyes that Trilby had inherited. From him, too, she had her slim height and her high-held head. And perhaps her stubborn rebellious spirit. Back at the mission she was considered a spitfire, cheeky and almost unmanageable. The other kids teased her about her strange light eyes, but Trilby was only acting when she bit back at them. At fifteen she was not yet brave enough to tell them she liked to be different. And that she liked most to be different from coloured people. The lovely velvet-brown eyes of most of the other children went unadmired. She preferred her own long secretive eyes.

She flung a careless arm across the tree and leant her soft cheek against its hard satin trunk. The sprays of delicate pointed leaves dipped and danced about her face. Across from her, in the very centre of the dry river-bed, a tortured gum grew almost parallel with the earth but its foliage strained towards the sky, lifting and rippling as the wind drove it ever downward. The coarse white sand

7

rose in clouds, the wind went flying through the leaves, and presently Trilby, in tune with her surroundings, flung straining arms tightly round her tree. Happiness leapt in her heart like a living thing so that laughter was caught in her throat and strangled there. The hardness of the wood crushed her chest but she only pressed closer to it, as if this were life itself she held in her arms. But at last there were tears as well as laughter, and the tears slipped down her cheeks and were bitter and salt on her tongue.

There were two who sat on the steps of the schoolhouse in the late afternoon, and the faces of both were bleak and still. All the comfort Noonah had to give had been given, and the boy Bartie was not comforted. Sitting on the step below her he pressed himself against her legs, empty eyes watching the antics of a group of small boys rolling over and over in the red-dusted sand. Tomorrow Noonah would be gone. There was no thought more important than that. And so it was for Noonah. Tomorrow she must leave Bartie and Stella behind to get on as well as they could without her. And the more she thought of the little things she had done for them, which nobody but an older-sister-turned-mother would ever think of doing, much less have time to do in this crowded and busy mission, the more desolate grew her thoughts. They would miss her so! And how cruel that she, who loved them, should be forced to withdraw herself from them and leave them alone. She slipped an arm over Bartie's shoulders and when the boy looked up at her inquiringly she smiled at him—the unutterably tender and reassuring smile of a mother for her child. Bartie questioned her with

8

his eyes, and the girl searched swiftly for words that had not been said before.

'What you have to remember is that it isn't going to be for long, see? I'll ask them as soon as I get down there and tell them you and Stella have to come down too. And if there isn't any room where they are, I'll make them shift somewhere or build another little place just for you and Stella. See?' But ten is not a looking-forward age. Nothing the future held had power enough to drag Bartie's mind off the present. Mourning, Noonah watched his dark eyes fill and brim until the boy dropped his head in shame and she could see only the curling black hair. Unable to bear his misery she scrambled to her feet. 'Bartie, I have to say good night to Stella again. I want to see her just once more before—,' she stopped. 'Come with me,' she begged, 'before the bell goes for you too.'

Bartie nodded, blinking his eyes. The two walked off, and as they walked their hands brushed and would have clung. But not here. Not until they had left these others behind them.

'Mrs Gordon cut our hair, mine and Trilby's, and she let us use some of her shampoo,' Noonah said cheerfully. 'It smelt nice, too.'

Bartie cast a brief look at Noonah's hair, swinging like a bell over her thin shoulders and cut in a thick fringe across her forehead. Every hair glinted with lights that had nothing to do with its rich black. The glow of the setting sun was on her face, too, ripening the amber skin that belonged to all of these Comeaways.

'You look pretty,' Bartie discovered shyly, his eyes lingering.

'Go on!' Noonah's oblique glanced mocked him.

They were approaching the large central building where they ate and sometimes played if it was wet, and where they gathered together to sing in their clear sweet voices. There was always one mission employee to grow enthusiastic about the way these coloured children sang, and to coach them in hymns and old-time favourites, and to bring them on as a star turn on the occasion of important visitors.

A few of the bigger boys and girls came clattering down the steps as they passed. The fly-wire door crashed behind them and there was Trilby, long slim legs dancing; her hair, fresh-washed, springing alive and springing round her face. She caught sight of Noonah and Bartie straightway and came over to them. There were no doubts about these three and their relationship to each other. Wide low brows, broad and slightly flattened cheek-bones, strongly modelled noses with flaring nostrils and then the clear sweet curve of lips that parted on square white teeth. Only Trilby had those strange light eyes. The others' were warm brown with jetty depths, the whole of the iris showing between wide-open lids. Only Trilby's hair had that sun-struck look. The others had hair the colour of coal, coarse hair that curled softly round their faces.

'Still grizzling?' Trilby questioned, teasing Bartie with a glance.

Before Noonah could answer a man in a pair of knee-length khaki shorts appeared, brushing the palm of one hand rhythmically across his fat thigh with each brisk step. This was Mr Norton, the superintendent of the mission.

He bent an attentive look on the girls. 'One more night for you two, hey? Well, early to bed so you'll be fresh for the trip. It's a long trip, mind you, down to where you're going.'

'Yes,' the girls murmured submissively.

The man nodded approvingly, switched his attention to a boy who lounged indolently against a veranda post. 'Better give that kikuyi grass another sprinkle tonight, George. Can't have it dying on us, eh?'

The boy gathered up his languid body and moved away, unresponsive but obedient.

Trilby curled her lip after the man. 'Always so damn cheerful,' she muttered. 'Treating everyone like they were children. Gee, I'll be glad to get away from this place.'

'It isn't too bad,' frowned Noonah, reminding her sister of Bartie's presence. 'Lots of kids like it better than where they come from.'

'Like to know where they've come from, if they like this dump,' Trilby said shortly.

'All you kids are going out in the ute tomorrow, aren't you?' Noonah asked Bartie. 'Into town, Mrs Gordon said.'

Bartie nodded lifelessly.

'Now don't start howling,' Trilby warned him. 'You gotta stay here if you like it or not. We had to when we were your age. And we were younger when we came, too.'

Bartie tried a valiant sniff but a few tears chased each other down his cheeks. A couple of boys around his age stopped to stare.

'Lookatim cry,' the bigger one jeered. 'Ole Cry-baby Comeaway.'

Trilby turned on them furiously. 'Get, you kids. Go on! And don't forget Bartie isn't the only one around here cries. What about you two an the way you cried when your mummy come up to see you. Thought she wasn't ever going to get away from you, I bet.'

Her grey eyes sparked as the two children made sulkily off. 'Never can let anyone alone,' she fumed. 'Always someone around to stick their noses in someone else's business.' She swung round on Bartie. 'An you! You make me ashamed you're my brother. You're the big one, aren't you? That has to take care of Stella. Don't you understand that?'

'Shut up!' Noonah spoke sharply. 'Bartie's coming down with me to see Stella. He'll be all right if you just leave him alone and don't bully him.'

'Us two are leaving early tomorrow morning,' Trilby said gruffly to her brother. 'If you want to say good-bye you'd better do it now.' She bent towards the boy and gave him a hug. Her thin fingers with their oval nails and perfect moons, like delicate shells against the dark skin, slid into the black curly hair. She gave it a tug, a rallying gesture to him to keep his emotion out of sight. Nobody ever saw Trilby in tears. Her world was peopled with enemies waiting to pounce on any such weakness and turn it to their own account, and every observation she made confirmed this fact more fully in her mind.

'Come on, Bartie,' Noonah said gently. Trilby looked after them, undecided about accompanying them, then she shrugged and turned in the opposite direction, chin high and eyes narrowed.

Bartie had caught some of his sister's fierceness. 'I am not a cry-baby. I hardly ever cry, do I, Noonah?'

'You're all right,' Noonah said affectionately. 'Trilby just said that because she felt like crying herself. She was all worked up, and she doesn't know half what's she's talking about when she gets worked up.'

'About once a year, that's all,' Bartie still smarted, and his cheeks were still a bit wet.

A woman in a canvas deck-chair looked up in surprise as the two approached her. She was accustomed to Noonah's nightly visits, but the girl had already tucked her small sister into bed and kissed her good night.

'Can we have just one more look?' Noonah begged. 'I'm going tomorrow and I just thought—Bartie and I thought—.'

'They're all asleep in there,' the woman said doubtfully. 'You'll have to be very quiet. One wakes the lot sometimes.'

'We won't make any noise at all,' Noonah promised.

'Go on then,' the woman said. 'But no noise remember! My feet are killing me today.'

Noonah pulled her brother after her into the children's nursery. Usually, only the children under five slept here, but Stella was small and delicate, prone to chesty colds and barking coughs, so she slept in here with the babies where supervision was night-long. Noonah went over to the far corner of the room where she knew her sister slept. The little girl had tossed off her sheet, and her nightgown was twisted round her waist so that her small round bottom and relaxed limbs showed dark against the white cotton sheets. One small hand dropped over the side of the bed; the other cradled her head. She was breathing lightly and evenly, her soft mouth parted.

Forgetting Bartie for a second, Noonah kneeled. She took up the tiny relaxed hand and pressed it gently to her cheek. Beside her, the boy bent his head to look at his small sister. His mouth curved upward. Hands on knees, his breathing carefully controlled, he continued to gaze. Then brother and sister exchanged a long look. Bartie nodded slightly, his eyes shy.

When they were well clear of the nursery, Noonah spoke. 'You couldn't come with me and leave her behind, Bartie, could you? She's so little, and she loves you.'

She walked Bartie to the dormitory occupied by the smaller boys. Before he passed through the doorway he stopped and turned back to her. 'Remember,' he said expressionlessly, 'you promised.'

The door closed behind him, and it was Noonah's turn to blink.

They were in the train at last and Trilby was almost out of her mind with excitement, terribly afraid that it was all a dream. But the train gathered pace and the familiar things outside the window continued to pass from her sight one after the other. No dream sister could look as real as Noonah on the opposite seat, or the man and woman across the carriage from them. She could read the notices, too, that told her not to pull the communication cord and not to expectorate on the floor. She could even make out the inscriptions under the dusty looking pictures of tall timber. Convinced, she sat back in her seat and looked out the window again. It was all bush now. Miles and miles of wattles and drooping river gums vanished behind the line of the frame. She tried to stay their progress by fixing her eyes on one special tree but the train flew too fast. She gave up trying and fixed candid curious eyes on the other passengers.

Noonah did not take her eyes off the view outside her window. For a long time she watched it unseeing, but gradually her brow grew lighter and her mourning mouth took an upward turn. The thing was done, the separation complete, and she was still too young to distrust the future.

By and by the little train grew weary and its first fine burst of speed slackened considerably. It picked its way more carefully now and sometimes, though still between stations, it stopped completely. On the track, men walked up and down, intent and busy, and the passengers in the carriages rushed to watch them pass. Some complained, irritably and angrily. Others craned their necks and narrowed their eyes against the sun and passed low-voiced comments to their companions. The lucky ones were those at whose carriage the mechanics halted to peer and poke and get down on hands and knees to examine wheels more closely. Trilby and Noonah, politely flattened against the backs of their seats to make room for the watchers, waited patiently and trustfully for the wrong to be righted, and in the meantime they took the opportunity to observe unobserved.

Trilby knew of only two types of white people. Those who did not care one way or the other about you, and the others who, like the white children on the school bus, waited wet-lipped and bright-eyed for your reactions to

15

taunts dealing mostly with the colour of your skin. Towards the end, the mission had been given schoolrooms of its own and government teachers had come to teach in them, but in the beginning the mission children had attended the town school along with the white children. A school bus came out to pick them up and Trilby remembered well the twice-daily trips in and out. The mission children preferred to sit together but that wasn't always possible and then they might have to share a seat with a white child. Pinched legs and hair-pullings Trilby could deal with and she did, very effectively. Remarks such as 'Pooh! What's the stink around here?' and 'Wonder if she et up all her nice lizards this morning?' resulted in a win for the white children, most of them needle-sharp at detecting evidence of victory whether it were wet eyes and vulnerable soft mouths closing over sobs or the angry snarls and hating looks they got from some of the bigger mission children. Nearly always there were bumps and bruises and torn shirts and frocks. Half-smiling Trilby remembered the dreadful satisfaction of hearing a pocket tear away from the material it had been anchored to.

Once, a girl sharing a seat with Trilby had cried, 'Why, that's my old dress you're wearing.' Warmth and happiness had flooded over her. She had turned to smile at her neighbour because she had thought, knowing no better at that stage, that here among her enemies was a friend. And then the girl had laughed, and in her eyes there was no friendliness at all—just a look that Trilby could not remember even now without feeling ashamed. The girl had turned to the others in the bus and told them, 'The kid's wearing one of my old dresses. My mum must have given it to her because it's all worn out. See?' She had pointed to a patch on the skirt, and those nearest had left their seats to examine the patch. So Trilby had learned.

There were other things. Waiting at the side of the road for the school bus, hoping this would be a good day, when the mission children could sit together. Bracing herself, just in case. Not joining in with the chatter of the others because she had been too busy cautioning herself against showing those tell-tale signs of a bull's-eye for which her enemies waited.

Trilby turned a narrow-eyed gaze on the wispy-haired woman who over-flowed the seat in the corner diagonally opposite. From the safety of today she took a cool look at the days of her first brush with education. She and Noonah had been with their parents then, living temporarily in a camp on the outskirts of a small northern town. Dad, Trilby remembered, sometimes let her and Noonah go with him to help burn off the great yellow stumps of the gum trees. Often they had camped alongside a glowing log all night, and the red glow would still be there under the pale silvery ashes when they woke next morning.

At this particular town Mrs Comeaway had been seized with the idea of sending the two girls to the town school. She had had a little mission training herself, but in her case the training had been confined to kitchen chores, with an hour or two in the classroom whenever it was felt she could be spared. Maybe she would not have had the courage to break the ice, but there were other camps round about and other coloured children attending the school in the little township.

17

The girls had fallen in with her plan for different reasons, Noonah because she was an even-tempered child who usually did as she was told and Trilby because she was curious.

Trilby leaned her head back against the carriage seat. It had not been much of a school. A few little tables and chairs in a draughty old timbered hall. A square blackboard on three yellow legs with a shelf to take chalk and the yellow felt pad used for cleaning off writing. And a woman school-teacher with wispy dry red hair that stood up in peaks, and peaky eyelids to match. From narrow shoulders her body had flowed down to enormous hips and the black shiny stuff of her apron had given off a smell of bitter peaches. There had not been enough of the little chairs and tables to seat the coloured children, so they had sat on the floor at the side of the classroom. One of them was expected to keep the blackboard clean. Trilby had hated the choking white dust.

The teacher directed most of her attention to her white pupils, but she always knew if one of the coloured children wasn't listening to what she said. A ruler across the knuckles or a stinging smack on the leg was her answer to that. Every day one of their number was sent home for any one of a variety of reasons. Too loud sniffing if a child had a cold but no handkerchief, torn clothes, dirty clothes, unwashed hands or hair, inability to answer a sharply-put question. Some of the coloured children, Trilby knew, committed any and all of these offences on purpose, wanting to be sent home, but she had not seen things this way. When her nose was wet she wiped it on the skirt of her frock, if she had overlooked her skimpy morning wash she sat on her hands, and because she listened with stony attentiveness to all that the teacher said, she was able to give satisfactory answers to the questions. Because it was so much nicer to play around the camp or to accompany her father to the paddock to help with the burning-off, Trilby had never quite understood why something in her rebelled at being sent away from the schoolroom. Even Noonah did not mind. They had all been sent away in the end. A policeman had come out to the camps and talked to the parents, and Trilby had learned, after sneaking close to him and listening, that some of the white mothers and fathers did not want their children to sit alongside coloured children because they had too many colds and they scratched their heads too much.

When the policeman had gone Trilby heard her mother grumbling to her father. Mr Comeaway had only laughed, but her mother had been crabby for days. There had been painful scrapings of their scalps with a fine-toothed comb, and slatherings of kerosene and even dark suspicions directed at the other camps. That had been the beginning of the ending of the girls' wanderings with their parents. The bug of education had established itself firmly in Mrs Comeaway's head and, a few weeks after that, Trilby and Noonah had been dumped at the mission. 'Where yous lucky to be at,' was her final and firm admonition to them both.

The long years that had followed! Half a dozen times since then the girls had seen their parents; the last time had been when Bartie and Stella had been brought to join them. Trilby glanced over at the corner seat. The woman sitting there was staring at her. Trilby remembered that same look in the eyes of her long-ago teacher. Curiosity with no warmth in it. If she had only known, that teacher. The distaste she had felt for the coloured children and shown so clearly had been equalled by the fearful shrinking they had felt for her and her white-rimmed eyes with their peaky lids. And her face which was the colour of the underside of a sleepy lizard.

'Ugh!' Trilby shivered, and the woman turned her head away.

TWO

Just before they reached the last station, the cheerful guard
came to tell them to put all their things together so that
nothing should be lost. He dug in his pocket and bent over
them. 'An here's something for yous to spend on lollies,' he
whispered. 'You been good kids.'

To each girl he handed a shilling.

Noonah took her coin shyly, with whispered thanks.
Trilby looked from her shilling to the guard and back again.
Then she flashed a look of such pure gratitude at him that
the man's expression of easy benevolence changed to one
of surprise. 'It's only a bob, ya know,' he chuckled at her.
'Won't buy yous much these days.' And he hurried off on
other duties.

Trilby followed his progress down the corridor, still
smiling. 'I don't mind him,' she said softly to Noonah. 'He's
nice.'

'Yes,' agreed her sister. She was busy with parcels and cases. 'Trilby, where's the little bag with the soap in it?'

'Sitting on it,' Trilby said, after a search. 'Here you are.'

'I promised Bartie I'd ask about him and Stella coming back as soon as we get there,' Noonah worried.

'Let it go for a while,' Trilby frowned. 'Gee, *we* had to stay there, didn't we?'

'Praps I won't mention it the first day. But soon!' Noonah's cares were beginning to settle around her shoulders again. What would it be like, living with her mother and father? Would they be nice to her? Would they want to get the others back? How could she convince them that Bartie *must* come back? That she had promised.

'Can't you listen?' Trilby said impatiently. 'I said let's get up early tomorrow morning and go straight in to the town.'

'I'll see the hospital,' Noonah said, her expression clearing again. 'I want to see the hospital first of all. I'm going to train there, to be a nurse.'

'And no more school,' Trilby said, making a firm line of her lips.

'You told Mrs Gordon you'd go back until you got your Junior,' Noonah reminded her sister.

'She'd have gone on and on if I hadn't. I'm not going back but.' Her brows drew together, narrowing her eyes. 'I'm going to look at the shops first of all and get some new bathers and I'm going to swim and have some fun, and later on, if I feel like it, I'll get a job somewhere. Serving in a milk-bar, I think. With a pink uniform like those others had at the Rainbow Milk-Bar. You think I'd be all right for a job like that, Noonah?'

'Anyone could do that,' Noonah said.

'I don't mean that,' Trilby frowned.

'What did you mean well?'

'Ah, never mind! You go and train to be a nurse, and I'll do things my own way.' But Noonah was not listening. Her soft cheek was pressed against the glass as her eyes strained ahead. 'Look at all the lights, Trilby. We must be nearly there.'

There were a good many lights. The station looked big and important. On another line a big black engine puffed past, trailing carriages after it in a neat orderly line. There was clamour outside the carriage and bustling busyness inside it as the other passengers cleared the luggage rack and gathered their cases and coats together in tidy piles. Guards called directions, friends shouted greetings, people's faces flowed past the window like an animated mural, and a sharp stuffy smell seeped into the carriage.

'How will we find them?' Noonah panicked, slim dark hands clutching the edges of her seat. There was a last jerk, a gentle shaking, and their train was still. The girls stayed in their seats until everyone had left the carriage then walked out with their own cases. There was the business of stacking everything on the station platform, neatly, so that coats did not get dirty, and after that nothing but to stand and wait. Uneasily, darting questioning looks at each other.

'Here they is,' said a remembered voice, and the girls turned with brightening faces. Mrs Comeaway's hair was greyer than they remembered it, overhanging the collar of her coat. She was fatter, too, so that the hand holding the folds of coat had much ado to prevent them from flying free. But her wide dark face was alight with pleasure and her voice excited as she called back over her shoulder to the man behind her. Mr Comeaway came up grinning. His wet hair had been sleeked back from his good-humoured face, his clean white shirt was open at the neck to show the curly grey hairs on his chest, his cuffs neatly buttoned at the wrist.

'So big!' Mrs Comeaway said wonderingly, admiringly. 'You two big now, eh?'

'Outside we gotta taxi,' Mr Comeaway told them. 'For all this stuff ya got. You bring im along an that taximan take care of that lot.' He waited politely for the girls to pick up their cases, then he led the way, nodding encouragingly. Mrs Comeaway escorted the girls from the other side, beaming and panting. 'We gotta nice place right by Green's. An a bed each for ya. New beds straight fum shops. How ya like that, eh? Eh, I didn't even kiss yous yet.' She stopped the procession to deliver two resounding kisses. 'Gee, you girls got big.' Her plump face creased in folds of firm and shining dark flesh as she laughed. Outside the station, the waiting taximan took their cases and slung them into the boot. The elder Comeaways climbed into the back seat and sat forward, smiling broadly. 'Come on!' they beckoned.

Trilby and Noonah climbed in too. The girls sat very straight whilst their father and mother looked them over from the tips of their toes to the tops of their heads, smiling all the while, nodding approvingly, nudging each other.

And the girls' prevailing feeling was one of warm pleasure. It was nice to have a mother and father waiting for you at the end of a long trip. It was a good feeling to see

24

them acting so pleased just because you were there, it was by far the most satisfying of the day's experiences. They belonged again.

In between exchanging smiles with her parents, Noonah took fleeting looks at the scene beyond the taxi window. Perhaps they might pass the hospital.

'Was it nice on the train?' Mrs Comeaway inquired. 'Did you get looked after good? Them mission people writ us a letter and they said we wasn't to worry about ya because you was gunna be looked after.'

'These two didn't see a place this big before,' Mr Comeaway chuckled. 'Not a word outa them.'

'Can we swim?' Trilby asked.

'You can swim,' Mrs Comeaway told her. 'They give ya that for nothing here.' She laughed uproariously and her husband joined her.

'Will we go past the hospital?' Noonah inquired.

'You the one's gunna be a nurse, eh? You look out there now. That big place with all them trees. See?

Noonah peered through the window excitedly. There was nothing to be seen but a tallness of lights, but her heart leapt. There! Inside that tallness was the matron who already knew about Noonah Comeaway and how she was coming down from the mission to learn to be a nurse. She was expected there. Maybe even now the matron was saying to someone, 'Wonder when that girl's coming?'

'Gee!' she sighed ecstatically.

'An here's ole Heartbreak Hill,' Mrs Comeaway said luxuriously. 'An we don't walk up *him* tonight. Ya gotta walk up this damn hill ta know what it's like. Gunna get arkattack fum that hill one a these days. There, up we go an round the top. An over an down an up again.' She sat waiting for the dips and turns, enjoying them as would a child. 'An this is it.'

'We get out here,' Mr Comeaway explained kindly, letting himself out through his door. His wife eased herself out after him. The taxi driver opened the girls' door and stood grinning at them. From the road they could see nothing but the dim whiteness and a rise. The man got their cases from the boot and deposited them at the side of the road. 'That'll be four shillings,' he said impersonally.

There was a short wait.

'Go on!' Mrs Comeaway said firmly. 'Give the man is money.'

'Didn't you have the money?' Mr Comeaway asked in injured tones.

'I did not,' Mrs Comeaway said even more firmly. 'An why would I seein ya didn't give me none.'

'Ah well!' Mr Comeaway shook his head at the taxi driver, sorrowing for him. 'I better come down tomorrow and fix you up.'

'Making it as near a pound as don't make any difference,' the man said. 'Okay! See you tomorrow.' He got back into the taxi and turned it expertly. The Comeaway family stood there in the dark, watching the tail-light disappear over the hill.

'Well, up we go,' Mrs Comeaway sighed. 'Come on!'

Mr Comeaway had already started.

'Come back here, you,' Mrs Comeaway called sternly. 'Just you grab them girls' cases, first time they home.'

'Gee, all right,' Mr Comeaway said, coming back to the road on a small slide of sand. 'Jus thought I'd get a light goin for yous, that's all.'

'Yes, you did,' Mrs Comeaway withered him. 'Now come on, you two, an follow me. Then ya won't fall over nothin.'

Trilby and Noonah groped for each other's hands. Their sides were heaving with their efforts to giggle soundlessly. Their mother plunged up the sandy hill and they followed her closely. The blackness was lit by a dim yellow glow to the right. 'That ain't it,' Mrs Comeaway panted, ploughing on past the smudge. 'That's where the ole lady lives. We're a bit further back. You kids is gunna like the ole lady. Real nice woman. Lets us use everything she got, dub an all.'

Another patch of yellow sprang out of the darkness ahead. It shone through between sheets of galvanized iron and spilled over a doorway. 'Don't you get too far over that side,' Mrs Comeaway warned, 'or you'll be goin arse over tip down the hill.' She giggled. 'On top a Billy Grey's roof, maybe. Is camp just down there.'

In the lighted doorway, the girls stood blinking and smiling and looking around them. This was home. They walked into it thankfully.

The room they were in measured about twelve by twelve. A hurricane-lamp stood on top of a heavy home-carpentered table, and a black-handled frying-pan, some crockery, a milk-tin full of dripping and a couple of empty brown bottles crowded it for room. Against each outside wall was a small iron bed topped with a mattress and several folded army blankets. The floor of the room was of earth stamped hard. A black iron stove bulked large across one end, its top cluttered with dim objects. Wooden uprights supported an assortment of clothes crowned with hats and bags, and across another aperture at the back of the room hung a man's thick brown coat, presumably acting as a curtain. Trilby's gaze was caught and held by a single brown chop in the frying-pan. It was frozen in a pool of brown fat, but her mouth watered for it.

'Fixin that catch on the door certainly kep them dogs out,' Mr Comeaway said, picking the chop out of its fat and tearing off a piece. 'Didn't even finish me dinner,' he told the girls, 'the ole lady was so anxious ta get down that station.' He waved a casual hand. 'Hadda leave everything an rush.'

'These here are the beds,' Mrs Comeaway said proudly, bouncing happily. 'Good new beds these. I put a coupla rugs each for yous. Look in that tin on the table, you kids. Might be some biscuits left.'

Mr Comeaway took the lid from the tin himself. He searched through the crackling debris of half a dozen old biscuit wrappings and finally found a few crumby biscuits. He proffered them graciously.

'You kids look wore out,' Mrs Comeaway said sympathetically. 'An likewise us. So I tell you what we gunna do. We all gunna get some sleep, an in the morning you can tell us bout everything. What ya think, eh?'

'Ya hungry?' Mr Comeaway asked, a bit anxiously. 'I shoulda arst before I et me chop.'

'I give em a good big feed tomorrow,' Mrs Comeaway said, clearing her conscience and her mind in one swoop.

'Yeah, that's right,' Mr Comeaway nodded. He gave the girls a big smile. 'I better get out now, an let ya get ta bed.' He hesitated, slightly embarrassed. 'G'night!' He mooched into the next room, ducking his head beneath the army overcoat.

'An you leave all that stuff till tomorrow, too,' Mrs Comeaway said, waving her hand at the cases. Her pleased eyes sought the beds again. 'You gunna be real comforble in them beds. Now!' She moved over to her daughters and hugged each in turn. 'Inta bed with ya.' She moved off after her husband and disappeared behind the coat, returning, however, almost immediately. In a loud whisper she told them, 'If ya wanta use the dub it's round the side. Take the lamp so ya won't trip over nothing.' The coat swung back into place and the girls were alone in their bedroom.

Noonah perched herself on one of the beds. Trilby's eyes still brimmed with laughter, but neither girl spoke, aware of the two in the other room. Their ears pricked to the strange thuds and groaning sighs as their parents prepared for bed. Trilby caught Noonah's eye and gestured over her shoulder with a thumb. Noonah nodded. They took the lantern by its wire handle and crept outside. It was a while before they found the toilet crouching drunkenly beneath a tree.

'You think it's going to be all right?' Trilby said softly, on the way back.

Noonah nodded vigorously. 'I like them. Don't you?'

Trilby spluttered suddenly. 'Why do you think they made that hole square?'

Noonah choked. 'Shut *up*!' she begged. 'They'll hear.'

'And I'm so hungry,' Trilby wailed softly. 'That lovely chop!'

'I was just going to ask if I could have it,' Noonah giggled.

'We'll have a drink instead,' Trilby said, waving the lantern round. 'Where's the tap?' But there was nothing that looked like a tap. Inside again, she poked round on the stove for the kettle, but there was no kettle there.

Noonah thought longingly of washing her face, which felt dry and dirty, then she shrugged her shoulders. Tomorrow would do. She fished in her case for pyjamas and undressed as quietly as possible. Trilby did the same, removing one of the hats and hanging her clothes over the things that already hung from a nail. The arranging of the beds came next. Trilby's extravagant miming when she looked in vain for a pillow nearly set Noonah off again. The girls climbed at last between the grey woollen blankets, using their arms as head-rests. Noonah reached for the hurricane-lamp and blew out the flame.

'Good night, Trilby,' she whispered.

'Night,' Trilby whispered back. 'We'll get up early tomorrow morning and have a look round, shall we?'

THREE

Trilby was the first to wake, her face barred with sunlight
that slipped through the inadequate walls of the humpy.
She smiled almost as soon as she opened her eyes. This
was the real beginning of freedom. She looked across the
room at the still sleeping Noonah and smiled again, remembering the night before. There was no sound from the inner
room. She swung her legs over the side of the bed and sat
considering. Then she reached for her clothes and stripped
off her pyjamas. A few minutes later she crept out through
the doorway, breathing quickly through parted lips, her
silver-grey eyes shining.

Ten feet away tall sunflowers grew together in a great
golden mass. Already bees were climbing clumsily over
the pollen-dusted black centres. Behind the sunflowers the
ground dropped away steeply. Trilby walked to the edge and
looked down on a wattle-studded valley, tenderly, brightly

green. The smoke from a couple of camp-fires rose thinly on the quiet air. Trilby counted a dozen roof-tops sheltering beneath the green: galvanized iron painted white, the grey of weathered tarpaulin and the rust-streaked glimmer of scrap-iron.

She turned to examine her own domain. The humpy was as she had imagined it to be, a ramshackle arrangement of tarpaulins and scrap-iron nailed to bush timber. A bough shelter projected from one end and beneath it stood another rough table and two cane chairs very much the worse for having been sat on. Suspended by a string from a nearby wattle swung a wire safe, its door hanging open, its shelves bare. The ground beneath her feet was pure beach sand, but along one side of the humpy grew several tomato plants. Trilby lifted the drab green leaves, but the tiny red tomatoes were holed and uneatable. She picked one and threw it high over the valley, watching the red speck until it disappeared into the wattles.

Back from the humpy was a weathered house, its roof sagging and broken, its timbers silver grey and splintery. At its side a blackened copper stood on some red bricks, and a wooden stand held wash-tubs. A few elderly stocks grew in a line along the wall, and dusty-leaved honeysuckle clung to the rail of the front veranda. But a big old gum flung sheltering boughs over the entire structure and the effect was one of peaceful homeliness. Along the line of the fence, where now not more than a dozen palings stood, peppermint trees trailed dim green leaves and clusters of rose-pink berries. The house was set on the flat top of a hill which stood like an inverted pudding-bowl, dominating the rise to the left and the wide stretch of plain that lay behind it. Scattered over the flatness were tiny box-like houses set in fenced paddocks of gold and green. The sun turned their roofs to squares of colour from a child's paint-box. Towards the township a grey fortress-like tank squatted solidly into the gentle slope of a hill which half obscured it, and far beyond that Trilby saw the line of the sea, slashed with foam, its slaty-blue merging into the softness of the summer sky.

She stood relaxed and still, looking into the distance, content with a new feeling of peace and happiness. And as she stood, the miscellany of tiny bush sounds smoothed themselves into a vibrant silence.

Three silvery notes broke the spell. Trilby watched smiling as a grey dot of a bird pretended to lose its balance on a bough over her head.

A group of children straggled forth from the grey weatherboard house. And Noonah's voice sounded behind her. 'Why didn't you wake me up?'

The children came closer, staring at the strangers with wide almost black eyes, their scrutiny both competent and impersonal.

'Hello!' Noonah greeted them companionably.

The faces melted into grins. A bigger girl bent to pick up a small night-gowned figure and settle it over one hip. Two boys stood their ground, alert and sure of themselves. Another small girl maintained precarious balance whilst she scraped with one foot at the back of a leg. 'Mrs Green's,' Trilby said.

'That's our Gramma,' the little girl said. Noonah bent to look into her face and to pat her cheek.

'We stay with Gramma an go to school,' the older one volunteered.

'You don't go to school yet, do you?' Noonah smiled at the little girl.

'Her mother lets her stay here when she goes away working,' the same older girl said. 'She's Bonny, and this is her sister,' looking down at the very smallest one on her hip.

'Let me take her,' Noonah offered. She took the baby girl and smoothed her hair back from her face.

Trilby grinned. Noonah would be busy for an hour now if she knew anything about her sister. 'Look, I'm going to get washed,' she told Noonah. 'I've found a tap.'

Noonah only nodded, already engrossed with the children.

Trilby went back to the humpy and searched quietly for something to wash in. She found a basin underneath the table. A skinny grey washer hung over its side. Trilby wrinkled her nose and used it to wipe out the inside of the grey-rimmed basin. Then she took her new washer and soap from her flowered sponge-bag.

When she had washed herself she took the basin to the side of the hill and flung its contents in a silvery sweep over the hillside. A river of rusting tins and trash already littered the slope, and under a wattle just over the brow glinted a stack of amber bottles.

Down in the valley there were signs of life. Voices floated up—the high clear voices of children and the rounder, deeper notes of adults.

She replaced the basin and went into the humpy to change her frock. She was tying the laces in her shoes

34

when sounds of vast yawnings and luxurious stretchings came from the inner room. 'You girls awake yet?' called her mother.

Trilby stepped uncertainly towards the coat-veiled aperture. 'We've been up for ages.'

'Come on in then,' chuckled her mother. 'Nobody in here gunna bite ya.' So Trilby stepped past the coat.

The inner room was thick with gloom. The only opening in its walls was covered by a heavy jute sugar-bag. Occasionally this lifted a little with the breeze and a breath of fresh morning air stirred the atmosphere. In this room a thin strip of linoleum had been laid at the side of the big double bed that took up most of the room. Head and foot of the bed were festooned with garments, and from its sagging middle Mrs Comeaway rose to greet her daughter. Mr Comeaway was still asleep, and as his wife sat up in bed his head rolled down the slope to her back. Mrs Comeaway, using her husband's chest as a back-rest, looked with pleased interest at her daughter. 'Aaah! Nnnh! You all dressed up, eh?'

Trilby ducked her head and smoothed the skirt of her frock.

'Come an sit on the bed a minute while I get me circula-tion goin,' Mrs Comeaway invited.

Trilby sat on the end of the bed and looked curiously round the room. Across one corner stood a high, old chest of drawers, its cream paint striped with scratches. The inevitable clothing littered its top and scattered through the debris were two tins of talcum, a brush stuck with a hairy black comb, a xylonite tray from which flashed an

35

assortment of jewellery, and two large white plaster-of-Paris rabbits with pink-lined ears.

'Ya think ya gunna like it with us?' Mrs Comeaway asked, wringing a groan from Mr Comeaway as her elbow slipped into his neck.

'It's going to be lovely,' Trilby said, with warmth.

Mrs Comeaway looked pleased. 'Course, it ain't much of a place,' she said complacently, 'it does us but. Keeps the wet out.'

Trilby doubted that, but she did not care overmuch.

'Can I have a look at that stuff up there?' she asked, pointing at the brooches and ear-rings.

'Me jools?' Mrs Comeaway said, with a grin. 'Go ahead.'

While Trilby examined the array, she slipped from the bed and pushed her feet into a pair of black patent court shoes with alarmingly slanted heels. She waddled, lurching a little, to the chest of drawers, selecting a few articles of clothing from its top. When she had donned these over and under the petticoat she had worn to bed, she took down a tin of carnation talcum. Pulling out the neck of her frock, she shook some of the powder down over her chest and with one hand smoothed it across and under each armpit.

'Take what you want,' she told Trilby. 'Never can remember to use it meself. Woulda give it to the kids long ago except it comes in handy if ya run short a money.'

'How?' Trilby stopped in the act of screwing on a pair of bright red ear-rings.

'Playin cards, you can use anything,' Mrs Comeaway said matter-of-factly. 'Played for nails before this.' She

36

unstuck the comb and wrenched it through her hair. 'Now,' she grunted contentedly, smoothing the dress against her hips, 'we better get you girls somethin ta eat. Where you say that Noonah was? My word, you look real nice, Trilby. Come on outside so I can see ya proper.' She took the girl by the arm and then clapped her hand to her head. 'The old man,' she murmured. 'Did e or did e not say e was gunna go down the wharf this morning? Hey, you!' She walked purposefully over to the bed, and in one business-like gesture swiped two blankets and an old overcoat from her husband's peaceful form. Trilby stepped back giggling as her father's night attire was revealed in all its scantiness.

'Come on, you!' Mrs Comeaway said firmly.

Mr Comeaway kept his eyes tight shut. 'Not *this* morning,' he said thickly, his hand groping for and finding the covers. 'What about them girls? Gotta show em the place, ain't we?'

'Didn't you say today?'

'Tomorrow just as good.'

Mrs Comeaway raised her shoulders high and let them fall again. 'E never did like work,' she told her daughter philosophically, leading the way out to the other room. 'Now then!' She swayed over to the black stove in the corner and opened the oven door. 'Not a bloody crust,' she said disgustedly. 'I tell ya what, Trilby. You just nip over an tell Mrs Green we got damn all ta eat an will she let ya have something till we go down town. Ask er fa what ya want yaself, weeties or something. She'll have it. Has to with all them kids. An say does she want anything down town.'

Trilby was horrified. 'Gee, Mummy, I don't like to.'

37

Mrs Comeaway straightened. 'Why doncha? She's a nice ole woman, Mrs Green. Wouldn't hurt a flea.'

'You come too.'

'Yeah well, I suppose I could,' Mrs Comeaway said, as if she had been presented with some novel idea. 'Come along then.' She lumbered ahead, her tremendous bottom hoisting her over the ground with a sailor-like roll. She began hoo-hooing immediately, keeping it up with a sort of absent-minded persistence until they were inside the house. 'Hoo-hoo,' she called through another doorway. 'Anyone around in here? You home, Mrs Green? I'm outa tucker.'

Trilby followed her across the earth-floored porch, and stood behind her sniffing a warm, wonderful smell of food cooking. The inner room was gloomy, but a good big fire burned in the shining black stove and on top of it sizzled a huge frying-pan-full of eggs and sliced tomatoes. This much Trilby saw before she closed her eyes and made a brief wish.

A woman holding a bunch of cutlery in her hand looked over and smiled. 'This is the other one, eh?' She had a rich full voice with velvety overtones. Trilby smiled back at her, hopefully.

She saw Noonah, sitting at one end of a big table with a child on her lap. The other children were either already seated or busy dragging chairs out for themselves. The place looked like a home, and the centre of it, Trilby knew, was this elderly woman with the sparse grey hair whose voice sounded so much younger than she could be. Mrs Comeaway was talking to her and, under cover of the conversation, Trilby studied Mrs Green curiously, a little hesitantly, before she switched her gaze to the room and its occupants.

Against one wall was a horsehair sofa upholstered in shiny black, split a little here and there, showing deep hollows where springs were missing or broken. At the end of the sofa sat an old, old man. He did not look up at the newcomers because he was busy steadying a steaming cup of tea. Trilby felt an urge to go over and steady it for him before he spilt it on his thin shanks. The woman, Mrs Green, followed her gaze. 'That's Skippy,' she said. 'Don't you worry about him. He's all right.'

'How old is he?' Trilby said respectfully. The old man's eyes peered from beneath folded lids. His hands on his cup looked like dark brown claws, and his face was wrinkled and shrunken. He looked across at her as she spoke, growling in his throat, his eyes two wicked pin-points of light.

'I—I just thought you must be pretty old,' Trilby repeated.

'Mumblin away,' the old man grunted pettishly. 'An damn kids everywhere shoutin their heads off.'

'Drink up that tea,' Mrs Green said pleasantly, 'or you'll be grizzling because it's cold.'

'Too damn hot,' Skippy grumbled. 'Nemind bout ole man, givim tea still bilin hot.'

Mrs Green smiled over at Trilby. 'You sit down with your mummy an have a cup too.'

'If ya got some ta spare well.' Mrs Comeaway lifted the nearest child from his chair and sat down with him in her lap. 'You take Martin on ya knee or get yaself another chair,' she told Trilby.

'Go on!' Mrs Green nodded. 'In the room at the back.'

So Trilby picked her way carefully past the old man and went doubtingly along the passage.

'Don't take any notice of Honay,' Mrs Green called after her.

As well as a suite of dining-room furniture in dark oak, the further room held a rickety-looking wooden bed and a woman occupant almost as old as Skippy. Trilby darted one look at the woman's face, grim even in sleep, and snatched up a chair, returning with it to the warm dark kitchen.

'Honay still the star boarder?' Mrs Comeaway inquired, with a twinkle. 'Her and Skippy,' Mrs Green smiled.

'How'd the ole devil get on yesterday?' Mrs Comeaway asked.

Trilby placed her chair next to Noonah's and sat down. Mrs Green pushed a cup of tea across to her and laughed. 'How d'you think?'

'I dunno how e does it,' Mrs Comeaway marvelled. 'Seems e's got them monarch just where e wants em.'

Mrs Green looked at the two girls. 'Skippy got picked up for receiving. They caught him with a bottle of conto,' she explained. 'He got off all right, but he's still mad about sleeping down the jail. Said he got cold.' She turned to Mrs Comeaway. 'Wouldn't mind betting he goes to see the sergeant about that.'

'What happened down the court?' Mrs Comeaway's eyes were crinkled with amused anticipation.

'Let me tell, Gramma.' A young girl came into the room holding a baby in her arms. Noonah's eyes went straight to the baby, but Trilby's mouth opened in surprise. Gramma Green's roof seemed elastic.

'You go on then, Lee,' Mrs Green said comfortably, 'an I'll just dish up this stuff.' She bent to take some plates from the oven where they had been heating.

The newcomer smoothed her long curling hair with one hand and smiled a greeting at Noonah and Trilby. 'Ya here, are ya? Ya mummy certainly made a fuss bout you two.' She went over to the sofa with her baby and lay back with it against her breast. 'The crowd of us went up to the court,' she said gaily, 'an we was lucky we didn't get put out. Ya not supposed to make any noise up there,' she told the sisters, 'but we was all gigglin. Couldn't *help* gigglin. First of all the magistrate says to Skippy, "Now I want the whole truth, Skippy, in ya own words." Skippy gives them cops a look, then e says e picked up this bottle off the street an before he's even opened it ta see what's inside, e gets picked up. So the boss looks down at is papers and then e says, "But that ain't the way ya told it to the police last night, Skippy." An Skippy says to im, "Ah, I tell them pleece anything. I wait till I see the boss before I tell how I got that bottle." So the magistrate scratches his head and ya can see he's trying not ta laugh, an then e says, "That's the truth then, is it?" And when Skippy says that's the truth, e finishes up dismissin the case. Skippy gets off. An ya know the first thing e says ta them monarch? E turns round on em an yelps, "An now ya can just gimme back that bottle."'

Mrs Comeaway choked on her tea. 'Gawd! Wait till I tell me ole man,' she crowed. 'There's a man for ya, eh?' She looked admiringly over at the old man. At the end of the sofa, Skippy had been listening approvingly, nodding and shaking his head, his wicked black gaze flicking on and off like a snake's. He was half blinded with trachoma, his ears were so full of wax he only bothered to listen when it pleased him, he was older than anyone could remember, including the department, and both legs had been lamed early in life. But he was known and respected as a fighter for miles around. For his rights, that is. Nobody could stick up for Skippy the way he stuck up for himself.

'Nobody knows how he does it,' Mrs Green told the girls, with a shrug and a smile. 'He just does, that's all.'

'Them pleece put there in that horfice ta do things for us fellers,' Skippy said belligerently, 'an not go bossin us fellers round.'

'Skippy!' Mrs Green shook her head helplessly.

'They guvmint, ain't they?' he demanded.

Mrs Comeaway tittered. 'Lissen to im. Ya can't make im understand.'

'Look, now you're here, you'd better stay an have breakfast,' Mrs Green said, her glance taking in the three Comeaways.

'Okay!' Mrs Comeaway answered for them all. 'That suit yous girls?' Noonah and Trilby nodded.

Mrs Green began serving up the food already cooked. The tomatoes drowned in their own gravy and the eggs were edged with brown lace. Noonah and Trilby exchanged looks and felt their mouths moisten.

'Went up and seen that partment feller yesdy,' Skippy said in his cracked old voice.

'Eh! You think that partment man ain't got enough ta do thout ole rascal like you wastin is time?' Mrs Comeaway mock-scolded.

42

'E take care a me fum long way back,' Skippy said complacently. 'I got card up that office. All things bout me. Yesdy I showim new boots. You see im?' With difficulty he pulled up his trouser leg and shoved out his foot.

'More new trousers too,' Mrs Comeaway said, truly scandalized.

'An still none to fit him,' Mrs Green added wryly. 'We had to turn those cuffs up three times before he stopped tripping over them.'

'These good pants,' Skippy said indignantly.

'Yeah, good pants,' Mrs Green soothed. 'And you were probably lucky to get them with that young Mona and Lee here waiting about to give you a bit of soft soap.' She looked over at Lee, her mouth firming, but a twinkle at the back of her eyes. 'Pension day Skippy's that popular he doesn't know himself. Thinks he must be getting young again, eh, Skippy?'

'I didn't ask him for nothing.' Lee's eyes were innocent.

'Ah, young girls all the same,' Mrs Comeaway said tolerantly. 'Do the same meself if I thought I could get away with it. Pity *you* don't put the nippers in fer a few bob but,' she accused Mrs Green. 'Him sittin round here week after week fillin is belly up.'

'No good tucker down ere,' Skippy snarled before Mrs Green could answer. 'Gotta go out in the bush fa good tucker.'

'Seen a big fat goanna round here yesterday,' Mrs Comeaway laughed at him.

'You girls full of plans, I suppose,' Mrs Green asked Trilby and Noonah.

43

'Noonah's gunna be a nurse,' Mrs Comeaway answered for her. 'Trilby don't know yet what she gunna do.'

'What sort of jobs can a girl get down here?' Trilby asked casually.

'Jobs?' Mrs Comeaway considered. 'Lee had a job minding someone's kids a while back.'

'No kids,' Trilby said promptly, 'or housework.'

On the sofa, Lee sat up straight, her face full of interest. Over the table, the older women's eyes met in a quiet look.

'You wouldn't like to be a nurse like Noonah?' Mrs Green suggested.

'Nup! What about those milk-bars. Don't they have girls there?'

'I wouldn't set me heart on anything like that,' Mrs Comeaway said uneasily.

Trilby's hands were quiet in her lap. 'You mean they wouldn't have me?'

Lee laughed scornfully. 'Ya don't think they want *our* hands poisonin their drinks.'

Trilby looked at her, her young face hard, and there was a little silence. Mrs Green entered into the breach, her eyes on the frying-pan she was scraping. 'What are you, Trilby? Fifteen? Sixteen?'

'Fifteen, an her sister two years older. Ain't that right?' Mrs Comeaway appealed to Noonah. Noonah nodded, serious-eyed.

'It's smart, these times, to get some education,' Mrs Green said pleasantly. 'What about going back to High School for a while, till you think things over?'

'Yeah, you could do that easy,' Mrs Comeaway said eagerly.

The girl's face stayed as quiet as her hands.

'Don't let Gramma talk you inta goin back to school,' Lee scorned. 'She tried ta talk *me* inta that.'

'I reckon Gramma's right,' Mrs Comeaway defended. 'Wisht I hadda got more schoolin. Can't get the sense a them comics sometimes.'

'You girls like some more to eat?' Mrs Green asked.

'No thank you!' Noonah refused. Trilby had not heard.

Mrs Comeaway eased the little boy to the floor and slapped the back of his pants. 'Spose we better get goin,' she sighed. 'Make a cuppa tea fa me ole man.' She rose cumbersomely. 'An if ya want somethin down town, you send one a the kids over before we go.'

The girls picked their way through the kitchen and waited at the door. Mrs Green measured sugar and tea into a glass jar and handed it to Mrs Comeaway. 'That'll see you through this morning,' she murmured, 'and I'll just butter a bit of bread while I'm at it.' She buttered two thick slices and wrapped them in newspaper.

'Ta!' Mrs Comeaway said casually. 'See ya later. You girls say thank you fa ya breakfast?' she enquired. 'Then we be off.'

Noonah smiled her good-byes. Trilby's mouth smiled, but her eyes were still thoughtfully cool. They walked one each side of their mother away from Mrs Green's home.

'An now ya fed,' Mrs Comeaway said comfortably, as if some mammoth task had been satisfactorily completed.

The thoughtful look disappeared from Trilby's eyes. 'Gee, isn't it *lovely* to be away from that mission?' she asked Noonah.

'Isn't Mrs Green nice, Mummy?' Noonah said, affectionately slipping a hand through her mother's arm. 'She speaks sort of nice too, doesn't she? Different from'—she hesitated—'us.'

'Been most of her life up on one a them big stations,' Mrs Comeaway said. 'Yeah, I always like ta hear her talkin. No rough stuff about er.'

'Yes, I like *her*,' Trilby added, a note of decision in her voice.

A lot of people liked Mrs Green. Coming of a people to whom hospitality came naturally, there was a gentle kindliness mixed with Mrs Green's that set it a little higher. There were never less than a dozen of her friends and relations under her roof; some of them part-paying guests, some of them just 'staying' with Gramma until some better job turned up than the one they had left. And there were the children of school age, who represented a cross-section of Gramma's children's broods, whose parents took it for granted that the old lady would see that they got their education. Under the shaky, boy-trodden roof there were three outside rooms, built on and added to by visitors who were used to providing their own shelter, and four main rooms, the biggest of which was the kitchen. The two top rooms were labelled sitting-room and dining-room, and occasionally, on some special occasion like someone's wedding, they were used as such. Mostly, the genoa velvet

46

suite and the dining-room table were pushed aside to make room for beds. Not seldom, the bumpy old lounge served as an extra bed. Only two spots in the house were sacred to Mrs Green—her tiny bedroom that opened off the kitchen, and the oven-side of the kitchen table which she needed because nearly all her chores involved the use of both. There on the top of the stove her washing-water heated in a kerosene-tin, her irons grew hot, her big black kettle boiled, and her savoury stews and fries sent mouth-watering smells throughout the kitchen.

There was one hard and fast rule. No young males over the age of sixteen. They didn't mean to, but they always made trouble, specially with the teen-age girls. The high-spirited youths went down to the big camp in the wattle-studded valley, the reserve set aside for coloured people, where there was plenty of space for them to fight and rough-house each other without endangering their surroundings.

Mrs Green was old-fashioned about swearing. She had accustomed herself to the men's easy oaths, but she was quick to correct the children and the young girls, so the children and the girls hardly ever swore when Gramma was round to hear. Mrs Green thought fighting and swearing gave you a bad name with the neighbours. Her own neighbours were a couple of hundred yards away on each side, but the old lady kept on the politest of terms with them. It was never the neighbours who complained about the kids playing on the road in front of the house. It was the townsfolk and the visitors who did that. They never failed to yell angrily from the car window when they had swerved to miss a child, though Mrs Green could have told them there was not much to worry about. The children were quick as race-horse goannas, and mostly they ran the gauntlet of the road just to see what the driver of the car would do and say.

Mrs Green had acquired citizenship years before—before, in fact, she and her late husband had known or cared about such things. The owner of the station where she had spent most of her life had attended to the details for them. Mr Scott had talked of citizenship rights as something rather valuable, but it was not until Mr Green had died and Mrs Green had moved to the house on the hill, nearer to town, that she had appreciated to the full the distinction and convenience of possessing them. She rarely abused her privilege of buying grog, and when she did it was to benefit her friends and not her pocket. Mrs Green did not trust easy money, and she knew of more than one citizenship-rights holder who had spent a month or two in jail because his pals had split on him.

Mrs Green's own children had married well. One of her sons assisted with the management of a small station. Another owned a farm. Mrs Green went visiting whenever she felt like it, and her children and their families were always overjoyed to have her. They even arranged for transport, paying her fare on the train if they could not pick up a lift for her.

Mrs Green had a plan for living and she stuck to it. First you went to school and stayed there until some of the teachers' learning came off on you. And you didn't wag it from school because you'd rather go swimming or fishing or tramping over the sand-hills that bordered the beach.

Mrs Green had a special deterrent for the wagsters under her control. She treated them as if she felt sorry for them for not understanding better. Somehow, it worked. Mrs Green was philosophical when it didn't. She had quite a few successes to look back on. Little Nancy was a fully trained typist now, working in the department's office down in Perth. Joe was apprenticed to a signwriter, and his two brothers had gone into the army. The others were good boys and girls, even if they did come back every so often from their jobs on stations, as musterers and shearers' assistants and childrens' nurses, filled with complaints about their bosses and their bosses' wives and the dullness of life lived miles from anywhere. And wanting, as Mrs Green very well knew, just a bit of a holiday with the other youngsters before they took another job on some other station, mustering someone else's sheep and minding someone else's children.

More than a few romances had blossomed from Mrs Green's house. There were always a few young bloods down at the camp. Some romances ended well. Some didn't. You couldn't blame a boy who came down from a station ready for a bit of fun, and the girl more than willing, even if it meant having the girl on your hands for months before the baby was born. Besides, after the baby had arrived, the young started to take things, and each other, a lot more seriously. And if they didn't, well, a baby was as good a way as any to teach a girl that she had to carry it in other ways than in her arms.

Mrs Green loved babies, anyhow.

'She didn't act a bit as if we were nuisances,' Trilby said slowly.

'Why should she?' Mrs Comeaway asked mildly. 'She's me neighbour, ain't she?'

The girls sat with their backs against trees and watched the smoke-blackened kettle resting against a burning log. The stove inside the humpy functioned only as an extra hold-all. 'Smoke everywhere,' Mrs Comeaway had explained cheerfully. 'And outside just as good. Maybe the ole feller fix im up one day.'

Trilby agreed with her mother. It was fun to cook outside and there wasn't much wrong with sitting here looking down over the valley while you drank your second lot of tea for the morning.

'That big camp down there,' Mrs Comeaway pointed, following Trilby's gaze, 'that's the government place. Anyone come ta town an don't have some place to stop at, they go there. Can do washin if ya like. Them little places down there, they take their washin up the big camp. Have a shower—anything they like.'

Mr Comeaway came through the doorway yawning and yanking at his pants. He smiled amiably at the girls and sat down between them. Mrs Comeaway took him an enamel mug of tea, steaming hot and strong. 'This packet's fa you. Mrs Green give it to me for ya.'

Mr Comeaway took his bread and butter. 'You girls like this place?'

'It's so pretty here,' Noonah said warmly. 'Mummy!'

'Watcha want?'

'I told Bartie I was going to ask you could he and Stella come back,' Noonah said diffidently. 'They want to. They don't like being left behind.'

'The young'un, eh?' Mr Comeaway said, with pleased interest. 'How's e goin, up there?'

'Nnnh!' Mrs Comeaway cocked an eye at her husband, frowning. 'I dunno bout that, Noonah. That mission a good place fa kids. All right ta come back when they been there a while an got some education. When they bigger.'

'Not Bartie,' Noonah said. 'Bartie's different from the others and they laugh at him. He draws, Mummy. You should see the things he draws. And he says funny things all the time, not like other kids his age. He *needs* to come back.'

Mrs Comeaway's lower lip was pendulous, her smooth brow puckered. She kept her gaze on Mr Comeaway's face as if it acted in lieu of a hand over his mouth.

'It's like this here,' she said at last. 'You kids don't understand proper. I made up me mind ta send my kids to a mission a long while back. Up there, theys all the same, nothing ta choose between em. Nobody don't call em names just because they coloured. An even if they don't like it for a little while...'

'I hated it,' Trilby burst forth. 'All the time I was there I hated it.'

Mrs Comeaway's face was wounded. 'Ya never said well.'

'You didn't come up much,' Trilby said indifferently.

'We knew yous was all right but,' Mrs Comeaway said a little anxiously.

'The little bloke—he don't like it up there,' Mr Comeaway brooded.

'Now don't you start on about it,' Mrs Comeaway said angrily. 'There wouldn't be no place for em ta come, not like they got up there. I *seen* them little houses,' she half accused Trilby. 'Little beds with covers over em. A place ta go to school. Plenty a fruit an tucker. They just gotta stay there like yous two, an come down when they bigger. That's all about it.'

'If we got a place to live like Mrs Green's got?' Noonah questioned, her eyes wide and brown and sad.

'None ta get,' Mrs Comeaway said briefly. A deriding expression on her face changed to pity when she saw tears fill Noonah's eyes.

'Stop worrying about Bartie and spoiling everything,' Trilby said, her voice irritable. 'It won't kill the kids to stay up at the mission, will it?'

Mrs Comeaway bent to the kettle again. Her voice was more cheerful. 'Nah! Not gunna kill them littlies. Kids— they soon get over things.' She straightened, and with the steaming kettle in her hand, looked over at Noonah.

53

'I got ambitions for my childrens, just like Mrs Green.' She stumbled over her explanation. 'I put my kids up there in that place cause I think that a good place for coloured kids to be all together, see?'

'I promised!' Noonah was humble in defence. 'And it wouldn't matter, Mummy, except he seems different from the others. I *know* he won't be happy now.'

'I know those things ya mean,' Mr Comeaway said unexpectedly. 'That Bartie. He a funny kid all right. All those questions he asks a feller. Does leaves like blowin around in the wind? About how heavy's a cloud? An drags a man out of a good sleep to show im a bit a water with some oil on top of it. Pretty, too, them colours in it. Yeah, I know! Always comin out with something that sort of catches ya up because ya ain't expectin it. I tell ya something else. I miss that damn kid.'

'Don't you get worryin, Noonah. E gunna be all right.' Mrs Comeaway's back was to her daughter. There was a sombre note in her voice.

Noonah looked at her mother, at the uneven hem of her frock, at the run-over black patent shoes, at the strong arm lifting the heavy kettle from the fire.

'It's all right, Mum,' she said, as if it were her mother who must be comforted. 'It's all right.'

'Where do you wash the cups?' Trilby said practically when Mr Comeaway had had his fill of tea and bread and butter.

'Just take em over to the tap an give em a rinse,' Mrs Comeaway told her. 'Sure ya had enough?'

'Oh yes, haven't we, Trilby?'

54

'I want to hurry and go down and see things,' Trilby said gaily. 'I can hardly wait.'

Mrs Comeaway laughed indulgently. 'Course we'll hurry.'

She watched the girls as they went off with the cups. 'What ya think of em, eh?' she asked her husband.

'Coupla nice kids,' Mr Comeaway approved. 'Smart, too.'

'Didn't do them too much harm,' Mrs Comeaway half-questioned. 'Gee, when that Noonah starts talkin about young Bartie. As if I don't know. Terrible hard job it was ta leave im, that time I took the two littlies up. Had me cryin too.'

'The ole lady seems ta manage all right.' Mr Comeaway nodded in the direction of Mrs Green's house.

Mrs Comeaway looked stubborn. 'She got her ideas. I got mine.'

She set to work damping down the fire with the tea-leaves. In a little while her habitual expression of cheerful good will returned to her face. She hummed a bar or two of a song as she waited for the girls to come back.

Trilby was dancing with impatience.

'All right!' Mrs Comeaway humoured her. 'I gotta change me frock first. Get meself dolled up to match yous two.'

She walked through to the inner room and went over to one of the hanging wardrobes. From the drapes she picked out a blue silk frock she had once picked up at a jumble-sale. Mrs Comeaway went to all the jumble-sales, though she rarely kept what she bought. She looked on sales as a quick and easy way to boost her income. The dresses and overcoats and other odd items she bought always brought four times what they had cost—friends and acquaintances down for a holiday snapped them up quickly, if Mrs Comeaway got in early before their holiday pay had been gambled away or borrowed. This particular blue silk, though, she had marked out as her own. It was a bit tight, but good looking and almost new except for the split under the arm. She smoothed the dress down over the pendulous bosom that rested on her high, proud stomach. She kicked off her run-over shoes and felt round under the bed for the suitcase that contained all the things she couldn't hang from nails. Another pair of shoes appeared from the case and she sat heavily on the bed to pull them on. And that was a hard enough job. She winced as she stood upright and tried to wiggle her toes, but the toes were caught, squashed, imprisoned against the hard toe-caps.

Giving up, she teetered across to the chest of drawers. The drawers of this piece of furniture were never used. The slats for the drawers were broken and they were almost impossible to open. There was another swift flurry of Carnation talcum powder down the neck of her frock. And a careful application of oil to her hair.

'Someone bring me that flannel hanging out there,' she called.

Noonah, who had been taking a quick wash, came hurrying in with the blue-striped washer.

'Gettin flash,' Mrs Comeaway admired. She scrubbed the wet washer over her face and ears and handed it daintily back. Then she took up a vast black purse and scrabbled through its contents. Face intent and serious, she hid the dusty purple of her wide mouth behind a swathe of pale pink. With her index finger she smoothed the gummy mess into her lips.

'Now!' she said, with satisfaction. 'All yous ready out there?'

Noonah had changed her dress for a clean one. The two girls stood before their mother, young, slim, bright-eyed with excitement. Mr Comeaway's white shirt was on him again, wrist-bands buttoned. His hair had been wetted and sleeked down. Mrs Comeaway looked them over with approval.

'Come on!' Mr Comeaway pleaded from the doorway. 'Anyone'd think we was gunna see the Queen.'

The girls laughed.

They started off down the slope to the road, waving to Mrs Green, who sat with a child on her lap on the veranda of her house.

'Not too fast now,' Mrs Comeaway warned. 'I gotta remember my feet. These damn heels likely to send me over if I don't take things quiet.'

The other three slowed their pace down the dark blue road. Mrs Comeaway walked with bent head, her mouth pursed with discomfort, her eyes searching the road ahead for the smoothest path. From one hand dangled the over-stuffed black purse.

Down the road a bit a sandy track curled off into the bush. Mrs Comeaway stopped her stomping. 'I wonder,' she said, 'if we better not stop an see Hannie an Charlie a while. They lations, an I tell them bout these two comin down. They got two girls round your age,' she told the sisters. 'Nice girls, they are.'

Everyone changed direction. Mrs Comeaway stopped again as soon as she stepped off the hard road and into the softer track. 'An now I'll just take these damn shoes off a while,' she said with satisfaction. 'Gawd! That's good. Felt like I had me feet in a coupla traps.'

The girls followed the sandy track, their shoes sinking ankle-deep with each step. Pleasing itself where it went, the path turned and twisted like the bed of a creek. The bush crowded close. Branches of green wattle and wild hibiscus brushed the girls' clothes and stung their faces and legs. Cream blossoms covered the wild hibiscus, the smell of them wildly sweet. The ground beneath them was sown with patches of colour, amethyst, blazing yellow, deep bright pink—each star-like flower upturned to the sun. A delirious chirping filled the air.

Mrs Comeaway walked with a sprightly step, freed from her shoes. Mr Comeaway rolled himself a cigarette and smoked contentedly. Noonah, her mind on Bartie, stepped off the path to exclaim at the vivid blue of a trailing creeper. 'An what ya think a this?' Mr Comeaway grinned, pulling free a spray of white flowers with delicate green stamens. Noonah smiled happily. Today she would buy paper and pencils and a big black box of water-colour paints. There was tenderness in her smile. And a doll for Stella, with eyes that closed and opened.

Trilby looked ruefully down at her shoes. Their bright polish was lost under a layer of dust. The black sand had seeped inside them, making her feet feel hot and tight. She looked ahead at her mother and envied her.

Around the next bend they heard voices. The girls sighed thankfully. Ahead of them they saw a camp like their own, though here there were only two side-walls—both ends being open to the air. Sheltering beneath was a double bed with long thin legs of iron. A second shelter projected from the first, its roof a tattered travelling-rug. A length of wire tied between two wattles supported a line of still-dripping washing, the barbs acting as pegs. At the back of the camp, a sight which drew both girls' eyes, a man's bicycle hung in lonely state from the branches of a tree.

The chattering of the group had died away. Four people, an older man and a woman, and two girls, sat in watchful silence waiting the approach of the Comeaways. The older man and woman relaxed first. They grinned a welcome.

Noonah saw a fat baby kicking and gurgling in the middle of the sagging bed. With an exclamation of pleasure, she went to it, but Trilby remained, shy and strange, a little behind her parents.

'This is them,' Mr Comeaway beamed. 'Come last night. What ya think of em, eh? You, Noonah over there, an Trilby! This your Auntie Hannie an Uncle Charlie; an these over here is Blanchie an Audrena. You say hello now and make good friends. That's Blanchie's baby, Noonah. Good big one, eh? How old now, Blanchie?'

Blanchie rose, grinning with embarrassment. She sidled closer to Noonah. Blanchie's hair hung lankly to her shoulders. The dress she wore was old and shapeless, hanging almost to her ankles. She and her cousin showed square white teeth in shy smiles.

Uncle Charlie's gaze flicked back and forth between his own girls and his brother's children. 'They smart all right,' he admired.

Mrs Comeaway turned her prideful look on Auntie Hannie. 'Noonah's gunna be a nurse down that hospital, if ya don't mind. Nurse young Tommy next time e goes in, eh?'

'Thought you was goin down the wharf this mornin,' Uncle Charlie addressed Mr Comeaway. 'I was goin down too. Didn't turn out that way but. Got a bit tired last night when all them peoples was here.'

'Feller needs a holiday,' Mr Comeaway allowed. 'Sides, we gotta show the girls round a bit today.'

'Take my tip an don't go fa that road work,' Uncle Charlie said seriously. 'Did that a coupla days last week. Gettin a bit old fa that stuff. Better on the wharf. Easier on ya back.'

'Gotta work hard sometimes,' Mr Comeaway said judicially. 'Keep ya wits about ya too. Knew a bloke got loaded inta one a them ship's holds right along with the wheat one time. That manganese ain't a picnic either.'

Trilby and Audrena took each other's measure. Unsmilingly.

'You live here too?' Trilby asked curiously, turning to look at the shoddy camp.

'We got a mattress under that ole blanket,' Audrena said. 'Young Tommy sleeps in with Mum an Dad if it's cold. This is only tempry but. Dad's savin up the deposit fa one a them houses down the Wild-Oat Patch. Then me an Blanchie's gunna have new beds. No use wastin good stuff in this dump. Might get wet.'

Trilby was impressed. 'You mean you're going to have a new house?'

'Course it takes a while ta save up that deposit,' Audrena said wisely. She grinned. 'Specially when the old man gets on the plonk an keeps rattin what we got. Make ya laugh. It's im wants the house. Mummy don't care all that much.'

'Don't you want it yourself?' Trilby kept her eyes politely away from the present dwelling.

'Be beaut!' Audrena said simply. 'Sometimes the rain gets on Blanchie an me.' She gloomed at the thin-legged bed. 'Four's really too many fa one bed. All legs, it seems like.'

Trilby turned over the remark wonderingly. Her thoughts returned more gratefully to the two new beds that had been bought for her and Noonah.

'Let's sit down,' she said, collapsing on some grass. 'And you tell me what it's like in this town. Do you do any work?'

'Used to,' Audrena said laconically. 'Had a job once up at a station, lookin after a coupla kids. It was beaut ta start off with. Had a room to meself and everything. Got sick of it but. Nothing ta do at night. I wasn't supposed to have nothin ta do with the station mob, y'see. The missus said they wasn't good company for me. So I used ta sneak out down the camp when she thought I was asleep. Then one night I get caught an that was the end a that. I spose she thought I was gunna stay up there fa the rest a me life never

61

havin any fun.' She sat in silence for a while, brooding. Then her face brightened. 'Gee, there was a beaut chap up there. I had fun with him all right.' She giggled and looked away from Trilby's candidly curious grey eyes.

'Don't you have fun down here?'

'Not if the ole man can help it.'

'No one's going to start ordering me about,' Trilby stated definitely. 'Come on, Audrena. Tell me some of the things you do.'

Audrena was flattered. The girls' heads moved closer.

Noonah sat with the baby on her lap. He was rounded, cuddlesome, good-tempered—the sort of baby to draw your heart out of your body with love for him. His skin was cocoa-coloured, satin-soft. Noonah felt her hands too large and clumsy to handle him but, quite obviously, he liked to be cuddled. She gathered him up and pressed her cheek into the silk of his black curls.

'You really gunna work at that nursing?' Blanchie asked. 'That's pretty hard work I know, because I done it. Not proper nursing like. In the hospital but. An I hadda wear a cap. The things they make ya do.' She shuddered. 'Real dirty stuff like emptyin pots and helpin ta wash people. Wait till ya strike them old men up there. Little bottles, they got. An some a the nurses is that crabby. I left after a while. Didn't like it.'

'I won't mind,' Noonah said with all the assurance of no experience.

'An it gets on ya pip, all this washin and boilin things. Ya gotta be that damn particular. Every day—stuff that useta look all right ta me—all gotta be cleaned up again. An floors polished that nobody's hardly stepped on.'

'That's because of germs,' Noonah said earnestly. 'Mrs Gordon up at the mission, she got me some little books, and it's all in them, the things I have to learn.'

'Ya gotta have ya Junior. Ya know that?'

'I've got that,' Noonah told her cousin.

'I went ta the High School down here meself,' Blanchie offered. 'Got sick of it though. Couldn't be bothered goin on years more.'

Noonah opened her mouth and firmly shut it again. And anyhow, what did education matter to someone who was married already?

'Aren't you afraid Tommy will roll off the bed,' she questioned.

'Did a coupla times,' Blanchie said. 'Course, it's soft ground here. Doesn't hurt im—just gives im a fright like.'

The older women got up and went over to the line of clothes. Mrs Comeaway straightened a dress that was hanging by one barb. 'Ya wanta take care a that dress,' she told her sister-in-law. 'I coulda got ten bob fa that if I hadn't just thought a you.'

They came over to where Noonah nursed the baby. 'Ya like kids, Noonah, eh?'

Noonah nodded. Auntie Hannie's face mooned round and fat from her stringy dark hair. There were many gaps where there should have been teeth in her nervously smiling mouth, but her dark eyes were shy as well as kindly. Noonah smiled reassuringly up at her.

'I'm used to kids. I helped round the nursery up at the mission.'

'That mission—a good place?'

'Yes, not bad.'

'You look all right. Smarter than Blanchie an Audrena.' There was no envy in her voice.

'Can't we go down town now?' Trilby asked plaintively, behind her mother, and Mrs Comeaway turned to chuckle. 'Okay, we better get goin,' she told her assembled relations. 'Less she goes an leaves us behind.'

'I just can't wait to see everything.' Trilby begged forgiveness.

'We don't get no peace till this girl's been down the town, I can see that,' Mr Comeaway said.

There was a chorus of good-byes as the Comeaways made their way back down the path. 'Don't forget about the beach,' Audrena screeched. 'Might see ya down the wharf tomorrow,' Uncle Charlie called after his brother.

'Monday fa sure,' Mr Comeaway called back.

'I see now you might make a real good nurse,' Mrs Comeaway said approvingly to Noonah. 'Had that baby eatin outa ya hand in no time. Just the same, ya better get a bit a fun in as well. That Blanchie, she thinkin a gettin married soon. Gunna get married in a church. Maybe we have some sorta party after.'

'Blanchie is the one with the baby?' Noonah asked.

'She didn't count on havin im,' Mrs Comeaway commented philosophically, 'but she's got im just the same.'

'What a fool she must be,' Trilby said.

'She ain't a fool,' Mrs Comeaway said with mild surprise. 'She's a real nice girl, that. Bit slow, but nice. Her an that young feller that comes down, you know the one, Tim. Hannie tells me they thinkin a gettin married.'

'Is it his baby?' Noonah pursued. She was trying to set these facts inside the framework of the mission-teaching.

'Gawd no, that's not is,' Mrs Comeaway replied. 'That baby's a quadroon. Didn't you see the colour of it? Father's a white man. Blanche hadda go down ta the partment bout that baby. Fix up about is maintenance. They made er sign papers an Gawd knows what all. After a while, they find out she's said the wrong name. Course it wasn't er fault. All she knows is the man's name is Popping an it happens there's two Poppings up in this place. They arst er which one, Neil or Billy, an she says what with them up in the office there starin at er she got real nervous an said Neil thout thinkin it might be the wrong one. An then this Neil sends a picture down the partment ta prove it ain't im an Blanchie looks at it an she's never seen im before in er life. She thinks now it musta been Billy, so she tells em that an everything's held up while they get on ta the bloke that really done it. She was lookin forward ta that money too, poor kid.'

The girls exchanged a quick look which was the undoing of both.

'I said something funny?' queried their mother, quite startled. Then she began to laugh herself. 'Eh, Joe!' she called. 'You ever think a that bloke's face up there when the pleece got on to im bout Blanchie's baby?' She slapped her chest and her laughter ended in a fit of coughing.

After a while they went on again, the four of them welded together by amusement, anticipation and newly-found affection for each other.

'What if it isn't the other one either?' Trilby giggled.

'Gawd, don't say that,' her mother said, sobered. 'If it ain't one it's gotta be the other, isn't it?'

'Can't think how that lot get emselves in so many damn mix-ups,' Mr Comeaway mused. 'Take Charlie now. Just thumbin imself a ride landed Charlie in jail a while back.'

'Tell us, Dad,' Trilby begged, still alight with laughter.

'E's comin back ta town see?' Mrs Comeaway took over after a pause. 'An e's tired, so e waits on the side a the road for a car ta come along. When one does e yells out for a lift. So the ute stops an ole Charlie climbs in the back an, believe it or not, a pleeceman gets outa the drivin seat an walks round to where Charlie's makin imself comfortable an the first thing e wants ta know is what's in the bag. An ya know what's in that bag?'

The girls waited, deliciously apprehensive.

'Three chooks, that's what e's got.'

'And where did he get them from?'

'Pinched em, a course,' Mrs Comeaway said promptly. 'I don't mean e went in someone's place. E told us after, they was jus walkin down the road, these chooks, so e wrung their necks for em, looked round fa something ta put em in, an was gunna bring em home to me an Hannie.'

'Only Charlie,' Mr Comeaway shook his head, 'would pick out a pleece ute. Got a gift fa doin the wrong thing, ole Charlie.'

'An I was gunna get one,' Mrs Comeaway said regretfully. 'The ole fool.'

66

From the house, the greater part of the township had been hidden behind circling hills. Now, at the top of a steep rise, the girls saw it spread out beneath them, and stopped short in surprise and pleasure. The houses, and the streets that bisected them, the tallness of pointed pines, the grand columns of a rose-coloured building standing proud on a rise, the cathedral, golden in sunlight, a red and white striped lighthouse guarding the distance, every detail stood out delicate and pure in the crystal-clear air. Away on the outskirts, white combers broke on a curving coastline. Two ships, like visiting majesty, rode at anchor inside a piled-stone breakwater. To the two girls, used to one wide main street and a scatter of grimy houses, the town looked breathtakingly big.

'Well, there she is,' Mr Comeaway said modestly, vastly pleased at their reaction.

'Bit bigger'n what you been used to,' Mrs Comeaway commented, coming to a panting standstill behind them. 'So's this hill we gotta climb down. Look at it, will ya? Should cut the top off it before they started buildin all over it. All right fa them that's got cars an them that takes taxis. Gawd, I'm beginnin ta wish I hadn't wore these shoes.'

The two elder Comeaways went cautiously on down the hill that curved into the township, leaving their daughters still ecstatic at the top.

'Wonder if there's pictures,' Trilby breathed.

'Which way did we come last night?' Noonah wondered. 'Where's the hospital from here?'

'You and your old hospital,' Trilby laughed, skipping off down the hill like a young foal.

They reached the main street through another road that meandered past shops and business premises and shabby little old-fashioned houses built close to the footpath. Now that they were in the centre of the town, the girls edged closer to their mother. Mr Comeaway had sloughed himself at the very first corner, claiming important private business. Mrs Comeaway, now that the hill had been safely negoti- ated, was smugly conscious of her good blue silk frock and her two fresh pretty daughters. The slowness of her pace was calculated to allow everyone a good long look at them. In return, her friends and acquaintances received gracious nods, bestowed with the dignity of a queen.

'My bathers, Mum,' Trilby whispered. 'Can I have some to go swimming with Audrena?'

'Don't tell me!' Mrs Comeaway's promenade stopped short. 'If I didn't clean forget about money.' Her face cleared suddenly. 'That's where e went. Ta get some. You'll have ya bathers,' she promised her daughter. 'We'll pick up with ya dad again and get some money for em before e spends it all.'

'Where's he getting it from?' Noonah asked.

'Round about,' Mrs Comeaway said largely. 'Someone'll be owin im some. Or e'll borrow some. E knows I gotta pick up some tucker, anyhow. Can't do that thout money.'

'Can we go inside one of these shops and have a look round?' Trilby begged.

'I dunno!' Mrs Comeaway was uneasy.

'We can look, can't we?'

Trilby moved determinedly off through the doorway of a dress shop. Noonah and Mrs Comeaway followed.

'Can't move a step in these places,' Mrs Comeaway whispered stealthily, 'thout one a them tarts comin up. Give anyone the willies.'

Delightedly, the girls whirled through the dresses on a circular steel display stand. Mrs Comeaway, her back to her charges, a worried frown on her face, stood guard. But at the approach of a slim smiling salesgirl, her courage evaporated. 'Come on,' she ordered, 'we gettin outa here.'

Trilby's face was discontented. 'We'll go inta Coles,' Mrs Comeaway placated her. 'That's a real nice shop an nobody don't bother ya.'

'I don't see why...,' Trilby began rebelliously, but Noonah intervened. 'Come on, Trilby, we can go back to that other place tomorrow.'

At the entrance to the chain store a toddler, escaped from his pushchair, stumbled across their path. Instantly, Noonah had him on the crook of her arm. She was about to return him to his small jail when he was snatched from her arms. 'That's my baby,' a young woman said frowningly. 'I'll take care of him, thanks.'

The smile faded from Noonah's face. More than her arms felt empty.

'What did she think...?' she began helplessly, but Trilby cut her short. 'You're a nigger. Remember?' For the space of a second, the sisters' eyes met. Noonah forgot her own hurt in a flooding of sympathy for Trilby, who in some way had suffered a deeper wound. But she controlled a desire to express her sympathy. Trilby did not care for stuff like that.

Mrs Comeaway's expression spoke volumes but she too kept her mouth closed.

The chain store was fascinating. The glittering jewellery counter held both girls in thrall. Even the bored-looking girl behind the counter was moved by Trilby's unashamed wonder.

'I'm going to have lots of these,' Trilby said excitedly. 'Look, Mummy, ear-rings and necklaces to match.'

'Yeah! Yeah!' Mrs Comeaway exchanged a shy smile with the counter girl. 'She's not used ta stuff like this.'

'Well,' the girl was moved to be gracious. 'I wear it myself sometimes.'

'Do you have paints? And little sleeping dolls?' Noonah inquired.

'Two counters up,' the girl replied, and the Comeaway party moved reluctantly away from the bright display.

'That should keep em happy a while,' Mrs Comeaway said comfortably when Noonah had completed her purchases. 'That was a real good idea, Noonah. An lucky ya had some money ta pay for em.'

'Mrs Gordon gave me a pound for helping her,' Noonah said. Most of the pound had vanished. Mrs Comeaway, and Trilby too, had chosen gifts to add to Noonah's original selection. The whole transaction had been completely satisfying to them all.

'I could stay here all day long,' Trilby sighed, when they at last made their way out. 'Those bathers with the red spots, Mummy. Are you sure Dad will let me have them?'

'Course e will,' Mrs Comeaway reassured her. 'E's going ta work tomorrow. An this time I'll make sure e goes.'

Trilby's brow was unclouded again, her grey eyes shining with happiness. She stopped before a milk-bar, resplendently pink and white, a counter replacing the usual glass front. 'Oh, a milk-bar. Mummy, can we...?'

'Better not,' Mrs Comeaway said quickly, out of her depth again. 'Besides,' she remembered gratefully, 'we ain't seen the ole man yet, ta get some money off a him.'

'It'll be all right,' Noonah said, as dazzled as Trilby. 'I've got some money left.'

Mrs Comeaway stood her ground. 'Not fa me,' she declared firmly.

Trilby's eyes flared again, a danger signal Mrs Comeaway was beginning to know. Shoulders back, chin high, the girl marched into the shop. Noonah looked doubtfully at her mother, then followed. They waited behind a group of people who stood at the inside counter. Gradually, the group melted away until only the two girls were left waiting.

71

The attendant looked them over, coolly, casually. 'Shop at the top of the street serves you people,' he said. 'Go on! Beat it!' Whilst he spoke his eyes kept darting to his customers.

'Come on,' Noonah whispered, her face hot.

With the handle of a silver teaspoon the attendant began a quick tattooing on the marble-topped counter.

'Two vanillas, please,' Trilby ordered in a high clear voice. She kept her blazing eyes full on the man's watchful face.

Several customers looked over curiously.

'Look...I...all right!' the boy capitulated suddenly. He began spooning ingredients into two silver containers. 'Just drink em at the counter, will ya?' He shoved the tall containers beneath two electric mixers, watching the rest of the shop from a mirror that backed a display of chocolates.

Noonah placed a two-shilling piece on the counter as he slid the foaming malted milks over to them.

'You'll get the brush-off in here,' he warned them in a low voice, 'and don't say I didn't tell ya.'

Trilby's face was grey. Deliberately, she lifted her container from the counter and walked to a table. Helplessly, Noonah followed and heard an anguished 'Gawd!' behind her.

The table Trilby chose already had one occupant—a middle-aged man drinking a cup of coffee. He looked up when the girls sat down and for a moment his face retained its pleasant good humoured expression. Then his features froze. He shot a look full of irritation at the boy behind the counter. When he lifted his coffee cup again, it was to drain the contents at a gulp preparatory to leaving.

Just as he was about to rise, however, a voice came from the next table. 'It's to be hoped they use some sort of disinfectant on these glasses.'

The man resumed his seat. He looked again at the lowered heads of his table companions, as if he wanted them to look up at him. Then he turned and addressed the young girl who had spoken. 'That was a damned rude remark,' he said roughly. 'If you were my daughter, I'd take you over my knee.'

Grey eyes and brown looked up at him. Shy and startled. It was Trilby who caught his attention. He smiled uncertainly at her as he rose again. And Trilby smiled back at him, the brilliant dazzling smile whose effect Noonah knew well.

The girl at the next table had her back to them again, stiff, straight and offended. 'Trilby, do you feel all right?' Noonah whispered. 'Your hands are shaking.'

'I don't want this drink,' Trilby said distastefully.

'Leave it,' Noonah begged, 'and we'll just walk out.'

Trilby flung a quick look at the occupants of the milk bar. Nearly all of them were watching openly. Only the offended girl kept her back to them.

'Wonder if Mum's still out there,' Noonah said.

'I can see her,' Trilby said through stiff lips. 'She looks scared stiff.'

Noonah thrust back her chair. Trilby was forced to follow suit. They walked slowly and with dignity out of the shop. The attendant whistled softly as they passed. He was smiling, but they would not meet his glance.

Mrs Comeaway bustled over to them. 'Wonder they even served ya in there,' she scolded. 'I keep telling ya. Little places like that, ya gotta be careful. Them people got their places. We got ours.' She marched grimly along the street. 'An I tell ya something else. We like it that way, see?'

Their shopping was done. The presents had been posted to the mission, and a string-bag filled with groceries and meat dangled heavily between Trilby and Noonah.

Somewhere or other, Mr Comeaway had come across some money, and held carefully under Trilby's arm was a parcel containing two pairs of bathers, for herself and Noonah.

'I been thinkin,' Mrs Comeaway said. 'Spose we walk down an take a little look at them houses in the Wild-Oat Patch. You know, Joe. The ones like the Maybes live in. The ones Charlie keeps yappin about.'

Despite their load, the girls agreed happily. Mrs Comeaway considered her swollen feet and decided they might hold out if she walked real slow.

'Them houses are goin up special fa coloured folk,' she told the sisters. 'All scattered about, too, not in a heap like we was rubbish. That's what they call discrimination.'

Mr Comeaway laughed. 'Ya got that arse about,' he told his wife. '*Ass*-imulation, that's what you mean. An I ain't never heard what the nobs think of it. You seen the Maybes lately, Molly? How they getting along with them neighbours a theirs?'

'All right!' Mrs Comeaway said drily. 'They don't come out an beat em off with sticks. The trouble, I think, is with them Maybes. Stuck-up lot, them *an* their kids.'

'One wrong thing that partment did,' Mr Comeaway said pensively, 'they made our places different from those others. Seems ta me they shoulda all been the same.'

'Ours looks bigger,' Mrs Comeaway defended.

'Thinkin a the kids we gotta bed down,' Mr Comeaway commented. 'Beats me bout these white folks. Never seem ta have many kids. I reckon they got the money and we got the kids, eh?' He chuckled.

They had reached a part of the town where the streets were narrow and crooked, where mean little houses peered distrustfully through dusty windows, their untidy side-yards overgrown with weeds, only an occasional glory of sunflowers lighting their drabness.

Towards the centre of the town the level of the houses rose. They were bigger here and set well back from the road, freshly painted, steeply roofed, their cold polished eyes glaring arrogantly or hidden deep in the dimness of cool verandas. They had smooth green lawns and gardens where frangipane, flame trees and apple-blossom hibiscus took the place of the vulgar sunflowers. Along the next street, huge well-proportioned Moreton Bay fig trees threw thick shade on a dusty footpath, and when these had been passed the town gave up the struggle and allowed its streets to meet and mingle where they would.

Another steep rise led them to a second attempt at planning. Here, the streets stretched tidily away at right angles to each other, each lined with houses so neat they

75

might have been coloured drawings or children's models. Most of them were built of asbestos. Some were of timber, freshly painted in bright glowing colours, each just a little different from its neighbour. The whole area seemed treeless. The little tiled roofs could be seen stretching away and away into the distance, geometrically planned, efficiently finished. This was the Wild-Oat Patch which the town council had bulldozed out from undulating sandhills and sown quickly with the seed of the wild oat for protection from the wild southerly winds which swept in off the sea.

Along the outskirts of the area, several houses were in the process of being built. 'We been here seven years,' Mrs Comeaway marvelled, 'an all that time they been buildin these houses. Gawd knows where the peoples come from ta fill em up. Praps them emigrants come up ere. Ever hear em jabberin away, Joe? Wonder ta me they understand what they talkin about.'

'Everyone's got their own language,' Mr Comeaway said patiently. 'Same as us.'

'Sounds funny just the same,' Mrs Comeaway was obdurate. 'What's more they teach it ta their kids stead of learnin em ta speak proper. Little bits a kids talkin a lot a damn nonsense nobody can't understand.'

'Cept their mothers an fathers,' Mr Comeaway grinned. He turned to Trilby and Noonah. 'Look there! That looks like one a ours. Nice big place, ain't it?'

'Daddy! Mummy!' Noonah's voice had a breathless note. Her eyes were luminous and pleading. 'Why can't we have a house down here?'

76

The four stopped in their tracks and looked at each other in silence.

Trilby smiled her dazzling smile. 'Gee!' she said. 'Gee! could we?'

Mr Comeaway looked at his wife. 'I suppose we could,' he said wonderingly. 'I suppose we damn well could. If we wanted to.'

'And get Bartie and Stella down?' Noonah breathed joyously. 'Could we?'

Mrs Comeaway kept looking from the half-built house to her husband and back again, as if she needed to see material symbols before she could begin to grasp the potential.

'Nothin ta stop us,' Mr Comeaway said recklessly.

'The money,' Mrs Comeaway said in a rush. 'We got no money.'

'Forty pound,' Mr Comeaway said grandly. 'Charlie told me.'

'We could save it up,' Trilby planned.

Mr Comeaway looked thoughtful. 'Now that forty pounds is the deposit, an ya gotta pay that much before they let ya in the place. An Charlie says after that ya got forty year ta pay the rest. That's a good long time, ain't it?'

Mrs Comeaway beamed. She saw herself opening her front door and inviting her friends in. Plenty of room for everyone in a place that size. Bartie and baby Stella. They could all come—she could have friends staying with her as often as she liked and no crowding either.

Mr Comeaway's thought ran parallel with his wife's. He saw himself leaning on his own front gate, smoking, talking to his neighbours. He saw himself host to his friends. He was conscious of mild surprise that he had not thought of something like this before. Still, he'd thought of it now and he'd see that department man first chance he got and arrange everything properly. Tomorrow, maybe. Some time this week, for certain.

Trilby was off and away, climbing all over the half-built house, counting up rooms, comparing them for size, deciding which one should be her own, determining to have it to herself, planning the furnishing right down to the colour of the frilly net curtains she had seen in magazines.

Noonah's eyes were on her parents, loving them, thanking them. She saw herself meeting Stella and Bartie at the station, the way she and Trilby had been met. Already, in her mind, she was wording the letter they would write to the superintendent of the mission, telling him that Bartie and Stella could come home. Home!

'Ain't nothin' ta cry bout, that I can see,' Mr Come-away rallied her, but Noonah's mother said nothing, only moving closer to the girl's side to pat her shoulder and to smile at her.

SIX

On the corner of the main street stood an hotel and at the back of the hotel was a square yard marked off from the lane behind it by an old stone wall. In summer, the wind blasted in straight off the ocean, carrying clouds of sand from the beach that backed the shops. In the winter, the wind was less boisterous but it was keen and cold, cutting through clothing and chilling the spines of those who loitered.

Winter and summer, there was always a little group who sheltered in the lane at the back of the hotel, in the lee of the good solid stone wall. For it was here that Horace held court. Here that he untangled quarrels and deliberated and passed judgement and, incidentally, kept himself informed. Horace's position was not unique. For every group there is one who leads. Horace was the leader of the coloured community and the only time he absented himself from his duties was when he was locked up in the town jail. And no one of his friends felt less than uneasy until he was back at the helm again.

On his way up to his present eminence, Horace's nose had been knocked sideways, his ears had been as badly treated as a tom-cat's, he had lost three or four of his splendid white teeth, and the tear duct of one eye had been damaged. There had been talk of an operation to repair this last bit of damage, but as a certain party said, 'It's like this. The operation is going to be very expensive. And it's not as though Horace has ever been what you might call a "handsome" man.' The operation had been deferred, a most happy decision, for Horace's tears only added to his sympathetic and benign expression.

Mr Comeaway was one of Horace's friends and admirers. He admired Horace's strength especially. Many a time he had watched Horace being bundled down the street shouting and swearing, his foot slipping slyly out to trip an adversary, his iron fists flailing and, with all the commotion, looking as if he were having the time of his life. One bottle of port royal did a lot for Horace. Three gave him the strength of a giant.

When all was over, and Horace had had a good rest on his jail cot, he was a different man entirely, gentle and well-behaved, shocked and unbelieving of his doings of the night before, changing to remorseful amusement as his memory was refreshed by the monarch. In fact, such was the undivided attention Horace bestowed on those who refreshed his memory, so many were the grave shakings of his battle-scarred head, the officers of the police force quite often grew confused; feeling that they placed a case before a kindly but impartial judge.

True to the promise he had made his family, Mr Comeaway was on his way down to see the department man. But first he wished to have a word about the matter with Horace. It was not that his mind was not firmly made up. Perhaps it was an urge to astonish his old friend and, at the same time, to receive what undoubtedly would be Horace's stamp of approval on the venture.

Horace nodded affably. Mr Comeaway rolled two cigarettes and courteously left his friend's unlicked. Then he selected a good place to lean. They smoked a while in companionable and comfortable silence.

'Calling in by the partment chap today,' Mr Comeaway said at last, very casually.

Nothing about Horace betrayed that his attention had been instantly engaged. Being a semi-official employee of the department, he frequently called there himself. There was his weekly ration to pick up; there was his pound note to collect once a month; his buckets and brooms and mops wore out and had to be replaced, and when he was quite certain that evil-doers were well off and away, he reported breakages of equipment on the government reserve which was his sacred charge.

Moreover, being such a regular visitor, he was in a position to advise would-be visitors of their correct behaviour, particularly if such advice might be needed to smooth out mistakes and misunderstandings.

'Bout one a them houses down the Wild-Oat Patch,' Mr Comeaway said, eyeing the shaggy end of his cigarette.

Horace remained silent a while, after which he cleared his throat and spat.

Mr Comeaway waited. And then he became impatient. 'What ya think a the idea?'

Horace took out his own tobacco and cigarette papers and rolled another cigarette. When it was lit he fixed his back against the wall and squinted through smoke at a group of men emerging from a doorway on the other side of the street.

'Well!' Mr Comeaway said. His bottom lip jutted a trifle. 'Ya think something's wrong bout getting a house?'

Horace turned right round. 'Ya gunna regret it, boy. I think ya gunna regret it.'

Aggrieved and disappointed, Mr Comeaway threw his new cigarette down and ground it out half-smoked as it was. Regret it?

'You all right where ya are, ain't ya? Nice little place up on the hill? Mrs Green—an there's a nice ole lady—livin right near an handy so ya ole woman don't get running round fa someone ta talk to? And ya wanta shift out there? An pay rent an stuff?'

A sweet wash of relief cooled Mr Comeaway's injured feelings. If that was all!

'We got that worked out,' he said simply. 'I just keep goin down that wharf every day not missin out. We can pay that rent all right.'

The glint in Horace's eye could easily have been warm interest, and only Horace knew for sure that it came from a lack of illusions. Horace forgave because he understood. Now he settled himself into another more comfortable position and examined the sky.

'Rent days has a habit of comin up pretty regular,' he gave of his wisdom. 'Can upset a man's whole day, sposin e's been working out some different sort a plan fa spending is money.'

Mr Comeaway grappled with this in silence for a while, deciding finally on another tack. 'This ain't no new thing,' he said earnestly. 'Mus be two weeks now we went down an had a look at them houses. Showin the kids the town like. An we had a look at one just goin up, an Noonah—that's the one's gunna be a nurse—she said why didn't we just get one a them houses an live down there. So that's how we done it but we saved a bit a money first—that's for the deposit—to show im we was good peoples to let get a house.' He dragged a tobacco-tin out of his pocket and fiddled with the tight-fitting lid. 'That's what I got here. An that ain't all,' he continued, a little uncertain now. 'After we been there a while I been thinkin we might get our rights.'

Horace showed his shock. A look almost of unfriendliness passed over his face, though this was the only sign he gave that his friend had stubbed, with his big clumsy tongue, right at Horace's single sensitive spot. Citizenship had been in Horace's mind for many a long day, but so far it had remained out of reach, advancing and retreating in line with his periods of freedom and his periods of confinement to a jail cell. He had tried often to bring it within grasping distance, but when the time was ripe, which is to say, when his unbending determination was beginning to melt into a mere resolve to keep out of trouble if he could and when this first coincided with one of his many friends arriving at the camp with a big shearing cheque, then, as surely as

83

a punch in the nose brings close arrest, Horace got himself picked up.

It was the strength in him that did it. All that strength that a few bottles of conto lent him. A man couldn't use it all up in talk and it had to be got rid of somehow. Horace could never fathom his reason for seeking out uniforms but it always happened that way and he had never yet met the monarch who was as forgiving as a friend might have been.

These slips between cup and lip constituted the only infelicity in Horace's otherwise happy adjustment to life, and nobody who ever followed his sage counsel to stay citizenship-less ever suspected that the grapes were sour.

He now wagged a stern finger under Mr Comeaway's nose. 'Get that house if ya like, but leave them damn rights alone.'

'Why?'

A tear or two ran down Horace's left cheek. 'Because,' he said heavily, 'I'll tell ya for why. Me boy,' another long pause whilst Horace searched the street for advancing friends and inspiration, 'ya don't know what ya might be running yaself into.'

Horace was genuinely at a loss how to proceed from here. Only a week or so back he could have used his most potent argument—no more hand-outs from the department—but some busybody had changed all that now, and a man only needed a teaspoonful of blackfeller blood in his veins to be eligible for departmental aid.

'Ya know all them questions ya gotta answer?' Horace asked gravely, seeing his tack at last.

'What about them then?'

84

'Peerin and pokin round ya private life?'

Mr Comeaway's face took on a wary look.

'Ain't even sure they might want ya to confess.'

'What's that?'

'Things ya done,' Horace said airily. 'Any little thing ya mighta done. Robbin a bank, things like that.'

Mr Comeaway was definitely uneasy now.

'An I tell ya something else. Everyone say you good man, Joe boy. So why would ya go an think ya was better than other peoples, you tell me that?' Horace was convincing himself as well now. His heart overflowed with compassion for his friend. If *he* had been deemed unable to manage citizenship rights, how much less able was Joe Comeaway? Clearly, he must save his friend from all that worry and responsibility.

'Ever see the Maybes?' he asked quietly.

'Not too often.'

Horace nodded, his expression stern. 'That ole man wouldn't give ya one drop a conto, not if ya lay dyin. One time I arst im. Too good now. Think us fellers unrespectable, think trouble might come spose they look at a feller. An that ole woman a his, marchin round with er string-bag an that black hat on er head, telling the childrens ta come on an stop talkin when I know them kids since they was born. Lations a mine even. Arrk!' Horace spat disgustedly.

'It was them girls,' Mr Comeaway said humbly. 'They said about it.'

'I'm tellin ya well,' Horace said sternly. 'You leave them rights fa the foolish ones. Nother thing, I can get ya a bottle a conto when ya want it—cheap,' he weighed

85

Mr Comeaway's possibilities, 'seven bob? Eight bob? Real good stuff fa nine or ten bob. An that's without you landin yaself in no trouble.'

'Them Maybes,' Mr Comeaway allowed, 'act sometimes like they wouldn't spit on ya.'

Horace's nostrils flared. 'An nor us on them,' he declared vehemently. 'Don't you be forgettin that.' He snorted. 'Im with is wouldn't wanta get in no trouble. For a bit of a drink for a bloke that's been a friend to im *and* er.' His brown eyes twinkled. '*And* her,' he repeated.

Mr Comeaway's mind had wandered. 'By gee, I could *do* with a drink. Two or three.' He took out his tobacco tin again and carefully extracted two pound notes.

They melted beneath Horace's big dark hand. Horace smiled sweetly. 'That feller that gets me the stuff, lets me have it fa ten bob now. Cause e knows I don't tell where I get it spose I get picked up. Get yaself a name like I got boy an ya right.'

'An fa Gawd's sake don't drop the bag comin up the hill,' Mr Comeaway begged.

'I ad a haccident,' Horace said primly, 'that time.'

Mr Comeaway looked as if he might be about to comment, but he changed his mind. If Horace knew he had had a look about, just a squint, round the place where Horace had said he had had his accident, because he thought maybe the sugar-bag might have cushioned just one bottle's fall, and that he had found nothing at all at the said site, not even a bit of broken glass or a sugar-bag... Mr Comeaway's instinct and his long undisturbed friendship with Horace sealed his lips. He nodded understandingly.

'Bloody rock on the road,' Horace said, and again Mr Comeaway nodded.

'Jus fa Christ's sake be bloody careful,' he begged. 'I'm puttin me neck out just givin ya the money, ya wanta know. All the whole lot of em's talkin bout nothing but this damn house.'

It was Horace's turn to nod understandingly, but his eyes were on his next lot of visitors. He welcomed them with a smile. Careless but proprietorial, he moved a step away from the wall.

Mr Comeaway went on his way meditating, concluding with some relief that no matter what, it was a good thing for a man to have a friend who would take up his troubles, sort them through and return them to him all straightened out.

'Where's the girls?' Mr Comeaway asked later that afternoon, dumping a parcel of meat on the table.

'The skies'll fall,' Mrs Comeaway said, eyeing the blood-soaked package. 'What's come over *you,* bringin meat home thout even askin?'

'Ya need it don't ya?' There was an irascible note in his voice. Bad enough lugging the stuff home without being eased out of the rôle of benefactor.

'Course I do,' Mrs Comeaway admitted. 'Didn't need enough ta feed a flock a elephants but. Have ta give some ta Mrs Green I spose. Save it goin bad.' She sat down on one of the beds, leaving the meat where it lay on the table.

'Naggin womans,' Mr Comeaway confided to the ceiling, having lowered his weary body on to Noonah's bed. 'Where's the girls, I arst?'

'Trilby's around somewhere. Noonah's gone down to see that hospital woman,' Mrs Comeaway answered. 'Ain't she been talking bout it for a fortnight?'

'Yeah! That's right! Wonder if she'll be all right.'

'Course she will. Somethin wrong if she don't.'

'Where ya think I been?'

'Standin outside the pub talking ta ole Horace,' Mrs Comeaway said promptly.

'Well I ain't,' her spouse said, shooting out his bottom lip at this second piece of obtuseness. 'I been down to the partment an seen that man. Told you I was going this week,' he added, glumly reproachful now that he had Mrs Comeaway's full attention.

'Bout the house?'

'Yeah!' Mr Comeaway said triumphantly.

Trilby skipped through the swinging door of the humpy.

'Guess where ya father's been,' Mrs Comeaway said instantly, swinging round to face her.

Trilby's eyes went to her father. 'Where?'

'Been down ta see bout the house, that's what,' Mrs Comeaway said, simmering excitement in her voice. She turned back to her husband. 'Now! What happened? We get one?'

'Well,' Mr Comeaway said portentously, removing some obstructions at the foot of Noonah's bed simply by kicking them off, 'I'll just tell ya.'

'Did you ask if we could have one with red paint and little steps and a veranda on the side?' Trilby asked eagerly.

Mr Comeaway puffed out his cheeks. 'First,' he announced, 'we gotta save up another eighteen pound. That's the first thing we gotta do. Twenty-six pound the deposit is.'

'Wait,' Mrs Comeaway said, doing a little figuring in her head, 'we already got ten, ain't we?'

'Eight,' Mr Comeaway said smoothly. 'Horace is gunna bring a few bottles up tonight ta celebrate.' He kept a stern eye on his wife until he saw that she accepted this fact.

'Then, when we *got* this eighteen pound, we shift down there.'

Trilby hugged herself and hopped about on one foot. Mrs Comeaway beamed.

'Then when we *get* into the house,' Mr Comeaway continued, 'we gotta pay rent an we don't have ta get behind with it. That gotta be paid every week regular like a clock. I told im then bout me workin down that wharf an that rent business don't worry us. Told im few other things, too. Like how we keep the place clean an got Noonah goin ta be a nurse an all that. So he knows we's a good family an got nice childrens.'

'And what about the colour?' Trilby demanded. 'Can we have a painted house?'

Mr Comeaway shook his head. 'We gotta do all that.'

'I think they're just being mean,' Trilby said furiously. 'I wanted a painted house. Now everyone'll know it's just a nigger's place.'

Mr and Mrs Comeaway gazed at their daughter in frowning bafflement.

'Why, you just a young hussy, sayin things like that bout ya own people,' Mrs Comeaway said, raising to stand threateningly over her daughter. 'What you say a thing like that for eh?'

'It's not me—it's them,' Trilby said, angry tears choking her voice. 'They spoil everything for us. They try every way they can to make us feel mean and little. Even down at the post office they try. We've got a name, haven't we? So why do they have to lump us all under "Natives". What's so different about us? They're beasts. I hate the lot of them.'

'I oughta give ya a good clip over the ear,' her mother said, still frowning. But there was more worry than anger in her face now. She flung a look of appeal at her husband.

'Let er alone,' Mr Comeaway said, himself perturbed at the outburst. 'She's jumpin out of er skin with excitement. Ain't that the trouble, Trilby?'

Trilby forced herself to be calm, despising herself for her weakness. It didn't pay to lose your temper. It never had in the past. It never would. Her mother cuffed her gently on the side of the head. 'All right! You remember what I said, though, an don't go calling us peoples niggers.'

'Ya know what?' Mr Comeaway ruminated. 'We sposed ta keep this house only to ourselves. No lations, no peoples comin down for a holiday like. E says tell em we don't have no beds for em.'

'They ain't partickler bout beds,' Mrs Comeaway said dubiously.

Neither saw much sense in the advice. A good roof meant shelter, and the number of those who sheltered could only be limited by the size of the roof. To the Comeaways, twenty-six sounded a likelier figure than six.

'E showed me a thing e called a blue-print,' Mr Comeaway said at last, dismissing the matter. 'So I could see everything. Got little rooms an one big room fa livin in, got a stove an a sink fa washing up cups, an all the clothes get washed inside this house, an there's troughs to wash em in.'

'I seen them sinks,' Mrs Comeaway nodded. 'Stainless steel. That's gunna be a jump up, eh Trilby?'

'Are we allowed to paint it any colour we like?' Trilby asked.

'It's our house, ain't it?' grinned Mr Comeaway.

'Not yet it ain't,' Mrs Comeaway was more practical. 'We gotta save up more money yet.'

'The partment man's gunna do that,' her husband said comfortably. 'All we gotta do, we take im our spare money, and e puts it away somewhere and lets us know when we got enough.'

'Sounds safer than that ole tobacco tin,' Mrs Comeaway chuckled. 'Remember that time we was gunna save up and go an see the kids up the mission.'

'Always rememberin some damn thing happened years ago,' Mr Comeaway said irritably.

Mrs Comeaway chuckled again. 'An I got plenty a things ta pick from.' Seeing a storm gathering in her husband's eyes she relented. 'Good things, too. Spose I remember back far enough.'

Trilby giggled. Then she bent a persuasive look on her mother.

'Can I have a room all to myself where I can put things and not have people touching them? Can I please, Mummy?' Her grey eyes were limpid pools and did not disclose that on this point she had already made up her mind. The front room of the humpy had become, with the addition of the two beds, a comfortable sitting-room. Often, the girls had to wait wearily for visitors to depart before they could claim their beds. Oftener still, being healthy young animals whose activities took place during the hours of daylight, they tired of waiting and curled themselves up on the big bed in the back room. Sometimes the visitors would still be there when they woke next morning, and they would find their mother stretched out alongside them and their father sleeping on a pile of old clothes on the floor.

Trilby hated this disorderliness and tried to alter it, but she might just as well have saved her energy.

'They living way over in the bush,' Mrs Comeaway would say vaguely. 'Mighta missed their way in all that dark.'

'They should have left when it was light enough to see well,' Trilby would snap.

'Yeah! That's right,' Mrs Comeaway would agree cheerfully. 'An they meant to. They was going ta do that! It was just we got talkin an then someone wanted a game an there ya are.' An expressive shrug of the shoulders disclaimed responsibility.

'I don't want anyone to sleep in my bed but me,' Trilby pursued.

Her father chuckled. 'I would say the same.'

'Well!' Mrs Comeaway soothed. 'I should think ya can have a room to yaself. You an Noonah.'

Trilby considered. 'And nobody else, not even if they're cousins.'

Mrs Comeaway looked over at her husband. 'You sure that man meant real lations like Hannie an Charlie an them girls?'

'I hope he did,' Trilby said spitefully.

Noonah came through the door and stood there, hot, perspiring and happy. 'It's all right! I can be a nurse.'

'And we're getting the house,' Trilby said triumphantly.

SEVEN

Mr and Mrs Comeaway and Trilby sat listening to all that Noonah had to tell them. Mrs Comeaway's face showed surprised respect at the long medical terms which tripped so easily off her daughter's tongue. Mr Comeaway blanketed equal respect under a lavish display of casualness. Fortunately, he could leave all questioning to his wife, because Mrs Comeaway was willing to admit to any shameful degree of ignorance in order to find out what she wanted to know.

'An what would that thing be, that thing you said?'

'Vocational Guidance Test? That's to show if I'm going to be all right at nursing.'

'You *wanta* be one don't ya?' Mrs Comeaway said with simple faith. 'An what comes after that?'

'I have to go away for ten weeks to a training school in Perth. If I pass my examination when that's over I can start training at the hospital here.'

'Perth, eh?' Mr Comeaway said. 'My daughter,' he would say later, to selected friends, 'has to go to Perth. The government wants her to go to Perth for a while.'

'I get about six pound a week to start off with.'

His eyes widened. He had never looked on his children as potential money makers but the thought was not unpleasant.

'Two pound fifteen is taken out every week for board and stuff,' Noonah said.

Mr Comeaway did some mental arithmetic. Even after two pound fifteen had been taken out there was still a wad of money left over.

'Of course I'll have to buy a lot of text-books to start off with,' Noonah went on, 'and there's deductions for uniforms and insurance...'

Mr Comeaway gave up his mental arithmetic and philosophically went back to just listening.

'Now tell us about nursing,' Mrs Comeaway begged, settling herself more comfortably. 'What sorta jobs ya have ta do. I was in a hospital once. Fa bein ill, I mean. Always wakin ya up ta wash ya an if they not doing that they dosin ya up with medicine. Wake ya up when it's still *dark* just ta wash ya. I tole em not ta bother bout me, seein they had so much else ta see to. Didn't do no good. I hadda be washed just the same.'

'Me too, that time I broke my arm,' Mr Comeaway said feelingly. 'Made me feel real shamed, the things they done ta me. Didn't like ta say nothing, but by crikey, I dunno. Don't seem ta act like ordinary womans, them nurses. And will I forget the day I come in. Damn near took the skin

95

offa me, they did. "Fair go," I told em, "a man's gotta have some sort a cover fa the meat on is bones."'

Noonah giggled. Trilby, who had been listening in scornful silence, joined in. Obligingly, their parents followed suit.

Recovering, Noonah said, 'The scrubbing is to get all the germs off you, so they won't infect you with something.'

'Thought germs was little things you could hardly see,' Mr Comeaway said whimsically. 'Not stuff ya have ta take a great mop to.'

'That's one of the subjects I have to take in Perth,' Noonah said, her eyes alight. 'Hygiene, asepsis.'

'Come again!'

'I think we'll be taken to see the sewerage places and the water department and things like that.'

'I see,' said Mrs Comeaway, who could see no connection.

'Listen to these,' Noonah said, reading from a prospectus. 'Anatomy, Physiology, Theory and Practice of Nursing, Personal and Communal Health, and First Aid.'

'I know what that First Aid is,' Mr Comeaway said quickly, grateful in his knowledge. 'People faintin and all like that.'

'I haven't learned much about it yet,' Noonah said tactfully.

'So you'll be goin off ta Perth just when I'm gettin used ta having ya round,' Mrs Comeaway said, but without reproach.

'And when I come back I have to live at the hospital,' Noonah said anxiously. 'You knew that, didn't you? I'm allowed home praps three nights in two weeks. I'm not sure. Anyhow, I get some time off and I'll come straight home.'

'Oh well,' Mr Comeaway said, 'love ya an leave ya.'

'Mummy, you can have all the money that's left over,' Noonah said earnestly. 'And that'll help you when the kids get back.'

'I spose we better start thinkin bout beds fa everyone,' Mrs Comeaway said.

'Gee, I nearly forgot,' Mr Comeaway took her up. 'We can get beds all right. Might be a bit left over fa some other doodahs too. That partment man says we get forty quid ta spend on furniture, soon as we move inta that house. An that's fa nothin.'

Mrs Comeaway looked as if the entrance to her mind was getting choked up again. 'Beds!' she murmured. 'Fa six of us. An we got three already.' She gazed intently at the two new beds.

Trilby said nothing. There was plenty of time to take action. But her bed cover and frilly curtains seemed a certainty, now.

'How old would Bartie be?' Mr Comeaway mused. 'Nine? Ten?'

'Ten. And wait until you see his drawings.'

'Bartie's nuts,' Trilby said tersely.

'He is not,' Noonah flashed. 'He's going to be an artist.'

'If he's let,' Mrs Comeaway had been sitting very still. A minute or two passed before she said, with a sort of compassion, 'You think it can all be settled just movin into a house, buyin a coupla beds, don't ya, Noonah? You think I sent you all away when there wasn't no real need, eh? You come here

97

an look.' She took Noonah's hand and pressed the fingers against an inch-long scar running through one eyebrow.

'I didn't want my kids hurt,' she said quietly. 'An called names. They might get that, Bartie an Stella, at this new school.'

Mr Comeaway growled deep in his throat. 'Gawd! Ya don't wanta talk like that roun these kids. That little bit of a thing. That ain't nothin.'

Trilby laughed suddenly. 'You think it doesn't happen now?' she asked her father. She turned empty eyes on her mother. 'You think your precious children are safe up at the mission? We're not safe anywhere, you fools. There's always someone around to make us feel we're dirty—not fit to touch. They wouldn't even serve me an Noonah with a drink—until I made them.'

'That man wanted to be nice to us,' Noonah reminded her sister. 'They're not all horrible.'

'Yes they are,' Trilby repudiated roughly. 'All of them. Some let you get closer than others, that's all. They still keep a line between us and them. And when you look at the way we live,' her eyes swept over the room scornfully, like grey lightning, 'you can't blame them, can you? Pigs live better than we do. I tell you I hate white people because they lump us all together and never give one of us a chance to leave all this behind. And I hate coloured people more, because most of them don't *want* a chance. They *like* living like pigs, damn them.' She jumped up, wild-eyed and defiant, and ran from the room.

Mr Comeaway glowered after her. 'Gettin a bit cheeky, ain't she?'

98

'If she feels like that,' Mrs Comeaway said distressfully, 'what's she wanta live right in among white people for?'

'Wasn't like what she said, up at that mission?' Mr Comeaway asked Noonah, underlip out. Noonah hesitated.

'I thought you was all happy up there,' Mrs Comeaway said reproachfully.

'Mummy,' Noonah said impetuously, 'happiness isn't just food and a bed and clothes. Not for children. At the mission, they teach you to go into your class-room at the right time, and they feed you and teach you to brush your teeth and they give you a bed in a proper room, but they could never teach us to stop wanting our own mothers and fathers and our own homes. And it doesn't matter if the home isn't a very good one—it's where we want to be. It's like being sick all the time. Not in your stomach, but up here.' She placed her thin hand against her heart. 'The little kids pretend Mrs Gordon is their mother. Whenever she walks round they crowd up against her and hold on to her hands or her frock and make her bend down so they can hug her. I know they're pretending she's their mother, because I used to pretend myself. And I used to want to smack the other kids and pull their hair— anything to make them go away from her so I could have her all to myself. And sometimes when I saw kids walking along with their mothers and holding on to their hands I used to wish and wish it could be me, back with you.'

Mr Comeaway's eyes had kindled. 'Ain't that what I said?' he accused his wife. 'Didn't I tell ya the kids should stay with us?'

In her mind Noonah was back at the mission, remembering the babies who had come to them from time to time.

Infants of two and three or even younger. And one little chap who had drooped his softly-curled ungainly head that had seemed too large for the stem-like neck. He had sat on the floor silent, indifferent to cajolery, something stony and dead about him which had frightened her. She had picked him up and looked into his dark eyes and seen there something she could not forget. Not endurance, nor hopelessness, nor pain. It was as if this baby she held in her arms had travelled far beyond these things and only the shadow of them remained to quiet his mouth and dull his eyes. She had wanted passionately to undo the wrong that had been done to him, to wipe the remembrance of it from his heavy eyes. And something in her had known that she was helpless, that the hurt had gone too deep and that the shadow of it would remain, perhaps for ever.

Mrs Comeaway shook her head. 'Don't like what you said, Noonah. Bout them kids hangin on some woman's skirts. Not fa my kids I don't.' She straightened her shoulders. 'Looks like we better get them beds quick an lively.'

'An about time,' Mr Comeaway said needlessly.

'You!' His wife withered him with a look. 'Only reason *you* didn't want em ta be in that place was all the fuss an bother it was ta get em there. Men!' She sniffed.

'Ere!'

'An I'm talkin the truth,' Mrs Comeaway said belligerently. 'If ya hadda sat still in one place I mighta done different. Fine time they'd a had, shiftin bout from pillar ta post, never knowin when they was gunna sleep under a decent roof, an no sooner gettin set somewhere than you up an talkin bout goin somewhere else. Ya known damn well ya didn't think bout them kids no more than if they was a lotta billy-goats.'

'I'm gettin outa this,' Mr Comeaway said, heaving himself off his bed. 'Man only gotta open is mouth an ya jumpin down is throat. No good ta me.'

'That's right! Get out when the goin gets rough,' Mrs Comeaway taunted, malevolent-eyed. 'Jus like a man.'

'It's not that they didn't try to be nice to us, up there,' Noonah said nervously.

Mrs Comeaway patted her shoulder. 'That's all right. I'm glad ya told us what ya did. But ya don't think I'm gunna let that one get the laugh on me, do ya?'

EIGHT

Mrs Comeaway hoped that Mrs Green would be alone, though she knew it was as well to be philosophical about this. People went to Horace for advice on problems. They called in Mrs Green when they needed to have all their fears and anxieties resolved into one easy-to-deal-with problem. Mrs Comeaway was vaguely troubled about Trilby. Sometimes she was all brightness and cheek. She had her father twisted round her little finger—could wheedle him into letting her do or have anything she set her mind on. But the things she said—right in front of people. Things that made people feel uncomfortable. Walking towards Mrs Green's open doorway, Mrs Comeaway stopped to shake her head and frown, and ponder.

People coming in for a little visit. Trilby acted as if that was something bad, though where the badness lay—again Mrs Comeaway shook her head. You didn't push your pals off just because it was time to eat. And all this walking round town. Mrs Comeaway had a corn on her little toe that was giving her gyp. Trilby said if they stayed home someone was sure to come, so they'd go out. And out they went, dragging up and down that damn street, never stopped to talk to anyone because Trilby wouldn't let her—or else they went down to the Wild-Oat Patch and picked out the house with the prettiest paint because, Trilby kept saying, just as if her father hadn't already agreed, *their* house was going to be painted the minute they got into it.

There wasn't really much to worry about. Trilby was good company and the food bills were certainly a lot lighter. Mrs Comeaway paused to hope piously that she wouldn't need to cadge a meal for a while yet. The truth was, she missed her friends and her way of life. After all, she'd lived it a good few years.

Mrs Green met her at the back door, coming out with an armful of steaming clothes.

'Not out today?' Mrs Green twinkled, as Mrs Comeaway trudged back to the clothes-line with her.

'She's off out with Blanchie and Audrena,' Mrs Comeaway said, without her usual grin.

'Finding her feet,' Mrs Green said sympathetically, pegging out a faded pink frock.

'She's worn mine off up to the ankles,' Mrs Comeaway said gloomily.

'We'll have a cup of tea,' Mrs Green said comfortably, 'just as soon as I get this lot out.'

'Anyone around?'

'Polly's out there under the trees,' Mrs Green gestured with her head. 'Having a sleep.'

They went back into the kitchen. The big black kettle dozed at the side of the stove. Mrs Green moved it to where it would get more heat. 'Those girls, Audrena and Blanchie, they know their way about, don't they?'

'Bet that Audrena does. I like Blanchie better.'

Mrs Green frowned slightly.

'Ya think they might lead er inta mischief?' Mrs Comeaway said bluntly. 'Ya don't need ta worry bout that. Trilby's the one'll do the leadin. An not inta mischief. Just down ta the Wild-Oat Patch ta have a look at the houses.' She rubbed her foot with tender fingers.

'I just thought,' Mrs Green said delicately. 'Trilby isn't used to going round with a gang of girls and boys. And you know what these boys are like. Specially the ones down for a bit of a holiday.'

'Ya mean last Monday night,' Mrs Comeaway said. 'She would go. So I tole Blanchie. "Now you get that girl home early cause er father ain't gunna like it she comes home late." And I said for em to keep away from that wharf down there, with all them men off boats like. An they was all promises an big eyes. Dunno what time they got in.'

'You ask her next morning?' Mrs Green asked innocently.

'No, I didn't. An what woulda been the use? She'd a told me a lotta lies,' Mrs Comeaway smiled a little. 'Same as I'd a done at er age.'

'She's so young an pretty,' Mrs Green murmured, searching for words to fit what her heart knew without the need for them. 'Pity not ta keep your hands on the reins a bit longer. You let kids gallop off where they like and pretty soon they're going to think it doesn't matter where they go.'

'Gawd! You tellin me a wild one like Trilby's gunna take notice a me?'

Mrs Green poured some tea-leaves in the pot and lifted the boiling kettle. 'I had 'em like her before,' she said softly. 'Like a young brumby, you know? That you have to handle gently.' Her mind went back into the tender memories of the past, and she nodded her head. 'Yes. Those little wild ones with their eyes rolling and their long thin legs a bit shaky with fright. And you don't go near, but just stand there and talk to them and you keep on talking. They gallop off to start with, but you hold on to your patience, and every day you're there at the same place and after a while they stay and listen to you. And their eyes don't roll any more and their ears don't lay back on their heads, but perk up real straight. Trying to hear if you mean all that soft talk you're giving em. Patience? You hurry those little wild ones and you've lost em for good. They have to trust you. And there's nothing like a little wild brumby for finding out the ones it can trust.'

Mrs Comeaway nodded impatiently. This was way out of her depth. 'What I thought—I came over ta arst ya—couldn't you tell Trilby some a them things you tell ya own kids, like about education an stuff, an getting a good job. She likes you. She'd listen to you.'

Mrs Green set out the cups. And, as though summoned, two figures blanked out the light in the doorway.

105

'Look who's ere,' Mrs Comeaway said, brightening a little. 'What you two doin back ere? Thought you was lookin fa better company.'

'Mary!' The woman's voice was peremptory. 'We got no tucker.'

'Sit down,' Mrs Green said, reaching for more cups.

'Thought you was well on the way ta Carnarvon,' Mrs Comeaway rallied.

'You better let me an Enry sleep in that ole bed a mine,' Honay snapped. 'Till we think somethin out.' Each word left her mouth neatly clipped from its predecessor. She sucked in her bottom lip and waited.

'What about—you know?' Mrs Green looked meaningly at the silent Enry.

'We gunna start when we leave ere,' Honay said.

'You gunna let em stay here?' Mrs Comeaway asked, amused. 'Don't tell me.'

Honay shot her a vindictive look. She and outspoken Mrs Comeaway had had many an argument during the time Honay had stayed with Mrs Green waiting for the release of her Enry from jail.

'Go on!' Mrs Comeaway was baiting her now. 'Didn't you tell Mrs Green you wasn't gunna sociate with niggers? Didn't you say Enry said you was ta keep away from us after e come out? What you doing back ere again then? After Mrs Green kept you in tucker all the time ya ole man was in jail. Gawd!' Her uproarious laughter filled the kitchen.

Honay stood shaking with rage. 'This one,' she told Mrs Green furiously, 'she's a no-good nigger. No good ta Enry or me. I tole you before.'

'Eh!' Mrs Comeaway's mirth dried up as suddenly as it had begun. 'Oo ya think you callin nigger.'

'Honay!' The silent Enry spoke. His voice was reproving. 'Honay!'

'I'll give er Honay!' Mrs Comeaway snorted with indignation, though amusement was not yet dimmed in her eyes.

'Honay,' Mrs Green said. 'You and Enry better sit down and have a cuppa now I got it made. And I suppose you can sleep in that bed a night or two. If it holds together. But you did tell me yesterday Enry didn't want you to associate with coloured people any more.'

Honay tossed her head. 'We don't even got no blanket,' she accused. 'You want me an Enry ta sleep thout no blanket?'

Mrs Green sighed. 'I got one I can lend you. But remember, I have to have it back. I need all my blankets.'

'We givim back,' Enry spoke softly. 'Soon!'

'I hope,' Mrs Green said feelingly.

'We have cuppa tea now,' Honay bossed. 'Sit down, Enry.'

'And if Skippy comes back while you're here,' Mrs Green begged, pouring tea, 'don't you two start fighting, Honay.' She looked over at Mrs Comeaway. 'I thought I was all through with their fighting. The way they act they're not much better than the kids.'

Honay wiggled her nose from side to side, slid a finger over one nostril, and blew the contents of the other over the floor. She looked quickly and defiantly at Mrs Green.

107

'Honay!' Mrs Green's tone was exasperated. 'Don't *do* that. You go outside now and get a rag and wipe that up. You dirty old woman. Go on!' She withheld Honay's cup of tea.

Honay rose from the table without a word, walked outside to where a wet rag hung on a nail and returned with it. Sulkily, she got to work.

'And Enry!' Enry looked up obediently from his tea. 'You and Honay can stay a night or two, but you've got to see that old woman of yours behaves.'

Enry nodded. 'You git me bottle, missus. I give er smack on the side of the ead she don't behave.'

Mrs Comeaway leaned over and clapped the old man on the back with such force that the tea held to his mouth slopped over the side of the cup. 'Good on ya, Enry, ole man,' she said. 'Damned if I don't go out and get that bottle for ya meself.'

Honay looked down her long nose, pursed her lips, and sniffed.

Trilby's new bathing-suit was a deep vivid green. In the sunlight her skin had a dusky shimmer to it and her long, free-swinging stride only emphasized the delicious youthfulness of her body. She stopped to dig her foot deep into the hot sand, letting it trickle smoothly back through her toes. When Blanchie and Audrena caught up with her she moved off again, completely happy. It was good to have the late morning sun burning into her flesh, good to know that any moment she chose she could dash into the sea, fling herself into it and feel its coolness against her.

There was peace to be found along the lonely little stretch of beach too. The ageless and immutable peace that belongs to everything in which man has taken no part. A little way out from the shore, moulded green waves shattered to white froth over submerged reefs. Overhead, seagulls swooped and screamed and described their flights against a background of soft blue.

The girls were walking along the less frequented part of the beach. The tide had climbed high in a curving line, leaving the sand wet and firm. Where the girls walked, their footsteps followed after them, delicately perfect. Between the beach and the road grew thickets of grey-green salt-bush, scored through with a hundred paths leading down to the sea. The noise of traffic was muted with distance, no more disturbing than the wash of the waves or the soft chatter of the girls. Unheard in their ears, the deep strong pull of the ocean went on for ever.

'School for you soon,' Audrena said, looking pityingly at Trilby.

Trilby gave her cousin a long look. 'I can always get a headache.'

Audrena laughed.

'Wasn't you gunna get a job?' Blanchie asked. 'Serving or something?'

Trilby looked sullenly ahead. At one time or another she had been into every shop in the town. Foreigners she had found, some golden-skinned, some dark, a few of them hardly able to make themselves understood, but there had been none like herself. Trilby bit her bottom lip savagely. On one point her mind was firmly made up. There would be no housework for her, nor minding of kids. For another year she would go back to school. By that time she would know more about this town and then she would see.

She forced a casual air. 'I'm going to get my Junior first,' she told her cousins. 'So I can get a better job. In an office or somewhere.'

Blanchie stared admiringly at her not doubting for a moment Trilby would get what she wanted. Blanchie did not mind taking second place to her glamorous cousin. She found it exciting to be with her, swimming when Trilby decided to swim, looking in shop windows, sitting at the far end of the Esplanade at night with a crowd of young ones, laughing, gossiping, wandering home late at night with a few fellers to keep them company.

Audrena fell in with most of Trilby's plans, too, but sour envy made up a good proportion of her feelings towards her cousin. Even Trilby's untouched body was a source of annoyance to Audrena. It was as though she set a price on herself. Audrena had to admit that Trilby had had her opportunities. The fellers hung round her like ants after jam. It beat Audrena to know why, when there was herself with all her experience and none of this stupid hanging back from something that was bound to happen to a girl some time or other.

Audrena was always watching for a chance to get under Trilby's guard. Her tongue shot venom wherever she knew it would sting most.

'Better not set ya heart on no office job,' she said now. 'You could be the best typewriter in the world an not get a job here.'

'Typiste!' Trilby flicked back.

'All I'm saying, ya want one a them jobs you'll have ta go some other place where they don't know ya got colour in ya.' Her glance went spitefully to Trilby's dark gold skin.

'That's what I'm going to do,' Trilby said proudly. And in that second decided to do just this. Of course! She should have thought of it for herself. What she must do must be to leave everyone behind her; begin a new fresh life of her own. The thought of it excited her. With a sudden uprush of spirits she sprinted up the beach, turned a somersault and landed laughing and breathless in the odoriferous scratchy seaweed where a group of boys waited for them.

She had chosen this spot herself, because it was far from the popular beaches and usually deserted. Nearly every morning a crowd of youngsters swam and played about on the beach. There were dozens of tight-packed seaweed balls to throw at each other. Sometimes they formed a circle and played a regular game. The boys wrestled and fought and showed off their strength, and when everyone was tired they could lie on the warm, wet seaweed and talk, with the suffocating smell of it deep in their nostrils. When the sun became too hot there was the sea.

This morning they made straight for the water. Audrena and Blanchie shrieked with pleasure, dived deep and came up with seaweed in their hair. Trilby swam out a little way and turned on her back. Through half-shut eyes she watched Phyllix follow her. She smiled, satisfied. She waited until he was within a couple of feet of her then dived cleanly beneath him. The two raced for the beach.

Argosy Bell and his brother Nipper, who were staying with the Beemans, threw themselves enthusiastically amongst the laughing girls, upsetting them, grabbing their ankles, ducking them unmercifully. Two more young girls who ran down to the water's edge and stood there pretending fear were seized and dragged in by their feet. Like young animals they kicked and fought, giggled and splashed; smooth-skinned, lithe, their eyelashes sticking together in wet points, their round pink tongues showing between their square white teeth.

Phyllix fitted his hands to Trilby's waist and pulled her slowly, deliciously, through the coolness. In the water the feel of someone's hands on your body was nothing. It was when Phyllix stopped pulling and let Trilby's body drift close to his, when he bent his head so that his cheek brushed wetly against hers, when she felt the intimate warmth of his breath, that Trilby was suddenly shaken. Her own breath caught in her throat. She liked the feeling even as she grew wary. But those golden eyes so near her own—under their level look Trilby found she had no power to drop her own gaze. Each gazed deep, and there was no holding back.

Blanchie called, and obediently they left the water for the warmth of the piled seaweed.

'You nearly broke my leg.' Audrena pouted, watching Nipper from the corner of her eye whilst she stroked and smoothed her outstretched leg.

'Want me ta do that?' Nipper said slyly, reaching out a hand.

Audrena whisked the leg beneath her haunches. 'No, I do not. See?'

Nipper slid his hand further towards her leg. 'I can fix that leg easy.'

Audrena threw her head back and her voice husked over with sweetness. 'You'd like to, wouldn't ya? If I let ya.'

Seated a few feet away Trilby watched the little scene with calm eyes. This was a sort of play-acting to which she was new. Nipper was a great one for touching—running his hand over your leg, slipping an arm high up round your waist. With other girls—not with her. Trilby could not let him. His hands were hot and wet, his breath smelled bad and sometimes his body smelled bad too, as if it were never washed clean.

This was one of the things about which Audrena teased her most; what Audrena called her stupid hands-off attitude to boys. But Audrena could inflict no hurt here. Never, never would she let anyone touch her if the touch brought her no pleasure but only loathing. Not for any amount of experience. Yet she was curious. If it were only half so good as the girls said…She turned her head away from the goings-on, caught Phyllix's gaze fixed squarely upon her and was again unable to look away.

'I'm going ta sleep,' Blanchie yawned, burrowing her head into her arms. 'I'm tired.'

'Out late last night?' Albany teased. 'With Tom?'

'Not Tom,' Blanchie said innocently, and was just as innocently surprised at the laughter this brought forth from the boys.

Trilby clasped her hands tightly round her knees and let her own head droop forward. Behind the screen of her

gold-tipped hair she watched Phyllix and tried to understand her feeling for him.

She liked him, but why? He was not so good to look
upon as most of the others. He had a thin delicate frame.
When he walked there was a touch of the stalker in him. A
soft-footed easy lope. His features were not well formed.
The gravity of his expression was carried to sternness by the
dark thick slant of his eyebrows and his wide, thin-lipped,
unsmiling mouth. His eyes were like the eyes of a cat, tilted
at the corners, tawny, the pupils mere pin-points. Perhaps it
was those strange eyes that drew her. Phyllix did not laugh
easily, or play the fool like the others. He seemed a little
apart from them always. Almost, Trilby thought irritably,
as if he would not bother himself with their foolishness.

Nobody knew who was his father, least of all Phyllix's
mother. Older folk remembered much about his mother.
A happy one, that. Certainly not the kind to sit on the
outskirts if there was any fun to be had. It was likely that
Phyllix's father had been a sailor or a deck-hand off a boat.
Enough of them berthed here. His thin nose with its narrow
nostrils was more Indian than aboriginal. But there was
his skin, the smooth brownness of it blotched with tawny
freckles.

He was still watching her, Trilby saw through her hair.
She lay back, pretending to sleep, and was conscious of a
sudden deep wish that these others would go away, all of
them, and leave her alone with Phyllix.

Egoline Barclay squealed. Someone had thrown a
seaweed ball at her. She picked it up, ready to throw it back.
There was a scatter of sand and seaweed. Someone tripped

114

over Blanchie's hot sunburned body, and she came to her feet with a yell of anguish. She caught Nipper by an ankle as he rose and he went sprawling. Instantly, he was upon her, manhandling her into the water, seizing his chance to lay hands on a female body. And the game was on.

Trilby looked after them, pretending absorption in their flying figures, conscious only of Phyllix.

Blanchie screamed madly until water closed her mouth.

Trilby knew when Phyllix changed his position. She peeped through her lashes and the yellow eyes looked straight into hers.

'You coming down town tonight?' Phyllix asked softly.

'What d'you want to know for?'

'You and me might go for a bit of a walk. It's nice walking along the beach at night. Nobody about.'

'What do I want to go for a walk with you for?'

She dragged a ribbon of seaweed from the tangled mass of it. It was almost the colour of Phyllix's eyes.

'All right!' she answered his demanding silence. 'I'll come down for a little while.'

'People fishing,' Blanchie called breathlessly. 'Come and see, you two.'

The beach was not deserted any more. Looking along it, Trilby saw the figures of three people, a woman and two men, busy about a net.

'Let's come and see how many they get,' Audrena said eagerly. 'Might give us a few if they can't carry them all.' She laughed wildly and fled up the beach.

The rest trailed after her. They might as well have a look. Nobody could stop you from looking. The net was

115

half out now. The men were completing a half circle with it, their steps slowed, the pull of its weight showing in their down-bent heads and straining backs.

'They won't get anything,' Phyllix murmured. 'Too early! When the sun goes down, that's the time.'

But they had caught something. Trilby saw. There was a sudden threshing in the net. The men waded faster, hurrying to reach the beach before their catch escaped. The woman there waited, tense and excited, her clenched fists beneath her chin, her back to the coloured youngsters. Audrena grinned, made a wicked gesture, and walked over to her. She was close behind the woman before she asked: 'D'you think I an my friends could have some of your fish if you catch a lot?'

The woman's back stiffened. She did not turn her head. 'I don't know, I'm sure.'

'We'd pay for them, if you wanted to sell some.'

'You'll have to speak to my husband about that.'

Audrena made a face, then swaggered grinning back to the others. 'Says we'll have to ask her ole man,' she called loudly.

'Silly damn fool,' Phyllix said coolly, though there was heat in his eyes. Some of the others laughed. There was a long wait, whilst the net was dragged up on to the beach. Then everyone ran to see the black threshing body it held. They saw a giant stingray, the curved tail long and forked at the end. A vicious tail it was, trying desperately to attack. The hooded eyes of the stingray rose and fell with its breathing. The big black body heaved helplessly in the meshes of the net and the black seal-smooth skin rippled like water.

'Damn!' one of the men said ruefully. 'I thought we had a good haul there.'

'What are you going to do with it? Throw it back, or leave it here?' the woman asked nervously.

'Better kill it. That's a dangerous beast there. And it's too close to the beach where the kiddies swim,' the man answered. He took out a knife. The other man hooked the slippery tail. Once, twice, three times the man with the knife slashed before he cut right through it.

'That's the sting gone,' he said with satisfaction, as he hacked at it.

Trilby's eyes were large. How did this Thing feel without its tail? Both portions of the body twisted in agony. The eyes sank despairingly down, only to rise again in a frenzy.

'Perhaps if you push that stick through the eyes...,' the man suggested.

A heavy stick was thrust down through the rubbery mass of the creature's eyes. But life was still there, and now blood poured from the cut portions of its body, gushing quicker with every flailing movement.

'Oh!' the woman cried, clasping her mouth with both hands. 'Oh!'

The man stabbed again and again. More blood poured out from the mutilated parts. The eyes continued to labour up and down, up and down, despite their wounds.

The woman looked furiously at the group of coloured youngsters, and her eyes were hard and hurt. 'These niggers,' she shrilled, 'you can never get away from them.'

117

Trilby did not even hear her. She had had enough. She wheeled and skimmed off down the beach. She flung herself down on the seaweed again, hid her face in her arms and saw again the anguished eyes rising and falling, the blood gushing out to stain the white sand with red.

The others drifted back and sank down beside her.

'What ya want to run away for, old softie?' Audrena asked, amusement in her voice.

'If they leave that tail behind,' Phyllix mused, 'I might pick it up. Good meat in that—like whiting.'

Trilby jerked upright. 'No!' she said tautly. 'No!' And her eyes, too, were hard and hurt.

NINE

A moon the colour of water sailed frigidly through the tenebrous sky, shedding no beam of light on the beach nor on the black moving water lapping insistently at the line of the shore.

'You all right?' Phyllix asked.

'Yes!' Trilby said shortly. She was finding no magic in the night. Instead, she felt like a fool. To be stalking along this beach alone with Phyllix, on guard against being caught up into something she might not want.

Phyllix reached out and caught her hand. His own was warm and dry, and its grip was firm. After a while he slid his hand around so that his thumb was on her palm.

Trilby's loose thoughts, like dropped stitches, were knitted up into a single thrilling awareness of his touch.

Gently and rhythmically, Phyllix stroked her palm. 'Nice bein quiet for a change, isn't it?'

Like steel to a magnet, Trilby swayed closer to him. Here was the magic! It had been waiting, ready to leap to life at the touch of his hand. Yet there was shyness in her now. Wantonly, she dissipated the sweetness with words.

'Did you take the tail of the stingray, Phyllix?'

'You told me not to, didn't you?'

She sensed that he was smiling. 'I thought they were awful, those people. I *hate* to see anything helpless. Specially something like that stingray that was so big and strong. They should have put it back in the water.'

'Why?'

'They don't hurt anything—stingrays.'

'Why do you think about it?'

'I won't, any more.' For a moment she was lonely because he had not shared her pain. 'Where are we going?'

'Along here a way. Don't you like walking?'

'I don't mind walking with you.' The words came out unwillingly. Her shyness was back again.

'You never gone for a walk with a feller before?'

'Not just me.'

'I think you never been with a feller—any way at all. Have you?' His face was turned towards her, and though they kept on walking it was as if everything stood still, like a moment out of the wholeness of time to stay forever fixed in their memories.

'No!' Trilby breathed. 'I never wanted to.'

'I could tell,' Phyllix said expressionlessly. 'You can always tell.'

Trilby thought of Audrena. A small surge of triumph gave her face gaiety. After tonight she would know all that

Audrena knew. She need no longer feel like a silly kid when Audrena talked of fellers the way she did. Nor try to carry off her ignorance with a high hand. She dwelt with a little wonder on Blanchie. Even Blanchie knew what this was all about.

Noonah came into her mind as well. And with Noonah came more uncertainty. At the mission, there had been strict supervision of the elder boys and girls. At night they had been locked into their dormitories, and there had always been someone from the staff to keep an eye on them. Even so, things had happened. There was that time, her thoughts roved back, when a lot of them had gone for a walk and come across a swimming-hole. First a boy had disappeared and emerged into view splashing and laughing, leaving his clothes on the muddy bank, and that had started them off. One by one the fellers and the girls had flung aside their clothes and gone slipping and sliding down into the pool. And that was where Mr Gordon had found them all—or nearly all. A couple had disappeared. And another couple had been about to sneak off when the panting and fuming superintendent of the mission had caught up with them. Crikey, what a row! And what fun it had been! But afterwards, she and Noonah had agreed that the two girls had been stupid fools to go off like that, getting themselves into all that fuss and bother, having to submit to being punished like kids. And Trilby had thought contemptuously that all that sort of thing could very well wait until there was no danger of someone tailing you up and making a fool of you in front of everyone.

Well, and here it was, and she supposed she had a right to please herself what she did now she was home. She flicked the thought of Noonah from her mind. She felt as superior to Noonah as she had felt towards those two girls who had gone into this thing so greedily and unthinkingly. There was a time, and this was it.

'I bet *you* have,' she teased Phyllix, sure of herself now, feeling superior even to Phyllix.

'Have what?'

'Gone with girls.'

'It's different,' Phyllix frowned, 'for fellers.' He looked down at her again. 'Wish I hadn't, sometimes.'

There was magic again. Their feet slowed. In an opening up of warmth and wonder, Trilby claimed the night as her own. The moon, ripening slowly to pale gold. The blackness of the water, changing now to rippling velvet. The white beach lit by the pale moonlight. It was all for her, and it was all hers.

To their left as they walked were the mounding bushes, etching themselves grey against the sky. 'Let's sit here for a while,' Trilby begged, and pulled Phyllix over to their shelter.

'This is good,' Phyllix said, with a sigh, stretching himself out on the cool hard sand.

Trilby sat alongside him, her ankles crossed, her chin in her hands, dreamily content. The air moved clean and tangy, gently cool against her hot face.

'You like to be away from the others?' Phyllix asked softly.

'I like to be with the crowd better,' Trilby teased him.

'They talk too much,' Phyllix said disinterestedly. 'Noise—that's all.'

'Why do you go round with them if you don't like them?'

Phyllix moved his shoulders. 'Have to have someone to go round with, I suppose. Besides, you're there.'

'What's different about me?' Trilby fished.

'You don't yap.' Trilby laughed delightedly. 'And besides...'

'Besides—what?'

'You damn well know. You've got em all beat. That Audrena, she's jealous. They're all a bit jealous.'

Trilby's heart lifted. Of course she knew it, but it was good to have Phyllix say it.

A dark figure appeared, strolling close to the water's edge on the hard wet sand. Trilby put out a hand, pressed Phyllix's shoulder, warning him to be silent.

It was fun to sit there, themselves unseen, and to watch as this man walked by. Everything was fun.

Phyllix reached for her hand and held it, and she knew he was sharing something of what she felt. They watched the man out of sight.

Suddenly Trilby was restless. Something more was needed. She thought of the cool rapture of water against her skin. Remembered the first tingling shock of its touch and the calmness as it rose higher and higher.

She rose in a lovely fluid movement. Phyllix sighed and prepared to rise too, but she pushed him back. Behind some bushes she stripped off her clothes and walked to the edge of the water. She felt the splash of a tiny wave at her feet and walked through it. When she was far enough out she began to swim. And the water was as she remembered it, like the touch of hands.

She heard Phyllix's call. 'Trilby, where are you?'

She stopped swimming and floated on her back. She would not exert herself to call. Phyllix must come to her. She closed her eyes and waited, and opened them to find Phyllix swimming close.

'Take my hands now,' she said when they both were tired from swimming. 'Pull me in. Please!' But Phyllix placed his hands instead over her breasts and drew her smoothly through the water. Until the water became shallow. And then he picked her up and carried her over the beach to the bushes.

Trilby learned that that was how it was. Peace flowing through every limb, and languorous weariness. She turned to her lover and sighed, the smallest fluttering breath. At her side Phyllix breathed deeply and quietly.

The air was like a kiss on their bodies.

But not all of Trilby's vitality had been used up by the walking and the swimming and what had come after. When she had rested a while she felt a desire to talk with Phyllix and question him a little. She wanted to hear him murmur again the things he had murmured against her ear.

'I'm glad it was you,' she whispered.

After a while she raised her head and stared down at him because he had not answered. She put her face close to his. 'Phyllix! Phyllix!'

Still there was no answer. Phyllix slept deeply.

Trilby was conscious of shock. How could he sleep, when she was so near?

She rolled over, took his shoulders in her two hands and shook him. 'Phyllix!'

She put her mouth to his and waited for the response. There was none. Sitting, she gazed unbelievingly down on him. He could lie there and snore after saying those things. After...

She sprang to her feet, her hands on her hips, her mouth thin with temper. Viciously she kicked him in the ribs, but Phyllix only moaned and curled himself tighter.

Now—she would teach him a lesson, this snoring fool. But first to cleanse herself from every trace of her foolishness. Like a shadow she slipped into the water again, swimming far out, diving deep, threshing furiously at the water with strong young arms and legs. She had to search for her clothes when she came out at last, and her clothes were covered with sand. Uncaring she pulled them on over her wet body, intent only on her outrage. She would leave him sleeping, and he would wake to find her gone. That would teach him that Trilby Comeaway was not—in the act of tying her sash, she froze.

Would that be a punishment? Would he care if she went or stayed? Now?

She began to run, but her thought kept up with her and it was not her exertion that made her feel hot. Her hair streamed away from her face and the sand flew from her feet, but the waves of shame kept coursing through her body. She had thought to use a man and he had used her instead.

And he must surely have known, Phyllix, that this was the way of it.

She was gasping for breath when at last she slowed her pace to a staggering walk. But the needles of agony in her side did not hurt half so much as the humiliation in her heart or the tears that stung her eyes.

Overhead the moon hid its cool loveliness behind a trail of clouds. And the beach grew dark.

TEN

'I dunno! Seems like an awful waste,' Mrs Comeaway said doubtfully, surveying the humpy. 'We've kep adding bits and now we got it real comfortable. I went an promised Charlie e could have it, too. Till they get their own money saved up. An after that I thought the Thomases. They got all them kids an nothin but a bit a canvas to keep em dry when it rains. Mrs Green wouldn't mind. She an Mrs Thomas been friends a good while now.'

'Nup!' Mr Comeaway shook his head. 'The partment man says e's gotta come down less other peoples moves in. Says e don't want that.'

'No time ta pull im down now well,' Mrs Comeaway said practically. 'You'll just ave ta come up some other time, when we get set down there in the Wild-Oat Patch.' She looked at Mr Comeaway with limpid eyes. 'Spose they ain't no harm in Charlie livin here till we get the time, isn't it?'

'Ya want wood ta burn, don't ya?' Mr Comeaway pointed out what had been craftily pointed out to him. 'Ain't no bush stuff round the Patch. All been bulldozed. You take them uprights now. Good wood there.'

'Yeah! Yeah! Well, we ain't got the time, I tell ya. I gotta get this stuff sorted out.' Mrs Comeaway destroyed nothing and threw nothing away.

'What ya gunna take?' Mr Comeaway asked. 'Tim an me better get busy.'

'There isn't much worth taking,' Trilby said contemptuously. 'Why don't we just take the new beds and chuck the rest of that junk away?'

'Don't tell!' Mrs Comeaway said, shocked. 'Ya think I'm gunna leave me good safe an me chester draws and them chairs? I like my ole bed. Fits me. Wouldn't sleep so good in no other now.' She ruminated a while, kneading her chin with one hand. 'Joe!' she called. 'Best thing you can do—bring everything out an I'll look it over. Go on, now. An you come ere with me, Trilby.'

Trilby followed her parents into the humpy. She was sulking. She did not care much now if they went or stayed. The thought of the new house no longer enticed her.

Mr Comeaway made a great business out of heaving the table through the entrance. At one end of the precious bed, Mrs Comeaway heaved and pulled and hammered until the rusted spring came free. 'Get on one end, Trilby,' she ordered, 'and we'll get it outside.'

They stood the mattress against a tree and Mrs Comeaway bent to peer at it. 'Been gettin bites some nights,' she said critically. 'Maybe fleas, or else it's them

128

sand-flies.' She chuckled suddenly, diverted. 'That Annie. She tole me a man came out ta the place where they was livin in Perth an bought a jar of fleas offa one a her lations. Paid a pound a hundred for em. This man trained them fleas, so he said.'

'Ugh!' Trilby said disgustedly. 'Where did she get them from?'

Mrs Comeaway shrugged. 'Offa the dogs, offa the blankets, out of er ead. She said the man liked yuman fleas the best. Smarter! Easier to train.'

'They make me sick,' Trilby snapped. She looked suspiciously at her mother's hair. 'Why don't you give your hair a good comb? You'll be getting fleas in your own head if you're not careful.'

'Not me,' Mrs Comeaway disclaimed.

'How do you know?' Trilby sneered.

'I don't itch,' Mrs Comeaway said cheerfully.

'This bed looks awful,' Trilby frowned. 'All broken. Why don't you get another one with the money the department gave you?'

'We are gunna,' Mrs Comeaway said. 'Fa Stella and Bartie. Gee, I bet them kids is gettin excited bout comin down.' She straightened to beam at her daughter. Everything was turning out most happily. There were drawbacks. So-called friends who accused her of getting too uppity, guessed she would be too proud to speak to them when she had gone into her new house. At one stage—when it was pointed out to her that she would be a far walk from a yarn or a game of cards—she had almost been ready to back out of the deal. But Joe seemed real set on it, and she

129

hardly liked to think what the girls would say, particularly Trilby. Besides, there were always taxis.

Her only regret now was that all her friends and relations were not moving down to the Wild-Oat Patch with her, though this had been partly solved by generously distributed invitations to come down and visit.

'Young Tim should be here by now,' she pondered aloud. 'Bet something's gone wrong with that ute.' Tim was Blanchie's 'boy', whose offer to move their furniture had been sought and accepted.

'Ya don't wanta worry bout Tim.' Mr Comeaway sat down to rest from his labours. 'That one can make a engine go with more parts out than in. Last time I seen that ute e'd ripped the engine cover off. Said it kept fallin on is ead when e was working on it like.' He brooded for a while. 'I tole im but, you bring one a ya pals along ta do ya windin for ya. I ain't takin any more chances with that handle. Damn thing about knocked me out last time. Needs a expert at the game.'

'When do they get married, him an Blanchie?' Trilby enquired, with the faintest show of interest.

'They was talking bout it last time I seen em,' Mrs Comeaway said. 'Pity him an Blanchie can't get into a house like we got. Could start off all nice.'

'They won't get married,' Trilby said tightly.

'May not! If they change their minds. An there ain't no hurry for a girl ta get married, that I can see.'

Trilby shot her mother an irritable look.

Mrs Comeaway was examining the food-safe. 'Ya know, ya might be right bout this safe. E seems to ave broke it up a bit gettin it out, clumsy great elephant. Ya think it might do Charlie and Hannie?'

'It stinks. Burn it.'

'I'll take it,' Mrs Comeaway decided. 'I can still *put* things in it. An ya never know.'

Tim and his mate appeared, ploughing their way through the sand.

'There they are,' Mr Comeaway said unnecessarily. 'Tole you they'd come.'

'We ain't half sorted out here yet, Timmie,' Mrs Comeaway said. 'You come right in the nick a time ta help us get these things out an look em over.'

Tim chuckled. 'Reckon I'd a come in the nick a time if I'd left it another week.' He grinned at the recumbent Mr Comeaway.

'Im! Gawd, yes. E ain't much help.' Mrs Comeaway did not even glance at her husband. 'Thing is, we dunno what ta take and what ta leave, eh, Trilby?'

'Ain't seen ya round lately,' Tim ventured to Trilby. 'Whatsa matter? You too busy learnin books down that school?'

Trilby walked back into the humpy without replying. Most of her resentment was directed at Phyllix, but there was enough of it to cover the rest of the boys who had formed part of the group.

'What's bit her?' Tim enquired of her mother.

'Dunno! Gits like that. Doesn't do ta ask questions but. Comes down on ya like a ton a bricks. What ya think a this safe, Timmie? Ya think I should leave it now its legs is broke off?'

131

'Take anything ya like,' Tim said generously. 'Plenty a room on the back.'

'Ya want me ta give ya a hand?' Mr Comeaway asked anxiously.

'You make im help ya,' Mrs Comeaway said strongly. 'Don't tell me! Ow e gets on down that wharf I dunno. Hides isself behind the stuff, I suppose. Get up there! You get that safe on ya shoulders an be off down that hill. An don't do it no more damage either.'

'I offered,' Mr Comeaway said, with dignity. 'Anyone think I didn't offer.'

Trilby came out with some cups on her fingers. 'No school today?' Tim asked, passing her.

'I'm home to help,' Trilby said coolly.

'Don't ya like swimming no more?' This was from his mate, Albany Bell.

'Just don't get the time,' Trilby said loftily. 'I'm taking my exams end of this year.'

'Whadda ya know well,' Albany grinned, nudging Tim.

'*You* wouldn't know *anything*,' Trilby flared, glaring at him.

'I know some things pretty good,' Albany grinned again. 'You ask Audrena.'

Mrs Comeaway had trundled off down the hill with some things, and Trilby was glad. Perhaps both these boys knew. Perhaps Phyllix had told them.

'Don't see Phyllix no more now, neither,' Tim said casually. 'Think e musta went off ta Meekatharra with a shearin team.'

Trilby felt weak with relief.

Mrs Comeaway returned with Mrs Green in tow. She struck an attitude before the humpy, hands on hips, mouth turned inward. 'You see any sense in it?' she asked of her friend.

'Well I could use it myself, for the overflow like,' Mrs Green said, feeling her way delicately, 'but I think I see what he's getting at.'

'See a damn sight more than I do well,' Mrs Comeaway said sturdily. 'Place like this wouldn't go beggin long. Them Thompsons—got six kids parked under that ole bit of tarp.'

'Mrs Green might not want a lot of kids here,' Trilby interrupted angrily.

'She don't mind kids,' Mrs Comeaway said. 'Don't be silly.'

'I hear they're putting up some more of those little places down the camp,' Mrs Green said gently.

'That's the lot fa this trip,' Albany called, passing them with the table balanced on his head. 'Anyone comin down?'

'What about you comin down?' Mrs Comeaway urged Mrs Green. 'See the house. These boys gotta come back ta pick up the rest a the junk.'

Mrs Green looked pleased. 'You sure there's room for me?'

'Plenty,' Mrs Comeaway said magnificently. 'An there's no need runnin back an changin ya dress. No one's gunna see ya.'

'I'll wait here,' Trilby said coldly.

'Please yaself,' Mrs Comeaway said. The two women went over the sandhill and down to the road.

'Well!' Mrs Comeaway said admiringly. 'We got more stuff than I thought.'

'It ain't too secure,' Tim warned. 'Didn't have enough ropes. You two better sit in front with me an the other two on top a the load ta keep a eye on things. You think ya can climb up there?' he asked Mr Comeaway, grinning.

Mr Comeaway eyed the load. He placed a foot on the running board, steadied himself on a chair and worked his way carefully to the top of the load. Two saucepans, insecurely balanced, crashed noisily to the road.

'Look what ya doin,' Mrs Comeaway said indignantly. 'Them's new from the second-hand shop.' She picked up the saucepans and dusted them off. 'Here, ya better hold em,' she ordered, handing them up to her crouching husband.

Mr Comeaway moved slightly but inadvisedly. The already damaged safe collapsed with gentle cracks and enveloped him.

'E meant ta do that,' Mrs Comeaway said with conviction. 'E had it in is mind ta do that all along.'

Albany leaped with agile grace to restore the threshing limbs.

'Ya wouldn't know *why,*' Mrs Comeaway said sarcastically, pushing Mrs Green ahead of her into the front seat.

'Will it start?' Mrs Green asked, her eyes on the naked engine.

'She got up here,' Tim said. 'You two just hang on while I get er goin. Ignition's on, I think.' He went round to examine the engine.

'Don't blow us all up,' Mrs Comeaway giggled. 'Don't strike no matches around here,' she called to the two at the top of the load.

A car or two passed while Tim worked. The occupants peered curiously, especially at the assorted furniture. The car engine started up with a powerful deep-noted roar and the whole load swayed backward as it jerked off in top gear.

'Always like a hill ta start off on,' Tim grunted contentedly, after he had landed with a crash in the driving seat.

There was another crash from behind. 'Them chairs wasn't tied on proper,' Mr Comeaway yelled.

'Can't stop for em now,' Tim yelled. 'That all right, Mrs Comeaway? Pick em up on the way back.'

'Less they gets run over,' Mrs Comeaway said dubiously. 'Never mind, Timmie. We just gotta take the risk.'

'Hang on up there,' Tim warned as they breasted the second hill and dived down the curving road to the township.

'Take it easy fa Gawd's sake,' Mr Comeaway wailed. 'It ain't safe up ere.'

Mrs Comeaway turned a threatening glare on her husband. 'Shut that big mouth a yours an stop worryin Timmie. E's busy.'

The utility took a corner dangerously wide, and there was a sharp crack at the back. Mrs Comeaway's irritation got the better of her. 'You broke something *else?* What's got inta the man?' she inquired of nobody.

Mr Comeaway, with Albany's help, regained an upright position. He looked as irritable as Mrs Comeaway.

'We'll fix it,' Tim comforted Mrs Comeaway. 'Ya lucky the ole man didn't fall off.'

'Would be just like im,' Mrs Comeaway snapped. 'Right in the middle a movin. Don't you go fallin off now,' she warned her husband.

Mr Comeaway grinned. 'I'm trying hard *not* ta.'

'This here's the house, ain't it?' Tim asked. 'Come on, stop, you ole bastard.' He pumped at the brake, and the utility drew to a reluctant halt, only three houses past the right one.

'Gotta get them brakes relined,' Timmie murmured, leaping out. 'Don't seem ta grip good any more.'

'We're here!' Mrs Green said.

'You men can bring all the stuff in,' Mrs Comeaway directed, 'while me and Mrs Green has a look round.'

They climbed out of the utility and walked up the footpath. Mr Comeaway, slapping his pants, followed them.

'You get back an help them boys,' Mrs Comeaway said sternly, when she was opening the gate. Mr Comeaway went sulkily back.

The two women stood for a while admiring the house. Then they walked up the wooden steps and Mrs Comeaway unlocked the front door. She preceded her friend into the living-room.

'This here's the sink,' she said, walking over to it and running her hand admiringly over its glittering surface. 'It's stainless steel. What ya think a that, eh?'

Mrs Green touched it, also admiring. She turned on the tap over it and there was water. 'That'll save your legs.'

'What ya think a this stove?' Mrs Comeaway asked, leaving the sink for the green enamelled stove that was set midway between the walls. 'Nice an clean, eh? New, that's why.' She pried the iron circles off the top. 'See? Never been used.'

She walked over to the louvres. 'See these here? You want some air you put em like this. It's cold, ya shut em up.'

'Yes, I like these,' Mrs Green said raising and lowering the blades. Her face was full of pleasure.

'Now come out an see the rest,' Mrs Comeaway ordered, again preceding Mrs Green. 'This here's the place where I wash, an there's a tub fa baths. Anyone can have a bath that likes,' she said proudly. 'Get the water hot in the copper.'

Mrs Green amused herself turning on the taps. They all worked. Both women watched in a kind of trance as the water spattered in a strong stream against the cement.

On the other side of the veranda were the bedrooms, two long rooms with a connecting door, louvred on one side.

'And that other door on the front veranda leads to another room,' Mrs Comeaway said. 'Three places ta sleep, not countin the big middle room. We gunna keep that room fa eatin in.'

The men came in and out, piling furniture in the centre of the main room. Mrs Comeaway extricated two chairs and she and Mrs Green sat in them.

'You reckon Trilby'll like it down here?' Mrs Comeaway asked, a little anxious note in her voice.

There was a scuffle at the back door, and both women glanced over. Round the frame of the door appeared the head of a child. It withdrew and another took its place. Mrs Comeaway rose in surprise and the sound of the stifled giggles gave away to the sound of scampering feet.

'Young devils,' she exclaimed, smiling as she again lowered her bulk to the chair.

For a moment, both women watched the door, their faces amused.

The next sound came from the roof. And at the same instant a childish treble of voices called, from a little way off, 'Nigger!'

'They threw a stone,' Mrs Comeaway said slowly. The expression of amusement had faded. Her bulk melted. She looked smaller than she had.

'I think,' Mrs Green said, and her voice was firm, 'I think Trilby will *love* it here in this nice house.'

'What about—that?' Mrs Comeaway said after a while. She waited with a sort of polite interest for Mrs Green's answer.

It was not long in coming.

'I can't see anyone saying that to *her*,' Mrs Green said with composure. 'Not twice.'

ELEVEN

Bartie was happy. He liked the new house, and with his freedom restored, his world opened up for him again. At the mission the days had been neatly sectioned off—meal times, school times, bed times, Sunday services—the little patches of leisure time had never lasted long enough for him to lose his feeling of being hurried—of having to get things done quickly or not at all. He had been lucky only in that he had never been bored as most of the others had. The overworked staff had little time for organizing games or any other pleasurable pursuits. The feeling was that the least the children could do in return for all they were getting was to amuse themselves.

Mostly, the children proved ungrateful. Instead of organizing themselves they stood around picking their noses or they crouched over the ground and poked holes in it with a stick, or they gawped and giggled and followed, with their round brown eyes, the perambulating excursions of visiting patrons. But whereas the bored ones had also a sturdy endurance, Bartie was never free of a panicky fear that this state of things would go on for ever.

Sometimes, now that he was home, he would remember the emptiness of the days after Noonah had gone. If it was night-time, he would hold his breath and listen anxiously for the gentle reassuring snores of his mother and the heavy regular breathing of his father that told him he was back again, part of the warmth of living that made up a family.

Here, every day brought possibilities of joy. Of long expanses of time which he could fill as he wished. Even school could be escaped if he went the right away about it. Just keeping out of the way until it was too late worked most times. With so many people about the house his mother could not be blamed for overlooking one small boy in the morning's sorting out.

At the mission he had slept in one of a long line of beds. Another line faced him from the opposite wall. He preferred the big sagging bed in which he and Stella slept together. It was not even necessary for him to make his bed. Mrs Comeaway might remember to smooth the big grey blankets. More often than not he crept straight into the nest he had made for himself the night before.

At home the state of his teeth and his hair and his fingernails was a matter which concerned only himself. Noonah, when she had leave from the hospital, might make a laughing, joyful matter of a big steaming-hot bath for him and Stella. Less often, his mother might regret that little use was being made of the fine big tub in the laundry—and do something about it. He might clean his teeth and smooth a little water over his face if Noonah were due home. At other times, only his hands caused him much concern. Dirty hands left marks on the drawing paper with which Noonah kept him plentifully supplied.

There were other things he liked about living at home. The food was different—nicer. Sometimes there was a big plate of fried meat with onion rings festooning its rich brownness. Or he might be handed a twist of newspaper containing crackly fried fish and a handful of crisp chips. There was always spongy new bread to spread thickly with jam and often a whole packet of biscuits sandwiched together with cream. Fruit in tins was not the luxury it had been at the mission; nor was the fizzing drink in bottles. And at home he was allowed to collect the bottles and sell them back to the shop.

Some mornings when he left for school, his mother gave him two whole shillings to buy his lunch with—and that meant the warm steamy interior of Colour Mary's shop with its pyramids of buns and stacks of sandwiches and soup in little bowls and the hot penetrating breath of pies and pasties. For two shillings he could buy a pasty and two buns and a bottle of orangeade. Or six buns and a Coke. And often Colour Mary slipped a banana or an apple into his bag before she handed it to him. She called him her 'good boy'.

All the children knew either from experience or from having been thankfully-innocent bystanders that Colour Mary would not hesitate to come out from behind the counter to the children who were *not* good.

141

Outside the shop and away from her hearing, some of the children complained resentfully of discrimination and occasionally forced some of the fruits of it from unwilling hands, but there was no other shop near the school, and the township was out of bounds, so Colour Mary's shop continued to be well patronised.

School, with the exception that there were more teachers, was much the same. But there was after-school to look forward to and Bartie rarely went straight home. He went often to the beach at the back of the town. That was his favourite place. He had come upon it by accident one day when he had felt a longing to follow up his thoughts undisturbed. A curling road, following faithfully the curling line of the beach, had enticed him on. He had walked much farther than he had intended.

Bordering the beach was the grey-green salt-bush, and to his left were spreading acres of it—stiff, small, unyielding cushions. A lighthouse, remotely tall, shot from their midst. Beyond the border on his right sparkled the sea, restless, fretting at the reefs, which guarded the shore, surging triumphantly at last to the base of the sandhills that formed a second barricade.

The wind swept round and past him, carrying the tops of the waves that stood in its path, spreading them in a mist over the road and the grey-green salt-bush. It swished sand from the beach and sent the particles flying in a whirlwind dance and they struck against Bartie's face and tried to find his eyes. He licked his lips and tasted salt and he raised his face to the still-hot sun and felt the coldness of the wind rob the rays of their warmth.

He walked on past the lighthouse, slowly, his schoolbooks under his arm. Around the next curve he stopped, a small boy spellbound into stillness. His greedy eyes absorbed the sight before it could vanish.

The sea rolled lazily in from the horizon—the palest clearest lime-green streaked with soft dark sapphire where banks of seaweed floated just beneath the surface. Towards the shoreline two streams slapped lazily together and spilled in transparent green circlets on the clean slope of the beach. Wet seaweed clung to wet rocks, darkly richly red. And nothing Bartie had seen was so free-flowing and graceful as the sandhills that swept through the sea in a long sweeping curve.

Bartie came to this place often. There were days when the water deepened to jade; when the foam cresting the waves matched the snow-white sandhills, and he saw the sandhills when the setting sun touched them to warm, cream, beckoning curves.

There were stormy days, when tossed seaweed turned the whole bay to turquoise, when waves smashed angrily up the steeply-sloping beach and reached with lacy fingers for the purple pigface that grew high beyond their reach. Each time he came, Bartie worshipped.

'Where you been, eh?' Mrs Comeaway would demand sometimes, if Bartie came within her orbit. But she did not stop for an answer, nor would Bartie have given her anything but his wide and secret smile if she had. Yet he loved her for letting him alone and because she laughed with him.

For Bartie, there was something irresistibly appealing yet humorous in the sight of his mother laboriously spelling out some of the words in his school-books. He had a child's sense of achievement in knowing something still hidden from his elders, even though at these times, in some unaccountable way, he felt more love for her welling up into his heart.

'Aaah!' Mrs Comeaway would say, half-vexed, half in amusement. 'Once I knew how to read a little bit. Now no good, eh? An you think you clever, isn't it? More clever than ole Mum?'

Bartie was never deceived by her vexation. He knew she liked it that he could read so much better than she could.

'Read out some for me,' she would demand sometimes, when she found him with his nose in a book. 'Learn ya ole mummy something fa a change.'

Obediently, Bartie would read a few sentences to her, but sooner or later she would stop him, a look of scandalized unbelief on her face.

'You take your mummy for ole fool, eh? You think I believe in this little boy so big only as a thumb-nail? An he got arms an legs an a head still? That book so damn good, only tell lies.'

If Bartie giggled, her suspicion of him would increase. 'You tellin me that all writ down there in that book? Or you jokin? You tell me.'

Bartie, choking with laughter, would roll over and bury his head in his arms, and Mrs Comeaway, giving him up as a bad job, would stand over him with the nearest thing to a scowl she could ever call up on her smooth and shining face. There were times when she doubted the wisdom of education. To her it was cloudy with mystery. Real things

144

that you could see or feel, people, trees, the sun and the rain, good food and the comfortably distended belly that resulted from eating, the miserable gnawing feeling of hunger—all these she understood, they were part of the life she lived. Bartie's primers—the glimpse he gave her of their contents—often there was unease in her spreading breast. Sometimes it was hard to throw off. More often, pleasanter things entered her mind, and she forgot it.

Bartie began to trust his mother. Noonah was at home for only two days in a fortnight. When he had drawn or painted something he felt was good, he needed to test it through another's eyes. He showed his things to Mrs Comeaway and here she was on firmer ground. These things were real and, in gratitude for this quality, she gave them her whole attention, dropping whatever it was she happened to be doing, taking up the drawing or the painting and retiring with it to where the light was better.

'Aaah!' delightedly. 'That sea, eh?' Or 'Nice big tree that is. Pretty, too! You did that good, Bartie.'

Her praise was not discriminating. She liked everything he showed her. Nevertheless, she sent him back to his work with a smile on his lips and warmth in his heart.

There was a day when he ran home from school, jumping the little fence in his hurry. He went straight in to where his mother sat narrowing her eyes against the heat of her tea. He flung skinny arms round her comfortable waist and dug his hard little bullet head into her chest. And Mrs Comeaway's cup of tea went back on the table quickly so that she could throw her protecting arms about her boy.

She waited a while, smoothing his head, then she pushed him away from her. 'You tell me now, eh?'

'The kids blamed me. And it wasn't my fault at all.' Bartie shivered, wrestling to get close to her again. 'I didn't even know she was going to do it.'

'An who did what?' Mrs Comeaway asked patiently.

'It was Trilby,' Bartie said, quieter now. 'I was in the play-yard at lunch-time and she went past and I waved to her and she came over to talk to me a bit. Then, when she was just going out the gate another girl came along, a white one. She was holding her nose and Trilby stopped an started yelling at her. She called the girl a white-faced bitch. An she smacked her across the face, all the time yelling. An then she rushed out.' Bartie's breath sobbed in his throat.

'An what happened then?' Mrs Comeaway asked dully.

'An then a teacher come up, and the white girl's nose was bleeding, and she said she was sneezing and was just trying to stop it by holding her finger against her nose. She said Trilby went and hit her before she knew it.'

'She said Trilby's name?' Mrs Comeaway asked gently. 'She knew who it was?'

'She said "a coloured girl", that's all.'

'An did they do anything to ya?'

'Not the teacher, but the kids. The teacher took this girl away because her nose was still bleeding, and then the other kids started on me an called me a dirty black nigger. None of them liked me any more Mum an I didn't do anything.

146

Even Joe Wheeler that I was playing with, he wouldn't come near me any more.'

Mrs Comeaway's voice was heavy. 'There ain't anything I can do, Bartie. That girl, the one that said about sneezin, she mighta been, or she mighta been holding er nose like some do when they pass ya, some a these cheeky bits a kids...I dunno! Trilby shouldn't a hit er. She shouldn't a took no notice. That's just somethin they do— Gawd knows why. To make people laugh or something, that's all.'

'Why?' Bartie's expression was confused and beaten. 'Why?'

'I dunno,' Mrs Comeaway said tightly. 'Now what about I get ya a cuppa an we sit ere an drink it up an you don't go back ta school fa today, eh?'

'I'll sit on your lap if you like, Mum,' Bartie said carefully.

Mrs Comeaway's laugh hit the ceiling. But in her eyes was all that Bartie needed to see.

They sat there in the dim cool room a long time. And Mrs Comeaway talked to him. For Bartie, she recalled the days of her own girlhood, when she had been as young and younger than Bartie. She told him how she had ridden on the back of a camel from one sheep or cattle station to the next, with her own father and mother, and how they had carried everything they owned on the backs of their two camels.

They had stopped wherever there was work to be had, staying a week, two weeks, up to a month. And then they would pack up their things and she would take her place behind her mother on the camel called Daisy, who was so lazy she had to be switched often.

'An often enough it was me got a good smack instead a Daisy,' Mrs Comeaway finished feelingly, 'when Mummy didn't get er judgement right.'

One look at Trilby's closed face decided her mother to say nothing of the matter to her. She could understand the grief of a hurt child who ran to her for comfort. She was not brave enough to risk one of Trilby's hurting and puzzling rebuffs.

For her part, Trilby could not have told her mother of the sick dread that stopped her breath and weighted her legs when she walked through the gate to the High School next morning.

She waited throughout the day for a summons to the room of the head teacher. More than once she was reprimanded for not paying attention. And then the head teacher actually came into the room.

Trilby's mind as well as her fingers, froze. She could not look up whilst her own teacher and the head teacher talked together.

Her teacher's voice brought feeling and movement back to her. 'Trilby Comeaway? Please?'

Trilby stood, somehow pushed herself down the aisle towards the front of the classroom.

She could not force herself to hardness. She felt only fear.

Outside the classroom, following the head teacher down the wide echoing passage she felt better. A wind cooled her face and calmed her thoughts. Her head went back and her chin up.

In his study, the head teacher slid into his chair, leaned his elbow on his desk, and looked quizzically up at her as she stood before him.

Then he smiled. 'I brought you in here, Trilby, because I've a word of advice for you.'

Trilby did not return his smile.

'You smacked a girl across the nose yesterday,' the head stated. 'I wanted to tell you that the girl's mother wrote a note to the Primary School headmaster this morning.'

Trilby waited. The thing she had been dreading was happening—and the feeling was much better than the one that had preceded it. She felt able to manage anything in the way of anger or abuse which this man might pile on her.

The head teacher reached for his pipe. 'I think she must be quite an understanding woman,' he said almost casually. 'She wants the thing dropped. She doesn't want anything done about it. No punishment for you...,' he looked up under his lashes. 'You think that was a pretty nice gesture for her to make, Trilby?'

'Yes, sir,' Trilby said woodenly, a shade sulkily.

'Okay! Skip off,' the head said briskly, turning himself about to face his desk, beginning at once to riffle through some papers upon it.

Trilby's mouth opened and so did the narrowed grey eyes. She stayed where she was.

149

'Well!' the head said, looking up again, clear-eyed and polite.

'Yes, sir,' Trilby said gladly.

Only later she was ashamed. Not because of the hurt she had inflicted nor because the girl's mother had acted so generously in the matter, but because this was the way any ignorant coloured girl might behave, to lash out with tongue and hands, to lose control. Never, she vowed, would she let that most despised half of her get the upper hand again.

TWELVE

A termagant wind beat at the glass louvres and scattered fine white sand over every object in the room.

The object upon the wide double bed moaned fretfully and tucked its untidy grey head beneath a prune-coloured arm. The hips moved mountainously, in slow revolt against the dry, devitalised air. Hot it might have been in the little back room of the humpy—but dark and quiet, squealing wind and stinging sand defeated by the windowless walls.

And no loneliness! Ten yards to the liveness and laughter of other people. Big cups of tea, hot, sweet and strong. And more tea-leaves in the pot when the first lot was done.

Tea! She could taste the first hot draught of it in her dry mouth, loosening her swollen tongue, washing deliciously down to her waiting stomach.

Mrs Comeaway sighed deeply, remembering her carelessly emptied tea packet and the distance to the nearest shop.

The doorbell rang, and she raised her head in surprise. Too early yet for Bartie and Stella to be home and nobody else played with the bell—not with the front door standing hospitably open to all her friends.

It rang again.

Mrs Comeaway smoothed back her hair with one hand and stumbled stiffly over to the door of her bedroom. Caught unawares, because she had been peering into every corner of the big living-room, Mrs Comeaway's visitor swivelled nervously.

'Them kids,' Mrs Comeaway thought swiftly. 'She's seen them kids swingin on her fence an pullin up her flowers.'

'You're Mrs Comeaway, aren't you?' the woman asked, whilst Mrs Comeaway took mild note of the fact that the eyes and the mouth of this woman showed quite different expressions.

'Yeah! An if I've tole them kids once I've tole em a dozen times,' she rushed to defend herself. 'I knew you could see em out your window. I'll get to em the minute they get home fum school and I'll say you been in here an gunna get the pleece to em if they don't stop.' She stopped herself mainly from lack of breath.

'Get the—oh! Yes, I did see the children but never mind about that now.' The visitor stopped to compose a suitable expression. 'Mrs Comeaway, I've come to welcome you to our little community. As a member of my church! I thought perhaps we could have a cup of tea together and

152

get acquainted. We ladies of the Guild hope and believe that if we—if you—I mean…,' her voice trailed away. She searched for simpler words which might convey her meaning more surely.

'I knew you was in a stink about em,' Mrs Comeaway apologized. 'Specially that big pink one. But ya know what kids is. Don't take no notice however I yell at em. When they know you been over they might do different.'

'Don't you worry your head about a few flowers.' A little irritability here because of these flowers which would keep complicating things. 'I'm sure the children didn't realize— anyhow, as I was saying, I thought it might be nice if we…'

'You mean you wasn't in a stink after all?'

'Not the least little bit. Now, what about…?'

'That's all right then well,' Mrs Comeaway said happily.

'I made some hot scones on purpose,' the visitor said with a tiny quiver in her voice. She banished the quiver. 'The tea's all ready too. You will come, I hope.'

Mrs Comeaway's happiness shattered. She looked down at her feet, and they were bare. From her own feet she shifted her glance to her visitor's feet, shod neatly in black shining leather. There was something intimidating about the way those feet stood there, planted so firmly on the wood of the veranda.

'I should go in there—?' Mrs Comeaway's eyes turned fearfully on her neighbour's house, noting the open door and the speckless highly-polished boards of the veranda, the daunting neatness of green lawns and bright flower-beds.

An indulgent smile. Mrs Henwood recovering herself completely. 'Of course!'

'Comb me hair. Put me shoes on. Been having a lay down. I dunno! Didn't bother bout gettin dressed proper yet like.'

'That's all right!' Mrs Henwood said inexorably. 'I'll wait here for you.'

Mrs Comeaway moved back into a bedroom that seemed even less of a sanctuary than before.

'Now just don't bother about that,' Mrs Henwood said, just past the doorway of her house. 'My fault! I had no business putting a vase on that table. Come right through here to the kitchen and sit down and I'll get a cloth and mop up that water. Won't take me a jiffy.'

Mrs Comeaway moved with slow caution into the kitchen. As a butterfly alighting on a flower, she lowered herself on to a chair, sat with her body forward, her hands interlaced, her black patent courts pressed primly together. There was a tiny red pot of geraniums on the window-sill behind her. Oppressively close. She could feel its impact between her shoulders. She rose and inched her chair away from the danger zone.

Mrs Henwood came back, a little flustered. 'And now we can have our tea, can't we?'

Mrs Comeaway allowed herself one brief and comprehensive look at her surroundings. Everything was pretty. Bright colours everywhere. Shining things. White cups and plates on a checked tablecloth. Her hostess handed to her a plate with a tiny red check handkerchief on it. And here was bewilderment.

'What's this ever?'

Mrs Henwood laughed gently. 'That's a serviette. A little napkin. For you to wipe your hands on.'

Mrs Comeaway shook out the square of material and wiped her fingers carefully, one after the other. When she had finished she crushed the material nervously, got rid of it into her pocket.

The tea was hot and strong, the way she liked it, but the cup was small and held about two good swallows. She sat with it in her lap while the woman nattered. How she liked living down here in the Wild-Oat Patch. How Mrs Comeaway would like it—after she got used to everything. How much nicer it was than those terrible camps at the back of the town.

'And you'll find very little *colour* prejudice,' Mrs Henwood said gravely. '*You*, Mrs Comeaway, can help stamp it out where it *does* exist.' Her eyes held Mrs Comeaway's. Mrs Comeaway tried to remember what they reminded her of. She knew damn well she'd seen eyes like that somewhere or other.

'We all of us realize,' Mrs Henwood continued, still grave and solemn, 'that you have a lot to learn about our white way of life and that you probably need help. We are prepared to *give* you that help, Mrs Comeaway.'

'Yeah!' Mrs Comeaway said, her thoughts on the woollen-covered teapot.

'Let me fill your cup. And please, do try one of my scones.'

After that it was better for a while. They were very good scones. Mrs Comeaway enjoyed them.

'Tell me,' Mrs Henwood settled back. 'What was your life like up there in those camps?'

'Awright!'

'No, but –,' Mrs Henwood coaxed delicately, 'do tell me. I've often wondered what really happens in those places.' She leaned forward, eyes bright and still.

'Galahs!' Mrs Comeaway thought. 'They got eyes like that.' Aloud she said, 'Didn't have so much damn wind, that's one thing certain.'

'Oh!' It was snipped off, as though she had used scissors. Mrs Comeaway rattled her tea cup in its saucer, not very much.

'There are *some* people around here,' Mrs Henwood said with relish as she poured more tea, 'who might just give you trouble.'

'Had enough a that,' Mrs Comeaway said stolidly, as she might have refused another scone, if there had been another scone.

Mrs Henwood softened. 'If you've had experience of this type of thing, I only hope you have not let it harden you, Mrs Comeaway. You must not let yourself get bitter. Though nobody could blame you. Nobody!'

The moisture in the round hard eyes disturbed Mrs Comeaway momentarily, then Mrs Henwood blinked rapidly and the moisture was gone.

'Drunk that tea down too quick,' Mrs Comeaway guessed, relieved.

She began on the cake, just to be polite, though she felt uncomfortably full already. And when the cakes were finished she sat, comatose and languid, waiting for them to digest.

'Just to start you off,' Mrs Henwood said later, 'I have a little creeper in a pot. And I'm sure my husband would take cuttings for you if you wanted them. Shall I ask him?'

'Yeah!' Mrs Comeaway said obligingly. It was a word she had said a good many times that afternoon.

'I'll just run down and get your little pot now,' Mrs Henwood said excitedly. 'You sit here and wait. I won't be long.'

Mrs Comeaway waited obediently. Mrs Henwood pattered down the back steps. Mrs Comeaway reflected that now would have been a good time to slip a few cakes into her pocket for Stella, if she had only foreseen the opportunity and left some of the cakes.

'There!' Mrs Henwood said, thrusting a small pot into Mrs Comeaway's hands.

Mrs Comeaway examined her plant. She thought it was a funny-looking plant and a bit withered.

'It's a sweet thing, isn't it?' Mrs Henwood encouraged.

'Yeah!' Mrs Comeaway said, taking another look at the pale-green tendrils dripping over the side of the pot. She wondered uneasily if Mrs Henwood really meant her to keep it. Should she hand it back? She made a motion with the pot.

'No, you can keep it,' Mrs Henwood said gaily. 'You go home and pick out a good spot for it. I'll walk to the gate with you, shall I?'

Mrs Comeaway brightened, like a child hearing the school bell. The two women walked down the front steps and along the little green cement path to the front gate. Leaning on it, Mrs Henwood said, 'As Kipling says, Mrs Comeaway, we are sisters under the skin.'

Mrs Comeaway was knocked clean off her pins. She stood there, grappling silently, and everything else Mrs Henwood said floated right past her.

She walked three or four steps in the direction of her own front gate before the first question resolved itself. She stopped. 'Eh?' she called to her neighbour, 'You come fum up Mullewa?'

Mrs Henwood, who had not heard the question, nodded pleasantly. After a moment, Mrs Comeaway went on.

Bartie and Stella had arrived home from school. They had dragged a chair over to the safe and they were searching for something to eat.

'Gee, I'm hungry, Mummy,' Stella wailed.

Mrs Comeaway stood in the doorway, smiling with relief, well content to be back in her own home. She went over to the safe and reached into it for the bread and the tin of jam.

'What ya got in ya pocket, Mum?' Stella asked, pulling out the little red-checked square. 'Can I have it for my doll?'

Mrs Comeaway looked at the square without interest. 'Ave it if ya like. Do for a shawl, eh?'

She spread two thick pieces of bread with jam and, as she spread, a second question posed itself in her mind. She dismissed it impatiently. 'Never even *met* the bloke, far's I know.'

'Whose pot plant?' Trilby asked later.

Mrs Comeaway frowned. 'Her next door,' she said reluctantly. 'Comin over ta plant it too, so she says.'

'You mean she just came over here and gave you this plant?' Trilby was surprised.

'She didn't give it to me over here. She gave it to me over there,' Mrs Comeaway nodded in the direction of her neighbour's house.

'Did you go over there?'

'I didn't *go* over there,' Mrs Comeaway said coldly. 'I was took. She come over an took me.'

'What for, Mum?'

'She just come over here an arst me to go over there an have a cuppa tea with er,' Mrs Comeaway said, irritably for her. 'Don't ask me why, because I dunno why.'

'Afternoon tea, that was,' Trilby pronounced. 'She asked you over for afternoon tea. Don't you even know that? Up at the mission we used to have lots of people coming to visit us and have afternoon tea.'

'No need ta carry on,' Mrs Comeaway said. 'Course I know bout afternoon tea. Didn't think they done it in places like this but.'

'Is she nice?'

'Er? All right!'

'That's her husband, that runs the garage up in town,' Trilby said. 'I bet her house is nice inside. What's it like?'

'Ad a damn fool table just inside er front door,' Mrs Comeaway remembered indignantly. 'Right bang inside er front door waiting for people ta trip theirselves up on it an might be get a leg broke.'

'Mum you didn't knock her table over, did you?' Trilby asked, shocked.

159

'I didn't arst ta go over, did I? An what if I did? Shouldn'ta had that mat there. Serve er right, ask me.'

'Gee, I bet she was mad,' Trilby said gloomily. 'Why couldn't you be more careful? Now she'll never have you over again, most likely.'

'An a good thing too,' Mrs Comeaway's retort had spirit in it. 'Ya wrong fa once but. She behaved the way she should, puttin mats round fa people ta slip up on.'

'What did you do after you tripped over the mat?'

Mrs Comeaway did not like that. It made her sound like a clumsy fool. 'I ad me tea an come ome,' she said shortly.

'Come on, Mummy, tell me some more. How did her house look?' Trilby sat on the kitchen table and swung her legs. When her face was alive, as it was now, there were no doubts about her beauty. Mrs Comeaway thawed under the sweet conciliation in the long grey eyes.

'She ad another little pot a flowers on er winder-sill, an she ad a check cloth on er table, an before she gave me me tea she made me wipe me hands on some bit of a hanky. Anyone think I didn't wash meself proper.'

'That was a serviette,' Trilby frowned. 'Are you sure she said you had to wipe your hands on it before you could have your tea? Like her damn cheek if she did.'

'If ya don't believe me ya can have a look an see where I wiped em,' Mrs Comeaway said stoutly. 'Stella, just gimme that little bit of a hanky I give ya. Let Trilby look at it an ya can ave it straight back.'

'Mum, you didn't bring it home,' Trilby said on a great wail. She rushed at Stella and grabbed the napkin

160

from her. She held the piece of material up before her. 'You'll just have to pretend you forgot about it,' she said at last. 'I'll take it back and tell her you put it in your pocket by accident. She'll think you don't know *anything*, Mum.'

'What's all the carryin on about?' Mrs Comeaway asked, mightily surprised. 'She gave it to me didn't she? Same as she gave me that pot over there. An ya wrong bout it bein a serve yet. I ironed enough a them damn things in me time. Ya got things all mixed up.'

'She *lent* you this *serviette*,' Trilby said passionately. 'There's little ones as well as big ones. And you don't wipe your hands on it before you have your tea. You wipe your hands on it *after*, and even then you only pretend to. If you want to know how people do it, they just pretend to mop up their mouths and then they crush it up a bit—not hard like you did—and then they put it back on their plate. That's so it can be folded up again and put back in the drawer. Except you don't do that till everyone's gone. What you're supposed to do, you're supposed to wash it after every time it's used but if people only crush it up a little bit you don't have to. What's the use of talking to you though?' she finished scornfully. 'You just don't understand.'

'Seems a lot a fuss ta make bout a bit of a hanky,' Mrs Comeaway said, resignedly. 'All right! Take it back. I'm sure I don't want nothin I'm not supposed ta have. Take it back now if ya like.'

Stella's round brown eyes filled with tears. 'You said I could have it for my doll.'

161

'You can't then,' Trilby snapped. 'I'm going to take it back straightaway.'

'Let er have it, let er have it,' Mrs Comeaway soothed. 'I'll find somethin else for ya. You just come in the bedroom an I'll hunt somethin up.'

'Ole horrible thing,' Stella whimpered. 'I hate Trilby, Mummy.'

Trilby made a sound of disgust.

At the back of the house Bartie sat with his back against the veranda post. One hand smoothed the stiff red coat of a sprawling cat. The other held a beginner's book on water-colour painting. But the angry voices that came from inside the house kept tearing at the edges of his concentration, forcing him to spell out a sentence two or three times before he got the sense of it.

He felt no urge to investigate. Rows like this one could catch a boy up if he so much as put his head inside the door to see what it was all about. Better by far to push the cat aside and get out of range. Behind the patch of low-growing wattles at the end of the yard he would be out of sight, and the back fence was as good a place to lean against as the veranda post.

He gathered up his things and retreated quietly. At the bottom of the yard he sat down again and opened his book. Red Cat, who had followed him, stepped daintily round the wattles, her nose twitching nervously, her pale-green eyes perturbed. Already reading, Bartie raised his hand, palm flattened. Patiently, he waited for her to push her head beneath it. But first she must satisfy herself that no danger lurked. Stiff, straight, watchful, she stood at his side, her tail twitching gently. In a little while she relaxed her tautness, poured herself out upon the ground like a pool of honey. Her wide-open eyes slept as his hand began its rhythmic soothing.

At this distance from the house the voices blended into a background of other noises—car engines, the hard sound of iron-shod wheels and hooves, a mowing machine and overlaying all that the lazy buzz of flies round Mrs Comeaway's uncovered refuse bin.

Bartie read steadily on. Here and there he came across some fragment of knowledge which was already his and the excitement of recognition was almost too great to be borne. Then, both hands were needed to hold the book and the cat must wake and wait with regal displeasure for the caressing to begin again.

Until now Bartie's preoccupation had been colour—the velvety softness of petals, the luminous grey pearl of the little sandy-cows with their delicate black tracery of legs, the rainbow sparkles in a handful of sand, even the ruby sheen on the back of a cockroach. And there was the mystery of what made Trilby's eyes so brilliant and Noonah's so soft. The world was full of colour, and you could not rest until you had tried to capture some of them. For the deep glow of Trilby's skin he had mixed purple and sienna and yellow and the result had been dull and lifeless, not the tender lustre he had aimed at.

His teacher, Miss Simmins, had found some of his attempts inside the cover of an exercise book.

'But what do they represent?' she had inquired.

'You see that?' Bartie had pointed out, shyly. For once, he knew he had come near to success; had almost captured the glowing gold that burned on the edges of the clouds for one long and lovely minute after the sun sank into the sea.

'Yes!' Miss Simmins had said thoughtfully, after he had explained. 'Yes!'

It had been strange, Bartie remembered, to see this lively little woman so lost in thought.

She had not let the matter rest there. After school she had beckoned him and questioned him further. Her bright brown eyes had held his steadily, and her questioning had cut through to his innermost desires and thoughts. She had tried to explain form to him—and to tell him that this way of life would be hard, especially for him. Already Bartie had forgotten most of what she had told him. The words had been too big and strange for him to hold in his memory. But he wanted passionately to please her. Miss Simmins was not young, nor even very pretty. She did her soft greying black hair in a funny old-fashioned way, loose about her head and confined in a tiny bun near the top of it. But her voice fell pleasantly on his ears, and her words were strong words which lifted him from his dreams and set him face to face with facts.

There had been other men like himself, who had succeeded. Among them one called Albert Namatjira, who had painted the Australian bush and the rocky outcrops and the trembling blue of the skies, and people had paid him much money. But he had had to work hard at his painting.

Bartie smiled. Work? How could anyone call this work when it was the reason he woke each morning.

THIRTEEN

Trilby and Noonah sat, each on her own bed, and looked at the heap of clothes on the end of Trilby's bed. They were part of a great heap with which Trilby had staggered back from Mrs Henwood's house, after her visit to return the 'hanky'.

Trilby was annoyed. 'You should have seen her,' she told Noonah. 'The more I kept saying "No", the more things she kept pulling out of her wardrobe and throwing over my arm. She said she'd had them hanging there for years and she never wore them because some were too tight and some she didn't like any more. I don't know why I took them. If I'd had any sense I'd have chucked them straight back at her.'

'Some of them will look nice on you, Trilby, if you pull them in a bit at the waist.' Noonah got up to examine a blueflowered summer frock with a gathered skirt.

'They stink,' Trilby scorned, giving the dress in question the merest glance. 'And talk about pleased with herself. The more she threw at me the more pleased she got. Grinning all over her face.'

'You could wash them,' Noonah said. 'They'd be as good as new, some of them.'

'Wear her frocks?' Trilby frowned. 'Catch me! D'you know what I'm going to do with them? I'm going to give em away to anyone who wants them. That Carter woman, the dirty old one who looks as if she sleeps under a bush. She can have some, and Blanchie and Audrena can have the rest.' She propped herself up on her bed. 'And I wish,' she said viciously, 'I could see that old dame's face when she sees someone else wearing her dirty smelly old dresses.'

'I don't see why you want to do that.' Noonah stopped her inspection to gaze in perplexity at her younger sister.

'Because she's got a nerve, that's why,' Trilby burst out. 'You think *she'd* wear someone else's clothing? Course she wouldn't. New ones for her. So why give the things to me? I'll tell you why. Because she thinks someone like me should be grateful. See?'

'Gee, your mind works a funny way,' Noonah said wonderingly. 'I thought it was real nice of her.'

Trilby flounced into a sitting position. 'I've had enough of other people's clothes,' she said angrily. 'Up at the mission. And I'm never, never going to wear anything that isn't new from now on. Even if I have only one dress it's going to be new, bought for me, and nobody else worn it before.' She cast a look of loathing at the frocks on the end of her bed. 'Look there under the arms. Making

166

them stink just like she does. D'you think I'm going to have her sweaty armholes touching me?' She kicked the clothes on to the floor. 'And the ones I don't give away,' she said violently, 'I'm going to tear up and use washing the floor.'

'Trilby,' Noonah said disapprovingly.

Trilby turned her scorn on her sister. 'You're just a fool, Noonah. And you always will be. Didn't I say how pleased she was to be giving them to me?'

'What's that got to do with it?'

'You can't see?' Trilby was yelling with rage. 'It made her feel big, that's what. She wasn't giving something to me. She was giving something to herself. Oh!' Full of unbearable irritation, Trilby sprang off the bed, kicked once more at the clothes, and flung herself out of the room, slamming the door shut with a crack like thunder.

'What's the matter with you?' Mrs Comeaway said mildly. She had squeezed herself into one of the garments that had been given to Trilby—a shabby faded blue cotton cardigan with most of the buttons missing. The sleeves moulded her massive arms into sausages and her bosom sprang, unchecked, from the gaping front.

'You're going to wear that cardigan,' Trilby half-questioned, half-stated, breathing hard through dilated nostrils. 'I might have known it.' She stood with her hands on her hips. 'Encouraging them.'

'Now what?' asked the harassed Mrs Comeaway. 'Encourage who?'

'People like that, to give us their old cast-offs,' Trilby spat out.

167

'Ya want er ta give us er new ones?' Mrs Comeaway commented reasonably. 'I like this coat. Got nice big pockets. An you know I like a big pocket ta hold me money in when I ave a gamble.' She chuckled. 'When I *got* any money.'

'Ah, you make me sick,' Trilby said disgustedly.

'Ere, you shut ya guts,' Mrs Comeaway said, injured. 'Wasn't even me took em. Ya brought em back ya own self.'

'I didn't intend to *wear* them.'

'What, well! Eat em?'

'I was going to…Oh, what's the use of explaining to anyone. You never understand anything. I don't know how you can *be* like you are. If someone came up and asked you to lie down in the mud so they could walk over you, would you do that too?'

Mrs Comeaway, brow ridged, clutched for understanding. 'I ain't never laid down in no mud yet, an just you stop that shriekin at me, my girl, or I'll stop it for ya.' She advanced threateningly.

Noonah appeared in the doorway. 'Trilby, stop it!'

'You *won't* wear them, I'll see to that,' Trilby cried wildly. She snatched at the clothes on the table and ran into the other bedroom, where she scrabbled at the clothes on the floor and heaped them over her arm.

Noonah and her mother followed, to be thrust aside as Trilby passed them on her way out again. Mrs Comeaway received a sharp elbow in the softest and most pliable part of her anatomy which caused her to clutch and gasp.

'What's she gunna do now?' she muttered as she moved in her daughter's furious wake.

168

Trilby fled down the back steps and across to the rubbish bin. She thrust all the clothes deep down into the mess that was already there, then she raced back into the house again. Mrs Comeaway, having been shoved once, made haste to flatten herself against the railing, and in a flash, Trilby was back carrying a bottle of kerosene and a box of matches.

She threw kerosene on to the clothes and started striking matches. But she was clumsy in her hurry, and at least half a dozen matches broke off in her hand before she succeeded in lighting one. In that time, Mrs Comeaway had come alive to her daughter's purpose, had crossed the yard in a couple of bounds, and had reached one hand into the rubbish bin to rescue some of the clothes. The match ignited the kerosene at the exact moment that Mrs Comeaway's hand disappeared into the soft materials. There was a roar of flame and Mrs Comeaway leapt back from the conflagration with a shriek of pain that could have been heard half-way up the street. Her yowl continued even after Noonah, who had come to the rescue, had assured her that the cotton sleeve had saved her arm and that her hand was only slightly scorched.

Trilby watched her mother, narrow-eyed and tight-lipped, not even moving to examine the burn. With Noonah's arm round her waist as far as it would go, the upset woman moaned her way across to the steps.

Just as they reached the bottom step, while the fire in the bin was burning fiercely, a head appeared over the dividing fence. 'What's the matter over here?' Mrs Henwood called urgently.

169

'Burnt all the clothes ya give er,' Mrs Comeaway said dramatically. 'An tried ta burn me up as well, er own mummy. Me hand woulda went easy.'

'Mummy,' Noonah whispered distressfully. 'Come inside, quick.'

Mrs Comeaway turned one more shocked look on Trilby, began moaning afresh and, with Noonah supporting her, ascended the steps.

'An that'll show you what I think of your rotten old frocks,' Trilby said harshly to the face at the fence.

The face, scarlet and bulging-eyed, disappeared. After a while, when the flames had died down, Trilby went too.

'I spose ya wouldn't ave a bit a money in ya bag would ya, Noonah?' Mrs Comeaway said delicately. 'Ya father doesn't seem ta be getting much work down that wharf lately.'

She was sitting at the kitchen table drinking tea which Noonah had made for her. Her scorched hand was bandaged neatly and it lay in prominence before her on the table.

'You can have all I've got,' Noonah said cheerfully. 'But I don't think it's much. I had to buy some more stuff for Bartie, and then there was a kid in the children's Ward— he's pretty sick—and I saw these little koala bears in a window so I bought two. You go an look in Trilby's room, Stella, and see what's there.'

With the exception of Trilby, who was reading comics in a corner, the whole family followed Stella as she ran, shrieking with excitement, into the girls' bedroom.

'Ain't that nice now?' Mrs Comeaway smiled.

'Gee, it's soft, isn't it?' Bartie admired.

'It's mine,' Stella said importantly. 'Noonah bought it for me, didn't you, Noonah?'

'See how much ya got, will ya, Noonah?' Mrs Come-away said casually.

Noonah took some money from her bag and handed it to her mother. 'That enough, Mummy?'

'Hafta be, won't it?'

'I mean I can give you ten shillings more if you really want it.'

'This'll do,' Mrs Comeaway said comfortably. 'Now you come ere Bartie an find me one a them pencils an I'll just write down a couple things I want.'

'Can I have a Coke?' Stella whined. 'An a packet of chewy, Mummy?'

'I spose.'

Slowly and laboriously, in a heavy childish hand, Mrs Comeaway wrote out a list. Trilby came over to read it. She laughed. 'Gee, just look at the spelling, will you? I'll get it, if you let me get those white beads I want.'

'Ya don't deserve nothing,' Mrs Comeaway said strongly. 'Burning me hand like that.'

'I'm sorry I burnt your hand. I told you. But I'm not a bit sorry I burnt those clothes,' Trilby said impetuously. 'I *couldn't* keep them, Mummy. Don't you understand that?'

Mrs Comeaway gave up. 'Jus the same ya did a foolish thing there. If ya didn't want em yaself, I coulda got a pound or two for em. Why didn't ya think a that?'

Trilby looked helplessly at Noonah, then shook her head and laughed. 'Let me get the beads and we'll be even,' she teased.

171

'Get em. Get em,' Mrs Comeaway said with an ineffectual flap of her hands. 'Won't get no peace till ya do, I spose.'

'We're coming too,' Stella told Trilby threateningly. 'Me an Bartie's getting Cokes.'

Noonah laughed and sat down at the table. 'Wait till they go and we'll have another cup of tea, Mummy.'

'Does Trilby like school?' she asked her mother, when the trio had gone.

'It's a nice big school, ain't it?' her mother said. 'Never said she *didn't* like it. She's a hard one ta understand though, Noonah. Don't tell me!' She rolled up her eyes.

'Praps she hasn't settled down yet,' Noonah pacified. 'She seems a bit jumpy.'

'A bit jumpy,' Mrs Comeaway said, heavily ironical. 'More'n a bit, ask me.'

Mr Comeaway came through the back door smelling strongly of shaving soap. His thick black hair was slicked wetly back and his shirt was clean. When Noonah was home, he always shaved.

'One thing, ya got a good excuse fa not doin ya work,' he chuckled, eyeing the white-bandaged hand. 'Ya think it'll be all right, Noonah? Won't need ta get it cut off?'

Noonah smiled affectionately at him. Mrs Comeaway tucked a ten-shilling note into an old tobacco-tin and placed it on a shelf behind some plates. 'An don't you think ya gunna get that,' she warned her husband.

'What I want with ya ole money?' Mr Comeaway said offendedly. 'Keep it, all I care.'

'Tea!' Noonah said firmly.

'What's been happening?' she said, when the three of them were drinking their tea.

'Them Berrings in trouble again, that's one thing,' Mr Comeaway said.

'Yeah!' Mrs Comeaway chuckled. 'I think they musta been pinchin people's chooks an ducks, fum what I hear. Now them white people's worryin the guvmint ta make em go back further yet. They been moved back once already, few years ago, so's them white ones can build their houses out there, but now they're up to em, an they wanta build more houses. That's what they say. Ask me, I think the chooks an things done it. An them carryin on night-times, yellin and kicking up rows.'

'Wasn't one thing it'd be another,' Mr Comeaway said philosophically. 'Them Berrings is in bad everywhere. Always was. Always will be.'

'Got their rights, too. Think they a cut above us peoples,' Mrs Comeaway added. 'Funny, ain't it?'

'Don't see much of em, them livin out the opposite way,' Mr Comeaway said thoughtfully, 'but the things ya hear ya gotta laugh. Cheeky devils. Hardly a time one of em ain't in jail. An got enough kids between em ta fill a mission on their own. One thing but. They stick together. An they reckon they ain't gunna shift back no more'n what they have. I reckon them white people'd been better off buildin their houses way from there.'

'What's been happening up that hospital,' Mrs Comeaway asked Noonah.

The Comeaways liked to know about the hospital. Especially Mr Comeaway, who liked, in turn, to talk about

173

it with Horace. Yet none of the tales Noonah told them ever quite convinced him that she was not speaking about quite different people from those that were familiar to him: gangling Dr Graham, who had trouble fitting his long legs into his tiny black car; frowning impatient Dr Bentley, who had once stabbed him with a needle before he properly knew what it was all about; stately pigeon-toed Mr Meagher, who looked at people over the tops of his spectacles, more as if they were a lot of ants rather than people. They bore the same names, yes, but this lot that Noonah talked about acted like ordinary human beings, and ordinary human beings was one thing Mr Comeaway knew they were not.

He followed attentively when Noonah chattered hospital lore, and rolled T.P.R.'s and four hourly backs round on his tongue for the sheer pleasure of knowing what these things meant.

He had been in hospital once himself, afraid to move for fear of creasing his bedcover, asking for bed-pans only when discomfort became greater than the embarrassment he felt at using them.

'The old ones, they like a lot of fuss made of them,' Noonah smiled. 'One old chap first chucks his pillows out of bed, then he falls on them, just so we'll all come running. Makes sure he doesn't hurt himself but.

'And some like to help. They get sick of staying in bed and they're glad to be doing something. Last week I gave a man a tray of dirty crockery to put in the service hatch, and instead of waiting for it to come up he just dropped them—crash! I was near enough, so I heard a voice come up the chute, "Jeesus, who the hell did that?"'

174

The Comeaways roared with laughter.

A sudden thought struck Noonah. 'Mummy, the sister-in-charge told me some coloured mothers won't call for their children when they're well again. The hospital sends them a letter to tell them to pick their children up and they just don't come, some of them. Why?'

Mrs Comeaway sat stolidly on her chair, not answering for a moment. At length she moved restlessly. 'Look, Noonah. S'pose ya got no place ta bring that kid back and ya know it needs somewhere decent. Better for it ta stay in the hospital, ain't it? No good bringin it back somewhere it's gunna get sick again, isn't it?'

'Someone should *do* something,' Noonah said pitifully, not quite knowing what. 'Why do they let their children get things like enteritis and burns and malnutrition even?'

Mrs Comeaway pricked up her ears. 'That thing! That nutrition! I know bout that. Had some woman on me back one time when young Stella was a baby. You give em plenty a good tucker, I tole er, an never mind bout all this nutrition.' She sniffed. 'An I was right, seems. The damn thing's puttin kids in hospital now.'

Noonah spluttered. 'Malnutrition, Mummy.'

'That's somethin quite different see?' added Mr Comeaway, taking the cue from his daughter.

'Nobody's gunna tell me that little Tommy's got what you said,' Mrs Comeaway said doggedly. 'I seen im with me own eyes put away enough tucker ta stuff a elephant. Coupla packets a biscuits, jam slapped a inch thick on is bread—yet that's what they say e got all right. An been in an out that hospital three or four times now.'

175

'Gutsache, that's what,' Mr Comeaway grinned before Noonah could speak.

'They do say you have to have protein as well,' she got in when the two had stopped laughing. 'And vitamins, too.'

'Yes, ya ole fool,' Mr Comeaway teased his wife.

'I like ta know who *you* callin ole fool,' Mrs Comeaway said, half rising from her chair. 'An if ya think I'm gunna start feedin ya all them things Noonah says, ya make a big mistake.'

'But...,' Noonah said, laughing.

Mr Comeaway held up one hand. 'Let er go,' he said peaceably. 'I managed this long on the stuff she slaps together. I dessay I can go it a bit longer.'

'Ere's ole Skippy,' Mrs Comeaway said, looking over their heads. 'Just look at im, will ya?'

'Think it was a walkin heap a clothes,' Mr Comeaway guffawed, 'if ya didn't know ole Skippy was inside of em.' He got up and walked to the doorway. 'Someone tole me e was in hospital one time an they discharged im as being a uncurable. Been uncurable ever since an likely ta see the lot of us out, ask me.'

Noonah joined her father, watching the old man affectionately. All his clothes looked too big for him. His boots clopped loosely on the pavement, his trouser legs, even though folded over and over at the bottoms, still concertinaed round his boots, and the sleeves of his coat obscured his hands. Like the rest of his clothes, his hat, a wide-brimmed felt, was too big for his shrunken head, and at this moment it sat sideways on. Every now and then

Skippy gave it an impatient jab and it did a little jig on his head before sliding down again over his forehead.

He stopped inside the gate and looked towards the veranda. His dim old eyes peered anxiously from beneath the brim of his hat and his black cavity of a mouth hung open. He looked like an old prehistoric bird. His face brightened when he saw Noonah standing with her father. Noonah was kind to him, and gentle. He liked her.

'You've come down at last,' Noonah said, as she helped him up the steps.

'Gettin a house meself soon,' Skippy cackled. 'I come down ta see what this one like.' He fixed her with a stern eye. 'Ya got ya water on yet?'

'Water?' Noonah said, puzzled.

Mrs Comeaway laughed. 'I know what e means,' she told Noonah. 'Now fa Gawd's sake get im inside an let im sit down. Poor old bugger must be wore out traipsin down here.'

'Like a mug?' Mr Comeaway said loudly, waving a cup in front of the old man's face.

Skippy refused to be seated. Instead he rolled across to the sink. 'Let im go,' he commanded, looking at the tap.

Mrs Comeaway smiled into Noonah's mystified face. She gave the tap a twist and let the water stream down into the sink. 'Hunhh!' Skippy grunted, and rolled back to his chair. For a while he just sat, recovering the breath he had lost in his climb up the steps.

'What's that about the water, Mummy?' Noonah whispered.

'Some of is pals, up the road a bit. They get theirselves a house, an because they was in such a hurry ta move in the

177

water didn't get put on till a while after. Skippy was stayin with em, see? An nobody couldn't make im understand that that water was comin just as soon as the waterworks people got around to it. You know what I tell ya bout him thinkin the pleece do everything. So what he does, he takes his pension book up ta the station an throws it down on the counter an roars that the pleece can keep their damn pension if they ain't gunna put water on his lations' house. Went ta town on em, e did, an the pleece no more able ta make im understand they got nothin ta do with it than the Mungos ad been.'

Noonah laughed and sent a compassionate look at Skippy. 'So what happened then?'

Mrs Comeaway's bulk was shaking. 'The water gets put on the very next day. Don't ask me if the pleece done something bout it because I dunno. An don't try ta tell ole Skippy they didn't, either. E thinks that water got put on because he ticked off them pleecemen.'

'And what about his pension book?'

'Ah, they made im take it back. Gawd, that little ole bastard.' Mrs Comeaway looked admiringly at Skippy. 'Makin everyone crawl to im. Dried up little runt like im.'

'Ya hear?' Skippy asked Mr Comeaway. 'I tell ya I gunna get me place. I been arstin fa this ouse long time now. Long time. Now I get im.'

'Where's e gunna be built?' Mr Comeaway roared.

'I gotta place,' the old man tittered. 'Gettin old now. Time I go back, eh? I borned up there, ya know that? Now I go back. An my friend e build me ouse.'

'Who's his friend?' Noonah asked in an undertone.

178

'That's the partment man,' Mrs Comeaway said. 'No wonder e's buildin im a house. Glad to get rid a the ole bastard I s'pose.'

'Im friend,' Skippy said indignantly. 'My friend.'

'There y'are,' Mrs Comeaway said, amused. 'One minute deaf as a post. Next minute bitin ya head off cause ya said somethin e don't oughta heard.'

'Give im a cuppa tea,' Mr Comeaway said. 'Settle im down.'

'Hope e's got it right,' Mrs Comeaway said dubiously. 'Don't e come from up the Kimberleys? Seems funny ta me, sendin someone up all that way ta build im a house.'

Skippy mumbled happily over his tea. 'Git pretty colour on *my* floor now.'

Mr Comeaway grinned. 'You get new wife now you got new house?'

Skippy nodded amiably. 'For work. For cook,' he squeaked. 'Git plenty kangaroo tail now awright.'

'Puttin ideas in is ead,' Mrs Comeaway said disgustedly. 'Gawd elp im if one a them young ones gets old of his pension book.'

Mr Comeaway rose and stretched himself. 'Gunna take a little walk. See what's doin.'

'Ya gunna take im with ya?' Mrs Comeaway nodded at the drowsy old man.

'He's nearly asleep, poor old thing,' Noonah said sympathetically. 'Let him stay for a while.'

Mr Comeaway looked at his wife. 'What about a couple, eh?' He moved nearer the shelf on which Mrs Comeaway had placed the tobacco-tin.

179

Mrs Comeaway hesitated. 'Ah, go on then,' she said weakly. 'Be careful but. No gettin us in trouble.'

'Doesn't Dad still work on the wharf?' Noonah asked her mother when Mr Comeaway had gone and Skippy's old head was resting on his arms.

Mrs Comeaway shrugged. ''E goes down sometimes. I dunno! P'raps there ain't been so much loadin lately.'

'How do you manage well?' There was a little frown on Noonah's forehead.

'I get me little bit a dowment comin in now—fa young Bartie an Stella. All helps. You bring a bit home. Get a bit at cards. Tick up a bit down the corner shop.'

'What about rent?'

'Now don't you go worryin ya head bout us,' Mrs Comeaway soothed.

Noonah ran a hand over the knicked table-top, feeling its grooves and bumps. 'Audrena came up to see me this week. Auntie Hannie and Blanchie came up a couple of days after.'

'Money?' Mrs Comeaway enquired swiftly.

Noonah nodded. 'I don't mind, Mummy. But I get in trouble if I have too many visitors when I'm on duty. We're not supposed to.'

Mrs Comeaway sat stiff and angry. 'Ya don't have ta tell me. They on to ya now. They know they can go up an bite ya fa a bit every now and then, the cows. I like ta knock their blocks off, comin round gettin you in trouble. I'm gunna tell em ta keep away fum you.'

'Gee, Mummy, I don't suppose it matters as much as all that.' Noonah was a bit perturbed. 'It's just that I'm not

180

supposed to leave the ward when I'm on duty, and I have to, to get my money.'

'You wouldn't be the only one,' Mrs Comeaway said, still grim. 'Anyone knows ya got a bit, they on ta ya like a lotta seagulls. Even me an my bit a dowment.' She rested firmly fleshed arms on the table. An indrawn breath flared her nostrils, and curved her mouth into a line of irony. 'Not that ya can blame the poor bastards, I s'pose.'

'An awful lot don't work, and they don't seem to want to,' Noonah said diffidently. 'Why, Mummy?'

'Don't you go measurin us up against white folk, Noonah,' Mrs Comeaway warned. 'The men works, they get the rough stuff to do. They get tired a that. Many a time I helped Joe do the burnin off on properties round about ere. An that's a picnic longside a some other jobs e's had.'

Swift sympathy softened Noonah's face.

Mrs Comeaway was encouraged to continue. 'Can't really blame em, wantin ta take a bit of a holiday like, every now an then. Would meself, I hadda do half what the men do. Sides,' she chuckled suddenly. 'It's all in. Ya bite someone one day, ya gotta expect ta be bit back when it's your turn. Ain't that right?'

'Gawd, Noonah,' she said a moment later. 'I ever tell ya bout that time ole Bung Arrer's pension come through?' She settled back in her chair and swished her pink tongue round her smiling lips. 'It's like this, see? The ole bloke's been bummin round on folk long as I been here. And then someone sees bout a pension for im. E goes round tellin everyone e's gunna get this big lotta money that's been buildin up since e's reached the age where they give out

181

pensions, see? And the day e gets it, there they are, all of em. Seventeen! For a bit a fun I counted eads. All waitin outside the post office fa ole Bung Arrer.' She put her head back and held on to the rippling folds of her stomach until her laughter had spent itself. Noonah laughed too, but there was compassion in her laughter.

'It's all right,' Mrs Comeaway gasped. 'Some a them seen the funny side an they left im a bit ta get on with.'

'And what were you doing there?' Noonah teased, relieved at this not too unhappy ending.

Her mother was unabashed. 'Waitin ta bite im, a course.'

'You're awful,' Noonah giggled, but there was affection in the look she gave her mother. Despite their undercurrent of tragedy, these were the tales she loved to hear when she came home. These were her people. She would not have had them much different.

Skippy woke with a start. He pulled his lax old limbs and his bird-like head in, towards his skinny body, as though he must concentrate his strength.

'Come down ere fa a good cuppa tea,' he announced, an evil twinkle in his hooded eyes.

'Ya just had a cuppa tea,' Mrs Comeaway roared indignantly.

The twinkle vanished. 'Nice thing, ole man can't git a cuppa tea when e needs it. Nice thing that is.'

'All right!' Mrs Comeaway moaned. 'All right! Put the kettle on, Noonah.'

FOURTEEN

One of the things Mr Comeaway liked to do on these hot nights was to sit on the top step of the front veranda and from there to survey his new kingdom—neat, small gardens stretching away to right and left—neat, small houses behind them—little white picket fences marking off each quarter-acre block, and now that dusk was falling, the sweet and heady scent of Mrs Henwood's stocks to delight his nostrils.

'Them plants her-next-door put in, they growin?' he enquired of his wife, who was seated in a cane chair just behind him.

'Dunno!' Mrs Comeaway said. 'Ain't seen er for a week or more.'

'Thought ya said she was gunna come over an see to em.'

'She ain't and I ain't,' Mrs Comeaway said, kismet fashion. 'Tell ya the truth, I clean forgot about em.' She

183

leaned forward to peer over the veranda. 'Don't see em now, do you?'

Mr Comeaway heaved himself up and clumped down the steps to investigate. 'Nup! Nothin there.' He straightened and sighed. 'Woulda been nice, avin a few flowers.'

Mrs Comeaway shook her head in commiseration. 'Musta been somethin wrong with that pot-plant she gave me, too. Went brown an all the leaves come off.'

'Don't matter,' Mr Comeaway said nobly, climbing the steps again. After a while he said thoughtfully: 'Praps if you was to tell er them plants she put in went an died, praps she might put in some more.'

'An take better care next time,' Mrs Comeaway disapproved. 'After all, it ain't me that's the gardner. She was the one seemed set on a garden.'

Trilby listened without interest, leaning her head languidly against the wall of the sleepout. Bartie and Stella whispered and giggled together and dragged themselves round the veranda on their stomachs.

'Wouldn't mind a few peoples round tonight,' Mr Comeaway offered.

'An it looks as if ya gunna have em,' Mrs Comeaway told him. 'Here's a taxi comin now.'

The Comeaways peered hopefully through the dusk. Few of their friends owned cars. Most of them were forced to use taxis, unless, of course, they preferred to walk, and few of the Comeaways' friends preferred to walk.

The taxi stopped before the Comeaway house, and everyone on the veranda waited expectantly. Dark figures detached themselves from the cab and on the still air there sounded the sharp clink of bottle against bottle.

Mr Comeaway smiled gently, and contentment flooded his soul.

'Couldn't let ole Nipper go back thout comin down ta see yous an ya new house,' Charlie said jovially. 'Gee, we ad some times since e's been down. Goin back tomorrow.'

'Ole Nipper, eh?' Mr Comeaway's voice was full of welcome. 'Whadda ya know? An young Stoney Broke an Phyllix, ain't it?'

'An Hannie,' Mrs Comeaway said of the sad silhouette that followed the men. 'Come in then.'

Behind her mother, Trilby stood stiffly against the wall, her body pin-pointing with shock.

'An be gee, we gotta remember the time that train goes tomorrow,' Nipper grinned in warning. 'They short anded. Boss only let me come down ta get me back fixed. Thinkin a takin young Phyllix back ta help out, seein is own team's finishing up.'

'What's a coupla days between friends,' Mr Comeaway said hospitably. 'Should park yaselves down ere with us a while. Got plenty a room.'

'I'll say,' Stoney remarked, looking round admiringly. 'Trouble is, it wasn't zactly like the boy ere says it was. Boss didn't *let* us come. We just tole im we was comin. Cause a Nipper's back.'

'An bicrikey, was e mad!' Nipper chuckled. 'Thing was, we was just startin a shed, an me ole pal Stoney wasn't gunna let a bloke come down by hisself.' He winked. 'Not havin this bad back like.'

185

'E stacked on a turn,' Stoney grinned. 'Said if we went we didn't need ta come back because e'd get someone else in ta do the job.'

'So ya see ow it is, boy,' Nipper finished. 'We miss that damn train tomorrow, e just might *git* someone else ta do the job. An Mirrabilli's all right. Not real bad. What you think, Stoney?' He raised an eyebrow at his pal.

'Ah, e's not a bad ole bugger,' Stoney agreed tolerantly. 'Now—what about a drop a grog.' He reached into the sack and withdrew a bottle of wine.

'Don't think the young bloke's taken to me,' Hannie mourned, taking Stella up on her lap. 'Makes off soon as e sees me comin.'

Mrs Comeaway gave a great laugh. 'I know where that one'll be. Run off to is bed. Always does, minute anyone comes. We hadda put Maudie Mungo in is bed one night, couldn't very well let er lay out on the veranda fa the neighbours ta see in the morning. E didn't like it but. Said she kep im awake snorin. An took up all the bed. Course e's a bit shy, ya know. Give im time ta get used to ya, Hannie. Ya takes some gettin used to, you ave ta admit that. Eh, Charlie?' And her great laugh roared out again.

'I was just thinkin,' Mr Comeaway said, watching Stoney pour the conto into some cups, 'didn't I say to ya, Mollie, I could do with a bit a company aroun?'

Nobody noticed that neither Phyllix nor Trilby had followed them into the living-room. The two stood together on the veranda, Trilby striving for calmness.

Phyllix took her hand and pulled her gently away from the oblong of light. 'I been lookin for you since I came back.'

Trilby flashed him a sideways look.

'Didn't see ya on the beach or nowhere.'

'I wasn't there, I suppose.'

'Why?'

Trilby tried to achieve crispness. 'I have to study. I'm takin my Junior the end of this year.'

'You got ya back up still,' Phyllix accused. 'Bout that night on the beach.' His tone gentled. 'You didn't have to, Trilby. I wouldn't of made ya.'

Trilby's chin went up as her temper sparked. 'You didn't make me. Nobody makes me do things.'

'We could get married, the two of us,' Phyllix's eyes held hers steadily. 'If you wanted it.'

Trilby's grey eyes widened, then she jerked herself away from him. 'What makes you think I'd marry you? I would be a fool.' There was resentfulness as well as bitterness in her voice.

Phyllix's heavy brows met over his nose. 'What's wrong with me? You think you're too good?'

Trilby's self-assurance grew. She liked the feeling of having hurt him. She wanted to hurt him yet more. 'Marry you and live in a camp like the others up there on the hill? You must fancy yourself if you think I'd go back to that just because you asked me to.'

'I haven't asked you ta do that, Trilby.'

Trilby would not soften to the pleading in his voice. She would have liked to fight him physically, as well as with words. There would be satisfaction in tearing at his face with her finger-nails. For weeks the thought of him had

187

disturbed her. Why must he come back just when she had succeeded in putting him out of her mind?

Dismayingly, she felt her thoughts falter, her body lose some of its tautness, as Phyllix moved closer to her. He slipped an arm about her waist and pulled her towards him so that once again she felt his hard maleness. Her defiance crumbled. She felt the warm wetness of tears in her eyes before her head drooped to rest on his shoulder.

'Where can we go?' Phyllix muttered, and his warm breath was on her neck.

'No!' Trilby's voice was hardly audible.

'Come *on*,' Phyllix said urgently. And there was sweetness as well as shame at following him.

In amongst the grey-green salt-bushes they lay close together. Trilby had waited to pay her debt of remorse and self-loathing, but this time there had been no payment to make. Instead, knowledge had come to her that Phyllix had taken from her no more than she had taken from him. And with this knowledge had come tenderness for him, and a pity which included herself.

'Better I tell Nipper I don't go with him on that train tomorrow,' Phyllix whispered.

Trilby made no sound. There was a peace about them that she would not disturb.

'You know, I had girls before,' Phyllix said dreamily. 'Not like you, Trilby. You get in a chap's head, keep him remembering.' She felt his intensity as he struggled for words. 'That's why I think we better get married. I want you with me always. All the time.'

'I will marry you,' Trilby said vehemently. And she knew she spoke so because what she said was not the truth. She did want to be with him always. In one short hour he had become dearer to her than anyone had ever been—his strong hard body to which her own had submitted so joyfully, his warm dry hands which were so gentle, the rough feel of his hair—he was her own. Sadness was deep within her because she knew she would let him go, *must* let him go, or she could not fulfil the promise she had made to herself.

'You could come with me,' Phyllix told her. 'They got good quarters on Mirrabilli.'

Trilby was glad of the dark. 'No! Not yet.'

'Not me neither well,' she knew he was smiling. She kept herself still so that he would not rouse to kiss her. So that she could think.

'Phyllix, you know I don't want to live like they do in those awful humpies. I want a house, a good house. And stuff to put in it.'

'You got a house. Room fa one more, isn't there?'

'Not there.' Trilby was patient. 'I want my own place. Like other people.'

'You want to live like white people live, that it?'

Trilby was ready to stiffen in case he should laugh, but Phyllix did not laugh.

'And I want a garden with roses and things in it.' Trilby's voice was vehement.

Phyllix did laugh then, but tenderly. 'You got some funny ideas in ya head, haven't ya?'

'They're not funny.'

189

'Ya want a whole house to yaself?'

'Yes.'

'I dunno! I suppose I could save me cheques. Work a few more sheds if I wanted to.' He turned suddenly, caught her hands and pressed them down, one each side of her head. His face was close and she could imagine the golden eyes holding her own. 'You better be here when I get back,' he told her, his voice thickening again. 'An don't you let no one else touch ya, see?'

Trilby's lips parted. Relief mingled with shame. It had been too easy to fool him into believing she would wait for him. She knew coldly that she would not.

Mr Comeaway leaned his arms on the table-top and focused his benevolent gaze on his friends. It had been a good night, and he was mellowed through and through with good will towards men.

'You still thinkin a comin down ere, Charlie?' he enquired with kindly condescension.

'Yeah, we still thinkin,' his brother returned comfortably. 'Only thing, that damn money pretty hard ta get. That deposit ya gotta pay.'

Mr Comeaway turned out his bottom lip, nodded understandingly.

'The truth bein,' Charlie added in a burst of frankness. 'We gone an spent the damn lot. Gunna start again soon's I get a week or two down the wharf.'

Mr Comeaway's expression was sphinx-like. He wanted to express his good will in some magnificent and overwhelming manner. Because he liked old Charlie as well as he liked anyone, he decided his brother might as well be the one to benefit.

'Charlie,' he said, banging a fist on the table. 'You can put that money right out ya head. I got a better idea.'

'Yeah?'

Mr Comeaway took a breath. 'Ya can come down ere an live in *this* house.'

Charlie took him up swiftly. 'Ya mean the lot of us? The whole four an the kid too?'

Only for a second did caution overtake Mr Comeaway's generosity. Then his fine independent spirit took charge. 'My place, ain't it?' he asked, with a hint of belligerence. 'Anyone say it ain't my place? You lot can come ere soon's ya ready. Eh, Mollie, I jus said Charlie an is mob can come down ere an live stead a wastin a lotta money. Ya think that's all right?'

'Wouldn't mind stayin ere meself, ya say the word,' Stoney Broke grinned. 'She ain't a bad sorta camp.'

Mrs Comeaway had been nurturing a little good will on her own account. Her hesitation was even more fleeting than Mr Comeaway's had been. Trilby's objections, Noonah's, Bartie's—she dismissed them in the moment of considering them. Another woman right on tap, even though it was only Hannie, would do away with those long lonely periods when for some reason or other she was unable to get into town or up to the camps at the back of the hill.

'Plenty a room,' she declared. 'Plenty. Dunno why we didn't think of it before.'

'Trilby don't seem ta like peoples much,' Hannie contributed nervously.

'Ah, she won't mind,' Mrs Comeaway said largely. 'Long as nobody pokes their nose in er room.'

'Gawd!' Hannie disclaimed, even more nervously. 'Ya think I want ta go in there, with er waitin ta pounce? Not me!'

'Fixed it all up erself,' Mrs Comeaway told the others. 'Cover-ups fa the beds, curtains, stuff on the floor. Cleans it out erself, too. Looks real nice.'

Mr Comeaway chuckled. 'Where is she, anyhow? An young Phyllix, too? They musta gone off somewhere.'

'They was out on the veranda,' Mrs Comeaway told him.

'Down the Fun Fair, likely,' Nipper said easily. 'Ringin ashtrays an jugs. The lot of us went there last night.'

He had no sooner spoken than the two were at the door.

'Where you two been?' Mrs Comeaway asked, looking from one face to the other.

'I'm tired. I'm going to bed.' Trilby moved away from the doorway, and Phyllix stepped into the room.

'Ow many ash-trays tonight?' Stoney asked, grinning. 'This is the boy to ring em,' he told the Comeaways. 'They was chasin im away last night. Woulda went broke if e'd stayed much longer.'

'Eh, Trilby!' Mrs Comeaway called. 'Come back in ere. We gotta nice surprise for ya.'

Trilby came slowly back to stand alongside Phyllix. She looked sulky.

'How would ya like it if Blanchie an Audrena come down ta stay for a bit?' Mrs Comeaway asked, over-heartily.

Trilby gave her mother a straight glance from her silver-grey eyes. She did not speak.

Mrs Comeaway stuck doggedly to heartiness. 'Ya father an me, we thought it might be a good idea ta have Charlie an Hannie an the girls come down ere.'

'I don't call that a nice surprise,' Trilby spoke clearly. She swept the group with a look which scorned them, then she swung round. They heard her bedroom door bang shut behind her.

Phyllix leant against the wall, his face expressionless.

Mrs Comeaway looked round uneasily. 'Nice sorta thing ta say,' she said weakly.

'Some bark, eh?' Stoney was impressed.

Hannie quivered in her chair. 'If it's all the same ta yous, I think we stop up there by Mrs Green. It pretty comforble—an quiet like. We come down ere, I dunno— that Trilby, she just as well might break out on us.'

Mr Comeaway sat back in his chair and roared with laughter.

From the doorway Phyllix echoed it.

'Be gee,' Mr Comeaway gasped, casting a look of appreciation at the only member of the party to share his amusement. 'Look at em all, will ya? An that Trilby! Ain't any pleasin er. An she got ole Hannie shakin in er shoes thout even comin near er. Don't you take too much notice a that one, Hannie. We gotta big chain jus outside that door. After you an Charlie get down ere, we gunna chain that Trilby up, like a dog.' He roared again.

'Better we stay where we was,' Hannie said primly, 'then we ain't under no compliments ta nobody.'

'What gets into er, eh?' Mr Comeaway asked Phyllix as one intimate to another. 'Tramps over people like they was muck under er feet.'

Phyllix grinned. 'Ah! I dunno!' He slid one hand higher up the door jamb, rested the other on a slim hip. 'Maybe she thinks different than the rest of us round here.' There was a glow in the depths of the yellow eyes.

'She's a young huzzy,' her mother said, with an unwilling smile.

FIFTEEN

With hardly a discussion, the Comeaways dropped, for the time being, the idea of inviting their relatives to share their home. There had been no misunderstanding Trilby's views on the matter, and neither of her parents felt strongly enough about it to risk their daughter's continued disapproval. Mrs Comeaway, in particular, in the few short months since her daughter had arrived back from the mission, had found that falling in with Trilby's ideas paid off in a more or less peaceful atmosphere. Besides, Trilby always won in the end. Her mother was the first to admit that her daughter had a way with her, when she wanted something.

Right from the start, Trilby had done all of her own washing. And she spent hours pressing her cotton frocks and her school tunic with Mrs Comeaway's old flat irons heated on top of the stove.

There was a strong bond between Trilby and her father. Mr Comeaway saw nothing wrong in Trilby's pertness or her sometimes cruel criticism of her bewildered and harassed mother. What other girls at school had, Trilby must have too. Whoever or whatever went short in consequence was no concern of hers.

Not that she did not help with the rest of the house. Over week-ends especially she was ruthless about what she called 'rubbish', and many a time Mrs Comeaway was forced to sneak out to the rubbish bin to retrieve something she cherished. In lots of small ways, Mrs Comeaway's life had become more complicated, but her pride in her smart daughter most often outweighed any resentment she felt.

There were her other children, too, with whom to relax, and her friends who lived in the humpies at the back of the town.

Only Noonah worried about things like rent. On Saturday mornings off she would bath both children and dress them in clean clothes, settle her mother into her blue silk frock and comb her greying hair back from her smooth cocoa forehead, cajole her father for money, when he had it, and start off for town with them all.

That was the happy time that Noonah remembered most often in the years that followed. For a short time the Comeaways prospered. After harvest, the town was always busy, and wharf-work was easy to come by. In fact, if you were a wharfie you reported regularly if you knew what was good for you. The big boats must not be held up. Every hand was needed to fill the holds with wheat.

Mrs Comeaway had her eye on an oak dining-room suite she had seen in a second-hand shop. Noonah thought it would be nice for her mother to have a really big cupboard for the kitchen. Bartie wanted genuine camel-hair brushes for his painting, Stella wanted a bride-doll, and Trilby found something else she needed every time she went to town.

Noonah was business manager. Occasionally some need more pressing than mere signatures on tiny scraps of paper bobbed up and her calculations went astray but it was so good to be home she could never worry overmuch about rent. In town on Saturdays, it was milk-shakes and chocolates and cool drinks for the kids, and a whole heap of stuff from the grocer who delivered, and agreeable little gossips with Mrs Comeaway's friends and perhaps a taxi trip up the hill to see Gramma Green.

With the utmost good nature, the Comeaway family had exhausted Mrs Henwood's attempts at rehabilitation, and the only contact they now had was when Mr Comeaway caught sight of her and strolled over to the dividing fence to advise her on her activities in her garden.

In a secret corner of her mind Mrs Comeaway still cherished the idea of getting Charlie and Hannie down to live in the Wild-Oat Patch, but for the present she vanquished the bogey of loneliness by spending most of her day in the township where there was always a group of friends to join; at the corner by the barber-shop, sitting on hard garden seats outside the bank, or sheltering from the wind behind the stone wall where Horace held court.

During the evening, if there were no visitors, she fed her husband the morsels of gossip she heard.

197

'Knew well as anything ole Skippy'd got is talk of getting a house all mucked up,' she told him one night. 'Mattie up the camp tole me.'

'An Horace tole me,' Mr Comeaway added, 'they gettin a lot a little houses up the camp stead a them camps. An Horace, he gunna be first gettin one.'

'An that's where ole Skippy's house is gunna be built,' Mrs Comeaway said. 'Course it is.'

'They all been trying ta make Skippy understand proper, but e sticks to it e's gunna have is house built special, up where e comes from.'

'Poor ole chap.' Mrs Comeaway was sympathetic. 'Gawd, what a time someone's gunna have, gettin it clear to im.'

'Should do something bout it. Someone should,' Mr Comeaway said vaguely.

'Maybe cost too much.'

'Still, ole chap like e is. Wouldn't hurt em.'

'Nnnh!' Mrs Comeaway sighed.

There was no longer any doubt that a baby was coming. The knowledge overwhelmed Trilby at first. If he had been near, Trilby would have sought Phyllix out, flung hysterical accusations at him. All her resentment of him was back, multiplied into hatred. But he was gone from the town, and the only thing left to do was to try to hide her burning humiliating suffering from every eye. She hated herself, too. She, with her wonderful plans, to be such a fool. To know she had gone into this thing with her eyes wide open.

In bed at night she beat her belly with clenched fists, hating the thing it enclosed.

She told nobody because nobody could help her. She sickened when she thought of the future. Soon she would grow big, and everyone would know and laugh. She guessed how they would laugh, how glad her mother's friends would be to see her beaten. The thought of their gladness drove her mad. She would not bear it.

At school she stayed aloof from everyone, took a day off as often as she could without causing too much comment. Daytime was worst. Other people forever about, any one of them likely at any time to guess her secret. She had no clear plan except to meet each day and endure it until darkness came.

During the evening she left the house to wander round the curving road that followed the line of the beach. Alone, she penetrated deep into the acres of marshy salt-bush, sought out deliberately, once, the place where she had lain with Phyllix—and departed from there with the ache of tears in her throat.

Sometimes the older Comeaways would still be up when she reached her home. There would be lights glaring from the windows and the noise of voices and laughter on the air. Nobody noticed when she came in because she went straight to her room. Her room, which she would share with nobody, was her one blessing.

On other nights the house would be dark and silent, every occupant in bed and asleep. Trilby walked for miles, but rarely enough to tire herself so that she slept straightway. There were always the hot, lumpy pillow, the tangled sheets—and weary half-closed eyes.

She felt an overpowering need to confide in someone—her mother, or Noonah—and this feeling had to be fought and subdued, not once, but often. Mrs Comeaway would have been astonished and unbelieving if she could have known that there were days when Trilby would have given much to be in Bartie's place, or little Stella's, when Mrs Comeaway sat on the top step with a careless arm round each, or told them, with the object of keeping them amused and happy, some tale of her childhood, or, more rarely, when she gave each a quick hug or a kiss or a playful smack on the behind. Sometimes Trilby resented her mother simply because Mrs Comeaway did not guess her daughter's need of her.

The temptation to tell Noonah was even harder to resist, and Trilby did not truly understand why she kept silent, unless it was that she wanted her sister's regard for her to remain unaltered, not tinged with sympathy. When, in the long night hours, she worked things out, she knew she wanted sympathy from nobody—not even from her mother.

One night, prowling along a back street, the glass window of a fire alarm caught her eye. She walked over to it, idly, not too interested, and bent to read the instructions. The thought came into her head that this glass must have been broken often, perhaps not always because there was a fire in its neighbourhood. There were boys—mischievous, unafraid of the consequences.

And a girl!

Glass shattered round her feet. She looked with unbelieving eyes at the stone she held in her hand. Her heart almost stopped beating as she dropped it and pressed hard against the bell in the little saucer-shaped container. She drew her finger away sharply, but the little bell remained depressed and Trilby knew why. In the fire station at the other end of the town, an alarm was sounding, right this minute. And it would continue to sound until someone switched off the mechanism. Any time now the fire-fighting truck would come clanging and shrilling down the street, waking everyone as it passed.

Like a shadow, and as quietly, Trilby slipped down the dark length of the street. Her heart thumped and beat in her throat so that she felt choked. Why had she done such a thing? Could someone have been watching her? What happened to a girl who broke the glass of a fire alarm when there was no fire?

Quietly—quietly, she crept into her bed that night, and lay trembling beneath her blankets.

But that night she did not lie awake in bed, thinking. It was morning before she knew it. And nothing had happened to her.

At the end of a week Trilby felt safe from consequences, but it was longer than a fortnight before she dared revisit the fire alarm. She hardly questioned that she *must* see it again.

It had been mended. A new glass shone in the moonlight.

Trilby looked to right and left this time, to make sure she was not being watched. Then she picked up a stone and hurled it satisfyingly straight at the little glass window. The tinkling of the glass as it fell was like music. Music that exhilarated and excited her. Her heart beat and thumped as she held her finger to the bell. She laughed. And suddenly, the future appeared free of worry. The suffering burning ache that had been with her since she had guessed about the baby—it was gone. Where it had been there was left only a tingling and fusing of all her senses.

This time she could not tear herself away from the scene. More! She must have more! What happened when a fire alarm was set off? If she hid, she would know. The Moreton Bay fig tree, its branches hidden beneath big sheltering leaves! If she climbed up into it, hid herself in its darkest part, she would see and hear everything.

Trilby heard the truck approach, watched it stop, gloated as the men fanned out to look for the fire then converged once more on the truck. She heard them talk, heard every word they said. The exhilaration remained. It was like being born again. She saw and heard everything and herself remained safely hidden.

'Same one did it before, I'll take a bet on that.'

'Might be around still, too.'

A man with authority in his voice spoke last. 'Two of you men stay here. Have a good look round, everywhere, and I'll go down to the station and fetch a policeman.'

Trilby's heart gave a great lurch. She kept very still, almost too afraid to breathe in case she made her presence known. The two men angled out from each other, searching the dark doorways of shops, penetrating the night-filled lane across the street from the fire alarm. Trilby knew she must drop from the tree and take a chance on escaping, but she waited too long. The men came back. Trilby's fear grew. She wanted to believe that she was dreaming and that she would wake from this horror safe in her bed. Sweating, shaking still, but safe! It could not be she who perched in this tree while two men below searched only for her. It *must* be a dream.

A third man came. Trilby recognised his uniform. This was the policeman the other man had called. Despite herself, a sob of terror forced its way through her lips. The branch of the tree shook and a dead leaf detached itself and fell scuttering to the ground.

The officer was quick. This was something in which he had been trained, this lightning-quick note of detail. In a second he was underneath the tree, peering up through the branches.

He called: 'I see you! Come on down, whoever you are.'

Trilby clutched the branch tighter but did not answer. There was a chance that he was gammoning. How could he see her, through so many thick dark leaves.

He had a torch out. The beam was directed up into the tree. It moved slowly across and across, thoroughly exhausting the potentialities of one spot before moving on to the next. Trilby closed her eyes, endured the torture of waiting. Then she felt the beam of the torchlight strong on her eyelids.

'Hah!' There was satisfaction in his voice. 'Got you!' The fire-brigade officers followed the line of light, saw the material of Trilby's skirt and her dangling dark legs and her clutching hands.

'A girl!'

'You coming down or am I coming up to fetch you?' the police-officer called.

A wild rage surged through Trilby. 'No!' she yelled, lashing out viciously with her foot. 'And if you come near me, I'll kick you, you hear?'

'You will, will you?' The policeman grinned. 'I'm coming up just the same, young miss. Unless you change your mind and come down.'

'Go away!' Trilby shrieked. 'Go away! If you come near me, you bastard, I'll push you down. I'll make you fall. You'll get hurt.'

'Tut! Mustn't threaten police-officers. Mustn't swear, either.'

'I think you'd better come down, girlie.' There was a kindly note in the voice of the fire-brigade man. 'Can't stay up there all night, you know.'

'I won't come down. I won't. Go away, all of you.'

'Looks like I'll have to go up,' the policeman said. He moved over to the great round trunk of the tree, searched with experienced eyes for a foothold. Trilby saw him come up the tree with the agility of a small boy.

She froze with fear. He must not be allowed to touch her. She would not let him. She closed her eyes and her mouth opened in a grimace. Letting go her hold on the branch she jumped forward just before the man reached forward to stop her. A broken bough caught her skirt when she was half-way to the ground. She hung for a second, then the branch broke with a tortured crack and she fell the rest of the five or six feet to the ground.

She was up like a shot. Off and away! But the fire-brigade officers were too quick for her. She felt her shoulder grasped. She rammed her head into one man's stomach, putting all her force behind it. When he lost his balance and detached his hand from her shoulder she made off again, but the other one had her this time.

'I got her,' he called breathlessly to his mates, 'but you better come and help me. She's as strong as a young lion.'

The policeman dropped from the tree and came over to them.

"All right! All right! Break it up,' he told the terrified and struggling girl.

There were three of them. And they had caught her.

Trilby stopped fighting, relapsed into fatigue and hopelessness. She was in terrible trouble, another sort this time.

Between two of them she walked, docile enough now, to the police-station. She did not even hear the men when they spoke to her. She only heard their footsteps echoing along the empty dark street, saw only the dull gleam of glass in shop windows.

Inside the station, terror seized her stomach so that it knotted. She kept her head bent, knowing there was only one weapon left to her, silence.

'Look, don't you understand? All we want from you is your name, and your age and a couple of other things, and then you can go and have a sleep.' The young police-sergeant was getting impatient.

Each time he asked, Trilby's alertness increased. She felt danger ahead if she answered so much as a single question.

'Find out, if you want to know,' she snapped once, and when one of the officers had moved closer to her she had lashed out at him with her foot and caught him a crack on his ankle. He kept his distance after that.

'I've got an idea she's one of those Comeaway girls that just came down from some mission,' one officer said after a while.

'Your father Joe Comeaway?' the sergeant asked sternly.

Trilby maintained her sulky silence.

'Take her away, Ted,' the sergeant said at last. 'Lock her up until she's in a better frame of mind.'

Lock her up? Trilby marshalled all her strength for one last attempt to get away. Before any of the men knew what she was about she had darted back to the doorway.

She was nearly out into the street before one of them grabbed her arm and held it fast. She was jerked inside again, kicking and struggling. The man was strong. She felt herself shoved through a doorway, then a door slammed. She looked up. A light shone feebly through a barred space at the top of the doorway, illuminating a few objects. She picked out a bed against one wall. A chair stood alongside it. She swung it up and crashed it against the door and her wrists jarred painfully.

Once more she lifted it and smashed it against the locked door. Across her mind raced the words: 'Lock her up.'

Only when her strength was gone did she pause in her efforts to break down the stout wooden door.

'Bet she's broken that damn chair,' said a voice. 'Gee, some temper.'

Another sterner voice floated through to her. 'If you don't behave yourself you'll be made to behave. Get on that bed and lie down. Now!'

'I will not!' Trilby shrieked. She made a jab at the hole with one of the chair legs. There was a scuffling noise and a yell of pain. Trilby felt fiercely triumphant.

She looked round the room to see what else it held in the way of missiles. On a table in a corner of the room stood a glass jug of water with a tumbler alongside it. She swooped on it, crept with it to the door, standing to one side so that she should not be seen.

'Is she in bed yet?' someone asked softly. 'Have a look!'

Trilby let fly with the jug of water. From further sounds of snuffling and gasping she knew she had scored one more victory. Her upper lip was curled back from her teeth and her eyes caught the glow of the light.

Footsteps receded down the passage and there was silence. Like a cat, Trilby prowled round the room. Her thoughts darted here and there, seeking a way to escape. She had to get out—she had to put an end to this suffocating feeling of being locked up like a dangerous animal. There was no hope of escape through the door. There was equally small chance of squeezing her body through the narrow barred window. The walls were of crumbling stone and cement. The jail was old. The walls had been built by convict labour. Trilby did not know that. In one of her circuits of the room she stopped to lean against the old stone wall. Her hand reached out idly to crumble a little more of the loose cement. Others had been at work on the stones beneath her hand. It was almost free of the wall. A tug showed her that it was still too firmly embedded to be dislodged. But she could do it! She darted over to where the broken chair lay on the floor and took up one of the pieces of splintered wood. With it as her tool she worked doggedly away at the deep furrow surrounding the stones. Action—any sort of action was preferable to waiting and thinking.

At first she worked carelessly, but as her spirit quieted caution came and she knew that any loud noise would bring an officer up the passage seeking the cause. Every now and then she stopped to listen. Once she heard footsteps approach. Like lightning she made for the bed and dived under the blanket on top of it. And none too soon. The beam from the torch shone on the bed. Trilby closed her eyes and lay still. The light was switched off and the footsteps retreated. As soon as she was sure it was safe, Trilby was out of the bed again.

Soon the stone was almost free of the wall, and a gentle tug was all that was needed to move it. Pausing only to place it on the floor at her feet she started on the next one. Before the grey of coming day appeared like smoke in the square of the window, Trilby had removed three stones from the wall. She had not expected to tunnel her way through. The arduous work was meant only to occupy her mind and her strength, and to fend off the quivering madness that

208

had overwhelmed her when she had been flung into this room and imprisoned there. It meant, too, that she was not submitting tamely. If she could fight, she could hope to beat them.

SIXTEEN

When the grey was tinged with blue she curled up on the bed. At her side were the stones she had patiently chipped from the wall.

Later, when footsteps came near, she folded the blanket so that they could not be seen—and waited. The top half of a man's face appeared at the square hole in the door. Trilby gave stare for stare, her eyes shining silver-grey between swollen lids.

'Going to behave yourself this morning?' the police-officer asked banteringly.

Trilby did not reply. Her hand closed hard over one of the stones.

'I've got some tea and toast here for you,' the man said, and she heard a key grate in the lock of the door.

She was ready with her stone the moment the door opened and the officer, taken completely by surprise, dropped his little tray with a crash and stood for a second holding his shoulder whilst he gazed at her with shocked eyes. Trilby had time to throw another of her stones before he was on her, holding her down on the bed by the shoulders.

'Why, you young devil. You might have killed me,' he said when he had her thin young wrists in a bone-crushing grip.

'Let me alone,' Trilby said between her teeth. With her head she tried to butt him in the stomach. With her feet she kicked wildly at him.

'Hey! Les! Come here,' the young officer yelled, but another man had already entered the cell.

'See if there's any more stones in that bed,' Trilby's captor said. 'And if there are, grab them.'

'Gee!' The man gaped as he searched under the blanket and found the cache of stones. He took them over and dumped them outside the room in the passage. 'Where the hell did she get them from?' he marvelled.

Trilby screamed. She was flung back on the bed and the door banged shut again. One round-eyed face shoved another round-eyed face from the hole at the top of the door. Then both officers went back down the passage.

Trilby ran to the door as soon as they had gone. She banged on it with both fists. She screamed through it. She hurled names up the length of the passage. Names which she had heard but which she had never used in her life before. Nobody came near, and she went on screaming. It wasn't really herself screaming. A little calm spot in her brain told her that. The screaming came from a Thing inside herself, that squirmed, terrified and beaten, and used her

211

voice. Her whole body shook. The bones in her legs turned to jelly. Just above her eyes and back of them was a place that was stabbed with knife-like pains each time her body tensed itself to scream. After a while she stumbled to the bed and lay face down. She let the bed take the whole tremendous weight of her pain. She sank down and down so that the bed absorbed her. She was part of it. Not a girl at all but a rusty iron bed with a tossed blanket on top of it. And nothing would ever happen to her again.

'Ahoy there! Someone to see you.'

Unwillingly, Trilby came out from the twilight of peace. She heard a door closing. And that meant it must have been opened again. She tried to raise herself so that she could see but she could not care enough to make such an effort. She felt a weight settle itself alongside her. She waited wearily for the next thing to happen. And was unprepared for the sound of her mother's voice.

'Trilby! Wake up!'

'Too late now,' Trilby's thoughts formed themselves, slowly, achingly.

'Trilby, you look real sick. What they done to ya, love? Sit up an tell ya ole mummy, will ya? Ya daddy said fa me to tell ya e's comin later if ya wanted im to. Noonah's comin too, and Bartie. Don't worry, Trilby.' The heaviness at the side of her removed itself and her mother's voice spoke near her ear.

Trilby wanted to respond—to pour out the whole wretched story, beginning with someone called Phyllix. But things were all tangled up in her head. She dragged herself away from her mother, her stomach knotting at the movement. What was the use of words? Especially with someone like her mother. With anyone! Nobody would understand why she was here if she must fit the things she had done to words.

When her mother placed a timid hand on her shoulder she moved restlessly and it fell away.

'Dearie!' Her mother must be crying. Her words were choked. 'They want to know, outside, why you done it. Be a good girl and tell Mum why you broke their old glass, come on.'

Trilby wanted to laugh but she had no energy. A broken glass! As if a broken glass mattered. That was the end, not the beginning.

'Go away!' she muttered. 'I don't want anyone. Not anyone.'

'They're waitin,' Mrs Comeaway said in a frightened whisper. 'Ya got to tell em something, Trilby. They might keep ya here if ya don't.'

Why couldn't they just leave her here on the bed, Trilby thought desperately. She twitched away again as her mother moved closer to her. And to blot out the sound of Mrs Comeaway's pleading whispers she buried her head in the blanket.

After a while the bed creaked and her mother's weight was gone again. There were more voices—her mother's and some more. Then the door opened and shut and she was alone.

She had brought this aloneness on herself, but that did not stop the bitterness flowing from her aching throat into every part of her body. She pressed her hands over her eyes and tried to clear her mind.

She was taken from her cell to another little room behind the court and left to wait. She had but one dreary victory to contemplate. With everyone who had questioned her she had maintained a stony silence. The police, the man from the department, a woman welfare worker, her mother and Noonah—she might have talked with her sister if she had not suspected that Noonah would take the tale straight back to the police and the others who wanted to pry into her affairs. And Trilby had decided recklessly that she would rather stay at the jail for ever than give strangers the right to shake their heads over her.

She paced the tiny room restlessly, her impatience growing as the minutes passed. After a half-hour spent entirely alone she felt urged to one more act of revolt against those who held her a prisoner. A chair had served her before. It should serve her now. She snatched up the one she had been sitting on and swung it over her head. The crash of wood against wood broke the numbing silence. Breathing quickly, her grey eyes slits beneath her frowning brows, she waited.

The door of the little room opened. A strange startled face peered round the edge of it. 'Hello! What's going on in here?'

'Mind your own business, stickybeak,' Trilby snarled, and the face, looking even more startled, withdrew. Trilby did not recognize the man. She did not care who he was. But her act of violence calmed her a little. When finally she was led into court by one of the officers, she felt almost cheerful. The sight of her mother and her father sitting at the back of the courtroom added to this. She gave them her brilliant dazzling smile and watched their expression change from tired bewilderment to glad recognition.

Her part of the business was over quickly. She was a minor; it was her first offence and, moreover, the magistrate was favourably impressed by her slim uprightness and the smile that had given such beauty to her face. In justice, she could not be entirely spared, but the seven days she had already spent in the little jail was considered sufficient. She was free to go home with her parents.

Mr and Mrs Comeaway did not come off so well. Both were brought to stand before the clear-eyed magistrate and listen to his sternly-delivered homily. They were too confused and embarrassed to understand more than that this whole sorry affair might have been avoided if they had taken better care of their daughter. Neither was disposed to argue, and apparently the magistrate was satisfied to accept their wondering silence as agreement. With a curt nod he dismissed them. They were free to collect Trilby and to take her home.

'Your hands, Trilby,' Noonah cried when once they were home. The hands that Trilby had taken such care to keep out of sight were examined with compassion. Perturbed and impatient, Trilby saw that Noonah was crying.

She dragged her hands away and put them behind her back. 'That's nothing! I did it getting the stones out of the wall. I suppose they told you that.'

215

More tears waited to fall. 'Trilby, I hate them too. I know you didn't deserve to be put in jail. Those policemen were beastly. I hated them. And they'll never get you again.'

Trilby remembered her first night in jail and smiled wryly. 'Don't be a fool. I broke that glass, didn't I?'

'Never mind,' Noonah said passionately. 'They were horrible and Dad went mad.'

'He didn't get me out,' Trilby observed drily.

'He helped,' Noonah said swiftly. 'He called in at the office nearly every day, just to tell them about you and how you weren't a bad girl at all.'

Trilby smiled. Her eyes watched her sister narrowly. She wondered if now would be a good time.

'You know what's wrong with me, don't you?' she said roughly. 'I'm going to have a baby.'

With a sort of sour pleasure, she watched the shock in Noonah's face. And admired unwillingly when she saw that Noonah instantly conquered her shock and allowed only her affection to show in her eyes.

'Does Mummy know?'

Trilby shrugged. 'They soon will.'

'Do you want me to tell them? Trilby,' she reached for her sister with impulsive hands. 'Trilby, I'm sorry if you don't want it. What about your—the man...Does he...'

'He doesn't know and he's not here,' Trilby said shortly. 'He won't be back for a long time—and I don't want him back. See?'

'Yes.' Noonah's eyes were puzzled.

216

'And when it's over I'm going off somewhere,' Trilby said defiantly. 'The baby can go to a mission. It isn't mine really. I didn't want it. I don't even want to see it. Another six months of *this*,' she finished savagely, looking down at her still flat stomach. 'I'm sick—nothing I eat tastes good. I hate this baby before it's even born. And there's still six months to go.'

'Trilby, you shouldn't talk like that. You can't hate babies. It's not the baby's fault. Can't you see...'

Trilby interrupted her sister. 'You don't understand anything.'

'You can give it to us if you don't want it,' Noonah said childishly. 'We'll have it.'

Trilby gave her sister a long straight look. 'It's my baby and it's going to a mission.'

Noonah's bottom lip trembled. 'Don't, Trilby. Don't let's talk about it yet.'

'All right! I don't want to talk about it.'

'I'll get you some books from the hospital. You can read them.'

'Okay!' Trilby picked up a comic, lay back on her bed pretending to read it. She had just remembered school. Of course she could not go back now. She'd made a muck of things. Behind the comic the long grey eyes stared blindly.

'What'll er father say?' Mrs Comeaway moaned, when she knew about the baby. 'Blame me as usual, I spose. An I kept telling er not to go gallivantin about, specially night-times. Warned er bout them sailors too. Dunno what more e expecks. Gawd, no wonder she run amuck, always bein

217

full of erself and what she was gunna do after she took this exam. Poor kid! You listen ta me, Noonah, an don't you go getting yaself in no fix like that. It's always the girl's left ta look after the babies when they come.' She flashed a look of inquiry at Noonah. 'She tell you who done it?'

'Just that he's gone away and she doesn't want him back. I don't think she likes him, Mum.'

'Musta liked im one time,' Mrs Comeaway said with weary worldliness. 'You can't tell em but. Think ya just an ole fool tryin ta spoil their bit a fun.'

Noonah went over to the stove and pushed another piece of wood under the kettle.

'Yeah, that's right,' Mrs Comeaway said gratefully. 'We'll make a nice cuppa tea.'

'I wish it had been me,' Noonah told her mother fiercely. 'I'd love a baby.'

'Gawd, don't you start,' Mrs Comeaway said comically. 'Let's get this one over first. An you oughtn'tta talk like that anyway, girl. Ya might bring something down on yaself.'

'You don't have to worry about me,' Noonah said bleakly. 'All the boys I see round act as if they're frightened of me.'

'An a good thing too,' Mrs Comeaway pronounced.

Noonah was not so sure. If training to be a nurse cut you off from other youngsters, she was not so sure she wanted to be one.

Mr Comeaway reacted with a flood of anger that covered every inmate of the house, except the cause of it. 'I tole you,'

218

he said furiously, 'ta keep a good eye on er. She's just a bit of a kid and doesn't know what goes on. That damn fool Hannie oughta keep er two away fum ours, gettin Trilby mixed up with their bunch. Ya know the tricks they get up to, careerin round them sandhills, stayin out all night fa all that silly fool Hannie cares.'

'Don't you come that bullyin with me,' Mrs Comeaway defended herself, standing like a battleship before him. 'After all it's ony nacheral, ain't it? Happened ta plenty before Trilby. Gunna happen ta plenty more.'

'Who done it?' Mr Comeaway demanded.

'Ain't no father,' Mrs Comeaway said shortly. 'She don't want no father for it.'

'Ya mean she don't *know?*'

'He went away, Dad,' Noonah said nervously. Apart from the nights when her father grew uproariously argumentative after a night on the conto, this was the first time she had heard him in a rage.

'Bicrikey, if I get me hands on im,' he smouldered. 'Why wouldn't she tell ya who the bastard was? Dunno what everyone's gunna think. First jail, an now this.'

'All *your* pals is too busy thinkin bout their own mistakes ta bother much bout other peoples,' Mrs Comeaway informed him. 'An now shutup. I ad enough. I'm gunna drink me tea.'

'An you'll be next, I spose,' Mr Comeaway said unhappily, at Noonah.

'I just tole er,' Mrs Comeaway said imperturbably. 'Not till we get this one over. An not then less she likes ta make a fool of erself. Come on girl, stop starin an sit down. An

219

call that Trilby out. Won't do er no arm ta get a cuppa tea inside erself.'

Noonah's face felt hot. She got a few cups down from the sink and set them out on the table.

'You don't know bout things like that do ya?' Mr Comeaway's face was unhappy. His eyes had a wounded look.

'Keep ya big mouth closed,' Mrs Comeaway said sharply. 'She don't wanta learn fum you, anyway.'

Trilby would not come out. Noonah took her tea into the bedroom, then she returned to the living-room to have hers with her mother and her father. The three of them sat round the kitchen table holding the heavy cups, sipping the steaming brew.

'Saw Mrs Green today,' Mrs Comeaway said in a normal conversational tone. 'Know what ole Skippy bought isself last pension day? If e didn't turn up in one a them furry ats. An a feather in it, believe it or not. Said at last e's gotta at what don't fall down over is eyes. Real pleased with isself.'

Mr Comeaway broke into delighted laughter. 'I seen im hoppin down the main street,' he said. 'An later on I seen im goin ell fa leather up that hill. Dunno ow e does it with them legs a his.'

'Mrs Green says e's always yappin bout is house. What e isn't gunna do when e gets it. An ain't no one been able ta make im understand it's gunna be built up the camp.'

'Someone oughta go in an tell that partment man,' Mr Comeaway brooded. 'Ole man like im buildin up is hopes.'

Mrs Comeaway stared at her husband in derision. 'Ya think that man ain't in the same boat as us? Don't tell me.'

Mr Comeaway chuckled again.

Mrs Comeaway pushed her cup across the table to Noonah. 'Ya know, I miss that ole place we had, up there with Mrs Green. Ya feel a bit out of it down ere.'

'Trilby will be company for you,' Noonah reminded her mother.

Mrs Comeaway looked uneasily at the wall that divided the living-room from the girls' bedroom. 'She's me own daughter, an I wouldn't say a word against er, but I tell ya what. I ain't lookin forward ta that. Not the way she's feelin.' Her face brightened a little. 'Wonder what it'll be. Girl babies is nice—easy ta have, too. I always liked a little girl. Bet young Stella will too. Like another doll ta that one.' She stopped suddenly, looked at Noonah and at her husband in turn, and began to laugh.

'What's a matter with you?' Mr Comeaway asked heavily, looking up from his tea.

Mrs Comeaway lowered her voice to a whisper. 'Just thought of it. She's gunna make something on the deal. What about that dowment?'

Noonah looked worried. 'Mummy, she's going to send the baby away as soon as it's born. To a mission.'

'Send it away soon as it's born?' Mrs Comeaway was scandalized. 'She ain't gunna do no such thing. Bit later, if she wants to. Not while it's little.'

'I knew you'd say that, Mum.' Noonah's voice was jubilant.

'What's she comin at, sendin a baby off ta some mission?' Mr Comeaway wanted to know. 'Can't she look after it erself?'

'I spose I can help me own daughter raise er baby,' Mrs Comeaway bridled.

'She doesn't want it.' Noonah shrugged her shoulders.

'Lotta rubbish,' declared Mrs Comeaway. 'We gotta good house, ain't we? Plenty a room?'

'Got some idea in er head,' Mr Comeaway said darkly. 'Fum that Audrena, most likely.'

'You wait,' Mrs Comeaway told them. 'She won't wanta send that baby away once she's seen it. Look at young Blanchie. She was the same way, wasn't she? You try an get that baby away from er but.'

'I remember,' Mr Comeaway's face wore an embarrassed grin. 'Babies is funny all right, but when they belong to ya—I dunno. Something different bout em then. Remember when we was worried bout young Bartie, eh?'

'That was when e had the stummick trouble,' Mrs Comeaway said. 'Didn't think we was gunna keep im. An that woulda been the third boy I lost in a row, just because round that time, after we had you two girls, we was wantin one. Joe was, anyway, wasn't ya, Joe?'

'I spose.' Mr Comeaway was still embarrassed.

'How did you lose them, Mummy?'

'Stummick trouble mostly,' Mrs Comeaway said matter-of-factly. 'Ain't much ya can do bout that once they get real bad.'

222

Noonah nodded. She had seen many children hospital-
ized because of stomach trouble. 'Enteritis,' she told her
mother. 'It's caused through...'

'Damn thing,' Mrs Comeaway pondered. 'Seems ta
hop fum one to the other, too. There's seasons for it I spose,
just like ya get colds when it's wet and blowy. Nothin you
can do bout it.'

Noonah compressed her lips, and vowed silently that
the new baby wouldn't get enteritis, not if she could help it.

'Ya don't bring any of ya friends down fum the
hospital,' Mr Comeaway said suddenly. 'Why don't ya do
that, Noonah?'

Mrs Comeaway threw an uneasy glance in the direction of the house next door. 'Ah, ya either got em stickin to
ya like feathers ta honey, or they lookin down their noses
at ya like you was dirt.'

'I don't want them down here anyhow,' Noonah said
indifferently. 'I see enough of them all day long.'

'Eyein ya like you was a dog with two tails,' Mrs
Comeaway grumbled softly. 'Mind,' she told her daughter,
'you wanta have some girl down ere, you can have er. You
just let me know, an I'll be off out fa the day.'

Noonah laughed. 'Well you can just stay home, because
I'm not asking anyone.'

'Not ta speak of them serve yets, which I ain't got
any.'

Noonah was giggling. The atmosphere was clearing
again. Trilby's baby wasn't nearly as big a piece of trouble
as she had imagined it might be. Her mother would handle

223

that as she handled everything else. Comfortably, with no fuss and bother.

'I just thought,' Mr Comeaway brooded over his second cup of tea. 'I just thought.'

The last drop of bitterness in Trilby's cup was in having her Aunt Hannie and the rest of Hannie's family move in to the house in the Wild-Oat Patch. She thought the invasion had come about because her mother, no less than her aunt, now considered her no better and her opinions no more important than anyone else's.

In fact, Mrs Comeaway had felt an urgent need for company more cheerful than Trilby's promised to be during the next few months, and Hannie, never a strong opposer of other people's wishes, had at last allowed herself to be persuaded that life in a real house held luxury and ease far beyond her imaginings.

As far as the elder Comeaways were concerned, the enlargement of their *ménage* had been entirely successful. Mr Comeaway found that company right in the house was a fine and handy thing to have. It made unnecessary the long walk into the town and the longer and more arduous walk up Heartbreak Hill. He and his brother spent companionable hours discussing the things most important to them, and as the long summer days shrank to the cooler ones of winter they settled into a pleasant routine. In the mornings they sat on the back steps, and in the afternoon, when the sun moved over, they sat on the front steps.

Often, they planned to go down to the wharf and get themselves a job. Several times, they actually hitched their pants higher round their waists and set off, just a little too late to be among the men picked to work on the ships that day. They could always blame the women for their late start and even before they left the house they were openly pessimistic about their chances and self-righteously indignant that they had not been woken earlier.

When they found their pessimism most gratifyingly justified they walked on into the town, seeing they were this far already, and if they did not see anyone they cared for on the main street they most times took the bit between their teeth and bolted up Heartbreak Hill to the humpies and temporary camps scattered in the bush behind it.

Back home again some time in the late afternoon or evening, depending on hospitality offered, they shook their heads regretfully over their inability to get jobs. 'Never could expect to,' Mr Comeaway would say reproachfully, 'not *that* time in the morning.' And according to whether Mrs Comeaway herself had enjoyed her day, she either accepted the implied reproof in the proper spirit or counter-accused.

Not that there was any need for real worry about jobs for the men. Noonah's money came in regularly and so did the child endowment. And there were plenty of extras like relatives and friends arriving for a holiday with two or three months' pay in their pockets. Mr Comeaway thoroughly enjoyed acting as host, differentiating not a whit between friends and relatives with money and friends and relatives without. The main thing was having company.

It followed naturally, too, that the Comeaways' fame as hosts spread and there were weeks when the house seemed never to be free of guests.

In between times, Mrs Comeaway felt she could have done with a little more of liveliness in her chosen companion, but on the whole the two women managed to live together in the same house remarkably well, with an immense tolerance and good humour on the part of Mrs Comeaway and a noteworthy capacity for listening on the part of Hannie. Hannie never argued nor put forth her opinions. She was perfectly happy with Mrs Comeaway's even when these changed from day to day and sometimes from minute to minute.

'Better than the damn cat,' Mrs Comeaway told her husband. 'Even if she don't talk much ya know she understands ya lanwidge.'

On the other hand, her aunt irritated Trilby to the point of frenzy, and the girl would spend hours of her time in her own room rather than be forced to look at her aunt slip-slopping about the house in her draggle-tailed dresses, her hair hanging like greasy black snakes on her greasy fat neck, her shoes, when she wore them, too loose on her large awkward feet. Work, to Hannie, was a trap into which only the unwary fell, but in a household where

227

the accent was on comfort rather than on spotless cleanliness she annoyed nobody but Trilby with this deep-rooted dislike of exertion.

Blanchie's baby was the pet of the entire household, apt to find himself swung up from the floor and soundly hugged by whoever tripped over him. Since one of Blanchie's friends had just lately rolled over on her own baby one night and suffocated it, Tommy slept on a couple of chairs alongside his mother's bed, safe from this danger if not from falling through or over the edge of the chairs.

Audrena went into the double bed with Stella and Bartie, and with this bed wedged tightly against the wall, room had thus been made for the tall double bed which belonged to Charlie and Hannie.

Trilby had refused indignantly to share her room with anyone but Noonah, so Blanchie had to make do with the living-room, but as everyone who used the living-room made do with her bed as a sort of settee, the arrangement was really quite satisfactory. And it still left plenty of floor-space for the accommodation of out-of-town holiday-makers and casual droppers-in.

One of these out-of-town friends had recently embroiled the whole family in a lot of trouble. The Comeaways had had much difficulty proving to the police that they had had nothing to do with a certain robbery involving the premises of a golf club. Nothing, that is, apart from innocently partaking of the spoils.

The true culprit was eventually forced to take full responsibility, but on the day of his trial Mrs Comeaway still smarted. 'Ain't nothin ta say ya can't cook a few chops

228

if someone brings ya some,' she said indignantly, sweeping the back veranda with unusual vigour.

The line of men dangling their legs over the edge turned their heads away from the clouds of dust. 'Lucky fa young Willie it's gettin to the end a summer,' one of them ruminated. 'That jail gets awful hot some a them summer days.'

'Bicrikey, you was lucky ta get outa that, Joe,' Dusty Dodd said, shaking his head. Dusty had just come back from a trip to Perth to see his wife who was in hospital. Three hundred and fifty miles by taxi had chewed quite a hole in his pay packet, but there was still some money left, and Dusty was staying with the Comeaways until it had been spent.

'Ask me, that Willie's a real bad one,' Charlie said heavily. Charlie was remembering that his commands to Audrena to get off to bed had had no effect alongside Willie's invitation to her to go for a walk along the beach.

'Gee, it's got some kick, that stuff,' Mr Comeaway said approvingly. 'I ain't never tasted that whisky before. Jus as well them pleece didn't show up an start askin their questions after ole Horace got a taste of it. Woulda landed someone sure. I just knew e was ripe for a bit of a do.'

'You too,' Mrs Comeaway stopped to berate him. 'You'd a got us all in trouble if I hadn't kep pokin ya with me elbow. Talk bout Horace. You was lookin fa trouble two days after. An ya know them monarch have ya up soon as look at ya. That's the way they get ta be sergeants, pinchin people.'

'Not me,' Mr Comeaway said comfortably. 'They wouldn't pinch me. They know I don't go round makin trouble.'

'Dunno so much bout that,' Mrs Comeaway said acidly. 'Ya pretty free with ya fists when ya had a few.'

Hannie appeared in the doorway.

'That meat smells like it might be burning,' she said mildly.

'Fa Gawd's sake put a bit more water in it well,' Mrs Comeaway told her.

Hannie nodded amiably and disappeared.

'Better do it meself,' Mrs Comeaway said resignedly, following her. She grabbed for the saucepan whilst Hannie stood meditating before a shelf of crockery.

Mighty snarlings and cracklings filled the air as Mrs Comeaway held the saucepan under the cold water tap.

'Was just lookin for somethin ta get the water in,' Hannie said apologetically.

'I fixed it now. Ya can go back an sit down.'

The hint of worry disappeared from Hannie's brow. She settled herself gratefully on her chair before the stove.

'Never can make out what goes on in your head,' Mrs Comeaway said good-naturedly, stirring the contents of the saucepan. 'Always sittin about thinkin. Ya don't seem ta know alf what's goin on.'

'Dunno that you'd call it thinkin,' Hannie disparaged. 'I just like ta sit where it's warm.'

Mrs Comeaway chuckled. 'One thing, ya don't do much harm jus sittin. It's when ya up an about ya get in me way.'

Hannie listened attentively. Now that the move had been made, she had settled down into contentment again.

230

She would have been equally content in the humpy or back in the bush camp.

Trilby spent more and more time in her room. She hated anyone, especially men, to see her in her present condition, and the house seemed always full of visitors. Most of them she had never seen before, and she liked their rough good humour no more than she liked their curious glances.

The visits of the police had reawakened the nightmare of her own stay in jail: heightened the feeling she had of being caught in a trap. So far she had found no way out.

Examining her face in the mirror she brooded over the shape of her features and the colour of her skin. She was lighter-skinned than many of the others. She had seen white girls with deeper toning. Perhaps, down in Perth, she might be accepted as a white person. Would her flattish nose give her away, or the short square white teeth? Fretfully, anxiously, she would peer at herself in the mirror; colour her lips with red to hide the tint of dusty purple that she hated; try out a trace of pink on her cheek-bones, varnish her shell-pink nails the same bright red as her lips.

She practised walking, holding herself high and proud. A lot of the girls she knew walked like old women, shoulders forward, knees bent, in a kind of shamed shamble.

Sometimes she would rise from the bed sick with herself, seeing herself besmirched with the colour and the features of the aborigine, certain that nothing but frustration lay ahead of her.

It was during one of the latter periods that she first accompanied Bartie on one of his rambling walks. She had followed him on a swift impulse, and when he sat a short distance from a tree that had blown almost horizontal with the ground and proceeded to draw it, she thought him quite mad. Bartie acknowledged her presence with a shy grin, presently losing himself in his work, so that he forgot she was there. Trilby drew closer, watched the wind-swept tree appear again on paper, and was interested in spite of herself.

After that first time she went with him often, and a sort of comradeship grew up between them. Gregarious by nature, Trilby craved company even whilst she shunned it. Bartie asked no questions. He was quite simply uninterested in anything outside his drawing and painting. He had to be quicker than lightning to catch the curl of a wave before it broke. And he needed all his concentration to get down on paper what that wave meant to do. Trilby's interest grew, and whilst she was with Bartie she shared, in some strange way, his inner peace and his quiet happiness.

At home she rebuffed every attempt at friendliness. She could endure neither her mother's frank comments on her changing shape, nor Audrena's sly eyes that always slid to her belly. Once, in answer to a sneer, she rushed at her cousin with a hot flat-iron, but her mother grabbed her wrist and made her drop the awful weapon. She fled from Mrs Comeaway's impatient and irritable scolding, though if she had stayed she would have heard a second being delivered to Audrena. There were no flies on Mrs Comeaway, and she had not missed any of Audrena's attempts to upset Trilby's hard-won control.

Towards Noonah, Trilby felt an impatient and grudging gratitude. With gentle consideration, Noonah skipped side issues and concerned herself only with present problems. She informed her sister of all that lay ahead of her, what she could expect in physical changes and sensations, and she anxiously minimized the pain of the actual delivery. Trilby was interested in spite of herself in a book Noonah gave her about methods of painless child-delivery.

Noonah gave her other things, too. Small-scale clothing for the new arrival, half a dozen napkins, a dainty pink and white frock. Trilby was not interested in these things. She stuffed them away in her drawer, out of sight.

Sometimes, lying on her bed in the dark, hearing Noonah's quiet breathing alongside her, Trilby fought out a private war inside herself. In the hiding dark she wanted to pour out all her doubts and fears—tell her sister exactly what had happened—question Noonah, why? Sometimes she had to bite her lips to keep back the flood. She would not give in. She would not allow anyone to see the weakness in her.

Allow Noonah to know that she had gone into this thing with eyes only half open, like any stupid, ignorant black-nigger girl? No! And again, no! It was the stupidity Trilby could not forgive in herself. Badness, wickedness, anything was excusable except plain downright stupidity.

In her own bed, Noonah was always conscious of Trilby's tenseness. She thought it was because Trilby hated to share her room and, though this was no fault of hers, she tried to make amends. She told her sister amusing things that had happened at the hospital, coaxed Trilby to tell her what went on at home. Once she was started, Trilby

233

could keep Noonah amused and entertained for a couple of hours. It took only a description of Hannie sitting in her chair nodding her head and agreeing with everything Mrs Comeaway said for Noonah to have to stifle her giggles in her pillow.

'And lazy!' Trilby said one night on a breath of scorn. 'You know everywhere she's been by the stuff she leaves behind her. She doesn't even pull the chain in the lav. If she puts on a dress and it's inside out she just leaves it that way. She's always wrapping up little parcels of rubbish and leaving them on the sink so she won't have to go outside to the bin. And Mum is always coming across them and stuffing them away in the food safe. I found three lots of tea-leaves there yesterday. Mum seems to like her but I think she's crackers. She falls off her chair asleep every time she has a bit of conto, she lets people cheat her at cards, she just smiles when Uncle Charlie yells terrible things to her, and one day she let Stella eat a whole tin of condensed milk so that she was sick. Mum says her trouble is she's too good-natured. I think her whole trouble is in her head.'

'She *is* kind,' Noonah decided. 'What's Blanchie like?'

'Blanchie's like a young Auntie Hannie. Tommy nearly choked the other day on something she gave him to play with, and Mum had to pick him up and bang him on the back to make him cough it up. Blanchie just stood there giggling.'

'She was nervous,' Noonah said, with quick sympathy. 'I think she really loves Tommy.'

'Mum does,' Trilby told her sister. 'Every time she goes out she buys something for him. Every time she's got money,

234

that is. There isn't much around here except when you come home. God knows how we eat.'

'Doesn't Dad work at all?' Noonah asked, troubled.

'Doesn't want work, if you ask me,' Trilby said shortly. 'He keeps saying he's going to get up early and go down to the wharf, but he never does. That's since Uncle Charlie came. They don't do anything but sit around on the veranda or take little walks up to the town. Dad wins some money at cards sometimes. They gamble just about every night. If they don't have money they use matches or razor-blades or even their clothes. Dad lost his good trousers the other night, and he would have lost that big coat too if Mum hadn't hidden it. Not that she doesn't go mad about cards too. She's as bad as the rest. She just likes that coat to put over her feet at night.'

'Does Dad lose often?'

'You've seen him,' Trilby said indifferently. 'All depends who he's playing with. Dad plays so fast I can't follow him, and sometimes I think he wins because nobody else can follow him either. When they've been at it a while you wouldn't disturb them if you dropped a cart-load of bricks alongside the table. The only time they talk is when someone's brought a few bottles. Then they start arguing and won't always pay up if someone else wins. I always go to bed, but I can hear them through the wall. If there's an argument I lock the door. One night some woman came wandering in looking for a mirror. She woke me up when she put the light on. She had her eyes all bunged up and her nose was bleeding. Mum told me her husband gave her a thrashing because she tried to take his cards.'

'What did she want a mirror for?' Noonah wondered.

Trilby sniffed. 'Said she had to breathe on it so she'd know she was alive. Told me she read it in some book she got hold of.'

Noonah let out a delighted giggle then she sobered. 'Do they wander into the kids' room too?'

'Mum keeps them out of there,' Trilby said significantly. 'A man went in one night and woke them up. They were playing for pennies that night and he'd been winning.' She smiled unwillingly. 'He said he had too many and they were too heavy to carry, so he was going to give some to the kids. Stella got frightened and yelled, and Mum rushed out and told him off, and then Dad came out and there was nearly a fight. I was scared stiff with all the noise and shouting. I thought the police might come because the whole street must have heard them.'

'Dad had a right to keep him out of the kids' room but.'

'Dad shouldn't have encouraged him to come here,' Trilby gloomed. 'We have some awful people here some-times. You should have seen some we had last week. All the women bring their kids, and so they'll get some peace they open up their blouses and let those kids feed from their chests right in front of everyone.' She shuddered. 'They make me feel sick.'

'It shouldn't,' Noonah said mildly. 'That's the best food most of those babies get.'

'These aren't babies,' Trilby said scornfully. 'They're up to three and four and five, and they sit on the edge of the table and hold those women's tits up to their mouths and suck and drool—I can't *help* feeling sick.'

Noonah was silent. In the dark, her hand went to her own small, firm breast. She wondered, with a little shamed thrill, how long it would be before she felt the warm mouth of a baby drawing its nourishment from her.

'Mum told me about a little boy who'd turned six and still wanted his mummy's tit. But even she thought he was too old, so she stopped him by painting a big black face on her chest. When she undid her buttons and dragged it out he got such a fright he ran screaming.' Noonah heard the distaste in her sister's voice and was glad Trilby could not see her own highly-amused expression.

'Noonah!'

'Yes?'

'I liked being home at first, and still can't help liking Mum and Dad—you know the way they are—we have fun sometimes still. And Bartie's not a bad kid, or Stella either. But I hate all those people who come round.'

'Mrs Green has a lot of people at her place, too. She says they just come, and how can she send them away.'

'Some of them look so rough and awful,' Trilby brooded. 'And they tell me they're my "lations".' She mimicked one of them. '"I'm your lation, gal. Ya mummy's my lation an so's you." Some of them want to give me money. A few have such big rolls of notes after they get their cheques changed at the bank. I suppose some of them aren't too bad.' Her voice was reluctant. 'I must say they make the place a bit more cheerful, the nice ones. But one old woman frightened the life out of me. She would keep talking about "hairy men". She said I must never go outside at night if I heard birds calling or whistling because likely they were "hairy men" waiting to catch me. She said you can always tell. She said she threw a stone at an emu once and the emu ducked, and that's how she knew it was a "hairy man" because emus are too stupid to duck stones. She said it chased her.'

'Gee!' Noonah said, impressed.

'She was so dirty, too. Even Auntie Hannie looked clean and tidy alongside her. She used to follow me about and get me to listen to these terrible stories that I just don't believe. She said she was staying at a camp once when there'd been a drought and there wasn't much food about, and she saw a man drag a baby away from its mother and throw it straight on the fire. And after—he ate it. That wouldn't be true, would it, Noonah?'

'That's silly,' Noonah said stoutly. 'You ask Mum. I bet if you'd told Mum what she was talking about Mum would have got her out of here.'

'Don't be silly,' Trilby derided. 'She frightened Mum just as much as she frightened me. And Mum believed her, specially about the "hairy men". She said she didn't, but I knew she did.'

'I don't.'

'And she told me the way to get rid of a baby is to put dirt in its mouth as soon as it's born, or chew up some bread until it's soft and mix it up with tobacco and let the baby suck it. And I could have killed her for the way she looked at me, as if she thought I might do the same. But she's gone, thank goodness. She must have started on Dad one day because he got wild and called her a dirty black nigger. She looked at him just as if next minute she was going to spring at him, then she went down the path yelling back at us and swearing every other word. And she shook her fist at Dad. I think it was what he called her that made her get in such a rage. She was just a fool!'

'A fool?'

'Yes, every time she talked about herself she called herself a black nigger, but because Dad said the same thing she went crazy at him. I thought she was going to have a fit. Right here. Her eyes...,' Trilby hesitated, 'and her mouth with white spit all round it as if she'd sucked soap. You know what, Noonah? I hated her then, but I was sorry for her too.'

'Why ever?'

Trilby's barriers were down. What she was saying now was coming from inside her, from the sore hurting spot that questioned and could not accept that a coloured skin made you different—and inferior to white people.

'Because I knew how she felt. I even know why she could call herself a black nigger. She had to keep saying it, to try and fool people into thinking she didn't care, and that it didn't matter to her if she was black or white or any other colour. And that was so they wouldn't call her that if they wanted to hurt her. I don't think she'd have cared what else Dad called her, so long as it wasn't that. Black nigger! Imagine, Noonah! Even a poor, dirty, skinny old witch like she is still doesn't want to be called a nigger.' Trilby sat up in bed and her voice was fierce. 'If anyone called me that I'd *kill* them.'

'I just hope she never comes back,' Noonah said worriedly. Her thoughts were occupied with Bartie and Stella. She had hardly heard Trilby's last words.

Trilby was instantly hurt and furious. 'Don't you ever think about the colour you are?' she demanded passionately.

Noonah was getting drowsy and was not so sensitive to Trilby's change of mood as she might otherwise have been.

'What's the use?' she yawned.

Trilby let herself trembling down on to her pillow. For a long moment she was bathed in humiliation. Again, her own fault. What was the use, as Noonah had just said? Of anything! Especially telling anyone the way you felt. She tried to stiffen herself to resentment, but a forlorn sense of betrayal brought a rush of tears to her eyes. Behind her closed lids they forced a way out, ran endlessly down her cheeks to her pillow. And Noonah slept.

EIGHTEEN

It was midweek, and Mr Comeaway was alternately yawning and wishing that the rain would stop long enough for him and his brother to take a walk down to the town. If he did get down there he was darned if he wouldn't go into that Employment Agency and try to get himself a job somewhere. A man got tired of sitting about the house, specially on a rainy day. Mrs Comeaway had kept the children home from school: Blanchie's Tommy was crawling around on the floor, Blanchie and Audrena were sprawled on the settee-bed reading magazines and comics, the women were sitting as close as they could get to the stove, and Charlie was taking a rest on his bed under a pile of old clothes. Besides not being able to take a step without falling over someone—Bartie was lying right in the centre of the floor—Mr Comeaway did not care for the company. He felt alert and restless, not in the least like taking a nap, and he was conscious of active resentment towards Charlie for leaving him alone with a lot of women and children.

He cast a hot, angry look about the room. Mag, mag, mag. Yap, yap, yap. And nobody else getting any warmth out of the stove with those two sitting almost on top of it. He hesitated, toying with the idea of pushing his chair between the two Mrs Comeaway and Hannie occupied, disturbing them from their seeming content. Then he grunted, rose and stamped over to the doorway, where he stood looking gloomily out at the slicing silver rain. And then a figure sloped up the street and turned in at the gate.

Mr Comeaway's face brightened. It was a man, anyway. And who? The figure reached the shelter of the porch and lifted its head.

'Phyllix Barclay!' Mr Comeaway welcomed warmly. 'Fa Gawd's sake come in an dry yaself off a bit.'

Phyllix moved over the veranda, smiling and shaking water from the coat he was taking off. 'Trilby home?' he asked eagerly. 'Thought I'd come down an see her for a bit.'

'Trilby?' Mr Comeaway said vaguely. 'Trilby's here, of course. Too wet ta be anywhere else, ain't it?'

'Course she's here.' Mrs Comeaway came over to the door and examined the visitor curiously. 'Bit wet, ain't ya? Better come in an dry off a bit.'

'Where's Trilby?' Phyllix asked, looking round the room.

'Layin on er bed readin, I spose,' Mrs Comeaway told him. She raised her voice: 'You in there, Trilby?'

'What's wrong?' Trilby called back. The door of her room opened and she stood peering out. Moving over to

242

the doorway of the living-room she caught sight of Phyllix and her face went ash-grey. Phyllix started towards her, but Trilby backed quickly, slamming the door shut in his face.

He stood there for a second stupidly, then turned back to the wondering Comeaways. 'What's the matter with her?'

'Don't take no notice a that,' Mrs Comeaway shrugged. 'She's actin funny lately. Gunna have a baby; that's why, I spose. Maybe she feel sick today.'

'Maybe all you women might get up off ya behinds an make a man a cuppa tea or somethin,' Mr Comeaway said testily. 'Shiverin cold e is, an ya don't do nothin but stand there an mag.' He winked at Phyllix. 'Get on ya ruddy pip, these old womans. Always having ta keep em up ta the mark, a man is.' He swept a clutter of clothes from a chair-seat and swung the chair over to the stove. 'There y'are.'

'There goes ya good coat,' Mrs Comeaway told Hannie, glaring at her husband.

Hannie looked hazily over at her daughters. 'Jus pick up me coat, will ya?' she asked. Blanchie reached down to the floor and yanked at the coat. She settled it round her feet and went on with her reading. Audrena sat back on her heels and looked boldly over at Phyllix, but Phyllix was unnoticing. 'Trilby married?' he said hoarsely.

Mr Comeaway looked back at him, surprised at his tone. 'Not yet she ain't.'

'You mind if I go in her room? I gotta message for her. Friend a hers told me ta be sure.' Each sentence was jerky.

243

'Won't get no change outa that one,' Mrs Comeaway said practically. 'Go in if ya like.'

Shining-eyed, moist-lipped, Audrena watched Phyllix as he went quickly back on to the veranda. She swung her feet over the side of the bed as if to follow him.

'No ya don't,' Mrs Comeaway ordered. 'You stay outa her room. Ya know she don't like ya in there.'

'What's e want, anyway?' Mr Comeaway asked of nobody in particular. 'Ain't e actin a bit queer?'

'An you keep ya nose out things too,' Mrs Comeaway said firmly. 'She don't want im in there, she don't ave ta ave im. You leave that to er.'

'If she don't want im in there, e's gunna come out with a flea in is ear,' Audrena snickered.

Mrs Comeaway swept the girl with a look of dislike and irritation, but she said no more.

There was something going on here which she did not entirely understand, but she was not going to buy into it until she had to.

Phyllix tried a soft knock at Trilby's door but this brought no response, so he quietly turned the handle.

Trilby was lying across the bed with an opened magazine before her. She looked up at him, and for a moment eyed him with a steady gaze. Then she bent her head to the magazine again.

Phyllix moved farther into the room. 'They said ya gunna have a baby,' he said slowly.

Trilby's body stiffened, but she would not speak.

'Trilby, what's wrong? What's the matter with ya?'

'I suppose I can lay on my bed if I want to, can't I?'

'Trilby, is it—was it me?'

Trilby raised her head again. There was scornful detachment in her face and a jeering at the back of her eyes. Whether directed at Phyllix or at herself even Trilby did not fully know.

'Not you,' she said carelessly. She laughed and leaned back on one elbow. 'What made you think it might be you? You're not the only pebble on the beach, are you?'

Phyllix's face was different now. He took Trilby by the shoulders and shook her. 'Who was it?' he asked softly. 'Who was it?'

Trilby tried to free herself. 'Leave me go,' she demanded indignantly. 'How do I know who it was? It wasn't you, that's all I know. You think I'd have a baby of yours? You get straight out of my room, you hear?'

'You been muckin round with other fellers,' Phyllix said, still in that quiet voice. 'Been muckin round with anyone liked to ask?' His fingers dug deep into the soft skin of her upper arms. He shook her again.

'Get out,' Trilby screamed. 'Mum! Dad! Come quick, he's hurting me.'

Phyllix slapped her across the face, not once, but several times. The pain of the slaps shocked Trilby into violence. Springing off the bed she went for him, kicking, biting, scratching, sobbing and screaming in turn. 'Don't you dare to touch me, you beast. I hate you, see? And I'll do it with whoever I like, but never, never you.' Like a cat, and as quickly, she avoided the hands that tried to pinion her and stood with her back against the wall, panting and fierce-eyed.

Her father, with the rest of the family solidly behind him, stopped open-mouthed on the threshold of the room, then he dived at Phyllix. 'For Gawd's sake,' he said, 'what's goin on in here?' He gripped Phyllix and swung the boy away from Trilby. The three were panting now. 'Whatya wanta do a thing like that for?' Mr Comeaway asked again, a mighty puzzlement outweighing all other emotions.

Phyllix switched his attention to Mr Comeaway. 'Who done it?'

'Who done what?' Mr Comeaway said irritably.

'Ya mean the baby?' Audrena said slyly from behind him. 'Why, we thought it was you, Phyllix. We all thought it was you.'

Trilby uttered a choked cry. Her face was grey again. She made for Audrena with upraised, clawing hands. Audrena yelped shrilly, with Trilby's hands twined tightly in her skimpy hair.

'You liar! You liar!' Trilby kept saying in a thin scream, and with each word she wrenched at Audrena's hair. Audrena recovered her wits, drew her finger-nails down each side of Trilby's face, leaving stripes of blood behind.

Phyllix's eyes went mad. He tried to get at Audrena. Mr Comeaway warded him off with one hand whilst he tried vainly to separate the two girls. 'You—get—out—of—my room,' Trilby said wildly, her fisted hands beating at her cousin's face. 'Dad, make her get out of my *room*.'

Mr Comeaway, comprehending no reason for the uproar, was out of his depths entirely, but his wife bounded into the fight with a wild cry, pulling Audrena off Trilby by main force. Trilby staggered, and Phyllix tried to steady her, but she flung him off.

In the background Hannie set up a wild caterwauling of her own.

'Fa Gawd's sake,' Mr Comeaway begged. 'Will everyone stop it.'

'*Charlie*,' he called desperately, '*Charlie!* Come in ere an give me a hand. *Charlie!*'

Charlie, wakened from a sound sleep, made Trilby's room in four jumps, pulled up sharp in the doorway and stood there pop-eyed with amazement.

'Don't just stand there,' Mr Comeaway puffed testily. 'Get that lot a yours quieted down, will ya?' He was having his work cut out holding Audrena back from a second attempt at Trilby. Phyllix was holding Trilby's struggling figure. Hannie had dropped her voice to a lower range and was yowling like a tired tom cat, and Mrs Comeaway was issuing orders to everyone in sight.

Bartie watched fascinated from behind a veranda post. Stella stood alongside him, holding two dolls by their legs. Blanchie had grabbed up Tommy and fled with him into the backyard.

Against the dividing fence, Mrs Henwood stood craning her neck, her mouth pursed and disapproving, her eyes, naked of their heavy lids, showing pleasure and awe.

It was a good ten minutes before Mr Comeaway and Charlie between them shouted the others into silence.

At the end of it all, Trilby was drooping with exhaustion, her wrists gripped in Phyllix's strong hands. From behind Mrs Comeaway Audrena still glared hatred at her cousin, her nostrils quivering, her hair a tangled whirl. Blanchie, with Tommy on her hip, ventured to peer round the doorway of the living-room. Hannie stood against a wall and examined with puzzled interest a foot that somebody had stamped upon.

'Now!' Mr Comeaway said. 'What was all *that* about, if ya don't mind?'

A utility with a monkey-cage at the back of it came to a standstill outside the front gate, and the atmosphere around the group changed to wary watchfulness. A policeman jumped out of the cab and came with business-like tread up the front path. 'Anything going on here?' he enquired menacingly as he approached. 'Neighbours rang to say you've been creating a disturbance. You better break it up or you can all come back to the station with me. Plenty of room in the cage.'

Mr Comeaway stepped forward, his smile conciliatory, his manner polite and deferential. 'No disturbance here. Just a bit of a quarrel between the family like.'

The officer glared disgustedly round at the dishevelled 'family'. He narrowed his gaze to the self-appointed leader. 'Saw you last week, didn't I? Weren't you connected with that breaking-and-entering up at the club?'

'We didn't have nothing ta do with that,' Mr Comeaway said with dignity. 'Not us.'

'H'm!' The man's eyes were sceptical. He gave the group another threatening look. 'Come on, now. Out with it. What was all this shindig about?'

Mrs Comeaway stood blank and frozen behind her husband. Charlie was as much in the dark as the officer and could only wet his lips and shuffle his feet. Audrena and Blanchie took slow steps backward, and Hannie took this new complication as one more mystery to be added to the rest. Trilby and Phyllix were half-hidden behind Mr and Mrs Comeaway.

Mr Comeaway took a deep breath. 'Ya don't want ta take no notice a the neighbours,' he said heartily. 'Gee, that wasn't nothin. Sort of a disagreement, that's all that was. We worked it out a while back.'

The officer took his heavy foot off the bottom step and placed it alongside its fellow. He seemed disinclined to relax any part of his monitory attitude. As if, now he had their undivided attention, his job was to hammer home his point so that they should never forget it. He grunted and swayed backward, still, however, holding them with a frosty blue eye.

The Comeaways held their breath and hoped.

'Look!' Mr Comeaway inclined his head with even more deference. 'I'll let it go this once, see?'

No one spoke a word.

'But no more rows, see? You kick up any more fuss around here and you'll end up at the station, the lot of you.'

'Yes, sir,' Mr Comeaway said meekly. He waited for a moment to allow his meekness to sink in before he added: 'Only this wasn't a *real* row, if ya get what I mean.'

'Real enough to have someone lay a complaint against you,' the officer said grimly. 'All right now! You lot keep the peace, understand?'

He flicked each face with his cutting look, swung round and stamped back down the path. The Comeaways

249

waited like statues until the utility had pulled out from the kerb and gone off down the street. Then they relaxed.

'There y'are, y'see.' Mr Comeaway swept his group with a disgusted eye. 'Nearly got us all in trouble.'

'How the hell did e get ere?' Charlie said, this last problem troubling him more than all the rest.

'That was er,' Mrs Comeaway said sagely, nodding her head in the direction of the Henwoods' neat house. 'Er an er pot plants,' she added scornfully. She moved to the edge of the veranda and darted a piercing look at the curtains that swayed gently behind Mrs Henwood's lounge windows. She took a deep breath, but before she could expel it in vituperation Mr Comeaway's black hand reached forth and plucked her back.

'You ain't had enough trouble?' he enquired fiercely. 'You wanta bring that monarch back?'

'None a her business,' Mrs Comeaway fumed, sailing majestically past her husband and into the living-room. 'An you keep them hands a yours off me.'

'All you women get inside an stay there,' Mr Comeaway ordered roughly. He turned back to Trilby's room and stood just outside, addressing himself to Phyllix and Trilby. 'An you two behave yaselves, see? Gawd!' he added to the attentive Charlie. 'I'm gettin outa this for a while.' He turned back to the two in the bedroom. 'An when I come back I don't wanta find no rows going on neether.'

A minute later, with Charlie in tow, he disappeared down the street, his old grey felt hat clapped on his head to keep off the last of the softly-falling rain.

Left alone, Trilby turned smouldering eyes on Phyllix. 'Well! You going to stay here all day long?'

Phyllix eyed the girl reflectively. 'You ain't been going out with other fellers. Why did ya tell me you had?'

Tears of weakness spurted into Trilby's eyes, but she blinked them back. Audrena's spitefulness had been a stab in the dark, she was sure of that. But she was equally certain that Phyllix would never believe, now, that the baby was not his. He could stand there and eye her with satisfaction and know that it was he who had done this to her—set a limit to what she could do, forced her to play a waiting game when she was so madly impatient for action.

She looked at him through a haze of nausea, and Phyllix stood there and, most hatefully, smiled at her.

With the quick dart of a lizard, Trilby spat in his face. 'You think I'd have a baby from you?' she asked, her eyes sick.

Phyllix wiped his cheek with his sleeve. 'I'm going now,' he said evenly. 'I'll be back when you've cooled off a bit.'

Trilby compelled her trembling legs to support her until he had gone, then she dropped on the bed. As she had done once before, she let the soft depths of it absorb her weight of misery.

'Ya think it mighta been him, that Phyllix?' Mr Comeaway asked his wife that night in the double bed.

Mrs Comeaway frowned into the darkness. 'Ya can bet ya boots I didn't arsk,' she said emphatically.

'What's gone wrong with er?' Mr Comeaway worried, 'ta carry on the way she did today? What's she got against that young bloke? Ain't e a nice enough feller?'

A thought flashed through Mrs Comeaway's mind, surprising her with the simple solution it offered to all Trilby's queernesses.

'She didn't want im. That might be it. E made er do it an she didn't want im to. Praps e hurt er. Gave er a fright. An then this baby started comin an frightened er worse.' She sat up in bed, half-inclined to go to her daughter with this new-found knowledge. 'Men!' she said, with tired disgust. 'Like animals the whole lot.' And as her husband muttered defensively, she added: 'I know. Ya can't tell me.' She still sat up. Her instinct was to gather up Trilby the way she would have gathered up any one of the others if they had been hurt. But Trilby was different. She frowned again in doubt of her ability to handle this thing. You never knew what was the right thing with Trilby. Might just snap at her.

How about if she had a word with Mrs Green and got the old lady to talk to Trilby?

As she sat there hesitating an icy wind blew through a broken louvre. That decided the issue. Mrs Comeaway lay down again and pulled the bed-clothes high up around her shoulders.

Alongside her Mr Comeaway was deep in thought.

'Ya know, ya might be right bout that,' he said at last. 'Seems ta me that stuff oughta be done the way it used ta be. Ole fellers takin the girls off inta the bush for a few days an gettin them used ta things slow an easy, so when they come back they know what ta expec.' He chuckled wickedly. 'Those times was here now I mighta got a few a them jobs meself, eh? Learnin the young ones round the camps.'

Mrs Comeaway gave her spouse a good poke. 'Ah, you!' she derided. 'Smoke stick better'n ugly ole bastard like you.'

NINETEEN

The house in the Wild-Oat Patch was locked back and front, and the silence surrounding it hit mournfully against Noonah's ears. The thing she loved most about her home was its cheerful clamour. A memory lit her eyes with laughter. Last time her family had gone off on a trip to a neighbouring town they had left Red Cat asleep on one of the beds and he had broken a louvre trying to squeeze his way out. She reached on top of the fuse-box for the big key, opened the front door and searched through the house for forgotten animals. She found a jug of souring milk in the food safe and poured it into a saucer and carried it outside to the veranda for Red Cat.

Then she locked the doors again and picked up her little case. She did not feel injured. She knew that her parents never missed a country show if they could help it. They liked to meet up with old pals, and at shows the card-playing was likely to be brisk and accompanied by real money.

Probably Bartie and Trilby would be waiting for her up at Mrs Green's. This would not be the first time Noonah had spent her days off with the old lady. The house on the hill was a second home to them all.

Walking along the crooked streets Noonah found time to ponder on her sister. Phyllix was almost one of the family now, though nobody, not even Audrena, dared to connect his presence with Trilby's baby. He had simply been absorbed in the same manner as other long-staying visitors.

Yet Trilby had certainly altered since he had come back. She was more cheerful and she took more care of her appearance. And she did not keep to her room so much as she had. She did not encourage Phyllix in any way that Noonah could see. Rather the opposite. Peremptorily, she made use of his services, ordering him to do this and that about the place, but rarely talking with him.

Phyllix showed no resentment. He had money, that was certain. The financial outlook of the Comeaway family had brightened considerably. Noonah wondered how long the money would last, what would happen when it was all gone. If Phyllix would go on another shearing trip to get more. And if he did, would Trilby's new cheerfulness disappear?

It had surprised Noonah to find good fellowship developing between Bartie and Phyllix. Phyllix was so quiet. Yet Bartie had told her he knew all about the aboriginal artists his Miss Simmins had spoken of. And Bartie seemed charmed to find that Phyllix shared his feeling for colour and the shapes of things. Noonah had been amused as well as a little hurt to have her opinions of Bartie's latest sketches brushed aside if they did not coincide with Phyllix's.

Noonah herself liked Phyllix. Gratefully, she had found a strength in him to add to her own. She felt that whilst he lived with her family nothing very bad could happen to them. Alone of the Comeaways, she doubted that the powers would allow them all to go on living in the house in the Wild-Oat Patch for much longer unless they paid more rent. Her thoughts swerved away from how much must be owing by now.

And there was no doubt about Phyllix's feelings for Trilby. Sometimes, watching his eyes as they rested on her sister, Noonah wondered how it would feel to have someone look at her like that. Her step had a different spring to it as she pursued the thought. How good to know you were important to someone, some man. And then she sighed. None of the boys she met ever looked at her except with wariness and distrust, as if she might bite them if they came closer. What was wrong with her?

Again she turned her thoughts from such unrewarding channels. A nurse's training was harder than she had thought. And she knew the reason for that. She could not concentrate as the others did. Stray thoughts of Bartie, her mother and father, Trilby, Trilby's baby, a particular patient in the hospital, the girls with whom she was training, even a patch of blue sky with the lightness of clouds on it, any one of these things was enough to detach her mind from her work. She was good at practical nursing. She knew the reason for that also. She liked handling patients, making them comfortable in their hot and wrinkled beds, setting the pillows the way they wanted them, cheering them when they were miserable. It brought real happiness to her to know that many of them were getting well under her care.

And guiltily, she knew that they appreciated her small departures from routine, the fact that she could be persuaded to pass over an early morning wash, skip a detail of diet, quickly rid their ash-trays of too many cigarette ends. She liked the other trainees, too. She was continually grateful to them because they got her out of trouble. One or two of them had even lied for her on the times when she had felt urgently that she must sleep at home instead of in her room at the hospital. She would have done the same for them, most willingly.

Nobody could save her from examination time though, she thought ruefully. That was coming, even though it was a long way off yet. Her step brisked again. She smiled with relief. Examination time was a long way off.

Bartie was waiting for her at the bottom of Heartbreak Hill. 'Nobody home,' she said cheerfully. 'Thought you must all be dead.'

'They went in the ute,' Bartie chuckled. 'And when they all got in there was hardly any room left for Horace. And it was him borrowed the ute. There's a show over at Marytown, Noonah, and Mum's gunna bring me back something from it.'

'Nice,' Noonah said as they struggled up the first steep rise. 'Mrs Green know I'm coming?'

'Yeah! I think she's glad. Her leg's bad. She's been in bed and all us kids hadda get our own breakfast. Trilby made the tea and let me make some toast by the fire.'

Noonah's pace quickened. 'Ah, poor old thing.'

Mrs Green was sitting on the front veranda in an old cane basket chair; Gramma's chair everyone called it, the chair nobody ever sat in because whilst it was empty there was always the chance that Gramma might come out on the veranda for a minute and sit down and maybe stay a bit longer than she had intended, watching them while they played, looking mightily surprised at their cleverness, encouraging the more timid, settling small fights, telling them the games she had played in her own childhood. And any game, if Gramma was there looking on, was more exciting.

'A touch of the screws,' she deprecated as Noonah climbed the sandy drive and sank down on the wooden step. 'Thought I'd just sit out here in the sun an wait for you.'

'You've got that wool wrapped round your leg?' Noonah asked anxiously. She had bought the wool herself.

Mrs Green gave her skirts a twirl. 'So much wool wrapped round me I feel as if it's shearing-time,' she declared.

Noonah laughed.

'Bartie tell you about the trip?' Mrs Green asked, amused glints in her eyes. 'You should've gone. Might've got yourself a nice young feller up there. All come down for these shows, they do, from the stations roundabout.'

'I wouldn't get one,' Noonah said frankly. 'They are different when I'm around.'

Wisdom was in the old lady's face, and a little sadness mixed up with it.

Noonah leaned against a veranda post and watched Bartie playing with the other kids. 'Gramma,' she asked, a small frown between her eyes. 'Why would a boy sling off at me because I'm training? Isn't it all right to train to be a nurse?'

Mrs Green thought before she spoke. 'It's different,' she said at last. 'That's about the only thing wrong with it.'

Noonah looked her enquiry.

'The different ones gotta pay a bit just to *be* different,' Mrs Green said.

'Why?' Noonah resented.

Mrs Green settled herself back with a sigh. 'I don't know how to make it plain, girl. It's just something I know. You go off and do something different from what the mob does, they don't understand. An what they don't understand they don't like. That's a thing that's true all round. You don't understand something, you don't trust it and you don't like it.'

Noonah rubbed with a forefinger at the splintered grey boards of the veranda. 'When people –,' she gave Mrs Green a swift upward look before she went on, 'and it isn't only the boys, Gramma—when people sling off at me for wanting to be a nurse, I feel the same way I used to feel with the white children on the school bus. As if I should be ashamed. As if I've done something terrible. On the bus it was because I wasn't the same colour as the white kids. Now it's because I'm doing my training. And there's no sense in it, is there?' Her eyes met the old lady's. 'Is there, Gramma?'

'You've got to be strong enough to get above em,' Mrs Green said steadily. 'And not let em hurt you. They don't *want* to hurt you, not really. It's just—they don't understand.

259

Praps, I don't know, they might feel you're going over on the other side. Going against *them*. That might be it.'

'I want to be like the other girls but,' Noonah said a little forlornly. 'They don't *see* me, up at the hospital. When I come home, why can't they forget all about me being a nurse?'

Mrs Green shook her head helplessly. 'Don't ask me. An don't blame them neither, Noonah, not too much. A lot of it's jealousy. You've had chances. They haven't.' Her eyes went to the group of children playing in the front yard. 'All these kids—I want them to get their chances too. That's why I stay here. Why I *have* stayed here.'

The slight emphasis was lost on Noonah whose thoughts were following another path. 'What would you think of the boy in the butcher's shop, grabbing hold of my hand when he gave me my change?' she enquired unexpectedly.

Mrs Green's eyes came alert. 'I'd say you better keep your wits about you an count that change,' she said drily.

'I've seen him up the street a few times. Once he walked a little way with me,' she told the old lady, her eyes round with questioning again.

Mrs Green's shoulders slumped a little in her chair. 'Noonah, I can tell you only one thing. I had a girl here once, like you. She wanted to be a nurse, too. Started doing her training up at that hospital, got on real well for a while.'

'What happened to her?'

'She had a baby,' Mrs Green said heavily. 'Like Trilby out there. But it was a white man's baby. After it was born,

260

you could see that all right. I knew, anyhow, because she told me. This white chap but, he wasn't like Phyllix is. This girl told him about the baby an you know what he said?'

Noonah did not move.

'He told her to go an find some other father to pin the blame on,' Mrs Green said. 'Went away about then, too. She couldn't find out where.'

Noonah's eyes were wounded. So was her mouth. She had the feeling of being punished for something she had not done, had not even contemplated doing.

'I didn't say...,' she began, her full bottom lip trembling.

'I know you didn't say,' Mrs Green told her, and there was kindliness and a great depth of understanding in her voice now. 'There's a lot of things a girl doesn't have to say, Noonah, to someone that's as old as me. The trouble is, there's so many ways a girl can take that's wrong, and that won't turn out the way she thinks. Trilby took one way. That girl I just told you about, she took another way. That's two you know about, an there's plenty more. What you want to be, my girl, is careful. Think what you're doing. An if you think real hard, maybe you don't do it.'

She leaned forward to stroke Noonah's hair back from her broad low forehead. Noonah caught the old hand in hers. 'I shouldn't have worried you,' she said remorsefully. 'I won't any more.' She jumped up. 'I'll cook the dinner instead.'

They went down the passage together. 'Where's Trilby?' Noonah asked.

'Down the yard with a pile of comics. Ruthie an Betty went out somewhere. Couldn't get her to go with them, of course.'

'Sit there by the stove, so your leg will keep warm,' Noonah ordered. 'And tell me what you're going to cook.'

She pushed a chair nearer to the still glowing fire in the big black stove. 'I should get up here more often,' she said, 'and I would if there wasn't so much to do always, when I get home.'

'You like being home, don't you?' Mrs Green twinkled.

'Too right!'

Mrs Green laughed.

'Go on now,' Noonah ordered. 'Tell me what you want done. What you really should do is get to bed, and I think I'll make you, too.'

'I'm fine just sitting,' Mrs Green declared, and when the girl was busy slicing vegetables into a big blue saucepan she added: 'Soon I'll have nothing to do but sit.'

Noonah glanced at her over the saucepan.

Mrs Green nodded. 'I'm getting old, Noonah, and I get a bit tired.'

'Ah!' Noonah threw back affectionately. 'Getting old now, eh?'

Mrs Green stopped to regard with whimsical amusement this slim youngster who was such a stranger to old age that she could not even understand it in another person. And it would come to her too, the old lady thought, so surprisingly fast, as it came to everyone. One day your thoughts filled only with the future and the next knowing that only this present day meant anything to you.

262

'Or maybe,' Mrs Green said aloud, 'it's just the pain in my leg that's troubling me.'

'Of course that must be it.' Noonah was perfectly happy with this explanation, Mrs Green could see.

'Gramma, why would a girl act the way Trilby acts with Phyllix, and still get herself up nice for him?'

Mrs Green smiled. 'She wants—she must have right now—something that Phyllix has got for her. That's why she dresses up for him. She doesn't want him herself, any more than a billy-goat, but she doesn't want anyone else to have him neither.'

'If she knew the way he looks at her,' Noonah said, cutting meat into thin slices.

'She does,' the old lady chuckled. 'Don't you make any mistake about that. Funny thing about Trilby. I've looked at those two many a time, and I thought a couple of times...'

'What?'

'He went the wrong way about things,' Mrs Green said seriously, as if Noonah was of her own generation. 'For a girl like Trilby he missed the mark by a mile. Easy an gentle does it with that one. You remember what I said about trusting, out there on the veranda? Wouldn't mind betting if he could get her to trust him— even now—!'

'Go on!'

'Ah, never mind,' Mrs Green smiled. 'Look, Noonah, I got something to tell you. I'm going away.'

'Why?' Noonah asked in consternation, dropping her work to gaze at Gramma Green.

'Partly the government,' the old lady went on. 'They came up the other day. Said I couldn't go on living here less I got that roof fixed.'

'Gramma!'

'One other thing they said. Seems this is a real good block of land this house is built on. Nice view and everything. They thought I wouldn't have much trouble selling the place.'

'They can't make you,' Noonah said indignantly.

'One of em happened to be looking for a block right now.' Gramma smiled a little. 'Wanted to fix up a deal there and then. I said I'd think it over and let him know. And now I've thought. I'm going to write to Robby and tell him he's got a buyer for his house and he can let it go because I want to go back home.'

'The kids! And their education,' Noonah appealed to what she knew Gramma held almost sacred.

'I don't know, Noonah.' There was a quality in the old lady's voice that made Noonah regard her more closely. She went swiftly over to the chair, took Mrs Green's head in her hands and pushed it gently into the crook of her shoulder. 'Yes,' she crooned. 'You want to go back to where you were born, don't you? Mummy's told me all the things you told her. She knows you love the north better than here. And the kids will be all right. Someone else will look after them. You don't have to worry about anything, Gramma.'

Mrs Green reached up and squeezed Noonah's forearm. 'I thought you'd understand without a lot of talking.'

Noonah patted her shoulder and went back behind the long kitchen table.

'I even had a white kid here for a while,' Mrs Green meditated. 'For a year or two.'

'You did?'

'The mother asked me to mind it for a day—and there were some thought she'd never come back and I'd have that kid for always. I knew she'd come back. She loved that kid of hers. Pretty, it was. Had a lot of red hair—same colour as a little pony I had once when I was a kid myself. I got real fond of that little girl, the time she was here.'

'She reminded you of your pony?'

'Ah!' Mrs Green laughed.

'And what did the woman say when she came to get her?' Noonah had finished making her stew and she came to sit alongside Gramma.

'Don't remember,' the old lady said, her smile tantalizing. 'Lot of silly things. Even wanted to pay me.'

'Didn't she say why she'd gone off and left it with you?'

Mrs Green looked surprised. 'Where else did she have to leave it?'

'Gramma!' Noonah slipped off the table. She turned to the door as Bartie came flying in. 'What do *you* want? Getting hungry?'

'What about you and me going for a walk—you know.' Bartie gestured towards the valley and Noonah nodded.

'All right!' She wiped her hands on the side of her frock and carried the big saucepan over to the stove.

'How's your leg now, Gramma?' she asked, whilst Bartie danced with impatience in the background.

'I'm going to sit here and think,' Gramma said. 'About the sun all hot on me, getting right through to my bones, and how I'm going to soak it up and let it get rid of every pain in every part.'

'We'll miss you but,' Noonah told her. 'It'll be terrible with no Gramma Green to stay with.'

'Off an go for your walk,' Mrs Green said briskly, 'before Bartie drags your arm off.'

TWENTY

Bartie had a friend of his own age. A real friend who liked him better than she liked anyone else. And she lived in the valley below Mrs Green's house.

Diane was the same age as Bartie, but she was a class below him at school. In contrast, Diane was all cheek and cheerful laughter and she had a disregard for authority that stunned Bartie into lasting admiration. She arrived late at school nearly every day, her stiff curly hair bouncing in two bunches on either side of her round shining black face. Diane was much darker than anyone else Bartie knew, and that was because she was part negro. Diane was nearly always in trouble, both at home and at school. The man who taught her class was an emigrant under the teacher-training scheme. His nationality was a source of continual conjecture for the children he taught, and sometimes the conjecture became ribald, especially if Diane was implicated.

Mr Jenzen was extremely slow-spoken and he had a passion for discipline. Once or twice a day he took Diane through her misdeeds and endeavoured, without success, to find out why she had erred.

'You know that school begins at nine?' His face was turned slightly, for this first question, his pale blue eyes fixed askance on Diane's lively little face.

'Yes,' Diane would nod.

'Then why,' with the air of one springing a trap, 'are you late?'

Diane's answer was always a shrug, with perhaps a beguiling little smile to soften it.

'You know you must be punished when you are late?'

'Yes!' The big brown eyes opened wide in innocence.

A quick lift of the heavy chin and the broad face with its high cheek-bones would come full-face, pale blue eyes glowing beneath down-drooping lids on which grew scant white eye-lashes. 'You fetch me my stick, please?'

This was the period the waiting children enjoyed most. Only Diane could pretend such concern and distress over the whereabouts of the stick. The diligent eyes searched in every corner where she knew it was not.

And there was the rising impatience of Mr Jenzen as he stood next to his table drumming a soft tattoo with the tips of his fingers. And finally, most exciting moment of all, the leap of anger to his face; the long stride to the cupboard inside which, suspended by its strap, hung his stick.

And there was the extra force with which he lashed at the small pale palm held out obediently in answer to his curt instruction.

To Diane it was all worth while, even the pain in her hand, because afterwards, during the lunch-hour, she could take aside a crew of selected friends and ape Mr Jenzen so perfectly that even her lively little face took on for the time being the dour cast of her teacher's.

Diane's mother was big and tall and calm, almost as slow-spoken as Diane's teacher, but whereas Mr Jenzen's voice was scratchy and ragged, words dropping from his mouth with a sound as of shell grit, Mrs Mongo's voice had the far-off sound of poured treacle, and it lingered on each word caressingly, as though reluctant to pass on to the next. Diane was the eldest of a brood of six, and Mrs Mongo had lately begun to think that the size of her family had got beyond a joke.

But it was well known that she would suffer no infringement of the rights of either herself or her children. She came often to talk with Diane's teacher, her soft brown heavily-lidded eyes gazing gravely into his. She begged the teacher to remember that he, too, had once been young. She spoke without emotion of the day when it had taken four grown teachers to hold her down because they had considered she needed punishment. Mr Jenzen, if he had troubled to inspect her tall strength, must have been under no illusions about what she could do to four grown teachers at her present stage of development. And finally, she reminded Mr Jenzen that her daughter attended the school in order to be educated and that she, and not Mr Jenzen, was the one who must deal out punishment to her own.

The wicked Diane always contrived to be within earshot at these interviews, with the result that her select

269

band was treated to yet another comic representation of what had transpired.

Noonah had heard much of Diane. Now she and Bartie were on their way down the hillside so that Noonah could actually see the girl.

They walked through the wattle-studded valley until they came to the Mongo camp. It was a fair-sized camp, this, to cope not only with the Mongo small fry, but with Mrs Mongo's old mother, her sister who had three children of her own, and Denzyl, who was currently acting father to her sister's children.

Mrs Mongo's mother sat on a chair in the doorway of the main erection, exchanging gossip with her daughter who had just finished washing and was now spiking clothes on the barbed-wire clothes-line. Diane rose from the midst of a squirming mass of children and came dancing to meet them.

Mrs Mongo stopped hanging up clothes long enough to shake her head at Noonah.

'If e took my tip,' she said in her lazy melodious drawl, 'e'd keep well away from that one. Mischief she's in all the time—an no one knowing what she's gunna be upta next. They tole you bout last week-end?' She raised black scimitars of eyebrows over her calm brown eyes.

'Nekked—no cloes,' cried the old lady in the doorway, rocking energetically and darting quick little looks at her daughter, at Noonah, at the children playing in the dust, and at Bartie and Diane.

'They hadda come back through the bush,' Mrs Mongo said, 'an wait till after it was dark, too. Couldn't think where she'd got to.'

270

'What happened?' Noonah said, curious.

'Ah, clothes is silly,' Diane said scornfully. 'You ever been swimmin without clothes? That water feels like little hands strokin.'

'These two's always goin fa walks,' Mrs Mongo said. 'Long that beach at the back where all them nasty men live. Talkin doesn't stop that Diane. Beltin don't neither. An Gawd knows where she left er good school frock.'

'I told you,' Diane said breezily. 'I put it under a bush in the sand-hills, but we forgot to mark the place, so we couldn't find it again. Let's go down now, Bartie, an have another look. Bartie, did your mother go mad at you too?'

Bartie grinned and the grin slid over to include Noonah. 'She didn't know,' he said simply. 'I just crept in to where I sleep and got into bed.'

'We ran along the beach,' Diane told Noonah. 'As hard as we could, and I beat Bartie, didn't I? And sometimes we went in the water. And we went nearly to the end of the sand-hills.'

'An them ole pensioners livin just the other side,' Mrs Mongo said, her eyes meeting Noonah's. 'All sorts goes on down there.' She shrugged. 'I tole er. Serves er right if they get er, some time.'

'Wouldn't get *me*,' Diane said, with decision. 'We climbed up the top of one sand-hill and we seen em. They got little places just like ours. We seen em, didn't we, Bartie?'

'An a good job nobody see you,' the old lady grumbled. 'Kids thout cloes.'

'Yes, you've *gotta*,' Diane said suddenly, pulling at Bartie's hand. 'Come on!'

Bartie looked at Noonah, who nodded. The two were off and away like rabbits, out of sight in an instant.

'They didn't mean the beach but, did they?' Noonah remembered, in a little alarm. 'That's not where they've gone, is it?'

'She found something. Forgot what it is, but she been talkin bout showing it to young Bartie. Guess they've gone where she found it,' Mrs Mongo said, draping more clothes over her homemade line.

Bartie went out of Noonah's head when she looked round to see Phyllix and old Skippy. As usual, Phyllix did not waste time on words when there was someone with him to do the talking. Noonah could see that Skippy was upset. His old voice shook with rage and the tone was so high it occasionally slid over the edge into a raspy croak.

'A full-blood, that's what I am,' he yelled, eyeing the group belligerently. 'And im down there in the town want me ta live up ere with all them arf-carse no-goods. Me live with fellers like that—carryin on—fightin all over the place. I tell im I'm a full-blood an wanta go back long my place. Nother thing,' his jaw shot out and back, 'who's gunna do me cookin up there, eh?'

Noonah gestured to the old man to sit on the kerosene-tin where she had been sitting herself. Skippy gave the tin a contemptuous kick with his heavy loose boot and stood breathing fire on everyone present.

'Praps they think you're too old to live too far away from everyone,' Noonah shrieked into his ear. 'What about up there. Anyone to do your cooking up there?' With her hand she waved vaguely towards the north.

'Yeah, an e said I couldn't ave me bike,' Skippy snarled, his thoughts turning to fresh injury. 'I got the money, ain't I?'

Noonah turned a look of enquiry on Phyllix. But Mrs Mongo answered for Phyllix. 'E went into a shop in town when he found e just gotta take this ouse up the camp or go without,' she said, amusement making her voice even richer, 'and blow me down if e didn't order isself a bike, so's e could ride back up north. With them legs a his.'

'Shopman rings up this partment bloke,' the old lady continued, 'an this ole man don't get is bike.'

Skippy glared round, half comprehending. 'Up outa this,' he ordered Phyllix. 'I want me tea. Fellers like this,' he glared at Mrs Mongo and then at her mother, 'no good ta be roun. Like them others up there in the camp.'

'Keep ya wool on,' Mrs Mongo said good-naturedly. 'Ya can live where ya like, as far's I'm concerned an,' she eyed her fighting brood, 'take some a these with ya ta keep ya company.'

Skippy stamped off, ploughing an uncertain path up the hill to Mrs Green's house, but Phyllix stayed behind.

'Been lookin at them new ouses?' Mrs Mongo inquired.

Phyllix nodded. 'Seen them?' he asked Noonah. 'If you haven't, come on back and have a look.'

Noonah smiled a good-bye to the Mongos, and Mrs Mongo looked with kindly interest from her to Phyllix. 'Don't see ya sister round no more. Someone tole me she's wild bout gettin a baby. Won't do no good now, I spose, but I could tell er a few things after she's ad it, if she wants ta know. I found out a few things.'

'I'll tell her,' Noonah said, feeling hot.

'Tell er I got all the dope in some book someone give me,' Mrs Mongo called after her as Phyllix led her back along the path he had taken.

Noonah peeped at Phyllix, but he was looking woodenly ahead of him.

The big camping area was soft with fresh green grass threaded through with bright wild flowers. Six or seven newly-built small houses sat in a prim circle in the middle of it.

'Not bad, eh?' Phyllix asked.

This was Noonah's first visit to the government reserve. She stared about her curiously, noting a bigger building at the back obviously intended as a laundry, with two smaller rooms each end.

'That's the showers, and so on,' Phyllix told her. 'That's for everyone.'

'It's nice,' Noonah said, more for something to say.

'Not a bad lot of people up here now either. Not much drinking and fighting goes on. A lot of young people, too.'

'Yes,' Noonah said, wondering.

'This was gunna be Skippy's joint,' Phyllix said, stopping at one of the little empty houses. 'One room, with a stove in it, and a bit of a veranda. All new, too.'

Noonah peeped through the glass louvres, admired the new wood stove inside the tiny room.

'You think Trilby'd like to live here?' Phyllix said abruptly. 'When it's all over?'

Noonah's face was pitiful. Mrs Green had mentioned something about Phyllix not knowing the right way to go about things with Trilby. How far out he was, she thought, if he meant to ask Trilby to live on the reserve with him.

'She wouldn't do it,' she told him. 'Trilby hates reserves. She thinks they're terrible places to live. You wouldn't get her on one if you built a castle for her.'

Phyllix looked away from her. 'It's all right. Just something I thought up when I heard old Skippy going hot and strong about not wanting the place. It'd be a start, is all I thought.' He kicked a stone at his feet. 'But I spose I knew she'd never come to a place like this.'

They turned away from the little house and moved down the track that led to it. 'Pity it isn't bigger,' Phyllix said. 'Mighta done for ya Mum and Dad and the kids.'

Noonah smiled, not really considering the idea. 'We've lived in places smaller than that.'

'Trouble here is they won't let ya,' Phyllix said. 'Skippy's place is for a couple at the most. No more. If ya Mum and Dad came here they'd have ta send the kids back to the mission.'

'No,' Noonah said in horror. 'They wouldn't do that.'

Phyllix shrugged. 'Just thought if they got kicked out down there. Because of the rent.' He went on in silence for a while, then added: 'Course they wouldn't have to worry bout Trilby. I could look out for her, if...,' he frowned, 'if she'd damn well let me.'

Noonah's mounting fear for the welfare of Bartie and Stella was drowned in a gush of sympathy for Phyllix. She touched his hand. 'It'll be all right,' she told him. 'You just wait. It'll be all right later on, between you and Trilby.'

275

'I got a feeling,' Phyllix said tensely, 'things aren't ever going right for Trilby an me.' He stopped to break two fly switches from a wattle, one of which he handed to Noonah. She took it gratefully and used it to beat off the horde of tiny bush flies that had come with the greening grass. 'I've tried. Done everything I could think of. She won't have a bar of me.'

'Phyllix,' Noonah said impulsively, after they had walked a while in silence. 'Why do you—you know?'

'Hang around,' Phyllix said hardly, giving her a brief look. 'Ever since I was a kid I wanted not to be kicked around when I grew up. You know how it is. Some a these white people don't seem ta think ya got any feelings at all. Just because ya dark. Talk right in front of ya face as if ya couldn't hear, or as if it didn't matter if ya did hear. Even the pleece. Ya gotta keep on the right side of em. Get in any sort of a mix-up an ya sure to be the one that collects. I wasn't sixteen when I had my first barney with the pleece. I was up for takin a drink a conto. Didn't even like the damn stuff. Did it for a joke sort of. But Trilby,' his head came up, 'nobody's gunna tell *her* what ta do. Not even the pleece. She makes all the others look like a lot of dead-heads.' His mouth curled in a grin. 'Even snappin an snippy the way she is, I still rather have her than any other one. Trouble is, she don't seem ta feel the same way bout me.'

Noonah's mouth smiled back at him, but her eyes were wistful. She wanted some feller to feel that way about her. Why should Trilby be the only lucky one?

'I tell ya what,' Phyllix said restlessly, 'I'm goin away again. For a while.'

The man who was keeping nit leaned easily against a tree, his heavy-lidded incurious gaze fixed steadily on the two men who approached him. Mr Comeaway stopped in order to hand over the pound note he had in readiness, and before the nit-keeper stuffed it carelessly into his pocket he jerked his head towards the gloom of the bush. Mr Comeaway nodded, and he and Charlie marched off in the direction indicated.

A quarter of a mile into the bush and past a clump of wattles, a bright yellow glare chased the night away. A burning pyramid of old motor-car tyres bellied flames and smoke both upward and over a sprawling group of people who sat close enough to breathe in the pungent odour and to peer through watering eyes at the cards in their hands and at the five that lay face up on a piece of old grey blanket thrown down in their midst.

'Manila,' thought Mr Comeaway pleasurably. He nudged Charlie's hip, and the two exchanged grins. Nothing like a game of Manila for excitement. Two cards dealt to each player and you made what you could of the cards in your hand and any three of those five in the centre.

Plenty of players tonight, Mr Comeaway noted approvingly. Old Mattie, her wide, flattish features and craggy brow outlined against the glow of the fire, her crutches placed carefully at her side so that she could get at them to aid her in rising or to lay about her if trouble threatened. Horace, sitting there quiet and dignified; Billy Gumnut and his shyly giggling bush black, quiet and subdued now as she listened to the betting; and more than a dozen others, all quiet and tense.

Mr Comeaway and Charlie sank to their haunches and waited patiently. When the dealing started again Mr Comeaway moved forward to the circle.

In his pocket, resting gently against his hip, were the ten pound notes Marty had lent him. The surprise and warm pleasure of watching Marty count out that money had not yet left Mr Comeaway. His lucky day all right, bumping into the young chap just, it must have been, after he had cashed his cheque at the bank and before anyone else had had a chance to get at him. Nice young bloke, that. Probably could have asked for twice what he did and got it. For a second Mr Comeaway's thoughts were tinged with regret. But no, a fair thing was a fair thing. You wouldn't want to clean a feller out on his first day, and what Marty had would go soon enough once he started flashing his money about.

278

'Hope the feller has a bit of fun before they all get on to im,' Mr Comeaway thought with expanding generosity. 'Damn well deserves it after doin that string a sheds.'

The next hand was dealt, and Mr Comeaway's palms were suddenly wet. The sweat sprang out across his upper lip and under his arms too. Yet his body pricked with coldness. Two aces in his hand. Two aces! And in the centre, a couple of kings, an eight of clubs—and two more aces.

The betting started, rapping from person to person as quick as the crackles of a bush fire. The hand in the middle was a dandy to bring up the betting. The peace that settled over Mr Comeaway told him that all would be well. He clamped down on himself. No flicker of excitement must show on his face—no smallest quaver of it in his voice. And it was him to bet. 'Ten pounds,' he said, allowing exactly the right amount of time for deliberation.

There were a few sharply-indrawn breaths. No one else bet now until it was the turn of the man opposite him. A stranger, this one. Big mean-looking chap with bunchy shoulders. He might need watching. The man's voice was a squeaky whisper. He had to clear his throat and start again, and this time he grunted deep. 'Ten pound—and thirty pound better.'

People sat still like statues now and the only sound came from the subdued roar of the flaming tyres. Nobody bet until it was Mr Comeaway's turn again. He hesitated just a bit longer this time. 'Thirty pound back twenty-five pound.'

The brightness of dark brown eyes was fixed in unwavering attention, weighing up, giving value to the slightest flicker to pass over the faces of the two men.

The big man cleared his throat again. 'Twenty-five pound back to another fifty.' Fifty? A sigh went round the table. Old Mattie clutched her wooden crutches tighter and eased her skinny haunches into a more comfortable position.

'Fifty pound,' Mr Comeaway said indomitably, 'back fifty pound.'

'Give us a look at ya cards,' said the dealer.

Mr Comeaway had been waiting for just that. An examination of his cards by the dealer meant that no examination would be made of his pockets. He handed them over, and the dealer scrutinized them through narrowed eyes and returned them. Now the dealer's face looked smooth and secret.

The big man shot the dealer a look of anger. His mouth formed a line of disgust. He threw fifty pounds in notes on the table, and whilst the dealer counted them he snarled: 'See ya.' But the flicker at the back of his eyes and the bad-tempered look of his mouth meant defeat, and everyone around the circle knew it.

Mr Comeaway, his mouth still under control, though not his eyes, threw down his two aces with a modest flourish. And the quiet was shattered. Laughter, jeers for the big angry man, shrill squealing from Mattie, back-slapping and more roars of laughter, and over the top of it all the big man's voice as he lurched to his feet and leaned over to accuse: '*Wunmulla jinagubby* Mt Magnet bastard.'

'Ya right,' Mr Comeaway grinned, and the laughter in his eyes leapt out to pile coals on the heat of the other's anger. While the babble went on and on the stranger tore more money from his pocket and threw it down on the old grey blanket. One hundred and eighty pounds in all. One hundred and eighty pounds!

It was months since there had been such a downright victory. The sight of the money stirred the whole crowd.

Mr Comeaway gathered it up and stuffed it deep into the pockets of his trousers. And he laughed and roared with the rest of them, feeling light-headed and almost sick.

A woman plunked herself down on his lap and held his head to her redolent bosom, and Mr Comeaway felt the good warmth of her soft thighs with outspread hand. She was plucked from his lap as suddenly as she had arrived, and an anguished squawk from the rear followed her disappearance. Mr Comeaway watched indulgently as she was cuffed into order.

He could have gone home right away. Nobody would have stopped him. But he stayed. He needed a few minutes more to gain control of the trembling in his legs. He played again, and again after that. And the last time he played he won more money with a full hand king high.

It was as he was gathering up his further winnings that the mopoke in the tree ten feet away gave voice to its lugubrious and mournful 'Morepawk'.

He concluded, afterwards, that it was Mattie who had started the commotion, but if this were so then she had but a split-second start on the rest. However it began, the tearing screams that followed the initial rending of the quiet night almost lifted the scalp from his head. People leapt to their feet and vanished. Almost between one breath and the next Mr Comeaway saw someone snatch the bird from the tree, chop it into small pieces with a knife, and stuff it into a hole clawed deep by frantic fingers.

'Bastard's after someone,' the man gasped, and then he was away himself, following the shrieks into the black of the bush.

The stamping crowd had gained a start on him, but Mr Comeaway pushed doggedly on, his eyes popping with exertion, his powerful legs flailing and, with all the excitement, both hands holding tight to the notes that bulked in his back pockets. Past wailing Mattie, whose legs had forgotten the need for crutches, past the big angry man and the little dealer of cards, past others who crowed for breath and those who still had sufficient for screaming. And at last he was running ahead of everyone, with Horace on one side and Charlie on the other, and the three of them caught up with the exhilaration of it all, wanting most to stop in their tracks and roar out their mirth now that that first panic had left them.

And at last they did. 'My Gawd!' Charlie wheezed and panted and chuckled. 'They got me in, with at damn yellin an carryin on.'

'Bicrickey,' Mr Comeaway agreed.

But it was left to Horace to nod his head in wisdom and thought and point out: 'Jus the same. Ya never know bout them things. Just as well we came away fum there.'

'Ya mean ya believe in all that?' Charlie scorned, still panting.

'All I'm saying,' Horace warned. 'Ya never know.'

And so they walked on.

After a while the thought of the money took precedence.

'Wouldn't mind spreadin that money out all over the table an havin a good look at it,' Charlie said.

'Yeah! No wakin up the ole lady but, spose she's asleep,' Mr Comeaway warned. 'We gotta think this thing out careful first.'

'Can't never trust womans,' Horace agreed, his thoughts playing lovingly with possibilities.

Near the outskirts of the town a taxi cruised past. Mr Comeaway hailed it with a peremptory gesture and all three climbed in.

'An if we call up the camp,' Horace said graciously, sinking into his soft leather seat, 'I might just find I had a bottle or two hid away.'

'If ya got the money ta pay for it,' the taxi-driver offered, 'I can get as much as youse three'll want.'

'Could do with a drink,' Charlie said wistfully.

'Yeah boy,' Mr Comeaway enthused. 'We might do that.'

But after all, the caution that made them stop the taxi a hundred yards away from the house in the Wild-Oat Patch was wasted. The night was younger than they had thought, and the women were still out of bed. There was nothing for it but the grand gesture, and Mr Comeaway made it not unwillingly. The pound notes, the fivers, the ten shillings, the silver, all fluttered and chinked and rolled and were caught and clutched and stared at by the dazed and delighted Hannie and Mrs Comeaway.

'An it don't mean trouble,' Mr Comeaway answered the look Mrs Comeaway shot at him. 'All come by honest. Ain't that right, Horace?' Horace nodded gravely.

'I dunno what ta do first,' Mrs Comeaway said, sinking down on a chair.

'Pork chops,' Hannie said tentatively. 'Wouldn't mind a pork chop meself.'

'Gotta nother letter fum that man bout the rent today. Least, I think it'll be bout rent. Didn't open it yet.'

'We can pay that,' Mr Comeaway said grandly. 'The whole damn lot.'

'An that sour-face butcher,' Mrs Comeaway added. 'An the grocer man an a coupla others. An what about we take a big heap a stuff up Mrs Green's an cook it up there an let's have a good feed, eh?'

'Where would a heap a money like that come fum?' Hannie said reverently.

Horace opened one of his bottles and poured the contents into cups. 'Seein it's early,' he said pleasantly, 'we might jus as well sit in to another little game while we drink this stuff.'

'Only first,' Mrs Comeaway said firmly, 'we put all this money away somewhere where it ain't gunna blow away.' She picked up Stella's little school case off the floor by the table and stacked all the money inside it, leaving out only a little of the silver. Poker-faced, Horace watched her.

Mr Comeaway took a good long swallow of his conto. 'Count *me* out,' he said lazily. 'I rather just sit ere an think.'

He smiled a beatific smile round the circle of faces and closed his eyes.

Horace said nothing.

The news of the win spread quickly. Auntie Milly arrived down from Mullewa for a little visit with her relations and two months later, when her husband got picked up for supplying, she decided she might as well fill in the time he would be away where she was. Neither Mr nor Mrs Comeaway was entirely happy about this arrangement because Auntie Milly was bossy and interfering and wanted to run the roost. Mrs Comeaway managed to put up with the old lady by living one day at a time which was all right with old Milly since that way her welcome lost nothing of its freshness. Mr Comeaway ignored her and slipped free of entanglement by pretending not to hear her when she spoke to him.

She was good with the kids, though, and could always be relied on to keep them quiet by some means or another, even if she had to frighten six months' growth out of them.

'You kids jus better be quiet,' she would warn, blazing eyes turned on the darkness outside the window. 'Wijari round here tonight. You see em dancin over that window—quick—up down, up down.' Her shoulders would rise towards her ears, and the children's fascinated eyes would follow her gaze to watch moonlight flickering among the shadows.

Having quietened them until their hearts beat fast with fear, she would lie down alongside them and comfort them with her presence. She believed what she said, too.

285

'Wijari after *me*,' she told Mrs Comeaway indignantly, one afternoon.

'Yeah!' Mrs Comeaway scoffed, whilst Hannie watched wide-eyed and nervous from her chair by the stove.

'They after me true. Sitting round in them wattles. I did see em, dancin backwards. Wijara them was. My word! An after ole woman like me.'

Mrs Comeaway straightened, half-believing. 'H'nnn!'

There were other visitors, too, to whom news of the win came like an unexpected dividend. Nobody could be accused of cadging who had visited only in the spirit of friendliness like Dora Dicker, because she was convinced she was dying.

Dora Dicker was a pest and a menace. Even Hannie was gently sceptical.

Only Mrs Comeaway's generous heart was touched. 'Ah, winyarn,' she murmured, when Trilby told her scornfully that Dora was just putting on an act.

'All that screaming and going stiff and putting her hand to her heart,' Trilby scowled. 'There's nothing wrong with *her*.'

'Anyone can get sick,' Mrs Comeaway said firmly. 'Might happen ta me one day.'

So Dora was humoured and pampered, and while there was a bit of money about she had special food and Blanchie's bed while Mr Comeaway fought valiantly all night against the threshing limbs of his two youngest.

'I'm gunna die,' Dora moaned one day. 'I can feel it. Here!' She rolled big agonized eyes. The skin on her face was wet.

286

'You gunna be all right. Ain't she?' Mrs Comeaway appealed to Auntie Milly, to the dumb and uncomprehending Auntie Hannie.

She tried to roll Dora down on the settee. 'No good,' Dora yelled. 'You gotta get the littlies down so I can see em before I die.'

Now this was a thing Dora mentioned often, and Mrs Comeaway would have complied long ago if it had not been for Mr Comeaway and Trilby and old Auntie Milly and even Noonah, who all believed that the limit of accommodation had been reached with thirteen people already under the roof more or less permanently. But there was only old Auntie Milly to defy today, so Mrs Comeaway took the bull by the horns and promised to get Dora's children down.

'The doctors say there ain't nothing wrong with er, don't they?' Mr Comeaway said irascibly, when told. 'Then that settles it, don't it? She can stay ere a while longer, turning the whole place into a madhouse, then she can get back where she belongs, an a damn good riddance.'

'I said she could have em down,' Mrs Comeaway said firmly, though wearily. 'Fa Gawd's sake let's get em jus so's she'll shut up bout em.'

'You go an send one a them tellygrams ta their gramma,' she ordered a reluctant Trilby.

'Don't know as I like so much womans bout a house,' Auntie Milly sniffed and tossed her head at the look she saw in her niece's eye.

The children arrived with their gramma on the following day, the children tired and cranky from their long trip down

287

by train and the walk that had proved so long and wearisome, from the station to the house in the Wild-Oat Patch.

Dora was languidly pleased to see them, and the children were hysterically pleased to see their mother. Mrs Comeaway's heart was touched. Even Hannie and Auntie Milly nodded approvingly, though the problem of sleeping everyone was still to be solved. It was a piece of good luck that Mrs Comeaway and the newly-arrived gramma liked each other and were pals of old. It helped lighten the atmosphere.

At night it was Hannie and Auntie Milly who complained least. Hannie wandered round until she found a spot that would take her bulk, and Auntie Milly was happiest sleeping in front of the dying fire anyway. Bartie and Stella slept in Noonah's bed, monitored by a vigilant-eyed and sharp-spoken Trilby, while Mrs Comeaway harboured the girls in hers. Mr Comeaway and Charlie made their own arrangements, sometimes not bothering to come home at all for their nightly rest, though there was one night when Mr Comeaway's loud-voiced complaints might have been taken to indicate that he had come to the end of his endurance.

Having got themselves into a game that had lasted most of the night both he and Charlie had decided that the long walk home to the Wild-Oat Patch was not worth the effort. They had bedded themselves down on the floor under a couple of old blankets that had been thrown to them.

'An I dunno what was in them blankets,' Mr Comeaway complained, 'but whatever it was, they had a bite on

288

em like a alligator.' He scratched vigorously. 'Got bit all over.'

'*E* did,' Charlie said. 'I couldn't feel much.'

'No,' Mr Comeaway glared at his brother. 'They was all on my side, seemingly. An there's Charlie tellin me ta keep quiet an lie still an when I did, that's when the buggers *really* started bitin. Gawd, no more a that fa me.'

Dora's children were sufficient only for a week or so. After that she felt she was getting worse and should have her husband with her to comfort her in her dying hours. Dora's husband had a good job with the Railways Department, a good permanent job at which he collected regular weekly wages, and it might have been this fact which helped Mrs Comeaway make up her mind to send for him. No win, however big, could long stand the strain of keeping a dozen or so stomachs comfortably filled every day.

She made a good decision. Dora's husband, already gloomy on the subject of his wife's health, immediately handed in his notice, collected back pay and holiday pay and arrived down by taxi to pick up Dora and take her down to Perth for further examinations. They left in the same taxi, with all the Comeaways except Trilby waving fond farewell from the front fence.

Mr Comeaway looked over the inmates of his house with a certain brooding dissatisfaction when he trailed them back again. There seemed a good big crowd of them and it sort of unsettled a man when he couldn't even count on a bed at night. Two or three pals, that was one thing. This great heap of womans, that was another thing altogether, specially when there were the kids as well.

He showed displeasure first by roaring at the startled children, who were quite unused to anything but kindliness and indulgence from the head of this house. When he had thoroughly disconcerted the children he turned his attention on old Auntie Milly, who had merely been sitting about meditating and minding her own business. Auntie Milly was so incensed she took Mrs Comeaway to task for marrying such a man.

'Ah, I dunno! He's all right,' Mrs Comeaway said wearily.

'You *good* woman, Molly,' old Milly said emphatically. 'That Joe there,' she darted a vindictive look in the direction of the bedroom where Mr Comeaway lay at rest, 'he a wijari hisself which I know.'

Mr Comeaway left the house quite early the following day. Soon after Charlie followed him. With both men and the ailing Dora out of the way, Mrs Comeaway felt easier. She made a swift decision to get out of the house herself, even if it meant taking everyone with her. Bartie and Stella went off to school. The visiting children went with them. And Mrs Comeaway made a pot of tea.

It was a comfortable fit round the table now, and everyone felt happier. 'I still got a bad feelin but,' old Gramma Dicker said, over her first cup of tea.

'Ya mean what?' Mrs Comeaway said, her mind set comfortably on the thought of staying round here until the children got out of school, then getting out and walking up the hill to Mrs Green's and maybe staying on there for a meal. If they did that they would only need to put all the kids to bed when they came home and there wouldn't be any need to bother with food. 'What was ya sayin?' she asked Gramma Dicker, absent-mindedly.

'That time I wanted someone else,' said Gramma surprisingly. 'Didn't even get im neither. I was sposed to meet im at the corner, but all e give me were a bash in the face an I hadda go back ta me ole man after all.'

Old Milly sat up straight and cupped a hand round her ear.

'Worried me a bit till I'd got it off me chest ta the ole priest.'

'What'd ya say?' Mrs Comeaway settled herself to hear another of Gramma Dicker's tales.

'Just told im all bout it, Molly. How after thirty years or more I gotta have that other man. An after all them children too. Jack's children. So after that I gotta say fifty Hail Marys—I forgot em a course—an something else. I hadda give em some money.'

'How much?'

'Ah,' Gramma winked. 'I tole that ole man I gotta pay some accounts. E lets me off at two bob a week fa five weeks.'

Mrs Comeaway laughed, as Gramma sighed, 'I still feel bad but.'

Auntie Milly lifted her cup and took a long drink, her dry old lips spread flat. 'Ya got outa that all right, didn't ya?'

Gramma sipped too, narrowing her eyes against the steaming tea. Then she looked across her cup at the attentive faces. 'It's me conscience,' she told them sadly.

'Go on,' Mrs Comeaway rallied. 'A change is as good as a holiday, ain't it?'

The wrinkled eyelids lifted in surprise as Gramma considered. She set her cup down suddenly. 'I think I ruther have that holiday.'

Even Auntie Milly's face was blank for a minute. Then everyone laughed. Mrs Comeaway's stomach rolled and bounced and hurt her until she held it. 'She rather have a holiday,' she gasped at the others. 'An ya know what? So'd I.'

Trilby came out of her room to see what was going on. 'We all goin up the hill when the kids come home,' Mrs Comeaway told her daughter. 'Ya wanta come with us?'

'I'll stay home and get a bit of peace,' Trilby said sourly. 'You don't get much around here.'

'Suit yaself,' Mrs Comeaway said easily. 'There's some bread in the cupboard an a new tin of jam. We gunna have tea out, with a bit a luck.'

They started the minute the children came home from school, all but Audrena, who had already left the house on a mission of her own. Blanchie carried fat little Tommy on her hip and when she got tired Mrs Comeaway gave her a hand. But before they got to Mrs Green's there were some others to look in on. Mrs Comeaway hadn't left the house for a fortnight and she wanted to see all her friends.

They came across Addie and Johnny Bean, just down from Carnarvon and busy building themselves a shelter alongside the Dowies'. They had found some good pieces of iron down on the dump, enough to make another little shelter after they finished the first one.

'Spose we got visitors,' Mrs Bean explained, 'it'll do to keep the wind offa them.'

Addie was peering into a big pot when Mrs Comeaway and her little band appeared. She acted annoyed and even though there were friends she had not seen for a time the scowl stayed on her face as she greeted them.

'Them dogs it is,' she declared indignantly. 'Come an et all the meat outa the pot.'

Mrs Comeaway examined the evidence—a pot scraped dry with only a few crumbs of bread adhering to the bottom. 'That two-legged dog,' she chuckled, 'ta scrape up all the juice as well.'

Johnny Bean, huge and majestic, frowned and scratched his head. 'Musta been when we was down the dump.' He looked along the rise to where the Dowies camped. 'That Tinker! E come along ere an eat my tucker, e find imself on the end a this. Im an is big dawgs always sneakin around.'

'Whyn't ya build ya place a bit farther away?' Mrs Comeaway asked. 'Ya know what them's like over there. Never got nothin an always hungry.'

'Ah gee, is done now,' Johnny said ruefully.

A tall skinny woman came climbing up the hill towards them, pushing a way through the stunted wattles. Her feet flapped, her brow was corded and in her arms she carried a loaf of bread.

She ignored Mrs Comeaway and the others and slopped her way over to Addie. 'Ya bread,' she said, handing over the loaf.

'That'll be somethin fa us ta eat,' Addie snapped, 'seein the meat's gone. You see any a that meat, Polly?'

Polly smiled ingratiatingly. 'An now we jus run outa potatoes,' she said. 'Ya wouldn't have none, would ya?'

Addie hesitated, considered and shook her head, and Polly looked with disappointment at the loaf of bread she had handed over. Addie followed the look. Her eyes swerved to where a couple of tins of meat lay beneath a fold of tarpaulin. 'Ah, take ya bread,' she said ungraciously, shoving it back.

Polly took it eagerly. She turned to greet Mrs Comeaway. 'How are ya sister? Ain't seen ya for a long time.' Her gap-toothed grin widened to include them all, then she began slapping back the way she had come.

Addie's mouth was thin. 'Needn't think she's gunna live offa us jus because we neighbours. Hey!' With her hand to her mouth she sent a call after the retreating Polly. When the woman stopped and looked back she yelled: 'I *guv* ya that bread and when I give ya thing I don't want em back. But if I borry things, then I *do* want em back. Ya hear that?'

'Awright!' Polly bellowed amicably. 'I remember, sister.'

'Ah, ya always was a bit snippy,' Mrs Comeaway said affectionately, when Polly had disappeared, 'but ya not a bad ole bastard an it's nice ta have ya back.'

Addie did not unbend, but a pack of cards appeared in her hand. 'Ya got the time?' she queried.

Mrs Comeaway looked uncertainly at the others. Auntie Milly was already settling herself on a patch of grass. Hannie waited patiently for orders. The children were chasing a lizard down the dusty road.

'Hafta be fa matches but,' she weakened, 'if ya got some.'

They all had cups of tea, too, at Hannie's camp. And a little game of cards hurt nobody, specially when it was only matches they played for. It was nearly dark by the time they got to Mrs Green's.

There was no light showing from the old house and that was strange because the Greens were connected up with the electric power and it only needed a finger to push down a switch.

'Hoo oo!' Mrs Comeaway called cheerily into the dusk. 'Hoo oo!'

They walked over to the side door that had hung apart from its hinges ever since Mrs Comeaway had first settled into her humpy at the top of the yard. The door was closed. Somehow someone had managed to pull it tight shut, and as well as being closed, it had been stapled and a big padlock hitched through the staples.

'What is it?' Mrs Comeaway asked blankly, looking at the silvery shining padlock as if it had been a snake. 'What'd she put a big lock on er door for?'

'Gee, I forgot,' Blanchie said suddenly. 'She went, Auntie Molly. She doesn't live ere any more.'

Mrs Comeaway turned slowly away from the door. 'Yeah!' she said flatly. 'Ya right. Noonah came an tole me an it went clean outa me head.' She stood for a while silently, her shoulders sloping sadly. Around her, the other women stood in a protecting group, waiting.

'I woulda liked,' Mrs Comeaway said at last, 'ta say goodbye ta the ole lady. She was a nice old lady, that one.' And she led the way back down the sandy slope and up on to the road.

Mrs Comeaway only wanted to get back home now. The heart had gone out of her as far as visiting went. She wanted to tell Joe about how they had all walked up to Mrs Green's and how she had thought it was funny that there had been no light and how she had remembered, after seeing the lock on the side door, that the old lady had been going and must have gone and not a good-bye or kiss me foot from the one who had been as close to her as if she had been a mother and not just a friend.

Mrs Comeaway ached everywhere and most of all in her heart.

'Ya just missed Joe,' Charlie said from Hannie's chair along-side the stove, when they arrived home.

'Jus missed im?' Mrs Comeaway said, puzzled. 'Where's e gone off to now?'

'E said for me ta tell ya,' Charlie began, and he wasn't comfortable about this telling, a blind man could have seen that. 'E said e was gunna write an tell ya soon as e got settled in somewhere. An ya wasn't ta worry bout him because e wouldn't be gone long. Just ta get a job like, an get a bit a money together.'

Mrs Comeaway just stood there, looking at him with dull eyes.

'An after that come straight back,' Charlie murmured. He got up from Hannie's chair. 'Time ya got a bit a tucker ready, ain't it?' he said roughly to Hannie. And then, finding that anger hid much of his discomfort from these others, he indulged it more fully. 'Get a move on, can't ya?' he snarled. 'Bout time ya got up off ya fat arse, ain't it, and did a bit round ere?'

'Leave er alone, Charlie,' Mrs Comeaway said absently. 'Leave er alone.' And without another look at anyone, she walked with her ache into her bedroom.

On the edge of the big double bed she sat staring before her, hoping that if she just sat still long enough, her thoughts would become clear again, and manageable.

Bartie came quietly through the door and sat close up against her. He took up her hand and held it in both small paws. 'Mum,' he whispered, 'Mummy.'

Mrs Comeaway did not stir.

'I'll help ya Mummy,' Bartie said, loving her. 'I'll help ya.'

She was herself again next morning, maybe because she had slept soundly and sweetly with Bartie and Stella curled up alongside her.

'Didn't come back I see,' she said, as she made the first pot of tea for the day. 'Thought e mighta changed his mind.'

'E say anything?' Auntie Milly asked.

'Said nothing,' Mrs Comeaway said shortly. 'Jus have ta wait an see I spose.'

'I reckon e mighta gone off up ta Carnarvon,' Charlie volunteered. 'E been thinkin there's lots a work up that way.'

Mrs Comeaway considered. 'Might be. Yeah, ya might be right, Charlie. An I spose we could do with the money e'll get.'

'Auntie Milly could help Gramma Dicker with the kids on the way back to Mullewa,' Trilby said calmly. 'They're a bit of a handful just for you, aren't they Gramma?'

'First I would hafta get some money fa me fares,' Gramma pondered. 'Didn't we see Willis yesterday? If he would still be here I might get it offa him.'

'I'll see if he's still round,' Trilby said coldly, pushing her point.

'A course ya don't need ta hurry,' Mrs Comeaway said, her eyes unhappy.

'I got me own fares,' Auntie Milly said proudly. 'Ya don't need go roun the town askin fa money fa me, I can tell ya that.' Her faded brown eyes that looked as if the colour had washed out of them and into the whites, glared angrily. 'I can take a int, too, if ya like ta know.'

'If it's a big enough one,' Trilby said, too low for Auntie Milly to catch what she said. She cut herself some bread and spread it with jam, poured a cup of tea and went with them into her bedroom.

'Takes after er father, that one,' Auntie Milly said sourly. 'What was that last thing she said Molly?'

'I dunno,' Mrs Comeaway said, stolid and determined.

From the chair by the stove Hannie said gently, 'Would ya like me ta run in an ask?'

Mrs Comeaway's mouth went broad in a grin.

'Er too,' Auntie Milly snapped. 'Mumblin so peoples can't ear.'

TWENTY-THREE

'No,' Mrs Comeaway said with determination. 'I'm gunna stick ta me ole man. E's been all right ta me, an you kids too. If you think I'm gunna make a big fool outa him your makin a mistake.'

'One thing, wouldn't cost anything,' Hannie put in, pouring what she imagined to be oil on troubled waters. 'An Joe isn't gunna mind gettin a bit of a letter, is e?'

Her comment was ignored.

'He's been away three months now,' Trilby said scornfully, 'and Horace told us he had a job. He can't just have forgotten about us. Look, all you have to do is write a letter and ask for maintenance like that man said, and if he doesn't send you anything you can get money from the government.'

'Yeah, an land me ole man in jail at the same time,' Mrs Comeaway said, still stubborn. 'I tell ya, ya don't ave to be worrying bout money all the time. E'll be back soon, when e feels like comin back, an then there'll be plenty fa everyone.'

'What about those letters from the Housing people?' Trilby said angrily. 'They won't wait, will they?'

'You ad no right ta go pokin round in my letters,' Mrs Comeaway said resentfully. 'They was mine, an sent ta me.'

'Someone had to read them,' Trilby said irritably. 'And you didn't.'

'An what would've been the use? No good reading things like them when ya can't do nothin bout em.'

'He had no right to run away,' Trilby said, 'and leave us all.'

'Ain't e done all right for ya so far? Gettin us all set up in a nice house an that.'

'A house we can't pay any rent for,' Trilby sneered.

'There's pounds an pounds gone off in rent,' Mrs Comeaway said hotly. 'I wouldn't mind a bob in me hand fa every pound e's ad ta give the damn guvment fa this house. An if you think I'm gunna put me ole man in jail...We ad enough trouble with them pleece already. We don't want any more.'

'That's right,' Trilby said bitterly. 'Sling off at me every chance you get.'

'You started, didn't ya? I didn't want any argufyin.'

'Ah, you make me sick,' Trilby said, moving her heavy body through the kitchen. As she passed Audrena, head bent over a comic, she shot out a hand and gave the head a push.

Audrena glared. 'Who you think you're pushing now, Miss High an Mighty?'

'Shutup, all of ya,' Mrs Comeaway said strongly, 'or I'll make ya.'

She was tired. Things had been this way for the last fortnight; everyone snapping and snarling at each other—everyone, it seemed, going out of his or her way to make more bother. And these everlasting rows about rent. Why was rent so important? The grocery man waited, didn't he? Mrs Comeaway's thoughts came to a halt and lingered uncertainly round the grocery man. Even him! Getting more difficult every day to get an order. What was the matter with the man? People had to eat. And a lot of good his stuff would do him sitting there on shelves.

'I just don't see how there could be so much owing,' Noonah said, fingering one of the worrying letters.

'I thought I'd burned those damn letters under the copper,' Mrs Comeaway said, giving the one Noonah held a fierce look. 'They just ain't added up right, that's all. An ya don't need ta worry. Ya father'll be back soon, and everything'll be fixed up.'

'This one came yesterday, Trilby says,' Noonah said slowly.

'Ho! Did it? An she couldn't wait ta show it to ya,' Mrs Comeaway said irritably.

'This is an eviction notice but,' Noonah frowned. 'You don't want to move out of here, do you?'

Mrs Comeaway gazed carelessly round her kitchen. 'Ah, I dunno. Course, it's bigger here. If Charlie hadda gone up ta Mrs Green's an picked up all that good iron an stuff, there woulda been no trouble. We coulda put up a nice place back fum the camp, like Mongo's. Ya can't get im up off is backside but, lazy ole devil.'

'Like the other one?' Noonah pursued, her eyes worried.

'It was nice,' Mrs Comeaway said, 'livin down here. But ya miss seein peoples ya know.'

Noonah giggled. 'Don't tell me you ever get lonely.'

Mrs Comeaway chuckled. 'Yeah, I know.' She pulled a chair round and sank into it. 'You got any money, Noonah?'

'Course I have. Nearly all of it.' Noonah reached into her pocket and pulled out a fat purse. Mrs Comeaway took it and sighed with relief. 'Just about have ta pay cash fa everything nowadays,' she said simply. 'Terrible inconvenient sometimes too.'

'Where's everyone?' Noonah asked.

'Went down the beach gettin that driftwood,' Mrs Comeaway said. 'We might get a quiet cuppa tea before they come back.'

'I see Skippy,' Noonah said, looking over her mother's shoulder. 'Hello,' she called, as the old man came rolling up the path.

He saved his breath until he reached the top, then he hung to the veranda post for a while, his open mouth like a dark hole in his shrunken face.

'I'm orf,' he greeted them, one eye obscured behind his hat, the other glinting wickedly. 'Orf on Mondy. E tells me give it a try an I give it a try. An it ain't no place fer a full-blood, that damn camp. Where's Joe?' He bent forward to peer into corners.

303

'Gone away,' Mrs Comeaway shouted, pointing north. 'I tole you already. Up there!'

'What?' Skippy was indignant. 'Where's e gorn?'

'Gawd,' Mrs Comeaway said helplessly. 'You tell im, Noonah. I tried to a hundred times.'

Noonah smiled at the old man and steered him into a chair. 'Dad went away. Coming back soon,' she said into his ear.

'Build nother house up there, where I come fum,' Skippy said.

Noonah knelt to tie the laces of Skippy's boots. 'You'll be falling over,' she scolded him.

Skippy jerked his feet away. 'Don't have ta deafen a feller. Like me boots comforble, so I can walk in em. Don't you go puttin a lotta knots in them laces,' He looked round the table. 'Cuppa tea?'

'Ya know, if e really is goin,' Mrs Comeaway said, pouring tea, 'it mightn't be a bad idea ta try an get that house a his.'

'You can't,' Noonah said tragically. 'Too many of you.'

Mrs Comeaway flashed her a look. 'I could fix that easy. Could say it's jus fa me an Joe when e gets back.'

'An what about Bartie and Stella?'

'I could say I was sendin em back ta the mission,' Mrs Comeaway said triumphantly.

'You wouldn't though, would you Mum?'

Mrs Comeaway shrugged. 'You think it's turned out so good down ere?'

'They love it. And there's Auntie Hannie too.'

304

'Ya, Auntie Hannie! She'd be just as happy sittin on a perch,' Mrs Comeaway said with finality. 'Just so long as she's sittin.'

'Eddication,' Skippy said suddenly. 'That's it, you gel there. You get eddication an you all right.'

Blanchie came in from the bedroom where she had been taking a nap along with Tommy. Noonah reached for him and Blanchie gave him up, laughing. At eighteen months, Tommy's eyes were black and clear and his eyelashes touched his feathery baby eyebrows. He suffered from no lack of food because someone was always feeding him something and his fat firm cheeks compressed his mouth into a wet rosebud. He was a good-tempered child, playing contentedly about under people's feet, sleeping soundly, though the house might be rocking with noise. Noonah adored him and brought him a new toy every time she came home. This week it was a yellow rubber puppy. Even Skippy was an interested observer as Tommy stared at the toy with big round eyes before trying it for taste. And whilst he played Blanchie watched him, her body curved towards him, her eyes and her mouth soft with love. When he dug into the soft rubber with a tiny forefinger, then looked up at her with his little pearl-like teeth showing between his pursed red lips, she snatched him up and buried her face in his fine black curls, gently biting the sweet soft curve of his neck.

'You two girls walk home with Skippy a way,' Mrs Comeaway said, when Skippy had finished his third cup of tea. 'No good a ole feller like him being out after it gets dark.'

'Tell Joe bout me ouse,' Skippy ordered, as the girls waited watchfully for his skittering feet to reach the bottom step. 'Where's e gorn, anyway?'

'Ave a good time up there,' Mrs Comeaway roared from the living-room. 'Don't do nothin I wouldn't do.'

Later, as the girls walked back from the end of the road, Noonah eyed her cousin thoughtfully. 'Blanchie,' she said abruptly, 'are you still going to marry Tim?'

Blanchie's eyes were innocent. 'What'd you do if you was me? Would you go up ta where Tim's workin an stay round them camps—or wait'll e gets a job down ere in town. E's always promisin e'll leave that place where e is now an come down ere. It's Tommy I'm thinkin about,' she said artlessly. 'If e got sick or something.'

'You could look after him.'

'It's easier down here than up there in them camps.'

'What camps?'

'Not camps exactly. Little sort of huts. An ya sposed to stay round there an not go near the homestead. Ya gotta stick round with all that mob that's hardly had any education ever. I never been used to living with people like that, always living round the town like. An spose I don't like it! After all, I got money comin in regular down ere. Me allotment an what that feller sends—when e sends it.' Blanchie's sideways look at Noonah was swift and sly.

'What about a job? Minding children, praps, or something like that.'

'Can't!' Blanchie said flatly. 'I already tried to get a job like that but they don't want Tommy. An Tim don't like me goin off an leaving im.'

'Does Tim send you money too, Blanchie?'

'E gives me some, when e comes down. E don't send me none because e knows bout that other.'

Noonah sighed. 'What about Audrena? Couldn't she take the job you nearly got?'

'Mrs Milton won't ave er. Audrena's a bit cheeky, an she don't like workin too hard neither. What's more, she says nobody's gunna make her stay in every night when she wants ta go out. The woman doesn't like that. She only lets ya go out once or twice a week an even then ya gotta be home early. Not like Audrena.'

'Where would she go every night?' Noonah wondered. 'What's there to do?'

Blanchie shot her another look, opened her mouth to speak then closed it again. She shrugged.

'I might try and talk to her,' Noonah frowned. 'We need girls like her up at the hospital, taking round trays and things like that. She'd get good pay, too.'

'You could try,' Blanchie said indifferently. 'Wouldn't waste me breath if I was you. That Audrena—she gets all she wants thout workin for it.'

Noonah felt burdened with care. But at home she forgot it. Trilby was in labour.

Outwardly calm, Trilby kept her eyes on the little wrist-watch Noonah was using to time her pains. They came at ten-minute intervals now, and as each one surged like a giant comber throughout the length of her body Trilby relaxed like a sawdust-filled doll and let the pain take possession of her.

Everyone was looking to Noonah, their own first-hand experience considered a trifle when set alongside the book-lore that was in Noonah's head. Trilby heard Noonah issue orders—Blanchie to go for a taxi, Hannie to finish packing the two battered old cases she would take to hospital with her. Trilby looked once at her mother's anxious face then rested her heavy head against her folded arms. She was drenchingly glad that Noonah was here to look after her.

'You'll stay with me all the time, Noonah?' Her voice was a thin thread. She had to strain to make it more than a whisper.

'Yes,' Noonah said briefly.

Trilby lifted her head to smile. She was afraid, but she hoped nobody would know just how much. It was not the pain. She could bear that, grindingly slow and exhausting though it was. It was the thought of Phyllix and what he might do—after the baby came. Trilby was blaming herself bitterly for having let him hang around her while she was pregnant. She should have snapped that tie—driven him off from her by some means or another. She could have done it—somehow.

She thought of the days when she would have to stay at the hospital. It would be like jail again. And outside, Phyllix might go ahead with his plans. Noonah and her mother might help him. They would try to stop her from going away and leaving them.

On the hard high bed in the labour ward, her head turned restlessly from side to side. She determined to rid herself of the baby the moment she left the hospital. And not only the baby. She would rid herself of the whole family, even Noonah. Step out of this life like she would step out of a dirty dress. In Perth everything would be different. It must be! And she would go soon. Neither Phyllix nor anyone else should stop her.

A nurse gave her an injection. After a while it was difficult for her to think clearly. She strove to identify herself with the fierceness of her desire, but her body was soft and weak. A while longer and not even the pain was real. She knew that Noonah's warm comforting hands held her own tightly and for that she was overwhelmingly grateful. Someone else was pushing down on her stomach with relentless urging strength, helping her weary body to push forth the weight inside it. How kind! How wonderfully, surprisingly kind.

'Here it comes now. Push! Push hard, that's the girl.'

Trilby put the last ounce of her strength into the straining muscles of her belly. She did it gladly, uplifted to the heights from sheer love of those kindly, helping hands.

TWENTY-FOUR

Again, surprising her, she found herself back in a perfectly ordinary world. She looked from her sister to the nurse, half-embarrassed, wondering if she had behaved like a fool—if these two would presently laugh at her.

Noonah was smiling. And the little nurse took up something and held it before her eyes. A white-wrapped bundle with a red wrinkled face at the top of it. An almost featureless face capped with damp, black curls.

It was Trilby who laughed.

When she woke again she lay in bed in a ward, of which she appeared to be the only occupant. There were two more beds, and their fresh virgin white, the neat and wonderful angles of their quilts enticed her to look again and again. It was enough, for a while, to see those beds or to watch the thin voile curtains blow in the soft breeze. It was happiness to move a slow hand over the flatness of her stomach and know that she belonged only to herself again.

Later, while she was still under the spell of the blowing curtains, the neat white beds and her own flat stomach, her mother came into the room. She disturbed its peace, breathing loudly, glancing nervously at the doorway behind her, whispering enquiries. But she did not stay long and Trilby watched her vanishing form with pale and complete satisfaction.

Noonah came, to lean over her and kiss her, and to tell her she had had a daughter and that it looked exactly like her. 'I bet you feel happy now, don't you?' Noonah added. 'Now it's all over?'

That last remark roused Trilby's dreaming mind as nothing else could have done. When Noonah went she was alert again and on guard. Phyllix would come soon. She must be ready for him.

She never doubted that he would come, even though he had taken a job twenty or thirty miles out.

The baby was brought to her and she was made to suckle it.

'And what are you going to call her?' the nurse asked pleasantly, showing Trilby how to feed her baby.

Trilby looked down at the minute head, at the unbelievably silky black curls and the little mouth fastening so knowingly on her nipple. She laughed, and the nurse laughed with her.

'You'll have to find a really pretty name for such a dear little baby,' she said in her cheerful friendly fashion.

Trilby's face was hidden by her hair, but the nurse saw the quick movement of rejection. The baby, losing the comfort of its mother's breast, moved its head blindly, mewed protestingly.

'Did she hurt you? Are you tender? I hope you're not going to have trouble with your breasts,' the nurse said anxiously, bending down to guide the baby's mouth once more to the nipple. This time the child fastened small hands in the softness of Trilby's swelling breast, kneading it, thought its amused mother, as a kitten might knead the belly of a mother-cat.

She felt detached, as if it were almost an imposition for this small creature to expect nourishment from her. And she was relieved when she could cover herself once more.

The regular visits of her baby brought nothing but a slight embarrassment until one day the baby refused to feed. It lay against her, sleepy and uninterested. Again and again its tiny mouth slipped unheeding from her breast. The nurse murmured vexedly, one hand cupping Trilby's full bosom, the forefinger of the other parting the baby's lips by pressing downward on its small chin.

To Trilby it seemed obvious that the baby was not hungry. She could not understand why the nurse persisted in her efforts to make it drink.

Suddenly the nurse gave her baby's leg a slap. The child woke and sobbed, and at the sound Trilby hugged it to her and swung it away from the nurse. 'Why did you do that?' she asked, her eyebrows almost meeting over her narrowed grey eyes.

'Here, let's try her again before she goes off to sleep,' the nurse said, trying to get at the baby's head.

'Don't you touch my baby,' Trilby quivered. 'Go away! Go on! I'll feed her myself.'

The nurse straightened and laughed.

'Good gracious, that didn't hurt her,' she scoffed, 'a little bit of a smack like that. That's what we have to do to wake them. They must be fed regularly, you know.'

'This is *my* baby,' Trilby scowled. 'She *won't* be smacked.'

'Okay.' The nurse gave up, her pleasantness undiminished. 'See she gets enough though, won't you?'

Trilby watched her walk from the room, and only then did her cradling arms relax. She looked at the bundle as though she were seeing it for the first time. And before the nurse came to take it back to the nursery, she had unwrapped it and taken off all its clothes and examined it minutely. She handed it to the girl with the greatest reluctance, and when she lay back against her pillows the mother in her was dominant over the girl. Her thoughts were of her baby.

She sensed danger in her changed attitude. She would need all her strength and energy to stand up to Phyllix and her family. She must not allow this tiny scrap to pull her from her purpose.

She tried to woo back her old attitude of detachment but despite her reasoning looked forward eagerly to the times when the baby would be brought to her. And the baby looked up into her eyes with boundless trust and contorted its small face into grimaces which should have been hideous

313

and were not, and the last of her clear-seeingness retreated before the evergrowing tide of her love for it.

Nobody could have had a baby like this before. So perfect! Why was it hers when she had not even wanted it? Why could she not have had an ugly baby—or one deformed in some way? Here was no difficulty which she had overcome and left behind her. Here was a living breathing baby whose demands on her were increasingly hard to ignore.

Phyllix came and brought her near to nervous collapse. He was harder to deal with than she could ever have imagined.

'You want us to get married now?' he asked, his eyes begging.

Trilby would not let herself respond, not even in anger.

'No. I'm going away. I don't want to stay here any more.'

'You taking our kid?'

'I'll put her in a mission. She'll be all right.' The contractions of Trilby's heart did not show on her face.

'That's my kid, too,' Phyllix said stolidly, resolutely.

'I haven't ever said that,' Trilby reminded him, feeling the great thump of her heart lifting her bosom.

Through stiff lips she told him: 'I don't know whose she is. There were others besides you.'

'There was only me. I know that.'

'You're a fool,' Trilby said tearingly. 'If I say so, there *were* others. How would you know?'

'I know,' Phyllix repeated obstinately. 'And I don't want my kid in a mission. A father gotta sign them papers too, remember.'

'I don't believe you,' Trilby panted. 'You're just making that up to frighten me.'

'I seen that department man about us. Told him we was gunna be married. Trilby!' There was pain in his cry. 'Couldn't you just think about it a while, Trilby?'

'Go away!' Trilby said desperately. 'I won't marry you. Nobody can make me do that. Nobody! And I hate you. Do you understand now? Dumb idiot. I hate you, and if you don't let me send the baby to a mission I'll run away from you, anyhow. I'll run away now. Now!' She thrust her legs from the bed and stood up, shaking with fury.

Phyllix was shocked. This was a situation he had no idea how to handle. In a flash he saw Trilby sick and ill, hurt badly perhaps because he had so excited and upset her. And perhaps, through her, the baby would get sick, too. He tried gently to force her back into the bed.

Trilby flung him off, her grey eyes big in her ashy face.

'I better go,' he said at last, helplessly. 'I'm sorry, Trilby. Sorry I made you angry. I won't come back in here again.' He dug into his pocket and dragged out two pound notes. 'That's all I got left,' he told her. 'I can get more if you want it but. For the kid or something.'

'I won't have it,' Trilby cried in a fresh panic. 'You want everyone to think it's your baby. That's why you're giving me that. You just take it back. I won't have it, see?' She threw the money back at him.

315

Phyllix ignored the notes. His look was both puzzled and sad. He went quietly out of the room.

And when he had gone Trilby dug her head into the pillow and wept tiredly because she wanted peace so badly—and could find none.

TWENTY-FIVE

Her sister's behaviour was deeply troubling to Noonah. She had put up with Trilby's moods of rebellion during her pregnancy, trusting that everything would come right after the baby was born. And here was her sister just as jumpy and irritable as ever—at one time showering her baby with loving attention, at another thrusting it into Noonah's or the nurse's arms as if it were something to be feared and disliked.

If Noonah talked of the future, however lightly, sullenness swept Trilby's face like a grey mist. She had not yet chosen a name for her daughter, and flared out at her sister in tempestuous rage when Noonah suggested names.

Noonah was not the only one who was perplexed.

Never had Mrs Comeaway tried so hard to please someone—and failed so dismally. Her bewilderment was the kind Bartie's school books aroused in her.

She supposed—pathetically—she was too far behind her different-thinking children. Just an old fool. Annoying instead of pleasing with her tremendous efforts to understand.

'What sort of a girl,' she asked Noonah indignantly, 'not even to give the littlie a name yet. We gotta call it "she" still, same as if it was a damn cat.'

'Trilby'll be all right soon,' Noonah reassured, as worried as her mother.

'She got over them idears of ers yet?' Mrs Comeaway probed. 'Sendin that baby off ta some mission an trackin down ta Perth erself?'

'I don't know,' Noonah said helplessly. 'She won't talk about anything like that.'

Mrs Comeaway regarded her daughter in a rich silence then, inevitably, went to the stove to fix a pot of tea.

There was only one way out of the mess she had got herself into. Trilby could not recall when first the chilling thought had struck her, but each time the baby was brought to her—so small, so helpless—it leapt again to ugly life. No matter if she tried to crowd out this thought with others—if she withdrew in shuddering horror—it stayed in the deepness of her mind, festering with possibilities.

To cover the baby's tiny face with a pillow until it suffocated, to roll a pellet of bread and stuff it into the open pink mouth, to unclose her arms and allow it to fall; this last would at least be quick and she would not have to watch it as it struggled for air, or choked on something too big for it to swallow.

Often Trilby lay with her eyes closed, the wind ice-cold against her damp and perspiring body, her hands clenching and unclenching in her anguish. Or she would gather up her child and stare into its face, her eyes tortured and wild.

For the better part of the day and night she was alone with her thoughts. Noonah could not visit every day. Her mother had concluded and dumbly accepted that Trilby was better left alone. Nothing she said or did seemed to please the girl. Trilby snapped her up as if she were being purposely annoying.

So in solitude the battle went on. With all that she knew herself to be, must she go back to the life she so hated? Because of this tie between herself and her baby which, despite the darkness of her thoughts, grew stronger every day?

She saw nothing good in a return, just a further sinking, a giving up of the fight before it had fairly begun.

For Trilby, the only good lay in this other life she would make for herself. Only when she had it firmly in her grasp could she walk proudly, consider herself the equal of anyone. She was so tired of fighting. With her whole heart she wanted to live in the certain knowledge that she was accepted completely.

There was no room in her mind to consider her family. She recognised no kindliness in them, no warmth of good fellowship, no loyalty nor generosity, not even gaiety. Her pity was all for herself. She blamed them for the feeling of desperate loneliness which was with her every waking minute of the day, promised herself that soon, after she had escaped from them, it would vanish.

319

The day was hot, with a careening wind picking up the dust from the streets and whirling it in through windows and down passage-ways. The baby had been fed and, whilst she had fed her, Trilby had drained her water-jug. Yet she was thirsty still and the skin on her face felt taut with dried perspiration.

No nurse came to take the baby away. Trilby looked at its sleeping face, deliberating between setting it down on the bed and taking it with her to the bathroom whilst she refilled her jug. She was frighteningly aware of the thought so firmly established in her mind, and to reassure herself was doubly careful of the safety of her baby, as if by examining safety-pins, loosening too tight clothing, touching the child with gentle hands, speaking to it in a voice that was low and sweet—she could ignore evil and cause it to vanish.

She made up her mind and, with the baby on her arm, took up her jug and left the room.

The bathroom was two doors down the passage. Trilby pushed the heavy glass door and let it swing shut behind her. And then she found she would need two hands to fill her jug.

She knelt and placed the jug at her side whilst she rearranged the baby blanket to allow a thick fold for the baby's head.

She filled her jug at the tap, feeling its weight grow heavier. Carefully, she balanced it in one hand whilst she bent to pick up the baby with the other. And in the act of picking it up the thought flashed across her mind that here was the time—and the place.

The shock of revulsion that raced through her body hastened her movements. The white rug, already disarranged, unwound itself. There was a soft crack as the baby hit the floor head first. And Trilby, staring down at it in fear and horror.

There was a crash and tinkle of glass and a great splash of water as the jug, too, fell from her nerveless hand.

Trilby reacted swiftly, in terror now of authority. To wrap the baby again in its rug, to hold it tightly, not daring to examine it for hurt—to wait with her heart in her mouth for the sound of running feet.

After a while she knew that the crash had gone unheeded. The nurses must be busy. Moving slowly and awkwardly, she picked up the pieces of glass and dropped them in the lidded tin behind the bathroom door. With the towel from the roller, she mopped the water from the floor as well as she could. She threw the soaking wet towel into a hand-basin and, on shaking legs, made her way back to her room. With the last of her strength she sank down on the bed, her clutching arms holding the baby tightly to her breast.

She could not look at it. She told herself that it would be all right, and that nothing could have happened to it. Mothers had dropped babies before. She had seen them. Seen Blanchie drop Tommy—and not only once. It had always been possible to charm away the bruise—or the cut—with a teaspoon of sugar or a suck at a finger coated with condensed milk. Why should her own baby suffer more than a bruise—or a cut?

All this she told herself while she waited with endless patience for the nurse to take her baby. And when the baby had been lifted from her arms she waited still, because she knew that what had happened to those other babies had nothing to do with this, and that her own baby would not have lain so quietly in her arms if she had not been hurt badly.

The nurse came back, as Trilby had known she would. Refuge was to be found only in silence.

The matron bustled in too, worried, perturbed, deeply shocked.

'Your baby is ill. Seriously ill. The doctor is with her now and he wants to know what happened. You must tell us.'

She waited for a reply, anger growing in her. Then she looked more closely at Trilby before turning to the little nurse behind her. 'Tell the doctor to come quickly. Here!'

So Trilby's breaking mind grew quiet under anæsthetics and the gleaming slits of her eyes saw nothing but blackness.

Noonah was there when Trilby woke. A Noonah who sat straightly on her straight-backed chair and whose knuckles showed pale on clamped hands.

This was it, Noonah thought painfully. This was the thing she had feared before it had happened, only the thing itself was so much more dreadful. She could not have imagined anything so dreadful as this. How could she, or her mother, or Trilby or even Phyllix, overcome something so big and full of trouble?

When she saw the dark lashes lift over the dreaming grey eyes she tried to smile and though questions sprang to her lips she fought them back, waiting until Trilby should be fully awake.

After a while she leaned over the bed. 'What happened, Trilby?'

Trilby's eyes opened wide and a wave of thankfulness passed over Noonah. Her sister's eyes were clear, not shuttered, as they had been at the jail. But the look in them shattered Noonah's composure and her tears would not be held back. She felt she could not bear that naked defenceless plea for help. That was the way Bartie had looked at her back at the mission the night before she left it. She dropped on her knees beside the bed.

'Trilby, tell me.'

'I didn't do it on purpose, Noonah, but...'

'But what?' Noonah urged desperately.

'You'll hate me. You'll go away.'

'Oh!' If Trilby only knew how far out she was, Noonah thought.

At that moment she would have sacrificed anything, and gladly, to help her sister. 'I won't go away,' she promised steadily.

'I'd been thinking about it. It was in my mind all the time—that I could easily drop her and pretend it was an accident.'

'Yes.' Noonah kept her voice gentle.

'And now I'll have it to think about for the rest of my life. That I wanted her to die. So she wouldn't be a nuisance to me.'

'Trilby, tell me the way it happened,' Noonah implored, and she took her sister's hands in hers and held them tightly to stop their trembling.

'I thought I'd end up like Blanchie—and those others,' Trilby whispered. 'And I couldn't see that it was fair when—I *wasn't* like them—not ever.'

'I know.'

Two tears showed between Trilby's closed lids. 'Blanchie's still got Tommy,' she said and her mouth twisted.

'Tell me,' Noonah begged. 'Just tell me, Trilby.'

'I told you,' Trilby wept, and her weeping was tired and hopeless. 'I wanted her to die and she died.'

'You didn't do anything to her?'

'I couldn't—it was the baby blanket—it slipped and she just rolled out and her little head…Noonah, I can still hear the sound of it—her little head on that hard floor. Her hair was always so soft and warm, Noonah, against my neck.'

'They let me see her,' Noonah said after a while, her voice dragging.

Trilby's eyes were wide open, imploring. 'And…'

'Her eyes,' Noonah said pitifully. 'They're crossed somehow. And she won't take any food. They think she'll die.'

Trilby went limp again. 'I won't see her any more. Not ever. And I love her so much—now. I always tried not to, but I couldn't help it. Noonah, this is all Phyllix's fault. Why didn't he stay away from me—leave me alone?'

'Was the baby—is Phyllix…?' Noonah stumbled on the words.

Trilby turned her face away. 'There was only him,' she answered her sister's question.

324

A nurse came, quick-stepping and business-like, her expression grave and remote. 'Matron would like to see you before you go,' she told Noonah.

Noonah was home, trying to quiet Mrs Comeaway's boundless fears when her own worry clouded her every thought.

'She's dead,' Mrs Comeaway crooned to herself, and her eyes were unbelieving. 'The littlie dead already, before I even seen er close up. Noonah, did Trilby say—ya think maybe she went crazy?'

'It was an accident, Mummy. She told me.' She told her mother what Trilby had said. 'But I had to see the matron after, and she said there's bound to be a bit of trouble about it. Something they have when people die in accidents. An inquest.'

Mrs Comeaway's voice was full of melancholy. Her eyes darted, seeking comfort from familiars. 'So much trouble ta come on us. It seem all the time trouble come after I get yous back. An now ya father away an nobody ta tell me anything what ta do. What we do, Noonah? What we do?'

Noonah's shock began to tell on her. She could give no comfort. She needed it so badly herself. With a little sob she sank to the floor at her mother's feet and pressed her head into that warm and comforting lap. And her mother's face cleared of its worry. This was something she could do; run her hands over her daughter's hair, murmur soothingly, lift the hem of her frock and wipe away Noonah's tears. The future, as always, must take care of itself.

The sun rose as usual—they ate, slept and woke—the children went off to school and returned—in all of these unchanging things lay reassurance, and the thought of Trilby's baby's death began to hold less horror for them.

Other things—visits from the department man and from the police, the questionings and their own reiterated answers, the quenched looks and quiet voices of Charlie and his wife and his children—had to be borne patiently until some decision arriving from unquestionable sources told them of change—for Trilby perhaps. Perhaps for all of them! Not even Noonah was entirely clear about what was going on.

But, from Mrs Comeaway down to little Stella, each felt that his neglect of some fact must have contributed.

'I just wisht I hadn't of gone in an upset her,' Phyllix said miserably to Noonah.

'If you tell,' Noonah warned, 'they might think she did it on purpose.

'I don't tell nothing,' Phyllix said, his face hard. 'I might say something wrong, so I don't say nothing. Not to anyone. Except you.'

'And it's no use worrying about anything. Not now,' Noonah said sadly.

On the day of the inquest, put off until Trilby had been declared fit, it was the girl's attitude, so aloof and uncooperative, which delayed the verdict for so long.

The coroner was puzzled. He had thought it a clear case of accidental death, but surely a girl would not act as Trilby acted if she had just lost her baby. She seemed utterly indifferent to all that was going on.

For the first time since they had come down from the mission, Noonah was seeing her sister defeated, without the fire of rebellion. Here again was a hurt that had driven deep and that would not be easily forgotten.

And for a fleeting moment, as the enquiry dragged on, Trilby thought of the girl she had been—the unknowing and happy dreamer who had leaned against a tree and planned for her future.

'An ya don't wanta worry bout what e said at the end,' Mrs Comeaway braced. 'Main thing is, ya got off all right.'

'I thought the matron at the hospital was so nice,' Noonah said diffidently. 'Saying all that about us loving our children and making more fuss of them than white people, and about you getting cross with that nurse for smacking the baby.'

'The doctor seemed a nice understandable sort of a feller too,' Mrs Comeaway added.

Trilby looked round at her assorted family, and for a second her old impatient spirit seemed about to leap out at them. Then her shoulders slumped. Without a word she walked away from them all, towards her room. Her door closed softly and definitely behind her.

TWENTY-SIX

The affair of the eviction notice had been shelved, not forgotten. Noonah was at home on the day Mrs Comeaway received her curtly-worded reminder. She urged her mother to visit the department man and find out if she could have the little house Skippy had scorned.

Mrs Comeaway applied to Horace for help, and Horace did not fail her. She returned from her visit to the department man with official permission to move straight on to the reserve.

'Wouldn't hear of Charlie an Hannie stringin a tarp from the side but,' Mrs Comeaway commented, 'so I spose they better move in with the Dickers till they find some place a their own. This place a one unit place, y'see.' She grinned at her daughter. 'I tole im we'd fit in smaller places an that an got on all right.'

'What did he say about the children?'

'I said we was gunna send em back to the mission after Christmas. By that time e mighta forgot about em.'

'I don't know,' Noonah worried. 'He'll probably write it down somewhere. Gee, I wish you could have got one of the big places.'

'Don't get worryin bout us,' Mrs Comeaway soothed.

'And there's Daddy,' Noonah revived. 'When he comes back he'll have enough money maybe to take another place for rent, and Bartie and Stella can stay down here.'

'That's right, too,' Mrs Comeaway beamed. 'We'll jus put one over on that bloke—an serves im right fa takin back all that stuff e give us.'

'What stuff?'

'Them beds an things we got with that forty pound,' Mrs Comeaway said, with indignation. 'Don't you remember e said it was a present from the partment? An now every single thing gotta go back. Beat that, if ya like.'

'Oh well,' Noonah soothed, 'you wouldn't have room for it up in the camp. Not in one room. And you've still got the big bed and the two stretchers.'

'Ain't that. It's the principle of the thing,' Mrs Comeaway said severely. 'Wastin our time goin an pickin it out an all the time it ain't really ours.'

'Only if we'd stayed here,' Noonah pointed out. 'Look, Mum, what say I help you get packed up before I go back?'

Charlie and Hannie and the girls and young Tommy had been accepted philosophically into the shelter of the Dickers' big camp, but they were not far from the reserve and Hannie spent most of her time hovering over Mrs Comeaway's

329

stove—a good thing, as it happened, because never before in her life had Mrs Comeaway had so much need of some living thing to talk at.

Trilby was difficult and moody. She had been hard to get along with before. She was even harder to understand now that she had to share her mother's bed during the night and either put up with Auntie Hannie or lose herself in the bush for the better part of the day. She would have nothing to do with the other young girls around the camp, and even kept apart from Bartie and Noonah. Her appetite was easily satisfied with a piece of bread and jam and a cup of tea, and she grew thinner.

She was jerked finally into more awareness by little Stella. She felt she could hardly bear the child's endless questionings. Stella had been looking forward to having a real little new baby as part and parcel of her family life. Aggrieved when this delightful thing had not come to pass she wanted to know the reason, and she asked not once a day but every time a fresh sense of her injury overcame her. Trilby began to think once again about leaving. And this time, she vowed to herself, nothing should stop her.

Bartie had suffered not a pang at his removal from the Wild-Oat Patch. He saw much more of Diane now, and for the first time in his life he was learning the meaning of a completely satisfying friendship. Noonah was on another plane. He almost worshipped his sister. Diane dipped round and about his own level, laughing, enticing, mischievous and strangely, perfectly tolerant of his curious hobby. So long as she could see herself in finished drawings and paintings, she would not pester him, using her time as model for the brewing up of fresh plans for mischief.

Mrs Comeaway was just beginning to find peace when Stella took sick. She complained and whined and drooped about the house, spending whole nights in coughing even after Mrs Comeaway brought her in from the cold little veranda and warmed her in her own bed. And it was something more than bad temper which caused Stella to refuse bottles of cool drink, cream-filled biscuits and the little bags of lollies which Mrs Comeaway would send Bartie to buy. After a night when the child had exhausted herself in fit after fit of painful coughing, Mrs Comeaway dressed herself and set off for the hospital and Noonah.

Noonah came, anxious-faced, to meet them.

'It's Stella here,' Mrs Comeaway said in a whisper, her surroundings affecting her as they always did with their cold cleanness and the echoing quality of the walls. 'She ain't been eatin good for a week now. I dunno! Maybe I been a bit worried bout other things an didn't take much notice. But now it's cough, cough, jus on all night. I thought maybe you could get a bit a medicine for er.'

Noonah dropped on one knee, her own conscience a bit uneasy. She took Stella's hot little face between her hands, and the child's dry skin burned her fingers. Bronchitis? she wondered uncertainly. Pneumonia? hearing the rales crackling in the little chest.

'Mummy, you'd better take her to the doctor straight-away,' she said, rising. 'He'll probably put her in hospital for a while. I'll ask Matron if I can take care of her. And

331

don't worry, Mummy. She'll be all right here with me. Just take her to the doctor straightaway though.'

'If that's what you think, Noonah,' Mrs Comeaway said, with relieved obedience. 'Gee, I'm glad you're a nurse an all like that. Always get a bit scared less I know something's real bad. Them doctors don't like it if ya waste their time.'

'Off you go then,' Noonah said, infusing a note of cheerfulness into her voice for Stella's sake. She bent to kiss the woebegone little face. 'You're going to stay here with me tonight, Stella. Won't that be nice?'

She gave her mother a quick hug, then stood to watch the two walk away down the drive, her mother self-conscious and dignified, with her old black hat pulled firmly down on her curly greying hair. And not until she was back in the ward helping with the afternoon sponges did she recall, with a throb of anger at herself, that she had forgotten just how far away from the hospital the doctor was, and how her mother and little Stella must already have been tired from their walk down Heartbreak Hill.

Why hadn't she given her mother the money for a taxi? And what change had been brought about in her mother that Mrs Comeaway had not, in her usually cheerful forthright fashion, asked for it?

Stella was admitted to the hospital that same day. Slipping into the children's ward as soon as she got the opportunity, Noonah was cut to the heart. On Stella's face as she lay quietly in bed was the same patient look she had seen on the face of Trilby's baby.

332

This time, she swore, it would end differently.

'We're going to start her on oxygen straightaway,' the little nurse said sympathetically. 'But it all depends on her resistance. She's not a very big child, is she?'

Noonah thought back to the week-ends she had spent at home and blamed herself for being unwilling to disturb the happiness she had always found there. 'I should have told her Stella is too thin. I should have told her what to do,' she thought in wretchedness. 'It's right there in my books and I didn't tell her.' She remembered the grocery orders, and the biscuits and cool drinks and pasties.

'This is my fault,' she thought, her eyes frozen in misery.

Noonah was not permitted to nurse her sister and, while she rebelled, she knew she could not have forced her little Stella to do the things she must do in order to get better.

However, no order could stop her from visiting. At night she had to be pushed out by the sister-in-charge so that she herself could get some rest before going on duty again. But because she was Noonah's sister, and because Noonah had made a place for herself in this great hospital, every little nurse who had anything to do with Stella's care put extra effort into her work. And of course the child took comfort from her sister's presence. Nothing could hurt her whilst Noonah was near. When Noonah nodded, Stella knew it was all right to submit to the prick of a needle or the paraphernalia of the oxygen-tent. Her docility under treatment endeared her still further with all the little nurses.

She did not, though, improve as everyone had hoped. She had too little resistance.

Occasionally Mrs Comeaway tiptoed in to pay a visit. More often she applied directly to Noonah for news, her awe of her surroundings making any contact with the nursing staff a thing to be dreaded. If Noonah had not been here she would have overcome her dread and perhaps obstructed the nursing with her suspicions and doubts. That had happened before where coloured children were concerned. But Noonah was here. Mrs Comeaway had perfect confidence in her daughter, if not in medical practitioners.

Each time she came she brought little parcels of food—big stripey all-day suckers, round hard rainbow balls, a package of chocolate cream biscuits or little bottles of Coca-Cola. There were quick visits from Hannie and Blanchie and even from Audrena. Bartie sent with his mother all the things most precious to him—a water-colour of waves, his game of snakes and ladders, a tiny dressed doll in a box, bought with money intended for an easel. And, behind the stone wall at the back of the hotel, Horace dispensed first-hand news to all who sought it. It took more than a nursing staff to awe Horace.

Only Trilby did not come. Still sunk in depression, she was miserably sure that nobody would believe in her concern for her small sister. The blame for this was hers, she knew that. She had never had much time for Stella when the child was well. It was too much to expect that Stella would want her now that she was ill.

Yet Stella did want her sister. The baby that Trilby had been going to bring home was still in her thoughts. Neither Trilby nor anyone else had given her enough of an explanation to satisfy her. She wanted to know. She asked in her thready little voice for Trilby, who must surely know what had happened to the baby.

So one day Trilby, too, visited Stella.

'Don't upset her,' the nurse warned. 'She has to be kept very quiet so that she won't waste any of her energy.'

Trilby promised.

The first heart-rending came when she saw how thin the little girl had become, and how big her brown eyes looked in her dry-skinned shrunken little face. Her heart was stormed completely at Stella's question.

'Tell me what happened to the baby. Please, Trilby.'

As soon as the tears filled her eyes, Trilby remembered the nurse's warning. She blinked them back and forced herself into calmness. She knelt by Stella's bed and put her head close to her sister's. As gently as she could she told Stella of the accident and how the baby had died. She told her more. Of the soft warm hair and the delicate and perfect limbs. 'Her hand was only half as big as my thumb,' she said, her eyes remembering.

'And she used to wave them about when I took her shawl off—and kick her legs, too.'

Stella's fathomless eyes held her sister's. These were the things she wanted to hear. After a while she sighed, so long and deep that her small chest moved the sheet above it.

'I wish you could have another one,' she said wistfully. 'Will you, Trilby, and let me play with it?'

Trilby took a deep breath. 'Yes,' she said steadily. 'I'll have another one for you, Stella, if you promise to get well.'

'Of course I'll get well,' Stella said in amusement. 'Silly!'

The crisis came and was past. It was certain now that Stella would get better. But it was weeks before Noonah took her sister home. Careful nursing and Trilby's visit had played their part in the graver issue. The nursing had to continue even more devotedly before Stella's health was completely restored. But at last she was allowed to go home.

Such happiness!

Noonah hired a taxi. The child was painfully thin still, her lengthening legs like sticks. And at home there was more happiness. There, at the door of the one-roomed house, his face a vast and welcoming grin, stood Mr Comeaway.

TWENTY-SEVEN

'Dad!' screamed Stella, scrambling from Noonah's grasp. 'My Dad!' Illness forgotten, she went leaping over the grass to her father, and Mr Comeaway waited to catch her and seat her on his shoulder.

Noonah followed, her eyes damp, herself surprised at the surge of love she felt for this returned traveller.

Mr Comeaway flicked a grin at the taxi-man and put one arm round Noonah's waist. Inside the small room Mrs Comeaway and Bartie laughed at the success of their surprise.

'Yeah, I'm home,' Mr Comeaway said. 'Took a lift all the way up to Wyndham an damn well hadda stay there for a bit. An what's all this stuff they been tellin me? Don't anyone know how ta behave their selves when a man goes off on a little trip? Get down here an I find I don't even live in the same place no more. Fine fool I looked, walkin in

337

that front door an practically landin on ole Mrs Mingo's lap.'

Noonah laughed and her eyes danced. She did not care how long her father had been away. Now that he was back, with his cheerfulness and optimism and unfailing good humour, everything would be all right again.

Mrs Comeaway was bustling importantly round the stove. She looked a different woman. The whole place, Noonah thought with satisfaction, felt like a home again.

'An where's a man like me gunna fit in here night-times?' Mr Comeaway enquired. 'Bit small after the other one, ain't it?'

'Stella'll come in ere with us,' Mrs Comeaway planned, 'an Noonah'll sleep out on the veranda with Bartie, eh, Bartie?'

Bartie nodded delightedly.

'Where's Trilby?' Noonah asked, looking round.

Mrs Comeaway sobered. 'I got somethin ta tell ya. Young Trilby's knicked off.'

'I seen er too,' Mr Comeaway said, a frown between his eyes. 'But the mob was round me an I couldn't get ridda them ta see what she's doin with a big case in er and. Anyway, when I got round ta findin out, she's gone. Never been back all day.'

'You got any idea where she coulda went?' Mrs Comeaway asked Noonah.

'She'd had her case packed a long time,' Bartie said, wide-eyed. 'But she just told me to mind my own business when I asked her what was in it. It was locked,' he added ingenuously.

338

'She couldn't have had any money,' Noonah said distressedly, her thoughts going straightaway to what Trilby had said about going to Perth. 'Would she try to get a lift to Perth?'

'What she wanta go ta Perth for?'

'The young devil,' Mr Comeaway said admiringly. 'Always told us she was goin. Probably half-way there by this.'

'I dunno,' Mrs Comeaway sounded dashed. 'That ole Mrs Green, she always said Trilby was gunna be hard ta handle. I wonder if young Lila—she's goin down by bus tomorrow—would she keep a bit of an eye out for er. What you think Noonah?'

'You could ask her,' Noonah said doubtfully.

'Or I could go in an see that partment chap,' Mrs Comeaway frowned.

Noonah frowned too. 'Trilby would hate that, Mum.'

Mr Comeaway moved on to the bed. 'Ah, she's gone. Bring er back an she'll be off again, soon as she gets the chance.'

'I wish Phyllix was here,' Noonah said, feeling depressed. 'He'd know what to do.'

'She never even spoke to im, when e come up here,' Mrs Comeaway said definitely. 'Acted as if e wasn't around.'

'Let er go,' Mr Comeaway insisted. 'She'll come back when she wants to, soon as she gets tired of bein away.' His face lightened in a grin. 'Like er ole man, eh?'

Mrs Comeaway smiled. 'Laugh on the other side a ya face if ya got put inside,' she said threateningly. 'Running out like that. An I can tell ya I damn near signed that paper

339

bout maintenance. Close as a stick of chewie, I was. Spose *I* go off when I like an have a holiday. Nice if I went off like you do, eh?'

'There she goes again,' Mr Comeaway said, still grinning. 'Nag at a man soon's e gets back.'

'Kettle's boiling,' Noonah said diplomatically. 'Shall I make tea, Mummy?'

'This girl,' Mrs Comeaway told her husband, 'she been real good ta us. Brung all er money home. An she the only one didn't get herself in no trouble.'

'What about me?' Bartie said, from the floor.

'You!' his mother said scornfully. 'You an that Diane. Less said bout you two the better.' She bent to take a good grasp of his hair, giving it a tug which made the boy yelp.

Noonah thrust this new trouble to the back of her mind. There was a thing she wanted to know.

'Daddy, did you do much work? Did you bring home some money?'

A look passed between her parents.

'Did you, Dad?'

'Well,' Mr Comeaway was uneasy. 'Off an on I did a bit. Off an on.' He picked up Stella and held her on his lap. 'An how's my girl, eh?'

Stella snuggled into his arms and Mrs Comeaway came over to look searchingly into her daughter's face. Stella's eyes were bright and clear now and there was no sign of listlessness. 'She'll do,' she said at last. 'They took good care of er up that hospital. You shoulda seen this one the day she went in, Joe. But er sister nursed er better.'

Noonah sat down alongside her father, disturbing a brown paper-wrapped parcel covered lightly with a blanket. A clinking came from the parcel.

'I thought,' she said carefully, 'we might be able to get a bigger place after you came back, Daddy. Did Mummy tell you about this being just for one or two people? The man at the department said you could only keep the kids here a little while.'

'Ah, ya don't wanta go huntin trouble,' Mrs Comeaway said, embarrassed. 'E's not a bad bloke, that partment feller. E'll let us stay here. You wait an see.'

Mr Comeaway rubbed his chin. And his brother chose this moment to join the family group.

Mr Comeaway greeted Charlie with relief. 'I was just startin ta tell Noonah what I been tellin you, Charlie me boy.' He turned to Noonah. 'It was all right, Noonah, but there wasn't all that much work about. Most a the money I got I hadda spend ta keep meself in between jobs, see? An then when I got stuck up at Wyndham an couldn't get a lift back I hadda pay out a good bit fa the taxi that took me down the next town. I got a few weeks' shearin there an thought I better come back while I still ad me pay. I got that bit, or most of it, but that ain't much. Still,' his voice grew hearty, 'now I'm back home me an Charlie's gunna go down the wharf again an pick up a bit down there.'

Noonah nodded, but she could not force a smile in answer to her father.

'Pity you couldn't a hung on ta that house down the Wild-Oat Patch,' Mr Comeaway brooded. 'Got a real shock when ya mother tole me bout that rent. An I wouldn't be

341

surprised if them blokes down that office didn't go an make
a mistake in their addin up. I could see the partment chap
about that. What you think, Noonah? You think I should
go in, maybe, an have a bit of a talk with im?'

Noonah swallowed the lump in her throat.

'I suppose you could do that,' she agreed.

Noonah and Bartie were sitting on the beach. Bartie's
favourite beach, where the green waves swelled smoothly
until they broke in lace-edged scallops on the sand.

Bartie had a silky-smooth piece of driftwood in his
hand. After a while he used it to make patterns on a strip
of wet sand.

'Bartie,' Noonah said. 'Would you mind going back to
the mission very much?'

'Do I have to? Why? Don't Mummy an Dad want us
down here any more?'

'Bartie, of course they do,' Noonah said warmly,
hugging the boy close to her. 'But it's a pretty small place
where they are now. They're not supposed to have you two
kids there at all. And if they keep you with them they might
have to shift out. That means another camp in the bush just
like the others. You wouldn't like that, Bartie, would you?'

'Wouldn't mind,' Bartie said easily. 'Have beaut fun in
a camp. Diane lives in one.'

That had been a stupid thing to say. Noonah tried
another approach.

'When I was up at the mission Mrs Gordon used to
wish she had someone even partly trained like I am, to help
her look after the kids when they got sick. I thought I might

342

write to her and ask her if I could have the job. What about that? Would you like to go if I was there too?'

Bartie considered. 'I like it down here better,' he said at last, 'but not without you. Why would you want to go back, Noonah?'

She did not, Noonah thought. But she had an aching longing for peace. There were still troubles ahead. If she went back to the mission and took the two children with her, that would settle a few of them. She sighed. Life didn't seem to be a matter of making up your mind and going ahead. Things happened, all sorts of things. Other people's lives got mixed up with yours and your thinking altered. And there was that other business she had talked about with Mrs Green, though with nobody else. Your own people got sulky with you if you didn't do everything the way they did it. Even training to be a nurse made them act differently towards you, as though they couldn't trust you any more. Why? She sighed again. And against her shoulder Bartie's head moved.

'Why didn't you answer me? What are you thinking about? You look as if you're crying, Noonah.' His hand touched her face. 'Without tears.'

Noonah laughed and held him closer. 'You wouldn't mind, if Stella and I were there too, would you?'

Bartie sagged. 'I spose I wouldn't mind as much. If you wanta go, Noonah, I'll go with you.'

The case was not large, but Trilby had been carrying it for hours. Now her shoulders felt as if they were being dragged from their sockets and the palms of her hands were sore. Plenty of cars had passed, but so far Trilby's nerve had

343

crumpled as each one approached and she had hidden herself behind the wattles that edged the road. She had had little experience in dealing with strangers and her worry over the right approach made her unwilling to begin. As well, she remembered hearing tales of girls being brought back home by the police after attempting to escape, as she was doing. Her father might have asked the department man to search for her. She shuddered at the mere thought of it, but for all she knew the very next car might contain her pursuers.

Her plans, after she reached Perth, were non-existent. She would take a look at the place and something would suggest itself. The main thing was to get there.

She had had nothing to eat since breakfast nor had she brought any food with her. Her only thought after her father had arrived had been to escape before he subjected her to questioning. The hurts that had taken so long to heal could not bear a fresh scraping-over. She would talk to no one about them. She had had enough.

She trudged on with her head bent, resolved to wait round the very next bend. Wait, and not fly like a coward the moment she heard an engine. This time she would walk out on to the road and hold up her hand.

She stopped and set down the case, intending to sit on it. But the case was very old. It sank inwards beneath her weight, so she got up and thumped it back into shape, then sat on the road at its side. She concentrated her gaze on the highway in the direction from which she had come. So intent was she that she failed to notice the noise of a car coming from the other direction. She was alarmed when it pulled to a stop opposite her.

Phyllix swung open the car door and jumped to the ground.

Instantly, Trilby's heart fluttered, but she was not afraid. At least this was someone she knew. She looked at the car from which he had jumped, and smiled. It was almost as decrepit as Blanchie's Tim's car. The driver of the car, a big stolid boy Trilby remembered from her days at the beach, sat staring at her with cool curiosity.

'Where are you off to?' Phyllix asked softly.

'I told you,' Trilby lifted her chin. 'I told you I was going to Perth.'

'You walking all the way?'

'I'm getting a lift with the next car that comes along.'

'Anybody stopped yet?'

'Didn't want them to. I thought I'd wait a bit.'

Phyllix nodded. 'You know you gotta be careful?'

'You mean the police?'

Phyllix hesitated. 'Praps. You're only a kid. The police might chase you up. I was thinkin of other things. Some men ain't too particular. Specially with a coloured girl.'

Trilby just stared at him. Her heart began to thump with alarm.

Phyllix shrugged. 'You want a lift, ya gotta take a chance. You gotta think of all things like that. Sposing you're miles from anywhere, who's gunna hear you if ya call out? And who's gunna believe you if ya tell about it?'

Trilby bent her head to hide frightened tears. She hated herself because she was afraid. She hated even more the idea of asking Phyllix's help.

'We're going into town,' Phyllix said smoothly. 'Tonight I'll be seein a man who might take you ta Perth if ya want. Praps tomorrow. You wanta come along?'

Trilby's feet dragged as she followed Phyllix over to the car. He flung her case on to the back seat. Then he motioned to the front seat and after she was in climbed in alongside her. The driver grunted and put the rattly old machine in motion.

'You want to come with me or go home?' Phyllix asked under cover of the noise it made.

Trilby hesitated. Of the two alternatives, Phyllix's company would offer most reward. 'Where are you going?' she queried.

'Tonight I reckon we'll be stayin up with the Berrings,' Phyllix said. 'We're on our way there now.'

'I'll come with you,' Trilby said. 'But I mustn't get in any trouble, understand?'

'You won't get in no trouble with us,' Phyllix assured her. 'They might have a few bottles up there, but you don't need to have any.'

He said nothing further and when Trilby stole a glance at him from time to time she saw only his profile. The yellow eyes were fixed on the road ahead and a slight smile lifted the corner of his mouth. Trilby wondered what he could be thinking about. A bitter little smile appeared on her own mouth. Whatever these Berrings were like—and she had heard plenty about them from her mother—she felt confident to handle Phyllix.

TWENTY-EIGHT

It was late afternoon when the old car churned its way up Heartbreak Hill. It turned into the bush track along which Trilby remembered walking on the morning her mother had taken them to visit Charlie and Hannie. The track was firmer now after the winter rains, but the car made heavy going of it. Trilby was bounced and bumped, flung first against Phyllix and then against the driver. Without a word, Phyllix took her arm and tucked it firmly beneath his and Trilby was grateful. A mile down the track the driver pulled into a sort of clearing. Trilby slipped from her seat and stood at the side of the road, staring curiously at the half-dozen humpies which made up the Berrings' camp. They were clustered on the outside edge of a half-circle of bare brown earth and behind them, shielding them from the wind, grew bushy stunted wattles.

The humpies were of wood and rusty iron reinforced with rotting grey canvas, and none of them looked large enough to contain any more than two small rooms. From each humpy projected the inevitable bough shelter which also served as a kitchen. Rickety tables fashioned from bush timber held frying-pans and saucepans and washing-bowls, and grouped around the shelters were receptacles to catch the rainwater which was directed into them by makeshift arrangements of guttering.

A thin acid smell pervaded the atmosphere around the camp-site, mixing with the sweeter smell of the surrounding bush. Following Phyllix, Trilby made her way to the first of the erections, picking her way carefully over the litter round the doorway.

The air inside the place was warm and full-bodied with a dozen separate smells. Burned cooking-fat, perspiration, the thick heavy smell of old clothes and, stronger now, the thin penetrating acid smell.

The gloom of the windowless room was offset by a hurricane-lamp swinging from a hook of wire which depended from a heavy piece of bush-timber beaming. Trilby recognised the woman inside. She was big, with a curling mop of black hair and in her bright black eyes was an alertness that turned to curiosity when she caught sight of Trilby.

'Trilby Comeaway,' Phyllix introduced them briefly. 'This is May Berring, Trilby.'

'I know er,' May said. 'Ain't she the one that killed the baby?' There was no trace of censure in her tone, merely pleased recognition.

'She dropped it. I told you that,' Phyllix said roughly, and the woman shot a surprised look in his direction.

'All right! All right!' she grinned. 'Keep ya shirt on. I was only askin.'

'I told Trilby she could stay the night here,' Phyllix said. 'That all right with you, May?'

'Why, fa sure,' May said with exaggerated politeness. She winked at Trilby. 'Any pal a yours, I'm sure.'

'I gotta go out again,' Phyllix said with an unsmiling look at Trilby. 'Be back later.'

'Come in then,' May told Trilby. 'Might as well sit down now ya here. On the bed'll do.' She moved up along the bed on which she herself was sitting and the movement disclosed the sleeping figures of two children, a small boy and a girl. The boy lay on his back, his mouth slightly open. The little girl lay on her side, pressed close to him, one fat hand cuddling her round chin.

'Will I wake them up?' Trilby asked nervously. Now that it was dark she was conscious of a deepening gratitude to Phyllix. At least she would not have to spend the night in the bush or, worse still, with one of the fellows he had told her about. She looked over her shoulder for another reassuring glimpse of him, but he had gone.

'He'll be back,' May said, amused. 'Ain't nobody gunna hurt ya here. Sit down, will ya?'

Trilby perched on the side of the bed. She took a quick look round the room. A cupboard made from wooden boxes stood uneasily alongside one bulging wall. Some food stood on its shelves—butter still in its wrapping paper, a knife interred in its yellow heart, jam in a tin, another tin labelled

349

powdered milk, a saucepan with rich brown gravy set in cold rivulets down its side, a loaf of bread on a wooden platter and below, along the bottom shelf, an assortment of cups, saucers and cracked brown plates. A shoe box at the end of the shelf held cutlery.

At the sight of the food, Trilby's mouth watered. She sped her gaze in another direction and caught the brilliant green of a set of canisters.

'They're pretty, aren't they?' she said, nodding.

'Jack won em down the Amusement Park. He's pretty good on them games. Yeah, they're pretty all right. Real handy ta put things in too, specially if I want a hidin place.' May laughed.

'Are these your children?' Trilby asked mechanically, looking down at the occupants of the bed.

'Yeah,' the woman said a bit impatiently, as if children were a poor choice of topic. 'You gunna stay with that Phyllix now?'

Trilby felt a fine perspiration break out on her upper lip and beneath her arms. 'I—I don't know,' she said weakly.

'Why'n't ya have a bit a fun first?' May advised. 'Once ya get running round with only one bloke ya fixed before ya know it. Seem ta think ya married to em or something. Take me. I been with Jack three years now. Dunno what started me off but I'm getting a bit tired of just stayin round here. I might go back home for a while, with me father. Me and me sisters used ta have fun up there.'

'Where does your father live?'

'Half-way up the road,' May said ambiguously. 'Hundred—hundred and fifty mile up. We got a big camp there. I got two sisters and we used ta have fellers stayin, helpin with the fencin. Us girls useta dig the holes, an the men come along behind puttin in the posts an stringin em together. We was the best team a fencers they ever had, some a the bosses said.' There was pride in May's voice. 'Could always get plenty a contracts. My ole man, everyone knows im up there, e useta do musterin too, us helpin. Gawd, we ad some fun. I miss them times. Satdy nights the fellers useta go inta the town and pick up a few bottles an we'd go on all night long sometimes. Nobody there ta kick up a fuss. Different ere.' The tone was moody now. 'Kickin up fusses all the bloody time. An now they wanta push us further back yet.' The black eyes sparkled. 'Jack says we moved all we gunna move. We stay put now. They can all just damn well move themselves, them white bastards. I'm gettin a bit sick of it but. Too many rows up ere, with the monarch comin out every time we make a bit a noise an stickin someone inside. I tell ya what. I might even take Jack with me. Dad can always do with fellers ta help an Jack's strong all right. Damn near killed me once when e ad a bit in. Took the axe off a me like no one's business an chucked it over in the bush there. Nobody ever found that axe yet. I spose I was lucky e didn't use it on me.'

Trilby's eyes were wide and fascinated. She hid her fear and distaste behind a tremulous smile. 'It's cold, isn't it? Do you think the kids are warm enough?'

'Them two?' May said off-handedly. 'They're all right. If ya like ya can help me shift em inta the nex room. No use wakin em up fa tucker now. They can make it up in the mornin. An the men'll be here soon. Once these kids

351

is awake they just make a nuisance a themselves.' She rose from the bed and bent across Trilby to look at the children. Trilby got a whiff of rose-scented hair oil.

'Young devils,' May said fondly, stripping a thready grey rug from the children's bodies. 'Get ya in trouble soon as look at ya. That man they send out fum the school, e's got is knife inta me because they don't turn up ta school some days. I send em off. Glad ta get rid of em. Gawd knows where they get to after that. Off down the beach I spose. Ere, you take Elvie an I'll take young Albert.'

Trilby picked the little girl up as gently as she could, trying not to wake her, but the long curling eyelashes lifted and Trilby looked down into sleepy brown eyes.

'Come on you,' May said good-naturedly to the little boy. She swung him up in her strong arms and led the way into the next room. 'Jus dump em on top of everything an I'll throw this blanket over em,' May ordered, and Trilby did as she was told.

Two single black iron beds pushed close together and further cemented by a dirty black and white ticking-covered double mattress took up a good deal of the space. The children settled into each other's warmth almost without stirring, and May flung over them the tattered rug.

'Hope they don't wet me mattress again,' their mother said. 'Buggers fa wetting the bed these two are. Jack's always sayin e'll get em sent away if they don't learn to behave emselves. That's because they ain't his but. E gets a bit jealous sometimes, an takes it out on the kids.' She laughed. 'E don't really mean it but. An I'd like ta see im try, anyway.'

352

The small room was chilly. Trilby cast a last look at the children on the bed and felt relieved that they still wore their clothes. She followed May back into the other room and as she did so another woman entered.

The new arrival straightened herself with a hand to her back and surveyed Trilby in silence, completely ignoring May.

'You're one a them Comeaways, ain't ya?' she said at last.

'The one that's baby died,' May said significantly before Trilby could answer.

'I know.' The newcomer nodded a bit impatiently.

'I been down ta your place plenty a times, playin cards. But ya always shot through an shut yaself up in ya bedroom. What's the matter with ya? Don't like ta play cards?'

'No,' Trilby said flatly.

'Or ya think yaself too good to sociate with us fellers,' the woman asked, though there was no annoyance in her tone, only amusement.

'I don't like all the arguing,' Trilby said stiffly.

'Ah, ya don't wanta worry bout a bit of argument,' the woman laughed. 'Sides, we behaved ourselves real nice down your place.' She turned to May. 'She oughta been up ere last night, eh?'

May laughed. The newcomer took a seat on a chair, swivelling it to face Trilby.

'What'd ya say if ya man got hold a ya arm an twists an twists till it breaks?' she asked, wickedness flickering in her eyes.

Trilby only stared.

353

'I'm Rene Riley,' the woman said. 'Ya heard a me, ain't ya?'

Trilby nodded. Of course she had heard of Rene Riley. In the last months the tale of Rene Riley had unreeled itself like a serial story. Not only Mrs Comeaway, but all the people who lived in the big camp and the others who tucked themselves away under wattles and rotting tarpaulins round the outskirts of the town, knew and discussed with varying degrees of admiration and envy, but always with absorbed interest, the doings of Rene Riley.

Rene was a Perth woman, and the story went that she had left a good house down there to follow her man up to Wilga, where he had a contract to fence. But Fred Riley's estimate had been low and the family had ended up in debt to the fellows he had employed to help him. Fred had taken the easy way out, doing a bit of supplying, but he had been caught and his son Robbie had tried to break into a small store to get some money to pay his father's fine and he had been caught too. A real old mix-up it had been, and through it all Rene Riley had moved with majestic force—speaking her mind to police and department alike—defying a threat of being charged herself, for contempt of court, by some means or other wresting her son from the clutches of the law and, finally, settling them all in a camp which sat on a small rise overlooking the town. And before the Riley family had been in the camp a month the town council had approved her request to have water piped up to her from the town supply.

Trilby had heard about the camp, its cleanliness, spaciousness, the garden that was bounded by dark bottles, the trees she had planted herself—there was more than curiosity in Trilby's grey eyes as she looked at the woman. A hint of admiration was there too.

It was rumoured, too, that this woman read all the books she could get her hands on, newspapers too, though, from the look of her, with her shapeless spreading body in its faded frock and heavy pocketed coat, her feet thrust into run-over slippers and her hair a frizzle of tiny grey curls, the reading had done nothing more than encourage a certain glint in her watchful eyes.

She made no secret of hating this town, but her husband had landed himself a respectable job as caretaker for an oil company and he refused to leave. Neither of the Rileys drank, preferring to gamble instead. It was generally agreed that what Fred lost on the horses, Rene picked up on the cards. It was certain that she was lucky at cards. Many a time she had played a man's hand for a stake in his winnings, if she happened to be broke.

Many more tales circulated. Kindness was never mentioned in the same breath as her name, but it was a fact that if a child shivered, Rene would find a warm garment for it and if a family had no food, they could always find a feed at the Rileys' camp. Rene was a good talker and whatever gathering she chose to join was never dull. She exchanged gossip with everyone and knew more of what was going on around the town than anyone except perhaps Horace. And what went in her ears came out her mouth, for the entertainment of anyone who cared to listen. She suppressed no incident that might accelerate the enjoyment of her audience, everything and everyone she talked about was stripped down to its bare bones, yet no one had ever heard her condemn anyone. She seemed to get her own enjoyment merely from contemplation and it was perhaps because of this fact that she rarely received just appreciation for favours bestowed. Though they were entertained, most people were a little afraid of Rene and her tongue, never knowing when they themselves might be found fitting subjects.

'What about a cuppa?' she said now, persuasively, to May, settling herself on the other end of the bed.

'Make it yaself,' May said. 'Ya know where the tea is.'

'Everything looks better after a cuppa,' Rene said calmly, getting up to poke at the sticks beneath the big black kettle. 'You got that big cup yet May, or ya broke it?'

May laughed. 'Ya lucky, Rene. I threw it at me ole man last night an only the handle came off. There tis, under the bed still.'

Interest was flickering in Trilby. There was something likeable about this woman Rene. If May had not been there in the room with them, she might have asked Rene about Perth and the things a girl like herself could do down there.

Rene had no such scruples about audiences.

'You on ya way somewhere?' she questioned later, pouring tea into three cups. Tea without milk or sugar, so that Trilby looked round, embarrassed, for at least a little sugar.

'Where's ya sugar?' Rene asked May. 'Don't take it meself. Makes things simpler,' she told Trilby. 'Now, where was we? You going off some place all by yaself?'

356

'Phyllix brought er,' May said, sipping. 'E'll be back soon.'

'Seems ta me,' Rene said, watching Trilby with intent dark eyes, 'ya wasn't keen ta have im round, a bit back.'

'I just met him on the road,' Trilby defended.

'What road?'

'I'm going to Perth.' Trilby lifted her chin.

'Nnnh!' Rene relished. 'Perth, eh?' She took a swallow of boiling hot tea. 'An what ya gunna do down there?'

Trilby opened her mouth, then hesitated. How could she tell this woman in two or three sentences what she intended to do? And, for that matter, why should she tell anyone anything? She withdrew, as if from a trap, and took up her cup.

'Ya got plans?' Rene said softly.

Trilby nodded.

'An I can tell ya what they are without ya even sayin a word,' Rene told her. 'Tell just by lookin at ya.' She shook her head. 'Don't you go, sweetie-pie. Won't do ya no good.'

Trilby frowned, but would not give significance to what this woman said by answering her.

Rene looked deeply into her cup. 'Ya look a sensible girl, that'd probably take some notice of a bit of advice I can give ya. I wonder now...,' she threw at Trilby a glance that was both mischievous and chiding. 'Ya gunna listen to me?'

Trilby nodded ungraciously.

'Use em,' Rene said promptly. 'That's it. Use em an don't let em use you. That's the only way you'll come out on top. But you try an break loose from these fellers an all you'll get's a kick in the face.' She looked squarely at Trilby.

'Not only from those white bastards. You'll get it there all right. But when ya come crawlin back, these fellers'll be waiting ta pick up the ball. See?' She held Trilby's gaze for a second, then dropped her own and shook her head. 'No, ya don't see. I mighta known. Too young! Too young!'

'I was just tellin er to have a bit a fun while she got the chance,' May broke in. 'You know. Before ya got a string a kids round ya all gettin sick or gettin in trouble somewhere, spoilin ya fun. An people comin sticky-beakin round wantin ta know how ya feed em an if they got beds an snatchin em off ya ta send up some mission if ya don't look out.'

'Kids gotta be looked after,' Rene said practically. 'Polly's kids got took because Polly an er ole man both got picked up the same night an the ole woman they left them kids with couldn't hardly look after erself let alone a couple babies.'

'Wouldn't mind bettin you had something ta do with that,' May said darkly.

'Wouldn't ya now,' Rene said equably.

'Ya always down that office,' brooded May. 'See ya comin outa there plenty a times. An ya been too bossy with me sometimes, too.'

Rene flashed a smile at Trilby, completely ignoring this further comment from May. 'What I mean by usin em, them white folks, I got two a my kids already in that place the partment's got in Perth. They go ta school from there. Get all their books, nice uniforms, hot bath every day if they like, nice little rooms ta sleep in.' She chuckled and looked sidelong at Trilby. 'Look after my kids all right, don't you

358

make no mistake bout that. Them kids can be what they like when they bigger. Go a long way further'n I ever went, with all me brains, that's a bit more than some silly buggers got,' she finished with a grin at May.

Trilby looked at Rene with a good deal more attention.

'My sister...,' she began hesitantly. Rene's head was slightly tilted. There was kindliness in the depths of the dark eyes. Trilby felt the words being drawn out of her. 'Mrs Riley, wouldn't there be some place in Perth where I could get a decent job? So I could live better than people do up here? I want to.'

'Course there's nice people,' Rene said calmly. 'But your not gunna come up against em. You'll be beat before ya get that far. The ones your gunna meet, spose ya go ta Perth like ya seem set on, they gunna be the small fry, the mean ones that likes ta have someone ta treat like dirt. Makes em feel bigger. Or ya'll maybe get friends with some white man that doesn't mind comin ta camps like this.'

'What was it like—where you lived in Perth?'

'Them!' Rene was scornful. 'They was a good lot, they was.' Her eyes were on Trilby, weighing, measuring. 'Kicked up a fuss before we even moved inta the place, before they even seen us. An it took a couple big dogs ta keep em fum pesterin the life outa us after we was there.' She laughed suddenly and then mirth took her over entirely, shaking her in its grip until her whole body bounced merrily, until May had been infected and even Trilby was forced to smile. 'Gawd! Will I ever forget that monarch flyin down the path with a bit outa his pants an then screechin at me over the gate. An me pretendin not ta understand.'

'Didn't you make any friends?' Trilby asked.

'If ya could call em friends,' Rene said. 'I minded plenty a kids for people that wanted a night out on the tiles. I didn't ask em to mind mine. An there was the ones like I said made em feel big havin someone ta look down on. Gave me all their ole clothes, too, that wasn't good enough for em no more. But we was all square there. Did a bit a tradin with me pals, an a bit a cash always come in handy. Nup! We didn't have em in our place, an they didn't have us in theirs. That way no bones got broke.'

Trilby stared ahead of her, her tea cold in its cup.

'I found out who me pals were—when I needed a bit of a help,' Rene continued softly. 'We wasn't let ta starve, up in Wilga. Always got a handout from the camps round about, an no questions asked. That's something ya gunna find out fa yaself, Trilby, ain't it? Ya not gunna let me tell ya. Don't think I don't know that, an Gawd knows why I been wastin me time talkin to ya. Eh, May, any more tea left in that pot?' She reached for the teapot and felt its weight.

'Gawd, she can drink tea,' May said with much amusement. 'Good job it ain't conto.'

'An that reminds me,' Rene said, apropos of nothing. 'Fred got my bit a money fa some horse e fancied. If ya got five bob, May, it'll do ta start me off tonight if I can get in a game.'

'Dunno why ya always come down on me,' May complained, reaching reluctantly for an oversize brown handbag and raking through its depths.

The canvas cover gave to the push of a hand. Phyllix walked in followed by a white man. The white man's dirty sweat-stained shirt billowed almost to his thighs before being confined in the skin-tight jeans that showed every curve of his fat swaggering body. In one hand he carried a sugar-bag that was full of clanking bottles. This he lowered gently to the table.

'Well!' he said, planting his pudgy hands on his hips, fixing his small piggy eyes on Trilby. 'So this is the gel that wants a lift down ta Perth. An me going down that way meself tomorrow. What ya think a that, eh? Like ta come with me?' He leered.

Trilby's eyes flew to Phyllix. His gaze met hers unblinkingly and she read the meaning in his eyes. If she wanted a lift to Perth this was the sort of man she would travel with.

TWENTY-NINE

'I can't go to Perth,' Trilby thought wretchedly. 'Phyllix will have to take me home again.' Questioning by her father seemed infinitely preferable to continuing with a plan which might end with her having to accept favours at the hands of such a man. She actually shuddered at the thought.

She moved towards Phyllix, but the white man cut across her path. Taking two bottles from the sack he waved them at May. 'What about a drink to warm ourselves up? These two's yours, May. That treacly muck you like.' He moved closer to Trilby. 'What's your name, gel? You can call me Teddy—or Bill—or anything else you like. I don't mind.' He laughed uproariously at the expression on Trilby's face, slapping his obscene hips.

'His name's George,' Phyllix said levelly, going to the make-shift cupboard and selecting some cracked cups and a couple of peanut butter jars. 'You wanta drink, Trilby?'

'Course she wants a drink,' May sniggered, while Rene looked disapproving. 'Looks as if she could do with a drink, that one. Go on, Phyllix, give us all one.'

Phyllix filled the cups. George lowered his bulk on to the sagging bed between May and Rene and put an arm about each. Rene shrugged him off irritably, but May giggled and widened her beautiful dark eyes at him. 'Now, you,' George admonished, 'don't you go puttin on a turn. I don't want to get in no trouble with *your* ole man. I had enough a that last time I was here. I'm gunna do a line with the little gel that wants to go to Perth with me.' He reached forward a paw and gave Trilby's waist a squeeze. His breath was already strong with alcohol and, as well, through the loose and flabby lips came the odour of decaying teeth. Phyllix cleared his throat and when Trilby looked over at him he gave her the smallest of beckoning nods. She went to him gladly and stood quietly at his side, her flesh remembering the hot clutch of the pudgy hand.

'You wanta drink?' Phyllix motioned towards the filled cups. Trilby hesitated, then picked up one of the glasses. It was uncomfortably full and took some balancing.

Before anyone could drink another man came into the room. Trilby had seen him around town. He had a broad good-humoured face and his flat widely-spaced brown eyes were rayed about with laughter-lines. He was grinning now and his smile disclosed an even row of square white teeth. Only for an instant, as his gaze fell on George, did his face lose its glow of good fellowship. But George exerted himself to be affable.

'Brought up a bit of the doings, Willis. Sit down an have one, man.'

'We got another visitor too,' May simpered, moving primly away from George. 'Look who's here, Willis. Young Trilby Comeaway. She's doin a bunk ta Perth tomorrer. With George.' She laughed shrilly.

Willis turned to Trilby. 'You the one that's just had ya baby die on ya?' he inquired with rough friendliness. 'Ne'mind, sister. You'll have more.' He grinned at Phyllix. 'If the young bloke has any say in the matter, eh, Phyllix?'

Trilby drank from her glass to hide her confusion. Phyllix bent to whisper. 'Ya don't have ta drink it. Just hold it.'

'I'm hungry,' Trilby whispered back. 'Is there anything to eat?'

Phyllix moved quietly over to the shelves and fossicked round among the tins. He came back with a few biscuits, soggy and smelling of mildew. Trilby pushed them into her mouth, grateful even for them. Her stomach ached with emptiness.

'What say we light a fire outside?' May said brightly. 'Then we can all sit round an get a bit warm. An Billy can come over an play is mouth-organ. C'mon.' She stood up, smiling secretly down on George, then turning wide innocent eyes on her big husband.

'An you jus behave yaself see?' Willis rumbled, his uncertain gaze on George.

'Don't you go lookin at me,' George said heartily. 'Come on, Willis. You and me'll hunt up some wood. I don't go muckin round with no one else's woman. Not when the

364

bloke's as big as you, anyhow.' He clapped an arm round Willis's shoulder and the two went out.

Trilby and Phyllix exchanged glances, then they too tried to sidle unobtrusively out through the doorway.

'Gunna play handies,' May's bright-eyed gaze followed them. 'You better look out fa that George, Trilby. I think e's got is eye on you.' She laughed again, and Trilby felt a flash of anger. She turned to give it vent, but Phyllix gave her a little push. She swallowed her anger and passed through the doorway before him.

'She don't mean any harm,' Phyllix said gruffly. 'Ya don't want to take any notice, that's all.'

'She's just stupid,' Trilby said proudly. 'As if I'd let a man like that touch me.'

'I've got a blanket,' Phyllix said. 'Here it is. We can sit on it.'

The two men had already lit a fire. In ten minutes it was a blaze of warmth. Trilby and Phyllix sat near a wattle, watching it. Trilby had placed her glass of wine on the ground nearby, but Phyllix held his and sipped at it.

Trilby was tired and her shoulders drooped. Perth seemed as far away as ever it had been. She thought of Rene and the things Rene had said. She lifted her gaze to George as he stood to pour himself another drink. As surely as ever, she knew what she wanted, but there were so many things in between. For the first time, there were miserable doubts in her mind. Above all, weariness both of mind and body. Behind her was Phyllix's shoulder. She felt she must keep away from it.

'Drink up your wine before it's spilt,' Phyllix whispered in her ear. 'One glass won't hurt you.'

Recklessly, Trilby picked up the glass and drained it. And having done that she resisted no more the impulse to lean against Phyllix. As her eyelids drooped and her lips parted on a soft sigh, Phyllix slid his hand round her waist, moving so that he was steady beneath her weight. For an instant before she slept, Trilby felt warmly safe.

It was quite dark when she woke. The fire still burned high and someone was singing. Lazily through half-closed eyes, Trilby watched the lit figures of women and men, and as she did so there was a scuffle on the other side of the fire. One of the big Berring men was holding a smaller man by the scruff of his neck. It looked so funny that Trilby laughed. A woman raised her voice in indignation. 'Only jokin, that's all e was doin. Put the pore bastard down. If ole Nosy Parker May over there hadn't told ya...'

'Did e or did e not ask ya?' the big man demanded.

'If ya wanta know e did and I said I would, like hell, with you around.'

'Ah! You!' The big man shook the smaller one as if he had been a toy. 'If you was half a man...' He shook him again, disgustedly. 'Go on, you just get.'

Strong legs set wide apart, hands on hips, he stood watching as the man scurried out of sight into the surrounding bush. Then he began, with calm unconcern, to upend a bottle over an enamel mug.

From the bush came a plaintive protest, 'Always pickin on me.'

A roar of laughter went up from the circle as the big man strode forward a few steps, bent forward from the waist and emitted a most realistic roar of rage which was answered by a frightened squeak and more frantic scufflings.

'That'll be the end a him fa tonight,' he came back grinning. 'The sawed off young runt.'

'Woke up at last,' Phyllix said, as Trilby laughed with the rest. 'You've been sleeping a couple of hours.'

'The little gel want something ta drink?' George said amiably, staggering a little as he plastered himself alongside Trilby.

Trilby stopped laughing abruptly and moved away.

'Come on. Less fill up ya glass,' George leered into her face.

'No, thank you,' Trilby said politely.

George snatched at her glass and poured from his bottle until the glass brimmed and spilled on her lap and her legs. Then he pushed it into her hand, spilling more of the strong-smelling stuff as he did so.

'Drink it down,' he ordered, 'an I'll come back an give ya some more.'

'That's right,' May yelled from her position against a man's shoulder. 'Drink it up girl, or there won't be none left for ya to drink.'

George leaned over and pressed her arm. 'I'll be back, kid. You wait here and George'll take care of ya.'

Phyllix followed George with his eyes. 'You still want that lift ta Perth?' he murmured and Trilby shuddered.

Another argument had started up opposite them, between the same couple.

367

'Ah, shut ya guts,' the big man said tiredly. 'Give a man a bit a peace. If ya gunna yap all night ya might as well go after im.'

'Awright well, I will,' the woman snapped, staggering to her feet with difficulty. 'Ya don't treat me like no bloody dog an get away with it.' She tried to draw herself up proudly but she had had just a little too much conto. The big man gave her a careless shove and she fell forward on her face. Again the group brayed with laughter. It was too much for the woman. On her back, she lashed out at the big man with both feet, catching him on the side of the head with her high-heeled shoes.

Phyllix rose swiftly, blocking out the sight of the fracas which followed from Trilby's horrified gaze. 'Come on,' he said quietly. 'We're getting.' With one hand under her arm he pulled her to her feet. Trilby was shaking from the cold and from fear. With the whole camp now in an uproar, she clung desperately to Phyllix's hand as he dragged her after him.

She took one last look at the firelit scene as they plunged into the bush, one shocked and unbelieving look. These were the kind who had befriended Rene when she needed help? These fighting yelling madmen and women?

Into the chilly darkness Phyllix led her, far beyond the light of the fire and the raised and angry voices. Wattles stung their faces and the ground beneath felt soft and springy. When the silence of the bush was all about them Phyllix stopped and spread out the rug. Trilby sank down on her haunches and rested her weight on her hands. Phyllix would have pulled her close, but she resisted. 'I'm tired. Can't we just sleep?'

'No!' There was pent anger in the short sound. Phyllix moved so that his face was between her and the grey of the bush and sky. 'We're gunna have this out properly—now, if ya never listened to nobody before, ya gunna listen to me now. Ya saw that crowd back there? You go to Perth by yaself and that's the kind of people ya gunna end up with. An men like that George. Their own kind won't have a bar of em so they buy their way inta camps like the Berrings' with a bagful of cheap wine. You won't find nothing ya want in Perth. I'm telling ya.' His voice changed. 'Trilby, why won't ya stick with me? What's changed between us two? You said we was gunna be married when I come back from the bush that time.'

'I never meant it. I said it to get rid of you.' Trilby flung the truth at him impatiently and in the long silence that followed she was only relieved to have found so quick a way of ending the talk between them.

She was all the more startled and angry, therefore, when she found her shoulders gripped by strong fingers. Jerking upright, she saw bared teeth and a glitter of eyes before her head was shaken back and forth in a quick and relentless rhythm. The strong fingers bit even deeper into her forearms. A scream that rose to her throat was choked before she could utter it. Then her head hit the ground with a thud as the boy flung her from him.

Dazed and afraid, she rolled herself into a ball and covered her face with her hands. Her breathing was tangled with deep wrenching sobs. She heard Phyllix say, 'All right!

We're finished.' And there was such a note of scorn in his voice she shrank as though she had been slapped. She felt him withdrawing from her and instantly an insanity of fear possessed her. This was like the time when her mother had sat on the end of her prison bed and pleaded with her. And had risen and gone away because she would not answer. There was the same feeling of terrible loneliness, the same desperate need for something strong and unchanging to which she could cling. And in the moment of his withdrawal, Phyllix became that which she sought.

Like an agile cat, she grasped at his belt and hung on to it.

'Don't go, Phyllix. Stay with me.'

Phyllix did not move.

'Let me tell you,' Trilby wept. 'You don't understand, Phyllix.'

Slowly the boy slipped back to the rug. For a while he listened to the girl's tearing sobs, then, with her hand still clutching his belt, he moved her with his arms until her head rested on his shoulder.

'Tell me,' he said, and his voice was gentle again. With one hand he smoothed the side of her head, the warm soft skin of her face and the springing curling hair. He crooned over her and held her until at last she was quiet. They rested for a while in silence. Trilby's eyes were closed, and over her head Phyllix looked unseeing into the grey and misty bush.

'I'd stay with you,' Trilby said at last, haltingly. 'You don't know how easy that'd be. But it's not only me, Phyllix. It's something I live with, here,' her clenched fist struck her heart as though she would hurt the thing that lived in

370

her breast. 'It keeps telling me I'll end up like that old woman if I don't get away from you all.'

'What old woman?'

Trilby stared away into the bush, seeing again the witch-like body, the black eyes spitting sparks, the rim of foam that crusted the curled and snaking lips. 'Dad had to kick her out. And he called her an old black nigger. She hated him then. She would have killed him, killed him some awful way that would have made him suffer as much as possible. And I knew why too. I know she was filthy and old and horrible to look at, but she'd got so that she didn't mind all those things. She didn't mind anything but being called a nigger. Don't you see, Phyllix? She was as young as me once, maybe just like me, wanting all the things I want, and now—all she wants is not to be called a nigger. All the things she used to be afraid would happen, like I am, they've all happened. She's only got one thing left to be afraid of.'

'Go on,' Phyllix said quietly.

'If I stay with you, the things that happened to her will happen to me,' Trilby said pleadingly. 'I want a proper house to live in and I'll get a humpy. I want nice things to wear, my own things, not other people's cast-offs. And I'll end up with one single dress. If I have children I want them to be clean and pretty, not running round with dirty noses and no pants on because it's too much trouble to wash them. But after a while there'll be so many kids I won't care how they look so long as they don't bother me. I won't care about anything but gambling and winning at cards and sitting round talking with all the other women. And if we want to drink, we'll have to sneak it and drink it quickly, so the monarch won't catch us, and you'll get drunk and come after me with a bottle or break my arm on purpose like one of the Berring men did once. And we'll quarrel all the time and I'll end up like that old woman, not caring about anything so long as I'm not called a nigger.' She straightened a little in his grasp. 'Phyllix, I hate that name as much as she did. I could kill someone, too, if they called me by it.'

Phyllix drew a deep breath of the cool clean night air. His shoulders straightened.

'You don't have to stay, Trilby. I won't make you. I'll even help you get away and give you some money so you can stay somewhere decent. Just remember but, I'm waiting back here for ya when you want me.'

Trilby only looked at him, unable for a moment to take in what he had said.

Phyllix gave her a little shake. 'It's all right,' he told her.

Sudden tears wet Trilby's face again. 'What if I don't come back?'

Phyllix sighed. 'You might get tired of fighting, Trilby. An even places like the Berrings look good when ya tired.'

'Rene said that,' Trilby said slowly.

'One other thing,' Phyllix said, his hands firm again on her forearms. 'Don't you go thinking it would be like you said—with us. That's not what I want neither, that drinkin an gamblin stuff. That's why I always wanted you, Trilby.'

Because Trilby could see over Phyllix's shoulder she was the first to see the stumbling figure of George.

'Found ya,' he said triumphantly, weaving towards them. 'Come on, boy. I told ya. My turn now with the little gel.'

Trilby screamed in fear but Phyllix was up in a flash, between her and George. He snarled in his fury like an animal, his body crouching, his elbows crooked. Then the two figures merged and Trilby was alone, edging herself along the ground, her frightened eyes trying to distinguish between the two locked figures, the hard crack of blows on bare flesh making her wince.

The fight did not last long. One of the figures fell with a heavy crash and Trilby knew that it was George. Phyllix stood above him, still crouching, waiting to see if he should rise. But George only groaned and then lay still.

Trilby looked towards Phyllix, needing him near her still. She rose trembling to her feet, and the boy moved over towards her.

'It's all right,' he told her as she nestled against him.

Trilby drew his head down to her and closed her eyes, exulting in the hard firmness of his body, pressing so close to him that she could feel the pounding of his heart as if it were her own.

'Trilby, will you stay—for a while?' Phyllix said at last, his need as great as her own.

Trilby nodded. Phyllix found her mouth and tasted salt from the tears that once again were seeping through her closed lids. She wanted to tell Phyllix what she knew he most wanted to hear—that she would stay not for a while, but for always. And she could not. The thing that lived in her heart would not let her. So long as she had youth and strength and pride, so long would she seek to escape this life.

Text Classics

textclassics.com.au